INHERITING REDEMPTION

DAWN SMITH

ALSO BY DAWN SMITH

INHERITING TROUBLE

Copyright © 2019 by Dawn Smith
All rights reserved.
ISBN: 978-0-9850871-0-4
Library of Congress Control Number 2019907844
ebook ISBN: 978-0-9850871-1-1

Published by Dawn Smith
Learn more at: dawnsmithmysteries.com

Cover, illustrations and layout by Ben Gilliand
Learn more at: www.bgvisual.com

Printed in the United States of America

ACKNOWLEDGEMENTS

Many thanks to my pre-publication readers: J.W. Smith, Crystal Smith, Skip Donau, and Leann Gilliand. Thank you to Jeff Smith for mechanical and technical advice, and to Ben Gilliand and Gene Herzog for their aviation knowledge. Thank you to Jane Ryder, Beth Jusino, and Lindsay Guzzardo at The Editorial Department for cheerleading, nudging and directing my manuscript into a much better book. And to Joie Gibson at Wiser Words Editing for her copy-editing skills. Any mistakes in this book are the author's alone.

ABOUT THE AUTHOR

Dawn Smith lives in Texas with her amazing husband JW, and Rumor the spoiled cat. When not traveling or fishing, she is writing. She can be reached through her website www.dawnsmithmysteries.com

For my husband JW Smith,
whose loving support, encouragement
and occasional badgering made this
book possible.

Redemption does not come so easily...

Psalm 49:8

PROLOGUE

The single-engine Cherokee Six climbed through gray clouds and leveled off at cruising altitude. The pilot, Kinnon MacKendrick, glanced at his wife. "It won't be long now, Megan. The hospital is a quick drive from the airport in Perth."

"Then we'll know soon what that phone call was about." She smiled. "I'm glad we're going home."

The worry constricting Kinnon's chest eased. God had given her an amazing smile—he'd never tire of it. "So, Miss Junior Texas is now calling Scotland home?"

Megan laughed. "That pageant was years ago. And yes, my love for you is definitely bigger than Texas." The plane jumped. She braced a hand on the top lip of the instrument panel, but her eyes stayed on him.

"What did I ever do to deserve you?" Kinnon asked.

"We've been married twenty days; you don't know what you're getting yet."

"Promise me the next fifty years to figure it out."

"I'm feeling generous. I'll give you seventy." She touched a finger to the windshield. "Is it raining?"

Kinnon looked from the plane's windshield to the falling oil pressure and rising temperature gauges.

"No, that's oil. We have to land. Give me a moment."
He keyed his mike. "Control, this is G-VOPK declaring an
emergency. Over."

"G-VOPK this is control. Your nearest airport is East
Fortune Airfield. Over."

Kinnon pressed a button on the GPS. "Confirmed.
Changing course. Starting descent."

"What is the nature of your emergency?"

"Loss of oil pressure. I estimate about two minutes
before we lose power." He heard Megan's quick inhalation.
He gave their heading and called out altitude readings as
the plane descended into clouds and turbulence.

The oil temperature gauge pegged its upper limit. Lethal
silence replaced the engine's growl. Kinnon watched the
slowing propeller. "Control, I've lost power. East Fortune
Airfield is out. I am looking for a suitable landing area. My
estimated glide range is about ten nautical miles. Over."

"Roger, G-VOPK. We are contacting emergency services
in that area."

Kinnon looked at Megan. "I love you."

"I love you back." She touched her fingers to her lips
then pressed them to his.

"The landing will be rough," he said. "When we break
out of the clouds, we'll have about a minute to locate a road
or a pasture. I'll tell you when to open your door. Wedge
something into the opening to keep it from jamming closed
when we land. Protect yourself as best you can."

Megan pulled their coats from the backseat. The plane

cleared the clouds. Kinnon's stomach knotted. No roads. No pastures. Just rolling hills with rocky outcrops. And then— "That's our spot," he pointed.

"Beside those rocks?"

"Aye." He pulled full flaps. "Open the door and jam the coats in place." He shut off the fuel and ignition. The closer the ground came, the rougher it looked.

The plane touched down, bounced high, touched down again. Purple heather battered the wings, fuselage, and windscreen. They were going to make it.

Another bounce launched them toward jutting boulders.

"Jump," he shouted. "I'll follow you."

Megan disappeared out the door. Kinnon released his seatbelt as the plane's left wingtip sheared off on a boulder. As the plane spun, the propeller struck granite.

CHAPTER ONE

I set aside a report and answered my cell phone, "Lyssa Eastin."

"This is Darach MacKendrick."

It took a few seconds for his name to click and a few more to wonder why Kinnon's brother was calling me.

"There's no easy way to say this, so I'm just saying it. Kinnon's plane crashed. He's dead, and your sister is in critical condition."

My heart stuttered, and my suddenly clumsy fingers almost dropped the phone.

"Can you fly to Edinburgh?" Darach asked.

"Of course. I'll call you back at this number with my flight schedule."

"Goodbye then."

"Bye," I managed, but he'd already disconnected.

The overnight Dallas to Edinburgh flight left me disheveled and sleep deprived. The uncomfortable seat hadn't kept me awake—it was my brain replaying Darach MacKendrick's words.

A cab ride later, I rolled my luggage into the intensive therapy waiting room of the Edinburgh Royal Infirmary.

The tall, broad-shouldered man with dark hair who stood up and walked toward me looked nothing like the photos I'd seen of Kinnon—the brother-in-law I'd never met in person—and now never would.

"Lyssa? I'm Darach. Megan's physician is coming."

His warm handshake thawed some of the chill from my fingers.

"How is Megan?"

"Fighting. They told her you were coming. Perhaps that encouraged her."

Hope flared. "She's conscious?"

"No." He massaged his stubbled jaw. "They put her in a coma. Given her injuries, the doctors say that's best. But they encourage speaking to her. The nurse recommended this." He handed me a tattered copy of *Pride and Prejudice* with a bookmark sandwiched close to the middle.

"Call if you need anything—or when you're ready to be picked up. I've a spare room you can use. Shall I take your case to the house?"

"You're leaving? I have questions—"

"I can't stay. I have to finalize Kinnon's wake tonight and his funeral on Wednesday."

"Of course. I'm so sorry." Embarrassed I hadn't offered condolences immediately, I took a good look at him. Judging by his rumpled clothing, his day had been as difficult as my night. I handed him my suitcase but kept my carry-on.

He looked past me. "Here's her surgeon."

A man wearing blue scrubs smiled. "Miss Eastin, I'm Doctor Lewis. I'll take you to Megan."

"Thank you." I turned to say good-bye to Darach, but he

5

was walking out the door. I clutched the book and fell into step with the doctor. "Has she improved?"

He rattled off a list of injuries until it sounded as if the damaged bones and organs outnumbered the whole. "We've done everything medically possible. The rest is up to her and God." He flattened a palm against a door bearing Megan's name. "Are you ready?"

"Yes." I swallowed and followed him into the private room.

Tubes and leads linked Megan to a frightening array of machines animated by muted blips and bleeps. Bandages, casts, and contusions marred her frame and face. I pressed my hands to my mouth then lowered them. "Can I touch her?"

"Aye. She's in no pain. Just don't touch the bed rails or equipment."

The door closed behind him. The nurse carried her clipboard to a chair by the window. I sat on the bedside chair and eased my palm under Megan's, careful to not jostle her IV.

"Megan," I whispered, "What did you get yourself into?" I drew a breath. "You know what? We'll figure that out later. Right now, you need to fight, and I'm here to help. So, let's get you started on healing."

I pushed suspicion to the back of my mind and, instead, spoke encouragement. I made outrageous promises, prayed, and recounted every happy memory I could recall.

Two hours later, the nurse came over and said it was time to "help" Megan with a few things. I visited the restroom to splash water on my face. When I returned, I took Megan's hand and settled into the chair as my brain replayed last week's call from Megan. I'd recognized her number and scooped up the receiver.

"Hi, sis."

"I know you're at work, Lyssa, but we're signing wills today."

"Leave me your cherry-red Versaces." I'd marked my place in the report I was reading and leaned back, grateful for the break.

"They're yours if I don't wear them out first. In the meantime, I have a favor to ask."

"You want me to fly over and sign as a witness? I hear Scotland is lovely in April."

"It is. But can you come the first week in May?"

"Absolutely!"

"Great! Full disclosure: While you're here, we want your opinion on a business matter."

I picked up a pen. *"Give me a general idea so I can assemble research."*

Her overlong pause activated my 'big-sister antennae'.

"Kinnon discovered something at work, and I've convinced him your analytical brain will be helpful. I know you like to prepare, but he'd rather provide details when you're here."

I dropped the pen. *"This sounds ominous."*

"I promise it's not. Now, if you're ready to hear the favor, Kinnon's with me, and I'll put you on speakerphone."

Seconds later, she said, "Kinnon's family has this thing where only a MacKendrick relative can inherit the family business. In my will, I should leave it to Kinnon's mother or brother, but I don't know either well enough to decide yet."

"Split it between them," I said.

"I'm not comfortable with that option right now."

"OK. I presume you're Kinnon's primary beneficiary. Who's his secondary?"

"His mother. But I'm not sure she's the best choice."

"You barely know her," Kinnon said.

"That's my point. And you said you wouldn't sway my decision," Megan said.

Given the stories she'd shared about Kinnon's family, I understood her quandary. "What's the brother's name again?" I asked, bringing them back on track.

"Darach," they both said.

I looked at the energy prospectus on my desk. "Like oil derrick?"

"Pronounced that way, but spelled D-A-R-A-C-H," Kinnon said. "It means 'oak.'"

"A hardwood, huh?"

"Definitely a hard acorn to crack," he said.

"Be sweet," Megan told him. The sounds of a tickle fight made me grin. "Lyssa, can I name you my secondary beneficiary for now? I promise to update my will as soon as I decide between Greer and Darach," Megan said, breathless.

I woke with a jerk as the nurses changed shifts. Darkness fell while I read to and talked to Megan. The next time I looked, the clock's hands registered five-thirty. Tuesday morning.

My second wind kicked in. I'd nearly read Elizabeth and

Darcy to their happy ending when the cardiac monitor hiccupped, resumed its rhythm, and hiccupped again. An urgent alarm bleated, and a flat line replaced peaks and valleys. I jumped to my feet. The nurse rushed to Megan's side and started CPR. Another nurse rushed a crash cart to the bed.

"Wait in the hall, miss," she said as the defibrillator charged and a doctor ran in.

I couldn't leave Megan. Hands to my heart, I backed against the wall. Minutes later, the doctor's shoulders fell as he called the time of death. The furious activity stopped.

Wednesday morning passed in a blur of funeral arrangements. I didn't meet Kinnon's and Darach's mother and stepfather, Greer and Peter Rand, until the double funeral service. Both Kinnon and Darach had inherited Greer's deep blue eyes, but only Kinnon had inherited his mother's ashy-blonde hair.

The minister's eulogy evoked a beautiful sketch of two short lives. An hour later, we huddled beneath umbrellas in front of a granite stone inscribed "Kinnon and Megan MacKendrick." My sister had liked the alliteration of her married name. Its newness allowed me to maintain my composure—to pretend this was someone else we were burying.

Thirty minutes later, I followed Greer through the front door of MacKendrick Manor—two stories of massive gray stone, roofed in slate shingles, and surrounded by acres of green woods and fields. Though built for a large family,

Darach, his handyman, and housekeeper were the sole occupants.

We gathered in Darach's study where smooth plaster walls climbed twelve feet to a ceiling that hoarded much of the fireplace's heat. Greer and Peter held hands. Darach stood apart, his arms crossed. I paced beside a wall of bookshelves, pretending to read titles.

The solicitor introduced himself as Mr. Craddock. He made two short stacks of documents on the desk that dominated the study. "If you'll be seated, we'll begin," he said. His deep voice sounded out of place given his slight build.

I chose the chair closest to the door. Peter sat beside me, his kind, gray eyes grief-dull behind wire-rimmed glasses. Greer settled beside him, her lovely face as stiff as her posture. Darach sat beside her and focused straight ahead.

Kinnon's family had no idea what was coming. And I deliberately hadn't prepared them.

"Mr. and Mrs. MacKendrick met with me last week to update their wills," Mr. Craddock said. "I have copies for each of you." He placed a hand on a stack of documents. "Upon his death, Kinnon MacKendrick's estate passed to his wife." His hand moved to a second stack. "Megan MacKendrick's estate, passes to her sister, Lyssa Eastin."

I turned to witness the family's reactions. Darach met my gaze. When I didn't pretend surprise at the announcement, his eyes narrowed.

"But that would include Kinnon's shares of MacKendrick

Industries," Greer said. "She can't inherit MacKendrick Industries. The family has first right of refusal on company stock."

"That would refer to the sale of stock, not the inheriting of it," Mr. Craddock said. "Megan was a MacKendrick, and it is her will we are following."

"This isn't what Kinnon wanted." Greer's sharp words held the truth. I watched Peter touch his hand to her arm.

"They died less than forty-eight hours apart," Darach said. "Did Kinnon's will contain a survivorship clause?"

Mr. Craddock shook his head. "Kinnon declined to designate a time period that his wife must survive him."

"A gambler to the last," Peter said.

Kinnon gambled? I started to ask, but Mr. Craddock picked up something small, walked around the desk, and handed the item to me.

"The key to Mr. and Mrs. MacKendrick's Perth flat," he said, covering the key with his business card. "Your sister mentioned you have a key to her New York flat."

"I do." I slipped the key into my pocket.

"Lyssa, are you aware that you can refuse Kinnon's part of the estate?" Peter asked. "Being a partner in a manufacturing business may not appeal to you. I'm sure reasonable compensation could be made to you for Kinnon's shares."

Three faces—one undecipherable, one doubting, one hopeful—chipped at my composure. I couldn't share my suspicions until I knew why Kinnon's plane had crashed.

"Can we speak privately, Mr. Craddock?" I said.

Darach rose. Though I stood five-ten and wore two-inch

heels, he had the height advantage. "Use the room across the hall," he said. His burr carried the smoothness of the Scotch sitting on the sideboard. Controlled anger had replaced his courtesy of the last forty-eight hours.

Mr. Craddock escorted me to the sitting room and shut the door.

"Everything we discuss is confidential?" I asked before he'd turned around.

"It is."

I looked directly at him. "Do you have anything else for me from Megan?"

He held my stare. "I've given you everything she left me to give to you upon her death."

I relaxed. Maybe my worries were working overtime. Megan was smart. If an underlying reason for rewriting their wills had existed, she'd have created a way for me to find out.

"Megan said Kinnon's secondary beneficiary was Mrs. Rand. If I decline Kinnon's part of the inheritance, does his estate go to his mother?"

"Yes. Do you not want the MacKendrick Industries shares? Most of the estate's value is tied to the business."

"What I want is to wake up and discover this is just a nightmare." I paced the room and paused at a window. "Megan wanted the company shares to stay with the MacKendricks. She just wasn't ready to choose between Greer and Darach."

"She mentioned that. But Kinnon didn't object when she named you her secondary beneficiary. In fact, he seemed pleased with her choice." His expression softened. "Then again, he seemed pleased with everything about your sister. While they sat in my office, the only time they weren't touching—holding hands, him playing with her fingers or her hair—was when they signed their wills. Their marriage was brief, but it was happy."

I smiled. "Thank you for that."

"Will you keep the shares?" he asked.

"Only as long as I have to. Megan's marriage doesn't entitle me to half of Kinnon's family's business."

"It does from a legal perspective." His tone remained neutral, as if he were discussing the weather rather than millions of dollars.

"But not a moral one. I'll return the shares after I decide if they should go to Greer, or Darach, or both."

"They're grieving. You'll have to see past their pain and anger—and your own."

I nodded. "Did Megan or Kinnon mention why Greer was Kinnon's secondary beneficiary and not Darach?"

"I'm afraid not." Long fingers drummed a four-count on his pant leg. "I don't know your personal situation, but if you keep the company shares thirty days, you can sell them to Greer Rand or Darach MacKendrick for the 'reasonable compensation' that Peter Rand mentioned."

I shook my head. "That's not what Megan intended."

My gaze followed the lines of yellow roses that climbed the wallpaper to suffer an abrupt pruning by the wide crown molding. I had a week of bereavement leave, seven sick days, and seven vacation days. If I chose Greer, I could decline the inheritance and leave. If I chose Darach, or both, I'd have to stay thirty days. A month, or less, to wrap up two lives.

The hollowness in my heart crept to my stomach. "Thank you for your counsel," I said as I walked to the door.

When we entered the study, I noticed that the Scotch had been poured. Darach stood alone, staring into the fire. The Rands were at a window. Greer's head rested on Peter's shoulder, his arm hugged her close. I'd yet to see the grieving mother and son consoling one another.

All three turned and gravitated closer, as if I were the sun—or a black hole.

"I'm accepting the entire inheritance," I said.

Greer tossed the contents of her glass. I backpedaled, but the Scotch hit its mark. She slammed her glass onto the desk. "Kinnon is dead because of your sister," she accused, stalking from the room.

Peter's brow furrowed. He set his glass beside Greer's. My hands hovered over my chest. "Megan wasn't—"

"I know, lass, but she's lost a son," Peter said, squeezing my arm as he passed.

"And I've lost a sister."

Mr. Craddock picked up his briefcase. "Good day, Ms. Eastin. Call if you need me." Unfazed by the drama, he followed Peter.

There was nothing good about this day. Nothing good about the last four days. Nothing would be good again for a long time.

Unwilling to turn my back on another member of this family, I faced Darach. "Do you have a Kleenex?" He handed me his handkerchief. I blotted my dress. "Kinnon was the pilot—"

"Attributing fault won't bring them back," he said, raising his glass.

I flinched. But instead of following Greer's example, he swallowed his Scotch then aligned his empty glass with the Rands'. "I'll see them out. Then we need to talk."

I folded the damp handkerchief and laid it opposite the glasses. "I'm changing clothes."

His head tilt invited me to lead. At the staircase, I climbed to the second floor while his footsteps faded in the direction of the front door.

Five minutes later, wearing a sweater and slacks, I tossed my wet dress into the trashcan, shrugged into my coat, and hurried downstairs. I needed air. Darach would find me—sooner or later.

The study doors opened onto a patio bordered by grass. I headed for the informal garden sprawling beyond the lawn. The crushed-granite path meandered through a wisteria-draped arbor. Beyond, azaleas rioted in fist-size coral, yellow, and fuchsia blossoms. I inhaled a floral top note with undertones of rain. Unfamiliar birds sang unfamiliar songs in the late-afternoon sunshine.

I sat on an iron bench and closed my eyes. Twenty days. Megan's marriage had lasted twenty days. Their attorney had eased my suspicions, but I still had to decide who Megan would want to inherit.

I knew what factors and personality traits led to a profitably run business. All I had to figure out was who possessed them—Greer, Darach, or both.

Footsteps crunched on the rock path. I watched Darach approach. Like me, Kinnon was twenty-eight, four years older than Megan. Darach looked to be in his mid-thirties. Circumstances made it hard to tell. After the last few days, I felt older. And I doubted Megan's makeup lessons hid the desolation of her death.

Darach stopped in front of me. "You knew about the will," he said.

"Megan and Kinnon called me when they rewrote their wills in Newcastle."

His jaw flexed like he was chewing gravel. "I want to buy your half of the company stock. Will you sell?"

"Even if I were inclined to sell, according to Mr. Craddock, I first have to hold the shares thirty days," I said. A cloud slid across the sun. I drew the edges of my coat together. "I've put you in an awkward position. I'll move to Kinnon's and Megan's apartment tonight."

He stepped away, putting a welcome distance between us. "Tomorrow is soon enough. I'll be out this evening. Anice is preparing your dinner."

I didn't protest. If I left now, I'd reach the apartment after dark. I wasn't sure how I'd react to seeing Megan's things. In my experience, daylight served best for tackling painful tasks.

"I'll have your dress cleaned," he said, pulling a cigar from his pocket. I walked upwind.

"I threw it away. The Scotch didn't ruin it, the occasion did."

Shielding the lighter's flame, he puffed until the cigar tip glowed. As he watched me from behind fragrant smoke, I imagined his thoughts: Do I snuggle up to her for 30 days to encourage her selling to me, or do I treat her like the interloper she is?

He jerked the cigar from his mouth. "Have you any idea what MKI does?"

"MKI manufactures pipes and valves for the oil and gas industry," I said.

He frowned. At my knowledge? Or my understatement of a complex operation?

"My inheriting Kinnon's shares wasn't intentional," I said. "Megan didn't want to die, nor did I want her to die just so I could interfere with your business."

His arms crossed. "Aye, I know that. But I'm not sure what to do with you right now. MKI is my inheritance too."

Bluntness was a good trait in a businessman. I added a mark to his column on my mental 'who should inherit' chart as I stood.

"You're needed at the plant tomorrow," he said.

I needed to see the operation and how the employees behaved around Darach, but I didn't like being rushed. "I'm moving to their apartment tomorrow. I'll come in on Monday."

"You'll have to drop your luggage off on the way to MKI and settle into the flat over the weekend." He stepped closer.

I stepped back. My retreat granted him victory.

"You chose to accept Kinnon's stock," he said. "That makes you my partner. In the business world, the present and future always take precedence. Paperwork requires your signature, and you must be listed as a company officer before payroll on Friday. Do you know how many people MKI employs?"

"No." I looked away. My irritation evaporated as the legal ramifications of entwining myself with MacKendrick Industries hit me. "How many?" I looked back.

I was speaking to the air. Darach was halfway to the manor.

CHAPTER TWO

Thursday morning, I carried my luggage downstairs. Darach's housekeeper, Anice, met me in the foyer.

She shook her head, and her fading auburn curls brushed her cheeks. "Ian would have brought those down for you."

"Your husband has enough to do." I left my luggage and followed her to the kitchen. "Were you and Ian here when Kinnon and Darach were children?"

"Yes and no. We arrived a few months before Mr. and Mrs. MacKendrick divorced. The boys were sixteen and twelve. Darach grew up here. Kinnon left with his mother."

Megan had mentioned that the brothers grew up separated. I couldn't imagine my childhood without my sister any more than I could imagine growing old without her.

"Would you care for breakfast?" Anice asked.

"No, thank you. Just coffee."

Her concerned tongue-cluck warmed me. How long had it been since someone had cared if I'd eaten breakfast? I checked the kitchen clock. Seven a.m. "Is Darach down yet?" I asked.

"The lad left an hour ago." The concerned cluck sounded again.

Lad didn't fit Darach's Braveheart-broad shoulders and height.

"How long does it take to drive to MacKendrick Industries?"

She handed me coffee. "Thirty minutes. I don't know why he felt the need for such an early start."

I didn't blame him for wanting to avoid me. "In that case, can a rental company deliver a car?"

"There's no need. He asked Ian to drive you to the flat, and then to have you at MKI at eleven."

I wasn't letting Darach force me into his schedule. "Thanks, but I don't want to tie up Ian's morning. If he'll drive me to a rental service, I'll take care of myself from there."

Flashy didn't describe the Ford Focus I drove away from the rental lot, but its safety rating was excellent—my vehicle criteria since my parents' fatal accident.

Even with Ian's detailed directions, driving on the left side of the road from the right side of the car, and negotiating roundabouts, required the same concentration as applying lipstick during a downtown-Dallas Uber ride.

I parked in the lot in front of a Georgian-style townhouse that had been converted into apartments. I had two hours until I needed to be in Dundee at MacKendrick Industries—plenty of time to look around the apartment.

I carried my things to the entry and eyed the electronic keypad on the outer gate. Mr. Craddock hadn't mentioned an entry code. Neither had Darach or the Rands.

A brass plate framed a dozen round doorbells with adjacent names. Seeing *Kinnon and Megan MacKendrick* made me tear up. I pushed doorbells until a Mrs. Donnel answered. After a brief introduction via intercom, a short elderly woman with thick-lensed, red-framed glasses arrived and opened the door and the gate. I followed her inside and down the white-walled hallway, shortening my stride to accommodate hers.

"Such a tragedy," she said. "They were a handsome couple to die so young—and your sister a bride less than a month." She stopped at apartment 106. Her soft hand touched my wrist. "If you need anything, I'm next door."

"Thank you for your kindness," I said.

If she hadn't been watching, who knows how long I'd have stood there. I unlocked the door and found a light switch. A ceiling fixture revealed dark wood floors and a red-carpeted staircase. I rolled my bag inside. The door to my right was a closet, the door to my left a guest room. The main living area must be upstairs.

Goose bumps rose on my arms. Was the heating bill overdue? I locked the door, left my luggage, and climbed the stairs to the living room. A cork-colored sofa squatted between cherry end tables. The royal blue and dandelion-yellow sofa pillows undid me. Megan had loved bright colors. She had sat on that couch and called me from that phone twenty short days ago.

"Lyssa, I'm calling today because I can't call Sunday."

"What's happening tomorrow?" I asked.

"I'll be honeymooning in the Scottish Highlands. I'm marrying Kinnon in half an hour."

I sucked in air to fill the void in my stomach.

21

"Lyssa? I know it's sudden, but I'm so happy."

She no longer sounded happy. That she was marrying Kinnon wasn't shocking. That today was her wedding day—

I mentally put on my big-sister pants. "I'm glad you're happy. You just surprised me. I always thought—" I'd always thought I'd be her maid of honor. "Is the sun shining? I always pictured the sun shining on your wedding day."

"Yes! It's a perfect day. Oh! Kinnon just came in with the photographer. I have to go!"

"I want wedding photos emailed no later than Monday. I love you, Megan. Kick—I mean kiss Kinnon for me."

She'd laughed. "Love you, too, Lyssa."

I plucked a pillow from the sofa and massaged it hard enough to threaten the seams. Afraid I'd mangled something of Megan's, I dropped it. The pillow fell to the couch without sound or damage. I craved sound and damage.

A white vase—too bland to be Megan's—sat on a shelf. I snatched it, raised it over my head, and let go.

Crash and shards.

As I grabbed a mug commemorating a rugby tournament, I glimpsed the display of framed photos on the opposite wall. My heart stuttered. A similar *happiness gallery* hung in Megan's New York apartment.

I stepped closer. Greer and Peter, younger and happy, cutting a wedding cake. Kinnon and Peter standing between a red Porsche and a silver Jaguar. Kinnon playing rugby. I glanced from the logo on his jersey to the mug in my hand and set the mug on the floor.

I kept looking. Me at my company picnic—I'd emailed the photo so Megan could appreciate my attempt to hit a softball. Megan and me at the Dallas Arboretum last fall, lying between two massive beds of chrysanthemums planted to look like butterfly wings.

Another step brought me to Megan and Kinnon's wedding. Serious expressions as they spoke their vows, then smiles. Arms wrapped around one another, on the verge of a kiss. On the verge of life together.

I turned my back to the wall and slid to the floor. God, I hurt. I'd never again laugh with her ... see her ... hug her.

She was *gone.*

Pain ate me up with huge, tearing bites. A sob broke loose. Megan's voice echoed in my head.

Could be worse. Could be raining.

My strangled laugh threatened to descend to something darker. We had recited the saying since childhood: a legacy from our parents to put problems into perspective. How many times had we used it? Hundreds? Thousands? Not nearly enough.

Life wasn't just raining. Life was pouring buckets.

CHAPTER THREE

I woke suddenly and struggled to my elbows. Dark tables. White walls. Tan couch. The Perth flat.

I pressed my hands to my face. I wasn't refreshed. Naps and crying always left me lethargic and out of sorts. I looked at my watch. If I hurried, I could repair my makeup and change clothes before heading to MacKendrick Industries.

The suction-slap sound of a closing refrigerator made me swing my feet to the floor. Darach filled the kitchen entry before I could untangle myself from the blanket he must have tossed over me.

"You're awake. Good."

Of the people I might choose to witness the aftermath of my breakdown, Darach was my last choice.

He nodded at the vase shards on the floor. "Was it like that when you arrived?"

"No. I broke it." I raked fingers through my hair. When he didn't ask for an explanation, I gave him points for restraint. "Why are you here?"

"Your neighbor called me."

"You know Mrs. Donnel?" I stood.

"We met five minutes ago when she let me in."

"You don't have Kinnon's gate code either?"

"No. This is my first visit to his flat," he said, looking around.

A black mark appeared below his name in my mental

column. "You live twenty minutes away and never visited your brother's apartment?"

"We weren't close."

"Why not?"

His stare probably cowed others into submission. It didn't work with me.

"Not all siblings share your and Megan's apparent intimacy," he said.

And Darach and Kinnon had grown up apart. I squeezed past him into the kitchen and opened the only cabinet tall enough to hold a broom. "What did Mrs. Donnel say when she called?"

"That she'd come to offer you tea. You were pale when she let you in, so when you didn't answer, she grew worried and rang me."

I carried the broom and dustpan to the living room. "You said she didn't know you."

"It seems Kinnon gave her my name and numbers as emergency contacts." He frowned. "I don't know why. Mother lives closer."

I revised my earlier assessment. I'd rather Darach found me than Greer. She might have woken me with another baptism—if she'd bothered to come at all. I swept up my mess and turned in a circle.

"I saw a dustbin under the sink," he said.

I dumped the broken glass and replaced the tools while Darach filled the coffeemaker with enough grounds to stimulate a sloth then flipped the power button.

Three cabinets later, he found mugs.

"When you've had a cup, we'll drive to the office." He searched his pockets. "I took Kinnon's spare flat key from his office desk. Be sure you put it back or I'll have to find the landlord to open the door next time."

"There won't be a next time," I said.

The coffeemaker pinged. Darach poured. "Sugar or cream?"

"Neither." Red poppies adorned the stoneware mug he handed me. It had to be Megan's. I caressed the mug with my thumbs and lifted it in a salute. "Thank you, I needed this."

Thick, dark hair swept back from his forehead as if he constantly faced into the wind. He struck me as a man who actively controlled everything within his sphere.

"Did you ever try to buy Kinnon's half of MacKendrick Industries?" I asked.

"I offered him more than it was worth—more than once. He turned me down."

"So, it's not just me. You don't want anyone for a partner."

He nodded. "But that would be wishing for the impossible."

"I wish for the impossible. I wish Megan and Kinnon went to New York instead of flying to England. I would have flown up from Dallas to meet him—"

"But not to Scotland? You never visited your sister here."

"I was scheduled to arrive next Monday to spend the week with them. Megan wanted time to settle into marriage—time for you all to accept her." I blew across the top of my coffee, creating visible ripples to accompany the audible swells in our conversation. "I wish you'd all had

26

time to get to know Megan. She was special."

"Special in that she'd marry a man she barely knew and not invite her family to the wedding?"

She hadn't invited me either, but I resented his criticism. "Megan didn't love lightly. She wouldn't marry lightly. And it's not like she had any other family to invite."

"Kinnon mentioned she was orphaned young." His voice softened.

"We were fourteen and ten when an eighteen-wheeler forced our parents off the interstate, killing them instantly." I leaned against the counter. "Four months later, I was buying a birthday card for Megan and realized I'd no longer be choosing mother or father cards again. Now I've lost the sister section." I took a quick sip. "We lived with our aunt. I never felt like an orphan, until now."

"Your aunt couldn't come for the funeral?"

"She died two years ago. Megan was the last of my family. At this point, you're my closest next of kin."

His forehead creased. The relationship didn't appear to make him any happier than it made me.

"Shall I carry your bags up?" He seemed to take up most of the small room, though I passed him without trouble as I carried my mug to the sink.

"No. I'm staying in the guestroom. Give me five minutes and I'll follow you to MKI."

Black eyebrows drew together, daring me to cross the line. "You're in no shape to drive."

"But I'm in shape to sign legal paperwork?"

He added his mug to the sink and squirted dish soap. "That can't be helped."

I started down the stairs. "I'll follow you fine if you slow down through the roundabouts. People here seem to merge by faith. I haven't quite got the knack yet."

Inside the guest bathroom, I looked in the mirror and cringed. I didn't look like a professional model's sister. Megan and I had shared our mother's wonderful cheekbones, but instead of Megan's tawny blonde hair and rare green eyes, my hair fell somewhere between red and brunette, and my equally undecided eyes were golden brown.

I rinsed my hands and face, subdued my hair into its usual twist, and swiveled to check the back of my skirt. The wool had weathered my catharsis without obvious creases. I replaced my wrinkled blouse with a sweater and reapplied mascara. Briefcase in hand, I opened the bedroom door and stopped short.

Darach leaned against the hall wall. He jerked his gaze from the red-carpeted staircase. "Come look at the thermostat," he said. He opened a box and demonstrated the settings.

I nodded. "Got it."

When he looked at my sneakers, I held up my briefcase and showed him the shoes tucked on top. "I don't suppose you've ever tried driving in high heels?"

"Point taken."

He opened the front door. I stepped past him into the

hall. Mrs. Donnel's door opened. I gave her a thumbs-up and received a smile.

"What are you driving?" Darach asked as we walked outside.

"The brown Ford." A click of the key fob released the locks. I set my briefcase behind the driver's seat. Darach commandeered the passenger seat, forcing it as far back as possible. Not far enough apparently, because he looked irritated. So was I.

"What are you doing?" My scowl failed to evict him.

"If you're going to drive in Scotland, you need instruction."

"But your car—" Unsure what he drove, I waved a hand at the parking lot.

"Evening traffic is heavier. I'll ride back with you." He deliberately checked his watch.

I slammed my door, fastened my seatbelt, and pulled onto the street, overcorrecting to drive on the left. Darach's left hand braced the dash, the right gripped my headrest.

Vehicles zipped past on the wrong side of the road, but I'd eat a ream of legal-size spreadsheets before admitting I was glad he rode shotgun.

After forty minutes of his terse directions, I miscalculated the turn into the MKI parking lot. The car's tires scraped the curb.

"Take my slot by the entry," Darach said, sounding relieved.

I parked and looked up at my sprawling red-brick, chimney-studded, temporary inheritance. Darach would have been pleased to know I was suitably impressed. "What's the water behind the factory?"

"The Firth of Tay," he said as I exchanged my sneakers for heels.

"What's a firth?"

"You'd call it an estuary."

Conversation with Darach was like counting grains of salt, a task most would quickly abandon. Unfortunately for him, I needed to know more about the business. "Does the railroad track we followed pass behind it, too?"

"Yes." He started toward the building.

I caught up with him and continued my inspection. The MacKendrick Industries complex stretched the length of a football stadium. The building where I worked in Dallas was small in comparison. "How is it laid out?" I asked.

"The ground floor houses factory operations. The offices are above on the right." His voice held a hint of pride.

He ushered me inside and into an elevator that rose to the second floor.

Curious glances followed us through the large room filled with cubicles. I avoided eye contact until we stopped in front of an organized desk guarding a hallway. A smiling woman with light-brown hair handed Darach a short stack of messages.

"Mrs. Gibson is our office manager," he told me. "Mrs. Gibson, this is Kinnon's sister-in-law, Lyssa Eastin. She is replacing him as my partner."

Surprise battled with sympathy in the motherly eyes.

Sympathy won. "I'm sorry for your loss. Mrs. MacKendrick seemed a sweet young woman."

"Thank you. She was."

I faced a future full of past tense. I blinked as the watercolor seascape on the wall in front of me blurred.

"Mr. MacDonald and Ms. Cameron are in the conference room," Mrs. Gibson said.

I followed Darach down a wide, tiled hallway. He pointed at doors. "My office, Kinnon's—your office, the conference room." He opened that door. A large oak table dominated the room. Two people stood as we entered. Though I'd forgotten their names, I'd seen the beautiful black-haired woman and the tall man with aggressively graying hair and thick black eyebrows at the funeral.

"Lyssa, you met Gavin MacDonald and his daughter Sabrina Cameron at the service," Darach said.

Gavin approached and extended his hand. "Again, our condolences, Ms. Eastin."

"Thank you. Please call me Lyssa." I set my briefcase on the table and shook his hand. "I take it you two are more than family friends."

"I've looked after the MacKendricks' legal needs for decades," Gavin said. "Sabrina also practices law. She joined me here two years ago."

I extended a hand to the petite *femme fatale* version of Snow White. "Mrs. Cameron."

"I'm divorced. It's Ms. but call me Sabrina." When our hands clasped, her wrist turned, forcing my palm down.

A dominance gesture displaying loyalty to Darach? If discovering who the other employees preferred as boss was this easy, I'd decide between Greer and Darach in no time.

"Would you care for coffee or water before we start?" she asked.

"Water, thanks." My stomach was already acidic enough to dissolve the gold pen Gavin tapped against a notepad.

"Coffee," Darach said.

Sabrina walked to the head of the table and activated the phone's intercom. "Mrs. Gibson, hold all calls, please." Without waiting for a reply, she continued to the credenza and poured Darach's coffee. No offer of cream or sugar. She knew his tastes. She opened the mini-fridge and handed me a bottle of water. "Where do you currently work, Lyssa?"

The question wasn't inappropriate, but the assessment in their eyes made me cautious. I'd disrupted their work world. They behaved politely, but I wanted an idea of what was coming before sharing my talents. I loosened the bottle cap. "I've worked for the same company in Dallas since I graduated college."

Gavin flipped open a file and re-stacked the papers inside with a sharp crack. "Have a seat and we'll begin."

The troops aligned.

Darach claimed the executive chair at the head of the table. Sabrina sat to his right, Gavin to her right. I sat across from Gavin.

Sabrina pushed a pen and a two-inch paper stack

across the table. "When Kinnon died, we had these prepared for Greer. You were a surprise, but that doesn't change the contracts. You should initial each page and sign the tagged sheets."

I fanned the stack with a thumb. "Is this a joke?"

They all met my eyes, but no one answered. Not a joke then. I leaned back. As teens, whenever Megan and I waited together, we took turns creating taglines for passers-by. Now, I tagged Darach as "Does not play well with others." Sabrina got "Don't hate me because I'm prettier than you are." Gavin looked ready to inquire about the availability of fancy mustard, and I'd earned "Runs with sharp objects."

I scooped the papers into one arm and picked up my briefcase.

"Is something wrong?" Sabrina asked. Her wide-eyed stare didn't fool me.

"Are you recommending I sign papers I haven't read?" I said.

"Of course not."

"Then I'll be in my office. Reading."

CHAPTER FOUR

I read until my eyes threatened to cross. Fifty pages later, I circled a third sentence and dropped the pen.

My mental scoreboard weighed Greer's Scotch-tossing against Darach's paperwork ploy. In the inheritance race, both contestants currently ranked zero.

I kicked off my shoes and curled my toes in the thick carpet. A framed eight-by-ten of Megan sat front and center on Kinnon's desk. He'd chosen a candid photo that captured Megan the woman, not Megan the model, her arms flung wide, her hair windblown, her clothing weekend-casual. I liked him for that.

I glanced at the racehorse prints on the walls. "A gambler to the last," Peter had said. Megan had met Kinnon at a casino. Was he gambling then? I scooted a stack of accumulated mail, from his desk, into my briefcase.

Rather than face another page of the contract, I stood and stretched and then paced the office's generous perimeter, skirting a saddle-brown leather couch to pause in front of an oak bookcase where horse-racing forms outnumbered industry publications. I thumbed through a few of each. Only the racing forms showed use, but the newest was over five months old.

I tried the knob on the connecting door that separated

Kinnon's office from Darach's office. Locked, but not on my side. I turned around. Drapes, the dark tan color of wet sand, concealed the entire back wall. Logically, the windows would overlook the Firth of Tay.

I gave the cord a brisk tug. Dust motes danced as the drapes ratcheted open. My sneeze ended on a gasp. Instead of a water view, the floor-to-ceiling window exposed me to the vast factory below where people in hardhats purposefully worked around hulking machinery.

"Just a smattering of your 248 employees, Ms. Eastin," I said, though Darach wasn't around to appreciate my imitation of him or the knowledge I'd gleaned from a company brochure on Kinnon's desk. I reached for the cord and then stopped.

I was legally responsible for these people. Every decision I made or didn't make while I owned MKI shares affected them. I'd never been a supervisor, much less an owner.

The phone rang. "Lyssa Eastin," I answered.

"It's Mrs. Gibson. Ms. Cameron is asking how long you'll be."

I glanced from the wall clock to the papers on the desk. "Please tell her I'll return to the conference room at one. And I noticed there's no computer in this office. Did Kinnon have one?"

"Aye, a laptop. He carried it about with him."

"Did he back up files to a central storage device?"

"I'll check the cloud and see what he might have saved."

"Thanks." I hung up and returned to the wall-window. I wouldn't let the employees go without their paychecks.

Neither would I sign documents written to leave me hamstrung.

I opened the phone book and made a call.

Twenty-nine minutes later, I headed to the conference room. I was walking too fast, breathing too fast. I paused outside the door.

Our parents had taught Megan and me to do the best job possible, no matter what the task. Being parentless had taught us to stand up for ourselves. Business school and my job in Texas had taught me to prepare before every meeting. "Shoulders back," I whispered, turning the knob.

The others, already seated, looked my way. I handed Sabrina the first fifty pages. "I thought you'd like to check my progress."

"You're not finished?" Smile gone, she fanned through the stack. "None of these are initialed." She fanned again. "Some pages are missing."

The intercom buzzed. Sabrina slapped the button to engage the speaker. "We're not to be disturbed, Mrs. Gibson."

"Mr. Murray has arrived."

"Who is Mr. Murray?" Sabrina asked.

"Please send him in," I said to Mrs. Gibson.

"Yes, Ms. Eastin."

Father and daughter shifted in their seats. Darach looked like he'd gone on alert.

The door opened. I stepped forward, hand extended. "Mr. Murray, I'm Lyssa Eastin. I appreciate your coming on short notice."

"Not at all. Call me Evan."

He was younger than I'd expected—not much older than me—but his grip was firm, and he was punctual. Wavy copper hair and lively brown eyes behind black-framed glasses gave him the appearance of a myopic, eager-to-please Irish Setter. I had hoped for a bulldog. Introductions didn't take long. "Please sit down," I said.

He chose the chair I had occupied earlier, so I sat between him and Darach.

"Evan is a solicitor," I said. "I have retained him to protect my interests in matters concerning MacKendrick Industries."

"Lyssa." Gavin shook his head. "As MacKendrick Industries' solicitors, Sabrina and I also represent you."

"Not until I sign these papers and officially join MKI. After what I read, I felt the need for an outside opinion." I pushed a few pieces of paper toward Evan and tapped the top sheet. "If I sign this, Darach gains tiebreaking authority over any business disputes we might have. The next one would allow Darach to vote my shares during an emergency should I be unavailable. And the next page would allow Darach to decide what constitutes an emergency." I tugged the stack away from Sabrina and gave it to Evan. "I need to know what I missed."

Sabrina turned to Darach and shrugged a slim shoulder. "I still think it was a good exercise."

Darach continued to relax in his chair. I had read and recognized his power play. The least he could do was react.

"This wasn't your idea?" I asked him.

"I agreed to the strategy. I was curious if you'd pass their test."

With a coolness I found frustrating, Sabrina turned back to me. "If you had signed without noticing the conditions, MKI would run more smoothly."

Evan released a low whistle and circled a paragraph. "My, that was clever." He glanced at Sabrina with apparent admiration. I wanted to spit nails.

"What exactly do you do for a living?" Darach asked.

"I'm a financial analyst at James Wiseman."

Everyone's eyes narrowed. You'd think I'd morphed into the UK equivalent of an IRS auditor. I didn't have to ask if they recognized the name of the world's second-largest financial firm. They now realized I brought more to the table than they had anticipated.

"What market sector do you analyze?" Darach asked.

"Central and South American consumer durables. Things like appliances, home improvement stores, electronic and photographic equipment providers."

"Lyssa, do you have a will?"

Gavin's new line of questioning was the last thing I expected.

"If Megan was your beneficiary, we need to revise your will," he continued.

"I suppose you'd like to write the terms of that document, too."

"If he doesn't, I would," Sabrina said. "You need a proper beneficiary." Her gaze followed Darach as he walked to the credenza and pulled out a bottle of water.

"The company and employees don't need further unsettling," he said. "You need a new beneficiary, bearing in mind that Mother and I are your only choices where MKI is concerned." He loosened the lid and offered me the water. I took it and the opportunity he'd presented.

"I could also split the shares between you."

The three of them frowned. Now I knew where they stood on that scenario.

"Since I don't know you or your mother well, you won't mind my asking questions of and about you both." I faced Evan. "I'll let you know when I'm ready to write a new will."

Gavin stood, a genial uncle imparting information for my own good. "A will is an unpleasant reminder of mortality. But given recent events, surely you see the sense in planning ahead."

My ducks-in-a-row nature had my fingers itching for a pen to create legal order. "I see the sense, but I'm not rewriting my will today." Again, I faced Evan. "Please draw up a document negating my current will. I'll sign that."

He tapped his pen. "Easily done. That said, you should write another will soon."

"I agree. But not today."

Gavin and Sabrina conferred in low voices, presumably weighing the chances and consequences of my dying a sudden death. For about the hundredth time I wondered what Kinnon had wanted to talk to me about regarding MKI.

I looked at Gavin. "Speaking of wills, do you write them

for the MacKendricks and the Rands?"

"I do."

"Then why did Mr. Craddock write Kinnon and Megan's new wills?"

His face darkened. I couldn't tell if he was angry or embarrassed.

"None of us knew Kinnon changed his will until Mr. Craddock contacted Darach after the crash."

Before I could ask another question, Darach stood. "Let's go."

"Where?"

"The bank. Mr. Murray, throw those papers away and draw up a partnership agreement with your co-counsels. Keep it simple. We'll meet at nine tomorrow morning for the signing." He sounded as fed up with the last few hours as I was, but he'd probably taken time for lunch.

"What happened to papers needing my signature today so that payroll can be released?" I asked as Darach lifted my coat from the rack by the door and followed me into the hall.

"Mrs. Gibson will scan your signature into the computer and send it to the payroll department, after which you'll sign a signature card at the bank. Let me get my coat." He pointed at his office door.

Curiosity beat out frustration. I entered first. Inside, neat rows of books and periodicals lined the shelves. Without looking closely, I knew all the materials would pertain to the energy industry. The curtains behind his desk stood open, framing his window-wall. Darach seemed the kind of man who would want to know what was going on down on the manufacturing floor—a good trait in an owner.

"If you only needed two signatures, we wasted the last few hours," I said.

"Had you mentioned your occupation and employer when Sabrina asked, I wouldn't have let the scenario play out."

I crossed my arms. "She didn't ask for my résumé, and I wasn't expecting a corporate exam."

"You should have." He jerked a nod toward the factory floor. "Every man and woman down there depends on us. And we depend on them. I was trying to protect us all— including you—by ensuring MKI runs smoothly."

His fists punched into the arms of his overcoat. He tugged his lapels into order and threw a plaid wool scarf over one shoulder. When he held out my coat, I presented my back and accepted his help. The scarf floated across my shoulders, the wool soft against my neck.

"What's this?" I fingered the cashmere, a mixture of blue, green, red, and black.

"The MacKendrick battle plaid." He opened the door. "You've earned it."

He probably hadn't meant it kindly, but I felt proud.

Our brief bank visit was all business. Darach directed me back to MKI and pointed out the canteen. I guess he'd grown tired of listening to my stomach growl. The rest of the afternoon passed slowly.

I toured the cubicles, but everyone appeared busy, so I

worked on getting my bearings instead of asking questions.

The drive back to Perth was mostly silent as I concentrated on retracing the route's turns before Darach pointed them out. We both had plenty to think about.

I wandered the flat, making piles of items that reminded me of Megan. When I went to bed, I lay awake while my brain hummed on the electric clock's frequency. I turned onto my side and looked at the illuminated numbers.

I figured the time difference between Scotland and Texas. It wasn't too late to call a friend, but the only one who came to mind was no longer an option. Megan had been my best friend. When we'd lost our parents, we'd shared a tragedy that none of our friends had endured. Megan quickly regained her ability to make friends while I'd concentrated on helping raise my younger sister.

I sighed. If I were home, I'd read reports until my eyes drifted shut. I didn't have any reports here, so I threw back the covers, groped for the lamp switch, and blinked at the sudden brightness. Kinnon's office mail bloated my briefcase, waiting to be sorted. I grabbed the letters and a nail file to use as an opener and stacked pillows behind me.

Piece by piece, I flipped obvious junk mail onto the floor. The relatively small pile of letters that remained bore postmarks up to a month old. I would check Kinnon's apartment mailbox tomorrow.

One envelope of expensive paper stock stood out. The Edinburgh return address bore the Spanish consulate's crest.

I turned the letter over several times. The mail was legally mine, so I slit the flap and removed an embossed card.

"The Spanish Consulate General invites Mr. Kinnon MacKendrick and guest to a reception for Alonso Alba de Espinoza, Minister of Energy, on Saturday, May 8th, at eight o'clock in the evening. RSVP."

Next Saturday. Megan would have sparkled among the black ties and gowns. I set the card aside and blotted my eyes with the cotton sheet.

A long envelope, postmarked Muirhead, Scotland, bore Kinnon's name and MKI's address in computer-printed capital letters. I flipped it over. No return address. I slit the envelope and unfolded a single sheet of unlined paper with the same block font.

"LAST WARNING. CHOOSE LIFE. MAINTAIN THE STATUS QUO."

CHAPTER FIVE

Friday morning, I picked up a duplicate mailbox key from the flat manager. As I tucked Kinnon's personal mail into my briefcase, Darach pulled up beside me in a gray BMW sedan. The somber color matched my mood.

The driver's window slid down. "You look exhausted," he said.

"Just what a woman wants to hear first thing in the morning."

I locked the mailbox. Truthfully, I *was* exhausted. After their attorney said Megan hadn't left a personal letter with her will, I'd put the idea they were in trouble out of my mind. Finding the threatening letter brought it all back. *Last warning* implied there had been at least an initial warning. I hadn't found another note while searching the flat last night, or I'd have called the police.

I had found items I'd take a closer look at once I got to work, but nothing that supported a death threat.

"Are you feeling all right?" Darach asked.

"I'm okay. I'm not on your way to MKI," I said.

"I thought you might want to follow me in and then make your own way back tonight."

"That's a nice offer, but why are you making it? The truth, please."

He rested an arm in the open window. "The truth is you're not yet comfortable driving here. So, until you are,

I feel some responsibility for you."

Yesterday's fighting spirit had deserted me, and my ability to negotiate roundabouts on my own after five hours of sleep wasn't a skill I wanted to test, but I felt like I had to.

"I put the address in the car's GPS, but I'll still follow you." I raised both hands to cover a jaw-stretching yawn.

"Bad night?"

"Bad week."

Darach frowned.

"What?" I asked.

"I can't say I'm happy you're my partner, but I appreciate that yesterday, when you could have mucked up payroll as payback for our test, you instead, behaved with integrity."

He was trying to be nice. Because he wanted me to sell in a month?

"My favorite economics professor taught that the fairest exchange is my best efforts for yours," I said. "I won't deliberately hinder MKI's operation."

His nod came slow. I guessed the jury was still out.

"Are you ready to go?" he asked.

"Lead on."

I followed Darach onto the street, mentally noting landmarks. A familiar shop and sign from yesterday's route slid past. In the morning light, the idea of murder seemed far-fetched. Kinnon and Megan rewriting their wills wasn't unusual. Our parents' unexpected deaths had made Megan and me cautious about leaving legal issues unresolved.

I solved nothing during the drive to MKI. Darach and I walked in on Evan, Sabrina, and Gavin passing documents across the conference table. I set down my briefcase and poured a brain-clearing cup of coffee.

"This won't do," Evan said, circling something on the page he was reading.

"What?" Sabrina snatched the paper from his hands and read as we all looked on. She glanced at her father, who continued reading the page in front of him with intense concentration. "Sorry, we missed removing this," she said.

Darach and I each held out a hand. Sabrina's lips tightened as she handed the paper to Darach. He read it then passed it to me. Evan had marked a paragraph that would have allowed Darach to vote my shares in the event of an emergency. I glanced at Gavin. Was its inclusion a mistake or deliberate? Since Evan had caught it, I didn't press the issue.

"I'll make that revision," Sabrina said, pulling her laptop closer.

I pulled the invitation out of my briefcase. "Darach, I found this in Kinnon's mail. Did you receive one?"

He scanned the embossed crest and nodded.

"Is that the party at the Spanish consulate?" Sabrina asked.

"Yes," I said.

"Don't worry. Darach and I represent MacKendrick Industries at social engagements. I've already RSVP'd. I'll take care of that for you."

She reached for the envelope.

"Thanks, but I'll do it." I stuffed the invitation into my briefcase wondering how much time Sabrina and Darach spent together outside work? I'd need to factor spouses and potential spouses into my decision for Megan regarding MKI. Greer had Peter, who obviously supported her. If Darach and Sabrina were an item, they made an impressive power couple.

Sabrina printed a page and passed it to Evan. Evan read, and then passed it to me to read. I signed then tapped my pen on the table. "Darach, what does MacKendrick Industries have to do with the Spanish Ministry of Science and Technology?"

"We're manufacturers, and they're looking for product. I'll be on the floor," he said, and walked out.

My face heated at his oversimplified answer. *So much for being partners.* Plus, I'd had another question. Reluctantly, I turned to Sabrina and Gavin. "Besides his visits to vendors, what can you tell me about Kinnon's duties?"

"They were greater than his desire to perform," Sabrina said. "Anything you do will be an improvement, but the best direction for MKI is for you to let Darach run the day to day aspects, as he's always done."

If I'd had hackles, they'd have raised at her criticism of Kinnon. "He had work files at his flat. So, he wasn't entirely a silent partner—or lazy," I said.

Sabrina opened her mouth and I watched Gavin put a warning hand on her arm.

"That's a question better asked of Darach, Lyssa.

He has the best knowledge of where you might fit in," Gavin said.

"Good idea." I faced Evan. "Am I through here?"

"Just sign this document to void your current will."

I read the short statement and signed. Gavin and Sabrina added their signatures as witnesses. I left the lawyers to finish up.

Back in my office, I opened the mail from Kinnon's apartment and read everything, including advertising circulars and junk mail. Nothing threatening lurked in the stack.

The phone's red message light glowed.

I called Mrs. Gibson for Kinnon's passcode and listened to a man say Kinnon's Porsche was ready to pick up at Clapton's Garage in Perth. Wondering about Kinnon's car hadn't occurred to me until now. Why was it in the shop? Maybe he'd hid other threatening notes there!

I called the garage. No one answered, so I left a message that I'd stop by over the weekend. I looked up the address and wrote it down.

At loose ends, I stacked the files and personal papers from Kinnon's flat on my desk. I started with his bank statements. He spent a lot of money, but he also deposited a lot of money. My monthly salary didn't come close to the twice-monthly deposits I interpreted as Kinnon's paychecks.

In January and February, he'd also deposited the odd amount. Gambling winnings? March and early April listed substantial outgoing checks made out to CASH. Paying off gambling debts? Megan's engagement ring?

The top drawer of Kinnon's desk held a chaos of paper

clips, pens, rubber bands, and sticky notes. *Leaving soon,* I told my fingers before they could sort the clutter into order. Personalized stationery occupied the top side-drawer. The bottom drawer held an electric razor, eye drops, nail clippers, peppermint breath spray, and a woodsy aftershave. I opened every drawer and read every paper without discovering another threatening letter.

I opened the MKI files and flipped through them. What *had* Kinnon done to earn those hefty paychecks? Nothing obvious jumped out at me, so I buzzed Mrs. Gibson.

"Yes, Ms. Eastin?"

"I found MKI files at Kinnon's flat and wondered if you needed them for company records." I read off the dates.

"No. I have the originals. Those are copies Mr. Kinnon requested a few months ago. Oh, and I checked the company cloud. Mr. Kinnon has a few files there. I'll get his password for you and have a computer installed."

"Thank you." I hung up and glanced at my watch. Eleven a.m. in Dundee made it 4 a.m. in Dallas—too early to call work and let them know I'd be adding my sick days to my bereavement leave.

I closed my eyes. The last time I'd talked with Megan she was at the hotel in Newcastle.

"Hey, sis! What's up?" Megan said.

"The usual. Work, reports, Dallas traffic. Tell me more about wedded bliss."

She giggled. "It involves a lot of cuddling and kissing—or snogging, as Kinnon says."

"Snogging? You're right out of a Harry Potter book."

"I know, weird word, but fun—and incredibly accurate."

We'd talked for an hour while Kinnon visited with a vendor. They were going out to dinner when he returned. And Megan had said—

I jumped up and scanned the manufacturing floor. Darach wasn't in view, so I buzzed Mrs. Gibson and asked for the Rands' phone numbers. I called the house first. Fortunately, Peter answered.

"It's Lyssa Eastin. This might be difficult, but I have some questions. Do you have a moment?"

"I do." Kinnon's stepfather didn't sound happy to hear from me, but he also didn't hang up.

"Kinnon and Megan flew back from Newcastle on Sunday afternoon. But when I spoke to Megan earlier that day, she said they'd start home Monday morning. Do you know why their plans changed?"

"No. We expected them Monday as well. We were away from home Sunday afternoon and only found out they were traveling when Darach called and told us about the crash."

"Do you think Kinnon was worried about the weather?"

"No. I paid particular attention to the forecasts when he flew. There was light rain, but nothing dangerous. No one knows why they left Sunday. Even if we did, it wouldn't change the outcome." Peter's voice cracked. "Why are you asking, Lyssa?"

"I'm sorry to upset you, but I'm trying to work out the sequence of their weekend."

"Understandable. And if you need to call again, use my mobile number. Greer already dwells too much on the crash and Kinnon's death. She doesn't need to be reminded any more than necessary."

I recited the number Mrs. Gibson had given me. He confirmed it, and we hung up. I walked to the connecting door and knocked. No answer. I tried the knob. Still locked.

I needed something to do, so I made notes on Megan and Kinnon's weekend time line. Then, since my reason for staying was to decide who to give my MKI shares to, I started a list of Darach vs. Greer qualities. It was short. I needed more information.

The factory floor drew my gaze. For the next five minutes, I watched. All those workers. Bosses probably received hate mail. Out of two hundred-plus employees, someone might have harbored animosity toward Kinnon. Especially if innuendo proved right and he hadn't pulled his weight.

Then again, what about those sporadic deposits and the large outgoing checks from his account? If he'd continued gambling but quit winning, maybe the note related to a debt.

I kicked off my shoes and kneaded the carpet with my toes. I flipped Kinnon's desk calendar to January and read forward. This week, Kinnon had two appointments. I dialed the listed numbers and canceled both. The masseuse and the barber offered sympathy over Kinnon's death, but neither indicated they'd seen it coming.

I picked up a paper clip and flicked the curved metal with my thumbnail. Did Darach indulge in a weekly massage? He'd probably benefit from a regular loosening of his stiff shoulders to give his type-A uptightness a breather. The two brothers brought to mind the fable of the industrious ant and the hedonistic grasshopper. I imagined Darach's head on the ant and Kinnon's on the—

A sharp tap on the door startled me. As the paper clip flew under the desk, I clasped my hands on the desk top. "Come in."

Evan entered and handed me a short stack of documents. "Your copies." He smiled, and then donned his business face.

"Have you given thought to writing a will?"

"I'm still considering my options."

He nodded. "We'll draw one up when you're ready."

"Thanks." I leaned back as the door closed behind him. Maybe I should go ahead and write my will. If I forgot which side of the road to drive on—

I pushed away from the desk and searched for the paper clip. A bright yellow square caught my eye. Someone—Kinnon?—had slapped a sticky note on the desk's knee hole. I tugged the note loose.

"AHD1132223124552." The numbers ran off the edge of the paper, where a torn corner suggested it had been ripped off in a hurry. The twos featured the same distinctive *Z* shape as the writing on Kinnon's calendar.

Another quick rap on the door caused me to jump. My head hit the bottom of the desk drawer. "Ouch!"

"Lyssa?"

One palm to my head, I backed out. The open door

framed three curious men. "Yes?"

"Drop something?" Darach asked politely.

CHAPTER SIX

As Darach approached, I held up the paper clip and stood. His left eyebrow elevated then fell to neutral. Gavin and another man followed him into my office.

"This is Frank Blevins, our foreman. Frank, Lyssa Eastin, my new partner."

I tucked the yellow note into my pocket and extended a hand. "Mr. Blevins."

The foreman's large hand swallowed mine. "Miss Eastin." The deep smile lines around his eyes weren't currently in use.

Darach's stare dropped to my shoeless feet. He'd have to get used to it. I did my best thinking while barefoot. "Mrs. Gibson is copying current job files and proposals. She'll have them for you soon," he said as if he'd read my mind about finding something to do.

Frank nodded at my desk. "Looks like she got a head start on you. She already has files."

"I brought those from Kinnon's flat. They're duplicates of completed jobs."

"Kinnon took work home?" Darach ran a finger across the date tabs.

"I guess wonders don't cease." Gavin's chuckle sounded forced. "I'll see you later today, Darach. Lyssa." He nodded and turned.

Frank tapped Gavin's shoulder. "I'll walk out with you. We need to talk."

"Of course, but I'm late for another meeting. Call me later?" Their voices faded.

Darach straightened. "I'm going to the floor. Would you care to come?"

"Yes, I would." Ready to observe Darach in action, I stepped into my heels and followed him from the office. Darach pointed right. "We can take the stairs at the end of the hall."

I matched my stride to his. Just past the conference room, he opened a steel fire door. Our steps echoed down the metal staircase.

"How long were you and Kinnon partners?" I asked.

"Since our father died four years ago."

"What were Kinnon's duties?"

"He flew his plane to goodwill meetings where he wined and dined clients, and he came in twice a month to pick up his paycheck."

I waited for him to elaborate. When he didn't, I thought about the size of that paycheck. "Why did Kinnon join MKI if he wasn't interested in the business?"

"It wasn't his decision. I received fifty percent of the company on my twenty-first birthday. Father knew Kinnon wasn't interested in MKI. He told me I'd eventually receive the other half. But he changed his mind and left it to Kinnon." His tone was neutral, but this family had a history of being surprised by a will.

"Did you and your father have a falling out?"

Darach shook his head. "We shared a common goal. Our means to that end differed, but we both believed in manufacturing a quality product that creates a demand that benefits the company, our employees, and our customers."

"Did Kinnon know your father was giving him half?"

"He said not." He opened another steel door. We stepped into a room with brick and mortar walls painted a happy yellow that held energizing-red rows of lockers.

Darach stopped in front of a shelf and handed me a hardhat. "Always wear one of these when you're on the floor."

I settled the hat on my head and followed him into the plant.

"Your education begins at receiving," he said, leading me to an open office adjacent to the loading docks. I looked up. I could see our office wall-windows.

"Is this how you learned?" I asked.

"From receiving to shipping. Father brought me in when I turned fifteen."

"What was he like?"

Darach didn't hide his grimace. "He enjoyed control."

"Then you come by your power fetish honestly."

To my surprise, his lips lifted enough to constitute a smile. "When our discussions grew so heated people could hear us through closed doors, Frank would "borrow" me to do something on the floor. He taught me more than anyone."

I did the math. "What is retirement age in Scotland?"

"Frank doesn't want to retire. And he knows the factory front to back so I'm not insisting."

We stopped at an open loading bay with a view of the afternoon sky. A hint of sea air diluted the machine-oil smell. Darach pointed at the flatbed trailers that filled the holding area, each loaded with steel beams nearly as long as the trailer. "We store the raw steel here. The real work begins behind us."

He walked me through pipe-forming, explaining the process. If he expected me to yawn, I disappointed him. His narration stopped mid-sentence. "Hang on."

I followed him across a yellow safety line to a machine that, even to my inexperienced ear, lacked mechanical rhythm. Darach pulled a phone from his pocket. "Frank, eighteen is out of sync. Bring Ted. I'll wait on you."

I took a cautious step back. My heel caught in the rubber mat and I pitched to the concrete floor.

Darach crouched beside me. "Are you all right?"

"My heel's stuck. My shoes aren't designed for these mats." I slipped my foot free, giving him room to jiggle the heel out of the rubber grid.

Frank jogged up. His "What happened?" sounded more like an accusation than concern.

"Lyssa fell." Darach lifted my arm, exposing my elbow. "She's bleeding."

Frank sighed. "Does she need stitches?"

"It's only a scrape," I said. I turned my leg and my knee came into view. "Or two."

Darach stood. Each man held out a hand.
I got my feet under me, stood on my own, and stepped

into my shoe. Darach took my arm. "I'll walk her to the nurse while you check the machine."

A man pushing a tool cart stopped. "What's that about?" I heard him ask Frank.

"The end of our non-reportable injury record. The lads and lasses were working hard to break that one. I heard plans for a cakes-and-biscuits celebration next week."

I read dismay on several faces as I limped across the plant. I'd reviewed enough manufacturing business reports to know that any type of injury could affect a safety rating and draw government scrutiny. Darach opened a door bearing a red cross. Without looking at me, he turned and left.

In the bright white room, the nurse set her clipboard aside and helped me onto the examination table. "What happened?" she asked.

I explained as she scrutinized my scrapes. When she turned and opened a drawer, I said, "What's reportable versus non-reportable?"

She turned back, antiseptic pads and band-aids in hand.

"Non-reportable means I don't have to file a report with the safety commission." She opened the pads and scrubbed my elbow and knee.

"What am I?"

"Non-reportable." She glanced from me to the dry erase boards on the wall. On the top one was written REPORTABLE and beneath it, 437 days. The bottom one said NON-REPORTABLE with *99 days* written in green.

Patched up, I thanked her, knowing that when I shut

her door, she'd replace 99 with a zero. I'd officially canceled the cakes-and-biscuits celebration. I was not making a good first impression.

I headed to the locker room, left my hardhat on a bench, and trudged upstairs to my office. Mrs. Gibson had placed current job files on my desk. I flipped through the pages but didn't know what to do with the information, so I set them aside and toggled the intercom.

"Yes, Ms. Eastin," Mrs. Gibson said.

"Thank you for the files. Do you have the name and phone number of the hotel in Newcastle where Megan and Kinnon stayed?"

"Let me uncover my calendar—here you are."

I wrote down the information. "Thanks. Do you have a copy of the hotel bill?"

"No, but I'll ask them to email it."

"I'll take care of that." I glanced around. "When can I expect a computer?"

"It's coming. Until we set up your email address, have the hotel send the bill to mine."

I wrote down her email, thanked her, and dialed. A woman picked up after the third ring. "Newcastle Inn."

"Hello. My name is Lyssa Eastin. My sister and her husband stayed at the inn last weekend, and then they died in a plane crash on their way home. Kinnon and Megan MacKendrick? Perhaps you met them?"

"Oh, sorry; I saw that crash on the telly."

The woman sounded genuinely distressed. "I checked

them in. I knew right off that they were newlyweds. They had that glow, like the sun shone directly on them."

I swallowed the lump in my throat. "Were you there when they checked out? They left earlier than planned, but I don't know why."

"No, I wasn't here. Call back tonight and ask for Kevin."

"OK. In the meantime, please email a copy of the bill. I'm the executor of their estate." We wrapped up the conversation.

Another wait for information. I picked up the trashcan and limped to the bookshelf, needing to accomplish something. Page by page, I checked each gambling sheet then threw it away. None bore handwriting or hid a threat.

Saturday, I cleaned the apartment and discovered reminders of Megan everywhere: her mugs in the kitchen, her throw pillows on the couch, her wall of happiness, and her coasters on the coffee table. I made tuna salad for dinner by tossing together most of the meager contents of their pantry. The meal sat untouched while I called the Newcastle Inn again. Kevin, the afternoon desk clerk, wasn't there yet, so I spoke to the shuttle driver.

"Aye, I took them to the airport. He was upset about something; I don't know what. She was the calm one—kept telling him it wasn't his fault and they'd be OK." The shuttle driver paused. "Hang on; Kevin's arrived."

After a moment I heard, "This is Kevin."

"Hi, Kevin, this is Lyssa Eastin. Megan MacKendrick was

my sister." I launched into my reason for calling, ending with, "I need to know why they left Sunday, instead of Monday."

"Miss, unless you can prove you're her sister, I can't help you." He sounded ready to hang up.

"Kevin, wait!" Everyone else had talked to me easily. "Check their bill. Megan called me Sunday; we talked between one and two your time. I didn't recognize the number, so she must have used her room phone. It's an outgoing call to—" I recited my cell number.

"Just a moment."

Seconds dragged into a minute. "Miss, that number is on their bill, but that doesn't prove you're the one she called."

"I have that phone with me. Please ask the operator to dial that number and tell her to reverse the charges. You'll hear my voice message and my name. Will you talk to me then?"

Silence met my request. Grief and the real threat of tears shook my voice. "Megan Eastin MacKendrick was 24, blonde, green-eyed, with a smile that made you immediately smile back and suddenly feel happier. She treated everyone she met like you'd been friends forever. She was full of joy and light. I buried her three days ago, and I need to know why she left your hotel early. *Please help me!*"

"I'll have to put you on hold," he finally said.

Minutes ticked by. If he hung up on me, I'd call Mr. Craddock and ask him to call Kevin.

My cell phone rang. Seconds later, Kevin was back and talking.

CHAPTER SEVEN

Sunday morning, I dressed in my slacks and Megan's long-sleeve Henley, leaving the top buttons undone to ease the snug fit. I'd need to shop for clothes soon. We were the same height, but even with my recent lack of appetite, I couldn't fit into Megan's size-six wardrobe.

I checked the time. I'd fallen into a deep sleep last night—the best I'd had since the crash. My thoughts flitted between the ominous letter I'd found, and the night clerk's revelation. I hadn't found a connection, but I knew who might. I dialed Peter's cell.

"Hello?" he answered.

"Hi, it's Lyssa. Do you have a moment?"

"Let me step outside. Greer is sleeping, and I don't want to disturb her."

I heard a door open and close.

"What is it?" he asked, sounding tired but alert.

"How is Greer?" I asked.

"She's having difficulty shaking off the grief."

"That's going to last for a while." I thought of Mom and Dad, Aunt Sally, and Megan. Life's lessons in loss didn't get any easier.

"Why are you calling?"

"I spoke to the Newcastle Inn clerk. He said Megan and

Kinnon were upset when they returned from lunch Sunday. And that Kinnon cited a family emergency as their reason for leaving early. And the shuttle driver said Megan kept telling Kinnon that 'they' would be okay."

"Kinnon and Megan *they* or someone else *they?*"

"I don't know." I tucked an arm against my stomach. "Was there a family emergency that night? Maybe someone in the extended family?"

"Not that I'm aware of. Most of the family attended the funeral, and no one mentioned anything amiss. But given the deaths, perhaps they wouldn't. I'll make calls." He sounded animated. I'd piqued his interest.

"Thank you. Megan said you were kind."

He hesitated. "I'm glad she thought so, but I don't deserve her tribute. She was lovely, sweet and genuine—the sort of girl we hoped Kinnon would fall in love with. Only, it happened so fast, and we knew so little about her. I'm afraid we made it obvious neither Greer nor I appreciated their marrying without telling us."

"That's understandable." At least Megan had called and saved me from feeling entirely left out. The rugby coffee mug caught my eye. "This is awkward, but do you think Greer would like to go through Kinnon's clothing and personal items?" *And maybe give me a chance to know her better?*

"Actually, I'm glad the task fell to you. I haven't the heart to go through them, and she may be upset with me later, but I don't think she's ready to deal with the finality of dispensing Kinnon's things."

I glanced at Megan's pillows. "I understand."

"Have you asked Darach?"

"It hadn't occurred to me. He said he and Kinnon weren't close."

Peter sighed. "Sadly true. He might surprise you, though. And it might offer him an opportunity for closure that he doesn't know he needs."

I waited, but Peter didn't elaborate. "I'll think about it," I finally said.

After we hung up, I considered Peter's suggestion. *Would Darach like a chance to sort through Kinnon's things?* The only way to find out was to ask. I dialed Darach's cell. It rang once.

"MacKendrick," he answered.

"It's Lyssa. Do you have a moment?"

"Yes."

"I'm ready to pack Kinnon's things. Peter doesn't want to go through them, and he doesn't think your mother should. He suggested I ask you. I'm capable of doing it alone, but I thought his family—"

"I'll be there in thirty minutes."

"Today?"

The dial tone sounded. So much for my plans to buy a late breakfast, grocery-shop, and pick up packing supplies.

My stomach growled. No food remained in the pantry. With luck, Darach would skim Kinnon's belongings and I'd eat soon. In the meantime, I drank a cup of coffee while creating a shopping list. That chore done, I looked around the flat. Megan's photos were going home with me, so I'd start there. I'd mostly avoided the master bedroom, but I'd seen something there I wanted to save.

I opened the bedroom door, crossed to the window, and opened the curtains. Sunshine flooded in, reflecting off black-lacquered furniture topped with a thin layer of dust. The room felt masculine—in the Asian way of clean lines and frugal decoration.

I walked to the dresser and picked up a silver-framed photograph of Megan and me at the last dinner we'd shared. I'd flown to New York at Christmas, and we'd asked our waiter to snap the shot of us hugging. I caressed the image and carried it to the living room. The doorbell rang.

I ran downstairs and opened the door. Darach was wishing Mrs. Donnel a good morning. She must keep her eye pressed to the peephole the way she knew every time someone walked down the hallway.

It was the first time I'd seen Darach without a suit. The jeans and blue chambray button-down made him appear more approachable.

"Hi." My stomach growled a welcome for the yeasty scent emanating from the paper bag he carried. "If that's breakfast, you're a lifesaver."

His gaze shot from my cleavage to my face. Blood rose to my cheeks. I should have changed shirts. He handed me the bag. "Anice sent baps. You haven't eaten?"

"The cupboards are bare. I'll shop after you've looked through Kinnon's things." I opened the bag, inhaled, and admired the golden rolls. "She sent enough for both of us. I made coffee, and there's jam in the fridge."

He followed me to the kitchen. While I poured coffee, he microwaved the baps. "Eat, and I'll take you to the shops before we start packing," he said.

"You want to help me pack?" I stopped mid-pour. I didn't want to spend the next few hours striving for polite conversation, knowing that the next little thing I found might start me crying. "That's not necessary. If you'll pick out whatever the family might want to keep, I'll shop later."

He pulled a piece of paper from his pocket. "Anice gave me a short grocery list. I'll take care of hers while you do yours. Where is the nearest grocer?"

My list was also short. "I'll ask Mrs. Donnel."

Darach looked in my shopping basket. His eyes rose directly to my face. I hadn't changed shirts. I liked him being the perturbed party for a change.

"You bought eggs for your breakfast?" he asked.

"Yes."

"Do you want bacon or sausage?"

"Bacon."

He put a pack in the basket. "What else do you need?"

"Salad dressing and soup."

"Is that what you eat for dinner?"

"For the next couple of nights, yes. After work and packing, it's quick and easy." My appetite, though returning, wasn't demanding much. I craved comfort food, and soup was the closest I'd found in the small grocery. As soon as I hit Texas, I was heading for the nearest Mexican restaurant for cheese enchiladas, heavy on the onions, black olives, and sour cream, with a salt-rimmed margarita on the rocks.

"Do you need bread?" Again, he fixed his gaze on mine.

"Yes. Are you sure you have everything Anice wanted?" Why couldn't he suddenly remember something he needed from another part of the store and give my blush response a rest?

"Aye."

We checked out and stopped by another shop for packing boxes, tape, and bubble wrap. The overly-attentive male clerk earned one of Darach's hard stares. Silence riddled our drive back to the flat. If the tight-lipped expression Darach assumed whenever we were together continued, it would be a long month.

Darach left his purchases in his car's trunk and carried the packing supplies inside while I toted my groceries. Two men in suits stood at the end of the hall. Mrs. Donnel popped out of her flat so fast I nearly dropped my bags.

"Miss Eastin, they showed me their warrant cards, so I let them in the building."

"What? Who's serving a warrant?" I looked from Mrs. Donnel to Darach to the approaching men. As far as I knew, I hadn't done anything wrong. Because I traveled to Central and South America, I had an international driver's license, and I didn't think I'd broken any traffic laws. But this was Scotland, and my driving, while improving, still required concentration.

"Miss Eastin?" said the man with a weathered face, fashioned along the same solid lines as his body. Thick gray hair brushed his broad forehead.

"Yes," I said.

Darach stepped forward. "Let's see your warrant cards."

Each man displayed identification. So *that* was a warrant card. Detective Inspector White and Detective Sergeant Gilly of the Tayside Police. I studied the IDs as if I'd recognize a real warrant card from a fake.

"What do you think?" I asked Darach.

"What do you want with Lyssa?" he said, ignoring me.

"Who are you, sir?" Detective Inspector White said, polite and all business.

"Darach MacKendrick."

The detectives exchanged a glance. They appeared to communicate telepathically; a handy talent for policemen.

"Is everything all right? Should I call more police?" Mrs. Donnel still stood in her doorway.

"That won't be necessary," Darach said.

Mrs. Donnel shifted from foot to foot. "This is the most exciting to-do since the SS Politician ran aground with over a quarter-million whisky bottles. That was in forty-one off the coast of Eriskay. We townsfolk collected as much whisky as we could before the excise men arrived." She goggled at the officers. "You can't arrest me for that, can you?"

"No, ma'am." To his credit, Detective Inspector White didn't show a hint of a smile.

"I've never seen the inside of a jail," she said. We all stared at her.

"Would you prefer the living room for this conversation?" White said.

Though I wasn't nearly as excited about their presence as Mrs. Donnel, I nodded and led them upstairs.

"Where can I speak to Mr. MacKendrick privately?" White asked.

"I thought you wanted to talk to me."

"Detective Gilly will visit with you. Mr. MacKendrick, if you'll lead the way."

Darach looked at me and shrugged. "Which room?"

"Kinnon's office." I pointed.

Detective Gilly glanced around. His wavy, dark brown hair was combed back off his forehead. His blue eyes returned to me. "Can we sit down, miss?"

"Of course." My pulse raced. I'd never been questioned by the police, much less in a foreign country. I sat on the couch. He chose an armchair. "Why are you here?"

"We're here at the request of the AAIB."

"The AAIB?" I shook my head.

"Air Accidents Investigation Branch."

Just like that, suspicion became fact. "This is about Megan and Kinnon's crash."

"Yes." He leaned forward, hands clasped. "I'm sorry to inform you that the AAIB has determined the crash was the result of sabotage. Mr. and Mrs. MacKendrick's deaths are now a homicide investigation."

CHAPTER EIGHT

Homicide. *Murder.* My peripheral vision blurred.

"You've had a shock. Would you like some water, Miss Eastin?" Detective Gilly repeated the question until I shook my head no. "Ms. Eastin, please focus. Help us find their killer."

I put a hand to my mouth and then lowered it. I'd suspected, maybe, but that hadn't prepared me. "Why are the investigators sure the crash wasn't an accident?"

"The oil-filter safety wire was cut."

That didn't help me. "Did this wire cause a malfunction? Is that what brought the plane down?"

"Indirectly. Loss of oil pressure caused the crash."

I curled my fingers, grasping for a solution to an unchangeable outcome. "But wouldn't an oil pressure or temperature gauge register a problem?"

"Mr. MacKendrick flew a Piper Cherokee Six. According to the investigator, in that plane the oil filter sits higher than the oil reservoir. The gauges would read normal until the reservoir emptied."

He must have noticed my blank stare because he kept explaining. "Had they flown on a sunny day, they might have noticed the oil leak earlier, though not necessarily in time to return to the airport."

He pulled a notebook from his pocket and flipped pages. "It

appears someone opened the cowling, cut the safety wire, then loosened the oil filter. About a minute after the engine started, the oil heated and began pumping out. Judging by the distance traveled, the engine seized roughly eight minutes after takeoff."

A mechanical heart attack. "Fingerprints?" I asked.

"Forensics is running what they found. If we're lucky, the saboteur won't have worn gloves, but we're rarely that lucky." Gilly glanced at his notes. "Why were Mr. and Mrs. MacKendrick in Newcastle?"

Sabotage. I shivered. "Megan was traveling with Kinnon on company business. She said he attended a meeting. Darach probably knows who he saw. Do you have any suspects?" Speaking the words felt strange.

"The Newcastle constable reported a tall, slender Caucasian male, mid-twenties with short black hair, on the airport tarmac near Mr. MacKendrick's plane on Friday. He ran when confronted. Do any of Mr. or Mrs. MacKendrick's acquaintances fit that description?"

I shook my head. "I met some of Kinnon's friends at the funeral, but I don't recall anyone specific. As far as I know, Megan had no close friends here yet, and the description is too generic to know if he's someone I might have met in New York."

"Several Newcastle Inn employees said you'd called."

I pushed a hand through my hair. "I realized Megan and Kinnon left the inn a day early. The night clerk said Kinnon mentioned a family emergency. Kinnon's stepfather is checking with family members."

Detective Gilly offered a piece of paper. "This was recovered at the crash site. Does the paragraph mean anything to you?"

"It's Megan's writing." I ran shaky fingers down the Xeroxed words. She'd written a date, April 8. "It's the day before they married."

I read her open-looped handwriting: *Kinnon is ready to redeem himself. His plan is dangerous, but I approve.*

Redeem himself how, I wondered. And for what? Slacking off at MKI? Marrying without telling Greer and Peter?

I shook my head and handed the paper back. "The only secrets Megan and I didn't share were other people's secrets. If Kinnon asked her to keep quiet about this, she would."

"Did she keep a regular diary?"

"No." I suddenly remembered the letter. "I'll be right back."

I hurried downstairs, retrieved the threatening letter, climbed the stairs, and handed it to Gilly. He read the envelope through the plastic bag I'd placed it in, and then opened the letter, holding it by the edges while he read the single sheet. When he looked up, his stare rivaled Darach's.

"Why didn't you notify the police?"

"I told myself it wasn't connected." I paced to the window and back. "The envelope has a postmark."

"We'll look into it." He walked over and tapped on the office door.

Darach walked out more slowly than he'd entered. His eyes locked on mine. DI White followed, and DS Gilly held up the letter.

"Ms. Eastin gave me this, sir."

White read. Expressionless, he motioned Gilly to show the letter to Darach.

I'd memorized every word. *LAST WARNING. CHOOSE LIFE. MAINTAIN THE STATUS QUO.*

"Where did you get this?" Darach asked, looking at me.

"I found it Thursday in Kinnon's office mail."

"What was *status quo* for Kinnon?" White asked Darach.

"That's a better question for my mother or her husband. I need to ring them."

"Detective Gilly and I spoke with her and your stepfather before we came here. She retired shortly after our arrival." White faced me. "Is there anything else you'd care to share?"

I glanced at Darach. "Kinnon asked for my help on a business matter, but he didn't want to discuss specifics until I arrived next week." I felt Darach's stare burning a hole in my direction.

"If you've no objections, we'd like to search the flat while we're here," White said.

"Do you want to call Gavin or Evan?" Darach asked.

This was as much about his brother as my sister, but he didn't seem alarmed by the request.

"No," I said. "I looked through everything already—after I found the note." The detectives frowned. "Please search," I urged them. "This investigation is already days behind the killer."

Darach and I sat on the couch. His closed expression stifled the questions I wanted to ask as the detectives moved from room to room. Not quite an hour later, they left with Kinnon's answering machine, address book, a list of his and Megan's phone numbers, and my promise to be fingerprinted at the police station tomorrow to eliminate my prints from any others on the note and envelope.

I locked the door behind them and climbed the stairs. Each step required a greater effort than the last. Who had killed Megan and Kinnon? I cleared the last riser. Arms crossed, Darach stood in front of the photographs on the wall—like a viewer at a gallery.

"That's Megan's Scottish 'Wall of Happiness,'" I said. "She has a larger display at her New York apartment. It was her way of keeping family and friends close and in her thoughts."

"Why didn't you tell me they had asked for your help with MKI?" Darach asked.

"Since I didn't know they were murdered, I didn't see the point in bringing up a now unknowable request. I also searched Kinnon's office without finding another threat. Either the note was a single occurrence, or we haven't found the others. Maybe he didn't take them seriously and threw them away.

"Before Kinnon changed his will," I said, "who were his beneficiaries?"

"Mother and then myself." He looked over his shoulder, his eyes cold. "You suspect us?"

"You've made no secret of preferring to not have to deal with a partner."

Darach nodded. "You're not reacting as I expected."

"What did you expect?"

"More along the line of what I found the first time I came."

He had no idea how close I was to breaking down again. "I don't mourn well. When I grieve, I go all out. I try to be alone during and after."

"Do you need to break something?"

My smile, though small, was genuine. "No." I needed to find out what else he might know. "Did the police show you Megan's note? The one from her day planner?"

He nodded.

"Any ideas on why Kinnon might seek redemption or need my help with something at MKI?" I asked.

"None worth dying for."

"Maybe he said something to your mother or Peter. Can we talk to them?"

Darach pulled his phone from his pocket. I couldn't hear what he said during the brief conversation, just his "good-bye" before he pocketed the phone. "We can drive over now."

It felt like progress. "I'll follow you in my car."

"It's not far. I'll drive you."

I wanted time to think.

"I've taken enough of your time. I can find my way back. Give me a few minutes to get ready."

He took his phone out. "I'll call Gavin and Sabrina. The press will want a statement."

CHAPTER NINE

I followed Darach's BMW through town and into a quiet cul-de-sac. Three large homes sat back from the street. An assortment of trees towered over each house, shading garden beds filled with plant species that wouldn't survive a Texas summer. I pulled in behind Darach as he parked in the driveway beside the silver Jaguar I recognized from the photo at Kinnon's flat.

Peter stood on the porch. He stubbed out his cigarette as we approached. The strain of the last few hours showed in his stooped shoulders. Because he looked like I felt, I hugged him. He patted my shoulder.

Darach's glance shifted from me to Peter. "How is Mother?"

Peter shook his head. "We're in the solarium." He led us down a wide hall into a room of windows that offered a view of the backyard. Greer rose, her eyes red-rimmed, her face drawn. She, too, had lost weight in the past few days.

"Mother," Darach said. They shared a socially correct air kiss and separated. Peter's awkward shoulder pat had held more warmth than their mother/son greeting.

"Miss Eastin," Greer said without looking at me.

Peter removed his glasses to polish the lenses. "Shall we sit?"

Darach settled beside his mother on the sofa.

I followed Peter to a love seat. None of them seemed willing to open the conversation, so I turned to Peter. "Was there a family emergency last Sunday?"

He replaced his glasses. "I spoke to everyone. No one was ill or injured, and no one had talked to Kinnon."

"Did Kinnon mention receiving threats?" Darach asked.

Peter and Greer shook their heads no.

Darach nodded at me. "Tell them about the letter you found in Kinnon's office," he said.

Detective Inspector White had kept the letter, but the contents I recited were fresh in my memory. Greer sat very still, gazing at her hands.

"Dear God," Peter said. His eyes closed and were slow to reopen.

While this piece of news sank in, I looked at Darach. "When was Kinnon's trip to Newcastle arranged?"

"Thursday of the previous week."

"Who knew his schedule?"

"Kinnon, Megan, me, Mother and Peter, Frank, Mrs. Gibson, Gavin, Sabrina, the sales and marketing departments, and any friends or co-workers we'd mentioned it to."

I turned to Peter. "Did the police show you the note Megan wrote about Kinnon's plan for redemption being dangerous?"

"Yes. Did she tell you why?" he asked.

"No. She called just before the wedding, but that's pretty much all we discussed."

Greer looked up. "She told you they were getting

married?" The words shot from her.

Too late, I remembered that Kinnon hadn't called Greer before the wedding. I nodded, as if not answering aloud could blunt my acknowledgement.

"Did you encourage them?" The coldness in her eyes flowed into her voice.

"I didn't discourage them. They were adults." And based on what I'd seen from the MacKendricks, my sympathy for Kinnon's situation increased. Why share his wedding plans if his family's happiness for him and Megan hadn't matched his own?

Greer rose. "Kinnon died because of her."

I tried to stand, ready to defend Megan, but Peter's hand gripped my arm. Greer's eyes filled with tears. She retreated to a bench on the other side of the room.

Darach followed and spoke gently, his words pitched too low to carry. When his cell phone rang, he checked the number. "Excuse me."

Trying to control my temper, I turned to Peter. "Can we talk privately?"

His forehead creased as he glanced at his wife. "Greer, I'm showing Lyssa to the lavatory. I'll be right back."

She didn't respond. The darkness of her mood seemed to isolate her. I followed Peter down the hallway. We passed the open entry door. Darach stood outside, his phone pressed to his ear.

Peter stopped at the end of the hall and shook his head. "Blast the police and the sabotage and blast your prior knowledge of the wedding." He stopped, stuffed his hands into his pockets, and hung his head. "I apologize. It's not your fault Megan confided in you while Kinnon kept us in the dark. What did you wish to ask?"

I sympathized with his predicament. "Why does Greer think Kinnon's death is Megan's fault? That's the second time she's hurled that accusation."

"Kinnon's original plan was to fly to Newcastle Friday morning and return Friday afternoon. When Megan offered to accompany him, they turned the trip into a weekend stay. It's not much of a reason, but Greer needs to blame someone." He rubbed his eyes. "And perhaps, like me, she's considered that if we'd been kinder to Megan—invited her to spend that morning with us—they might both be alive today. Grief and guilt are a terrible combination."

I looked away.

"We've not treated you well, Lyssa, but Kinnon and Megan's marriage came as a surprise, and then their deaths, and now their murders. Losing a child is outside the normal sequence one expects from life. And if, as the police say, the man seen Friday sabotaged the plane, Kinnon would still have crashed. Greer will realize that soon." He touched my arm. "I never thanked you for not reacting in kind last week after she threw her Scotch on you."

I attempted a reassuring smile. "That was a rough day for all of us."

"You're a sympathetic lass. How are you coping?"

"I'm still dealing with the fact they were murdered.

Like Greer, until this morning I was getting past the shock and working through the pain. Now I'm angry. Megan's note proves she knew whatever Kinnon planned was dangerous. And she chose to help him with it. Last week was all about reaction. Now it's time for action."

"You're very open about your feelings, Lyssa. Something the MacKendricks aren't known for," Peter said.

Whatever I thought of Greer, he clearly loved his wife, temper and all. That was a mark in her favor.

"You said 'the MacKendricks.' Do you still consider Greer a MacKendrick?" I asked.

"Only when she's around Darach. Something about his presence curbs her spirit. He's very like his father in appearance and behavior."

"I can understand how Darach's strong personality might overpower a less aggressive personality." That didn't bode well for Greer or MKI if they became partners. But murder put that decision on the back burner. "Before Kinnon and Megan left for Newcastle, did they act anxious?"

"No. They behaved like newlyweds." He smiled. "I believe Kinnon and Megan experienced love at first sight. I felt it the moment I met Greer. Did you know she was married at the time?"

"No," I said, intrigued.

"Whenever I was in Scotland, I arranged to attend the same parties and events that she did. I waited six months for her divorce to become final. And I spent most of the next year gaining her trust and convincing her that marriage to me would be good for her and Kinnon." He winked at me. "My work in the foreign service taught me patience as well as diplomacy."

"Do you still work for the foreign service?"

"No. I retired from all the travel and started a venture-capital business. Greer and I live a quiet, happy life—or at least we did until recently."

The front door closed. Darach joined us, tucking his phone into his pocket. "I spoke with Sabrina and Gavin. Among other things, we agreed that unless the police uncover evidence that Kinnon continued gambling, we'll operate on the assumption that he quit. We won't mention it unless the police ask."

"He told us he'd quit in February," Peter said.

"His bank statements support that," I added. "But the police can find out if he still owes debts."

"For Greer's sake, I'd rather keep it quiet unless the police ask us directly. Kinnon attended regular Gamblers Anonymous meetings and promised me he'd paid his debts." Peter ran a hand across his face as if he were trying to wipe away the week. "I considered Kinnon my son. I loved him, but sometimes he made it hard."

I was less interested in protecting Kinnon's reputation than I was in finding a killer. "I'm not comfortable withholding information from the detectives."

"If Kinnon owes money to a bookmaker, the bookmaker will contact you as Kinnon's beneficiary," Darach said. "If that happens, tell me, and I'll take care of it."

"I can deal with a legitimate bookmaker," I said, "but if Kinnon borrowed from a loan shark, or whatever you call them in Scotland, they could employ unorthodox collection methods."

Peter nodded. "I believe Kinnon used both, but I doubt they'd kill him. You can't collect from a dead man." He looked at me. "As you say, the possibility needs investigating. If I make the calls, will that satisfy you?"

"If one of them sabotaged the plane, they'd hardly admit to a debt Kinnon owed," I said.

"Agreed. But let me try. I'll be thorough, and I have connections that can make discreet inquiries better than the police."

"Fine. Let Darach and me know what you learn soon."

"Absolutely." Peter turned to Darach. "Let's prepare tea, shall we? Lyssa, we'll serve in the solarium."

I entered the powder room. When I emerged a few minutes later, the doorbell chimed. When no one appeared in the foyer, I answered the door.

"Good afternoon, Ms. Eastin. May we come in?" DI White said.

"Do you have news?" I stepped back and bumped into Darach. I hadn't heard him approach.

"Come in," Darach said. "We're this way."

In the solarium, Greer and Peter looked as if they were braced for a beating. DI White sat across from them. Peter nodded at the tea service on the table. He held Greer's hands. "Lyssa, would you pour?"

I managed the task without spilling. Darach distributed cups, cream and sugar, and then joined me on the bench.

DS Gilly pulled out a large envelope and passed us each a sheet of paper. "This is a sketch of the man seen near Kinnon's airplane."

My heart pounded as I studied the face of the man suspected of killing my sister. Dark hair, narrow face, pointed chin, dark eyes. I didn't recognize him. Neither did anyone else. "Sorry, no," repeated around the room.

"We're reviewing the calls to Mr. and Mrs. MacKendrick's mobiles on the day of the murder," White said. "There's one we can't identify, placed to Kinnon from a phone box in Muirhead."

"The letter I found was postmarked from Muirhead!" I said.

White nodded. "Do any of you know who they might know there?"

We all shook our heads no.

"We're checking security cameras in the area for a view of the phone box." White looked at Darach. "We need a list of your employees living in Muirhead, and we'd like to look through Kinnon's office. We'll stop by MacKendrick Industries at eight tomorrow morning."

Darach nodded. Hearing someone at MKI might be involved, wouldn't make him happy. I raised a hand. "I searched and straightened up Kinnon's office on Friday."

Neither Gilly nor White showed surprise. "Did you throw anything away or find anything that struck you as unusual?" Gilly asked.

"I checked each page for notes then tossed old periodicals." For now, I would honor Peter's desire and not divulge Kinnon's gambling.

"Did you find any notes?"

"Not in the periodicals. I did find a note stuck under Kinnon's desk. It looks like his handwriting, but who knows how long it's been there, or if it has meaning, or if he just missed the trashcan while throwing it away. Anyway, I kept it."

"Bring it with you Monday when you get fingerprinted."

I didn't have to look at Darach to know he was staring at me—and not in a good way.

White continued. "Kinnon filed a flight plan for Perth, and he called a Perth taxi service before leaving Newcastle. Prior to that, he dialed Darach, who was at a concert and couldn't respond. Kinnon left no message."

I glanced at Darach. He'd never mentioned missing Kinnon's last call. First chance, I'd get details about that.

White looked at the Rands. "Your son called this house Sunday afternoon. Did either of you receive that call?"

Greer gasped. Her expression made clear she didn't know about the call. Peter put an arm around her. "No. We attended the Dickenses' anniversary party. Darach and Sabrina were waiting. They told us about the crash."

"Did Kinnon know you were attending the party?"

Peter looked at Greer, but she stared at the floor. "No, I don't believe we mentioned it. And we left our mobiles at home."

"Do you have an answer phone?"

"Yes, it has taken our calls since that night." Peter's

shoulders fell. "Sixty-four messages are a grand tribute to Kinnon but listening to them is a task we've not felt up to taking on."

"May we see the answer phone?" White asked.

"It's in the library."

A sense of expectation filled me as we followed Peter and Greer to the library. "It's programmed to play the most recent message first," Peter said, "But Kinnon showed me how to reverse it." He pressed two buttons.

"Message received April twenty-fifth at 3:32 p.m.," a mechanical voice said. The day of the crash.

"Mother! Peter! Is anyone home?" I recognized Kinnon's voice. There was a pause, and then he said, "No one's answering!"

Greer sank onto a chair. Darach turned to stare out the French doors. In the recording's background, a second voice said, "Call a cab. I'll have us packed in five minutes."

I stepped back and collided with a bookshelf. Kinnon's voice I'd expected—but not Megan's response.

CHAPTER TEN

I cornered Darach while the detectives disconnected the answering machine. "Kinnon called you the day of the crash?" I asked.

"He did."

"Why couldn't you answer your phone?"

"I'd taken Sabrina to a film. Our phones were set on vibrate."

"Did you look to see who called?" I heard the accusation in my question.

"Yes."

"Did you call him after the movie?"

"He didn't leave a message. I presumed his reason for calling wasn't urgent."

Darach had certainly inherited his mother's icy stare but I wasn't giving up. "Did he call often?"

"Not since we were children."

Something in his voice finally got through to me. "Do you wish—"

"Every second of every day since."

He walked away, human after all. I felt bad about badgering him into the admission, but I made my living analyzing businesses. Analyzing people was similar: I did my research and asked annoying questions until I learned the truth.

"More tea, Lyssa?" Peter offered.

"No, thank you. It's time I leave. Please tell Greer good-bye for me." I noted his relief and hurried outside. The detectives were halfway down the sidewalk. "Excuse me!"

They turned. "Yes, Ms. Eastin," White said.

"I'm off to make arrangements to pick up Kinnon's car from his mechanic. Can one of you come along—in case Kinnon hid another letter in the car?"

"Detective Sergeant Gilly will go," White said, carrying the answering machine to his car.

Gilly followed me to my rental. "Where's the garage?"

I gave him the address.

Following Gilly's unmarked car made navigating to the neighborhood of haphazardly maintained cottages easier. I identified Clapton's Garage by the assortment of cars surrounding the closed doors of a windowless single-bay building detached from the adjacent house.

We parked then negotiated a gravel walk to knock on the house's faded blue door. After a few moments, the door opened, revealing a man whose abundant brown hair needed trimming. He squinted at us. "Aye?"

"I'm here about Kinnon MacKendrick's car," I said.

"About bloody time. I left a message Monday." He lifted a grease-stained denim jacket from a hook by the door. "Where's Kinnon? And who are you?"

His scent, a combination of ale and sweat, drove me back. "He and his wife died Sunday."

"Pity. She was a looker."

Gilly made a disapproving noise in his throat. Of all the times I'd said they died in the past week, no one had responded with such callousness. "She was my sister. I'm settling their affairs."

He shrugged into the jacket. "Kinnon owes me on this car."

"How much?" Gilly asked.

"Including a week's secure, covered storage, it comes to a thousand pounds."

I converted the figure to American dollars and swallowed hard.

Pulling keys from his pocket, he sauntered past us and fit one into the garage's hefty padlock. Double doors creaked open. The Porsche looked like a rich kid slumming amid the scattered tools and oily rags littering the workbench and floor. The detective sergeant exhaled an appreciative whistle.

"Will you take a check drawn on an American bank or a credit card?" I asked.

"Not even if you were the Queen." He pointed to a hand-lettered sign over his shoulder. "Cash only. I've dealt with Kinnon before. You get his ride when I get my cash."

"What did you repair?" Gilly asked.

"A nasty scratch on the passenger door," the mechanic said.

"Did Kinnon say how it got there?" Gilly asked.

"No."

"I'll bring cash tomorrow morning," I said. "And I'll expect a receipt detailing exactly what you repaired."

He snorted rudely.

"We'd like to look inside the car," Gilly said.

"Not until I get paid. Now leave off. I'm missing the football match."

Gilly displayed his warrant card. I got the impression he was enjoying himself. "I'd like to look inside the car now, sir. Unless you prefer to wait until a patrol car arrives with a court order. Those patrol officers certainly like to use their lights and sirens."

My estimation of Gilly skyrocketed. The nasty mechanic narrowed his eyes.

"I'll get the key."

When he returned, Gilly opened the trunk. I watched over his shoulder. He didn't take anything, just searched, closed it, and moved on to sit in the driver's seat. He explored between the seats and opened the glove box. He glanced at some papers and carefully tucked them into a plastic baggie.

"What are those?" I asked.

"Receipts. You never know."

When it was clear the car didn't contain a useful note naming Megan and Kinnon's killer, we left. I followed Gilly to the main road and, after one wrong turn, found my way back to the flat

Inside, Mrs. Donnel peeked out her door and waved. I waved back. Entering the flat, I trudged upstairs, scooped up the phone, and called Darach. "I may be late coming in tomorrow. I need to pick up Kinnon's car and drive it to a dealer for sale."

"You don't see yourself as the Porsche type?" He sounded

snarky.

"Do *you*?" I didn't wait for his answer. "Where's the closest Porsche dealership?"

"Edinburgh."

I already dreaded the drive. "OK. What time do banks open in the morning?"

"Nine. Why?"

"I need to transfer Kinnon's checking account into my name and withdraw cash to pay the mechanic." I briefly described my encounter with the hairy man.

"How much do you need?"

"A thousand pounds."

"How are you getting to the garage?"

Did this man do anything but ask questions? I let a little of my annoyance seep into my voice. "I'll call my attorney, Evan. If he can't help, I'll call a cab."

"Ian and I will be at your flat at seven. I'll bring the cash."

"That's not necessary—"

Once again, the dial tone cut me off. One day I'd leave *him* hanging during a conversation, although I couldn't imagine what circumstances would make him wish I *hadn't* stopped talking.

I entered the master bedroom and opened the walk-in closet. I'd put this task off long enough.

The night our parents died, after Aunt Sally arrived and the police and neighbors left, I'd found Megan in the master bedroom closet, asleep on Dad's robe, using Mom's as a cover. I'd joined her.

This closet was different, full of unfamiliar clothes, but the scent....

I tested fabric textures with my fingertips, reviving the remnants of Megan's musky perfume. I paused at a black velvet gown—the most formal item on the rack—appropriate for an evening reception at the Spanish consulate. Would she have worn this dress?

I held it to me and walked to the bedroom mirror. The gown would have been stunning on her. The flattering cut would even look good on me. If it were a size larger, I'd keep it. It would be one way of keeping her close.

After our parents' deaths, whenever I'd noticed Megan sinking into sadness, I'd taken her to the fanciest department store and boutiques the local mall offered and let her try on whatever she wanted. She'd also put together outfits for me to try on. Eventually, the owner of a modeling agency spotted Megan. A week later, she'd signed a modeling contract.

I ran a hand from bodice to hip, stroking the velvet like a cat. My fingers caught a loose thread. One tug added half an inch to the side seam, and the other seam revealed a second basted tuck. She'd planned to have the gown altered.

A late-afternoon sunbeam shot gold shimmers through the window's sheer under-curtain. I faced the light. "I can take a hint, Megan."

I hung the dress back on the rack and spotted a pair of black heels. We wore the same size. Those, I'd keep.

I finished exploring the closet and settled in the living room on the couch with a pad and pen. Peter was working on

Kinnon's possible gambling debt, but other likelihoods existed. Kinnon had died while on a company trip. He had brought company files home though he was considered work-phobic with few real responsibilities. And the threatening letter was delivered to Kinnon at MKI.

Why hadn't Kinnon used Gavin, the MKI lawyer, to draw up his new will? What did he want redemption from? Why were they killed? I underlined that one three times then moved on to a to-do list for tomorrow.

Wayward strands of hair tickled my neck. I tucked them behind my ears and tossed the notepad onto the coffee table.

Amid all this uncertainty, I still had to pack and donate Megan's and Kinnon's things. I got busy and worked steadily until nine, when the emotional-roller-coaster day demanded its due. I turned out the lights and descended the stairs to the dark guest room.

CHAPTER ELEVEN

Monday morning, I waited for Darach outside the flat. When he pulled up, his handyman Ian rode shotgun. I followed them to the customer-service-isn't-in-my-vocabulary garage, where Darach flashed a fistful of cash that instantly made up for our early arrival and improved the surly mechanic's attitude to the point that he offered us tea. After glimpsing the interior of his house, we declined.

I looked up from mentally adding the amounts scribbled for sanding, primer, and paint and tucked the receipt into my purse. "Thanks for the loan. Are you going to ask me for MKI shares as collateral?" I asked Darach.

"It crossed my mind, but no."

I sat in the passenger seat of the Porsche and stuffed what DS Gilly had left in the glove box—a bottle of aspirin, an unopened pack of cigarettes, and miscellaneous items—into my purse.

The cigarettes bothered me. Megan had never dated a smoker and imagining her marrying one was difficult. I hadn't seen an ashtray or smelled tobacco smoke at the flat, and the Porsche ashtrays were empty. Maybe Kinnon had been a social smoker.

"Will you drive the Porsche?" Darach asked.

"I've never driven one." I visualized myself racing low to the ground in the give-me-a-ticket red sports car—maneuvering through a roundabout—reaching for the—*stick shift*. I sighed.

"Ian can drive the Porsche to the dealership. I'll follow in my rental then take him back to the manor. You should go to work. The detectives will be there soon."

Darach's eyes narrowed. "Why aren't you driving the Porsche?"

I felt defensive. "A friend tried to teach me to drive his classic, manual-transmission Mustang. My first lesson was my last. I ground through gears, lurched through starts and stops, and got stuck on a hill because I was afraid I'd roll into the car behind us if I took my foot off the brake. If I drive, the Porsche will be back in the shop today."

"You seem to be a quick study. You probably only needed a second lesson." He turned away. "I'll see you at work."

I stared after him. Had he just complimented me?

In Edinburgh, Ian helped me negotiate a reasonable price at the Porsche dealership. I dropped him off at the manor then spent thirty minutes at Kinnon's Dundee bank changing his account into my name. It was nearly ten-thirty when I arrived at MKI and walked upstairs.

"I have no words," Mrs. Gibson said as I approached. Tears filled her eyes. "Why would someone tamper with Mr. Kinnon's plane like that? The world makes no sense anymore."

I had words for Megan and Kinnon's murderer, but they weren't fit for polite company, so I just nodded.

She handed me a message.

"A Detective Inspector White looked through Mr. Kinnon's office. He asked if you'd bring the note you'd mentioned to the police station when we get fingerprinted."

"We?" I looked up from her neat handwriting.

"I put Mr. Kinnon's mail on his desk. They want my fingerprints, too."

"I doubt it's what you planned for your afternoon, but I'm glad to have company. I'll drive if you'll navigate."

"Of course."

"Did they say what time we should be there?"

"That's up to us."

I looked at my watch. "I'll buy our lunch afterwards."

She reached for her calendar. "That sounds fine."

I waited until she finished her calendar entry. "Did you ever open Kinnon's mail or notice anything unusual among his letters?"

"The police asked me that. I used to open his envelopes. Then, at the start of the year, he asked me not to." Her chin rose. "I don't know why. I never looked at the contents."

"He was protecting you," I said. "I found a letter threatening Kinnon. He might have received others."

"Dear Lord." She turned a shade whiter.

I sought to distract her. "Is Darach in his office?"

"He's on the floor. The solicitors are in the conference room."

When I opened the door, Evan, Gavin, and Sabrina sat deep in conversation but quieted when they noticed me.

Evan jumped to his feet. "You were superbly controlled when you called yesterday. How are you handling the news?"

"Better sometimes than others."

I faced Gavin and Sabrina. "Did Kinnon talk to either of you about seeking redemption?"

Gavin shook his head. "No. Nothing like that." Sabrina looked at Gavin. He met her look and gave a single shake of his head. The MKI attorneys clearly weren't going to air MacKendrick family laundry in front of Evan. I had no time for subtlety.

"Gavin, could I speak to you in my office?" I said.

He walked next door with me.

"How can I help you?" he asked.

"You can tell me what that silent exchange between you and Sabrina meant. What did you both think of when I asked about Kinnon and redemption?"

"I'm sorry, but—"

I faced him. "If it impacts MKI or Megan, I need to know. Especially if it involves Kinnon's gambling."

He started. "Where did you hear that?"

"From Peter and Darach. Peter is looking into any debts Kinnon might still owe. Do you have any information to add?"

"No." He pointed to the horseracing prints on the wall. "Kinnon gambled for a while, but he said he'd stopped."

Another dead end. I opened the door for him. "Thanks for answering my questions."

I sat at my desk and opened drawers. Kinnon's address book and desk calendar were gone, but his personal-care items remained in the bottom drawer. I added the things I'd taken from the Porsche.

A phone message lay in front of me. Mr. Craddock had called and left a number but no message. It took five seconds for my brain to make the connection: Kinnon and Megan's solicitor—calling to offer condolences about the sabotage?

I dialed his number. His assistant asked my name and put me on hold.

"Miss Eastin?" His familiar bullfrog voice said.

"Yes. I had a message to call you."

"I have an envelope to courier to you this afternoon if that's convenient. I need a delivery address."

My heart surged into my throat, cutting off my words. I swallowed and tried again. "What's in the envelope? And why am I getting it now?"

"A sealed letter from your sister. I have not seen the contents. I was only to give it to you if they died under suspicious circumstances." He paused. "I saw the story in this morning's paper."

I struggled to form words. "Did she or Kinnon elaborate on why they thought they might die?"

"No.'"

"How long will the courier take?"

"It will arrive between one and two this afternoon."

I recited MKI's address. "Be sure it's marked to my

attention, please."

"Of course."

We rang off.

Shock iced my hands, but anticipation sharpened my mind. Would Megan's letter name a killer? I looked at the clock. Three hours until I found out.

I'd call DI White after I'd read the letter and made a copy. I reached for the phone to dial Darach's extension then drew my hand back.

What if the killer was someone I'd already met? Kinnon's family's faces flashed through my mind, joined by Gavin's, Sabrina's, and Frank's. I didn't want the murderer to be one of Kinnon's family or friends. I looked at the connecting door.

As if I'd called him, Darach stepped through. I gathered my scattered thoughts. So, he *could* unlock the door if he wanted to.

"Am I interrupting?" he asked.

"No, come in."

"Mrs. Gibson says you're seeing the police later."

"Yes, for fingerprints and to give them the note."

"May I see it?"

I made copies."

I handed him one. From now on, I'd be watching everyone more closely. His face didn't change expression as he read.

He handed me another piece of paper. "Peter emailed this list of Kinnon's licensed and unlicensed bookmakers.

Since you're waiting on a computer I printed his list for you."

I scanned the list. "Look at all these names. Maybe I can help him by calling a few."

"Your readiness to investigate bookmakers is admirable but unnecessary."

Since I wouldn't know what to say to a bookmaker anyway, I gave in. "Peter will call when he finishes?"

"Yes."

"I need to do something besides waiting for answers and news."

"I'd think you'd have enough to keep you occupied with the flat to pack."

"I've assembled boxes and packed a few things, but Megan didn't have much here." Her New York apartment would be the real trial. "Since the police interrupted us yesterday, I won't pack Kinnon's things until you can look through them."

"I'll make time soon." He turned. "I have bids to review now."

"Can you teach me the process? I'm good with analysis and numbers."

One hand on the doorknob, Darach looked over his shoulder. "When are you seeing the police?"

I checked my watch. "Mrs. Gibson and I leave in forty-five minutes."

"See me when you get back and we'll work on your duties."

He shut the connecting door behind him.

A sense of expectancy surged within me. I couldn't shake it, but maybe I could distract it. I fanned the files from Kinnon's flat across the desk and arranged them by date. Four files, one per month since last January. Each covered a manufacturing job from the arrival of raw material to completion.

To get a feel for the business, I studied the bid sheets and skimmed job-cost estimates, material deliveries, product-shipment manifests, and other job-related notes. Whatever significance the files held for Kinnon wasn't obvious to me. I'd check them against the originals to make sure nothing had changed or been omitted from Kinnon's copies. *And speaking of originals....*

I copied the letters and numbers on Kinnon's sticky note onto a note pad. AHD1132223124552. Too many digits for a phone number. Out of the first three numbers, you could make January first or thirteenth or November third. And what was "AHD"? Initials? A work-related abbreviation?

Since Darach was busy with project bids, I called Peter. He answered, and asked me to wait while he stepped outside. I admired his consideration of Greer and envied her having someone like him to lean on in her grief.

"Sorry to bother you again, Peter," I said.

He sounded resigned. "Given the circumstances, it's no bother, although I'm looking forward to a time when your calls don't depress me further."

"I'd like that, too."

"If it's any consolation, your calls also bring me hope. If

you're dredging up clues, the detectives must be making progress as well."

That perked me up. "I like your interpretation. I called to ask you about the note I found under Kinnon's desk. It says AHD1132223124552. Does it sound gambling related?"

"Read it again. I want to write it down." I heard him fumbling to balance the phone and whatever he wrote on.

I read it again.

Peter was quiet for a moment. "Frankly, no, I don't think it's related to gambling. But let me study on it a bit."

"Thank you. How are the calls going?"

He chuckled. It was the first time I'd heard someone from Kinnon's family laugh. "Seven said no, two disconnected, and one was no longer in service. On the positive side, so far, he no longer owes any of them money. The negative is I've been shouted at, disconnected, and told they wouldn't loan Kinnon or any friend of Kinnon's another pound because it took too long to collect. I'm appreciating Megan more and more. His recent solvency must be attributed to her influence."

"Megan was always frugal, even after her modeling career took off. Dad used to tell us, 'It isn't what you make, it's what you keep.'"

"An intelligent man," he said. "I told Darach I'd call when I finished. I'm nearly through."

"Then I'll check with him after lunch. Thanks, Peter."

"Not at all."

I walked down the hall to Mrs. Gibson's desk.

"Hi," I said. "Besides a computer, I need a calculator and printer."

She typed something into her own computer, adding a flourishing gesture when she hit the last key. "They'll be in your office when we return from lunch. Mr. Kinnon, God rest his soul, never asked for office machines. I suppose he kept his notes on his mobile phone."

To which the police had access. "Several people have mentioned Kinnon didn't have the same level of interest in MKI as Darach does."

She made a diplomatic noise.

"Did you compile the list of Muirhead employees for the police?" I asked.

"Yes. Mr. Darach said to, though none of them would tell me why."

I smiled an apology. "Sorry, but if Darach and the police didn't say, I probably shouldn't either. I'd like a copy, please."

She tapped a few keys. As two sheets of paper printed out, I handed her the files from Kinnon's flat. "At your convenience, I'd like to see the original files for these jobs."

She traded me the lists. "I'll pull them right now. Back in a moment."

I leaned against her desk and visually followed the line of cubicles that led to the elevator on the far wall. The doors opened, and Gavin and Frank stepped out.

"*Life* is a risk, Frank," Gavin said sharply.

Frank gripped Gavin's shoulder and brought him to a stop. "I know that better than you."

They caught me staring and stepped apart. As Gavin walked to the men's room, Frank approached and dropped papers into Mrs. Gibson's in-box.

"Hello, Mr. Blevins." Despite how Darach introduced him, my Southern manners didn't allow me to call the older foreman by his first name unless invited.

"Miss Eastin."

His face held less of a greeting than his words. Before I could think of another topic, Mrs. Gibson returned.

"Morning, Frank. Here you are, Ms. Eastin," she said. I accepted the files from her.

"What do you have there? Diving into work already?" Frank asked, reverting to politeness though he interrupted it to shoot a glare toward the men's room. I saw Gavin exit without looking our way.

"I want to learn how the jobs sequence, so I'm reviewing old job files."

"With a list of employees?" Frank's eyesight was sharp. "Is that the Muirhead list the police asked for?"

That shocked me. "How did you know?"

"Darach told me. The lad's near as angry as me."

"I understand. But I want the police looking at all possible leads."

Mrs. Gibson nodded. Frank's grunt might have meant anything.

"Are those the same files you brought from Kinnon's flat?" he asked.

"Yes. I want to review the originals."

"It's good to see you jumping right in, lass. Let me know if you have questions." He sounded sincere.

CHAPTER TWELVE

Mrs. Gibson directed me to the local police station—a compact red-brick building with meticulously trimmed flowering shrubs lining the sidewalk leading to the glass double doors. It looked too charming to be intimidating. We reported to the constable at the desk then took a seat.

My briefcase held the list of employees living in Muirhead. Forty-three names, none of them familiar. "Have you ever been to Muirhead?" I asked Mrs. Gibson.

She nodded. "Twice. Last year to take the grandchildren to the red squirrel sanctuary and several years ago after the UFO sighting."

"UFO?"

"Three lights seen by three people. Lots of us went the next night and sat up, waiting to see if they'd return. They didn't, but it was good family fun." As Mrs. Gibson smiled at the memory, the constable called us.

DI White and DS Gilly weren't in. I tapped my foot in frustration as we waited to be fingerprinted, until I realized their absence might mean they were searching for the murderer. I asked the desk officer to have one of them call me. I'd have more to share when the courier arrived with Mr. Craddock's envelope.

One officer scanned our fingerprints. Another took the

sticky note and placed it in an evidence bag. We walked outside just after noon.

"Where should we eat?" I asked Mrs. Gibson.

"Do you like fish and chips?"

"Never had them Scots-style, but I'm game to try. There's one condition."

"What's that?"

"You call me Lyssa."

Her eyes widened. "Oh, I can't. It's unprofessional. Mr. Darach's father insisted on professionalism."

I juggled my purse and briefcase until I found the keys and beeped my car open. "I understand. We Texans are big on 'Yes, ma'am' and 'No, sir.' You call Darach Mr. Darach. How about calling me Ms. Lyssa?"

A smile plumped her cheeks. "That I can do."

We ate at a tall table for two in a bustling shop and chatted about Mrs. Gibson's grandchildren and work.

"How long have you been at MKI?" I asked, reaching for a chip.

"They're better with vinegar," Mrs. Gibson said, passing the bottle. "Eighteen years. But I'm a short-timer compared to some."

I sprinkled malt vinegar cautiously and sampled another chip. "Not bad," I said, though I wouldn't have turned down ketchup. "Who's been with MKI the longest?"

"That would be Frank." She sipped her tea. "He's a good man. Like Mr. Darach, he puts in more hours than a standard workweek."

"I noticed he wears a wedding band. His wife must be very understanding."

"The poor dear has Alzheimer's. Her understanding is now fleeting."

"That must be rough and expensive for them."

Mrs. Gibson nodded. "Home nursing and doctors come dear."

I sprinkled vinegar on my fried fish, took a bite, and tasted the crispy, flaky, tangy mix. "Now *that's* delicious."

She beamed as I swallowed.

"Darach's going over my duties when we get back. What did Kinnon do?" I wondered how her loyalty would let her answer.

"It took Mr. Kinnon time to find his place, but this year he spent more time in his office and walked about the floor and the shipping yard. He frequently visited the sales staff for updates on what he needed to know for his marketing trips." She looked away, then back at me. "I'm not saying that he wasn't involved, mind you, just that his public relations training was more useful upstairs, just as Mr. Darach's engineering studies make him useful on the manufacturing floor."

That made me pause. Darach's engineering degree would also make it easy for him to tinker with a plane engine—I'd have to ask the detectives if everyone's alibis had checked out. I ate another fry.

"I'll visit the sales and marketing departments this week. I don't want Kinnon's responsibilities to go unmanaged."

I folded my newspaper cone down an inch to expose more chips. "Does Mrs. Rand visit MKI often?"

Mrs. Gibson sighed. "I haven't seen her since before her divorce. Is she happy in her new marriage?"

I smiled. Greer was well over a decade into her *new* marriage. "She is," I said. "Peter seems like a very attentive and loving husband."

She gave a satisfied nod. "I'm glad. It must make times like these more manageable."

"I'm sure it does." My fish suddenly lost its flavor, and I hid what was left in the newspaper wrapper. If all this had taken place a couple of months ago, I'd have had someone to comfort me, too.

Back at MKI, I checked for a courier delivery. Finding none, I familiarized myself with the computer on my desk. The tech had set up my email account and written my address and password on my notepad. I knocked on our connecting door before letting myself into Darach's office, pleased it was now unlocked. "Do you have a moment?"

He rolled the tension from his shoulders and stood. "Have a seat on the couch."

He joined me. "How did it go with the police?"

"The detectives weren't there."

"They were here, interviewing the Muirhead employees." An internal freeze iced his eyes. "They're wasting their time and ours. They need to search elsewhere for the murderer."

I made a noncommittal noise. With luck, I'd know within

108

the next forty-five minutes if one of the employees was to blame. Right now, I wanted to discuss other things.

"Have you given thought to my duties here?" I asked.

Darach raked a hand through his hair. "No. The morning's been busy."

"You may loathe having a partner, Darach, but I'm a hard worker, and I know what makes a manufacturing business successful. If you can't decide how to utilize me to MKI's advantage, I have suggestions."

He rested an arm along the back of the couch. "Let's hear them."

"I'm reviewing old job files, but I could use some explanation concerning job sequencing. I'll start studying company catalogs and talking to the sales staff to familiarize myself with the product lines. What else should I do to get up to speed?"

His eyebrows rose. "You have thought this through. You even sound as if you're looking forward to it."

"I am." Tackling something new felt good. "What else can I do?"

He glanced toward his paper-covered desk. "You said you were good with numbers."

"Numbers *and* analysis."

He stood. "Let me walk you through a bid-review. The engineers and sales staff work them up, but I like to review them before they're sent to clients."

I moved to the chair beside his desk. He explained his review process and was showing me how to check figures when

Mrs. Gibson called, looking for me. "There's a courier with a package for Ms. Lyssa. She needs to sign for it," she said.

Darach glanced at me. "She's here. Send him to my office."

Blood deserted my head then rushed back. Struggling to move calmly, I opened Darach's door, and met the courier in the hall. "I'm Lyssa Eastin."

The young man smiled. I signed and accepted the envelope. "Thank you," I whispered. Heart racing, I turned the envelope over and read Mr. Craddock's name above the address.

"What's that?" Darach asked, suddenly at my elbow.

"Papers from the solicitor," I said.

He frowned. "Are you about through with Murray?"

I allowed his assumption to stand.

"Not quite. Evan still has to write my will when I'm ready."

Darach turned to answer his ringing phone. I followed him to his desk, the envelope feeling like a flame burning my fingers. His conversation was brief. "Frank needs me on the floor," he said, hanging up.

I nodded, anxious for the privacy of my office.

I sat at my desk and stared at the envelope for a long minute. Fear and hope skittered up my spine. *And the murderer is*—I opened the envelope and removed the smaller envelope inside.

Megan had written my name on the front. I made a quick second slice, removed and unfolded two handwritten pages, and read.

Dear Lyssa,

If you're reading this, Kinnon or both of us are in trouble.

Okay, I'm laughing. That was way melodramatic. And, of course, you'll never read this, but Mom and Dad's sudden deaths taught us to cover our bases and behinds.

Kinnon discovered something at work a few months ago. He brought home files that I can't make sense of (yes, I snooped). He's pretty sure of what's going on but isn't sure who's involved. Because he's trying to protect me, he's not sharing details until he has proof (stubborn man). He's promised to share all when you arrive, so we'll both know shortly. That doesn't stop me from trying to convince him to tell me sooner.

I tickled out of him that whatever "it" is, involves someone high up at MKI. Here's what I learned from playing 20 questions: Darach is synonymous with MKI. When we meet, he's polite but darn near monosyllabic. Kinnon says their obvious tension comes from their growing up apart. (I feel doubly lucky to have a sister who cares so much about me— and I forgive you for hunting me down that night I snuck out with Karl Compton. You were right, it was stupid.)

I've met the head of sales. When I asked Kinnon if he suspected him, I got a definite NO. Frank Blevins, MKI's foreman, is nice but obviously Darach's man. I can tell that irks Kinnon. It's common knowledge among the family that Darach would prefer to run MKI solo. I get the impression those closest to Darach at MKI would prefer it too.

Which brings me to Gavin and Sabrina—father and

daughter lawyers. Sabrina has the good taste to compliment my clothing. Kinnon says she and Darach spend a lot of time together. I can't picture her as a sister-in-law, but maybe she'll grow on me. Kinnon said Gavin tried to talk him out of accepting the inheritance from his father. I saw Kinnon and Gavin arguing once but didn't hear what they said.

Everyone is cordial, but most of them seem to consider Kinnon a latecomer to the game since he didn't get his MKI shares until his father passed. Kinnon didn't expect them. I told him that maybe his father was trying to re-connect his sons. Kinnon laughed.

Maybe I'll learn more today when I grill—er—interrogate—er—make lunch conversation with my wonderful husband.

Love you,

Megan

I blinked back tears and read the letter through again. No murderer named, but she'd provided me and the police with a starting place.

At six, I aligned the files on my desk and gathered my purse and briefcase. I'd made two copies of Megan's letter and left another message for DI White to call me. Taking a chance, I knocked and opened the connecting door. Darach sat at his desk.

"I'm headed to the flat," I said, walking through.

He glanced at the wall clock. "I'll follow you. We can pack some of Kinnon's things if you don't have other plans."

Ah. He wanted to clear a chore from his to-do list—a

motivation I understood. But he could be a suspect. Did I want to be alone with him?

CHAPTER THIRTEEN

I'd already been alone with Darach several times and hadn't felt threatened. And when DI White came to my flat for Megan's letter, it could be a good thing if Darach were there. White might ask Darach about Megan's theories, and I'd be present to witness his reaction. I kept surprising Darach with information, and until I knew for sure who I could trust, that wasn't going to change.

"I'd appreciate your help packing things," I said. "If you want some dinner, I'll even share my soup and crackers."

He grimaced. "I'll pick up some takeout."

I set my briefcase on his desk and pulled my new checkbook out of my purse. "Let me reimburse you for the Porsche repairs." I wrote my first check from Kinnon's account and held it out.

Darach ignored my outstretched hand. "You don't owe me anything. The debt was Kinnon's."

"And the money is coming from Kinnon's account. I accepted responsibility for settling his debts when I accepted the inheritance."

Darach still didn't take it.

I raised my chin. "If you don't let me pay you back and I'm ever in a financial bind again, I won't ask you for help."

Another silence fell between us. He finally spoke, his

words slow and low with an emphasis on his *R*'s. "When you act honorably, you refute my initial theory that you're morally lacking. The only alternate theory I've constructed is that you accepted the inheritance for financial security."

He was fishing, but I wasn't biting. Unable to stare a response from me, he plucked the check from my hand.

I navigated the roundabouts without incident. A couple of blocks from the flat, Darach pulled into a shopping center. I continued home and greeted Mrs. Donnel when she popped out to welcome me home. I told her Darach was coming and left my door unlocked. I kicked my shoes off and hung up my jacket before heading upstairs to turn on lights and set the table.

Darach arrived about fifteen minutes later.

"I hope you like Indian food," he called from the stairs.

"I do. Come on up. I'm in the kitchen."

He walked in carrying a big bag that smelled of curry. This wasn't the first time he'd fed me. "If you keep showing up with food, my stomach's going to start growling every time I see you," I said.

His surprised look was followed by a quick smile. "A conditioned response?" He transferred six containers from the bag to the table and opened them. "I wasn't sure what you liked so I brought options."

"Tea or water?" I asked.

"Water."

He slipped off his suit jacket and eased his tie off, rolled it around one hand and slipped it into his pocket.

I poured two glasses and joined him at the table. "Tandoori chicken! That's one of my favorites." I spooned a helping onto my plate and explored the other containers while Darach filled his plate.

"Do you plan to stay here?" he asked, his attention on the containers.

"What?" I nearly choked on my first bite. Had I somehow telegraphed my plan to return to Dallas?

"In this flat."

"Oh! No."

Even if Darach assumed I was staying indefinitely, tying up the loose ends of Kinnon's and Megan's lives meant emptying this flat. It made sense to find somewhere else to live while I remained in Scotland.

"Do you know an estate agent?"

He lowered his fork. "How much do you wish to sell?"

"All of it but Megan's pictures and whatever you want to keep."

"Too many memories?"

I shook my head. "The wrong kind of memories. I don't want to constantly think, 'There's the couch I was sitting on when I learned Megan and Kinnon were murdered.'"

We ate in silence for several minutes. "An estate agent will pack and catalog everything for you," he said. "What did you want to pack tonight?"

"Anything you want to keep for yourself or your mother."

"She'll want the photos of Kinnon."

"Of course. Anything else?"

"No. She's particularly fond of photographs," he said.

The phone rang. "Excuse me."

I answered the living room extension. The conversation was short. When I returned to the kitchen, Darach was carrying leftovers to the refrigerator.

"Is there anything of Kinnon's that you'd like, other than his MKI shares?"

"I'll let you know." One side of his mouth definitely turned up this time. For the moment it lasted, he was handsome. The thought startled me.

I stacked our dishes, deposited them in the sink, and then broke the lingering silence. "Can you wear Kinnon's clothes?"

He shook his head. "I'm broader than he was."

"I can relate."

He trailed me into the living room. "Where do you want to start?" He picked up a box.

Might as well get the hardest part over with. "Their bedroom."

He followed me in and looked around, pausing at the dresser. "I'd like to keep this photograph of Kinnon and me as boys."

I'd been so busy looking for Megan in the room that little else had registered. I walked closer and studied the silver-framed photo of sand and sea and siblings wearing genuine smiles.

"Grandmother took the picture on our last vacation together. My parents divorced a month later. Six months after that, she died. But we had a good outing that day."

"You loved her."

"Aye." He looked away from the photo and frowned down at me. "You smell like her."

I took a step back, surprised by the intimacy—and accusation—in his comment.

"Chanel No. 5 was my mother's favorite scent. I wear it to remember her."

I handed him the photo, glad he had at least one happy memory of Kinnon. "Will an estate agent pack their clothes?" I asked, glancing at the closet.

"They will."

"Then since we're looking for things the estate agent won't want, I guess the bathroom is the logical place to begin."

Darach headed for the en suite bathroom. Dread held me in place until he turned to look at me.

"I'm sorry," I said, walking in after him. "This is more difficult than I expected."

He set his box on the vanity. "This looks like Kinnon's side." He slid a drawer open and thrust toiletries into the box without examining them.

I took a deep breath, opened Megan's drawer, and mingled her belongings with Kinnon's. It didn't take long; she'd probably taken most of her things on the trip. The cabinets held towels and linens. I checked the hamper.

A turquoise blouse lay puddled on the bottom. I brought the silk to my nose and breathed Megan's musky perfume. I sank onto the tub's edge, my eyes closed against tears.

I could tell when Darach sat beside me. His body radiated heat.

"I'll finish," he said. "There's not much, and it's mostly

Kinnon's. Can you start on the photos in the living room?"

Unable to speak, I nodded and walked out. The rely-on-me seduction of his offer threatened to undermine my strength. If I couldn't get through packing this flat, how would I manage Megan's New York apartment?

I grabbed a box and bubble wrap and started packing the photos of Kinnon, Greer, and Peter. I left Megan's photos on the wall.

Darach came out of the bedroom carrying a box. "Where would you like this?" he asked.

"Set it along the wall. The pictures for your mother are in that box." I pointed as the flat's exterior doorbell rang.

I buzzed DI White into the building and darted into the guest room to pluck Megan's letter from my briefcase before opening the door. "Come in," I said, letting him pass. "We're upstairs."

"After you." White motioned me up.

"Darach is helping me pack things for his family," I said.

"I noticed his vehicle in your car park," White said as we entered the living room.

Darach looked up from the box he was closing. His glance moved between us. "You expected him?"

"Yes," I said.

"Is that the letter?" White asked, pointing to the envelope in my hand.

"Yes." I handed it to him. He sat on the couch, slipped on glasses, and started reading.

Darach's eyes entered deep-freeze mode. I rubbed my arms for warmth.

"When and where did you find another threat letter? And why didn't you tell me?" Darach asked.

White held up a finger. "Quiet, please."

Happy to oblige, I sat in the armchair. Darach remained standing. White read the letter through twice then folded it and replaced it in the envelope.

"I'd like to read it," Darach said.

"I'm afraid that's not possible yet." White put away his glasses. "Miss Eastin, please keep the contents, and how you came by this, to yourself until I've contacted the interested parties."

"OK." I saw Darach's shoulders tense.

"Did my alibi check out?" Darach asked White. I looked expectantly at the detective.

"It did. Good night, Miss Eastin. Perhaps you'll walk out with me, Mr. MacKendrick?"

"Aye, I will." Darach picked up his coat without saying good night.

I followed them downstairs and locked up. The tenuous camaraderie I'd established with Darach was again nonexistent. Why had White walked Darach outside? He'd corroborated Darach's alibi—

I ran upstairs and peeked out the living-room window. The men exited the building and stopped to talk beside what I assumed was the detective's car. Darach's arms soon crossed. He glanced up and saw me. I flinched but stayed to watch. Five minutes later, both men drove off.

CHAPTER FOURTEEN

Tuesday morning, I noted Darach's car in its parking space when I arrived at MKI. I took the stairs, tossed a good morning to Mrs. Gibson, and entered my office. The connecting door opened as I set my purse and briefcase on the desk.

Darach walked in. Despite knowing his alibi had checked out, I couldn't behave normally around him. Kinnon's suspect list had included Darach, and I found myself wishing it hadn't. I needed an ally, and Darach had seemed the best candidate.

"White has contacted several people already, so I presume the letter you found contained more than just a threat," he said, advancing to stand in front of me.

"That's a fair assumption."

"Did you make a copy of the letter?" he asked.

My pulse skipped. "Yes."

"When White releases you from silence, I'd like to read it."

"You're not going to enjoy reading it."

"You're probably right." He handed me three files. "See what you can do with these. We'll review them after lunch."

He walked back into his office before I'd said "Okay."

I released a relieved breath and powered up my computer. Darach was being understanding. If he were guilty, wouldn't he have pressed to see my copy of the letter immediately?

I dug inside my briefcase for the notes I'd jotted last night and pulled out the Spanish consulate invitation with them. I reread the invitation. As MKI's marketing face, Kinnon would probably have attended. I stood the invitation against my printer. Mrs. Gibson called as I finished unpacking my briefcase.

"Did you see my email?" she asked.

I checked my inbox. "I have it. What's the Inland Revenue Office, and why do I have an interview with them tomorrow?"

"You need a National Insurance number before the next payroll. Because you're a foreigner, they want to interview you first."

"Okay." I tried not to worry about the eventual tax implications of receiving a paycheck from MKI. Instead, I thought about Kinnon's sticky note. "What does a National Insurance number look like?"

"Two letters followed by six numbers and another letter."

Too many digits. "Thank you."

"Not at all. And your badge is ready."

"Do employee badges have identification numbers?"

"Yes."

"How many digits?"

"Four."

I penned slashes between the numbers starting at the front and back. "Who has numbers 1132, 2231, 2455, 5542, 1322, and 2311?"

"Let me pull up the staff records," she said, sounding

curious, and tapped on her keyboard. "Here we go, 1132 was James Dermot. He worked on the floor and retired four years ago. Mary Lawson is 1322. She works in accounting. The other numbers aren't valid."

"Thanks."

"Not at all."

I hung up and picked up Darach's bids. Time to earn my paycheck.

Two hours later, I set the bids aside. Stiff from sitting, I arched my back. A chorus of pops accompanied the easing of my spine. I clicked on My Documents and smiled. Bless Mrs. Gibson, she'd had Kinnon's MKI files downloaded from the cloud. I opened a folder and skimmed a spreadsheet with familiar dates.

Aligning the original job files, I reviewed the sequential job dates: 1/15, 2/26, 3/19, 4/9. For each job, Kinnon had created columns for start and end dates, for units produced by type, for dates the jobs were bid, and for dates they were put into the system.

I sat back. As far as I could tell, the original files matched Kinnon's spreadsheet and none of the columns of dates corresponded with the numbers on Kinnon's sticky note. I renamed the file "KINNON" and made a copy named "JOBS" that I'd use to track job sequencing. Given Kinnon's limited involvement at the plant, I wasn't optimistic that I'd gain anything by it. Unless—

I sat up straight. He'd focused on marketing, so that was the investigative angle I'd take. He'd worked mostly with the sales team, Mrs. Gibson had said. Megan had written that Kinnon trusted the department head, but maybe someone else in the department was suspicious.

I picked up my badge from Mrs. Gibson and followed her directions to the sales department. I asked the secretary there to print a list of the jobs Kinnon had been working on. While I waited, I introduced myself to the head of sales and had him clarify aspects of the bidding process for me. The Spanish invitation invaded my thoughts. "How much of our business is domestic, and how much is foreign?" I asked.

"About eighty percent to twenty percent," he said, "though we're working on expanding our European and Asian markets."

"What can you tell me about our marketing plan for Spain?"

I didn't learn as much as I wanted to know, but I had another source to pump.

Back in my office, I picked up the bids files and carried them with me for one last review over lunch in the canteen. On my way to the stairs, I spotted Gavin and Sabrina waiting for the elevator and veered toward them.

"Do you two have time for a few quick questions?"

"We're on our way to lunch." Sabrina pushed the call button, which was already lighted. Was she still upset I hadn't signed her rigged contract, or had DI White been in touch?

"We can talk on our way to the car park," Gavin offered.

The lift opened, and I followed them in. "Has MKI ever had trouble with a job or with satisfactorily fulfilling a contract? Trouble that might have resulted in legal action or the threat of legal action?"

Gavin shook his head. "None that's required litigation. Most job-site problems trace back to the installer, and Darach personally troubleshoots any product complaints that come in. As for contracts, we get an occasional request for renegotiation on some point or another. So far, all have been settled amicably."

"Is this about the murders?" Sabrina asked. "Darach said the police found another letter, and they must have learned something because they're suddenly very interested in the workings of MKI. They've asked Dad and me for another interview this afternoon." One delicate eyebrow rose. "Did they call *you*?"

The lift doors closed, and we started descending.

"I spoke with DI White last night." I didn't give them a chance to ask for details. "Gavin, I thought Kinnon might be seeking redemption for his gambling, but you and Peter said Kinnon quit a while ago. Peter has called around and can't find anyone Kinnon still owes money."

Sabrina exhaled loudly. "I heard Darach call Kinnon and offer to cover his losses in exchange for MKI shares. Kinnon turned him down. That was the middle of last year, so one can hope that Kinnon did quit gambling. Still, he behaved oddly when he was here."

"Oddly how?"

"Keeping his curtains open during the day, for one. Darach mentioned that several employees commented on

Kinnon watching them and that he asked questions about operations on the floor. It made them anxious. They thought he was planning operational changes."

I faced her father. "Gavin? Any thoughts on why Kinnon's behavior changed?"

"No. Sorry." He didn't sound it. The lift opened. He placed a hand on the doorframe and let us exit first.

"Thanks," I said as they walked off.

In the canteen, I settled at a small table with my files, salad, and bottled water. Halfway through my review, a shadow fell across the table and my barely touched food. I looked up, expecting Darach but discovering Frank.

"What do you have there?" he asked, pointing with his cup.

"Would you like to join me?" I asked out of politeness.

"Thanks, but I've eaten. I saw you as I got up." He again looked at the files.

"I'm working on pending bids. I'll meet with Darach after lunch to review them."

His shoulders relaxed. As 'Darach's man', I must be pushing his buttons. "Do you have any questions?" he asked.

"A few."

This time he sat and listened and answered while I took notes. "Anything else?" He now bordered on downright friendly. Maybe he was glad I'd be helping Darach instead of hindering him.

"An unrelated question. Do you have any idea why Kinnon might have taken project files home? They don't hold any marketing value that I can tell, and that was his job."

"I've no idea." Frank looked toward the exit. "It's time I

126

returned to the floor."

"Thanks for your time."

He nodded and left. I returned to my office. Out of habit, I checked emails and found one from Evan, my attorney, acknowledging receipt of my email address. I glanced at the Spanish Consulate invitation propped against Megan's photo.

Sabrina had made it clear she and Darach would represent MKI, but the event was marketing-related. What if someone *expected* Kinnon to attend? Would that someone approach me in his stead? Might I learn something about Megan and Kinnon's murders?

I owed MKI, as well as Megan and Kinnon, my best efforts, and my experience with Central and South American corporations might come in handy. And, in the spirit of further researching who should receive Kinnon's shares, I could observe Darach and Sabrina in a social setting.

I picked up the phone and dialed. Evan's secretary put me through. "Good morning," he said. I heard the smile in his voice.

"Hi. I wanted to thank you again for your help and remind you I haven't seen a bill."

"Always happy to help. Unless, of course, it's something illegal. In that case, I'll advise you against it. As for a bill, I'll bring it over in the next day or two. I wish all my clients were calling and asking."

I nudged the invitation. "One more question. Do you have plans Saturday night?"

"Nothing important." I heard the curiosity in his reply.

"Do you own a tuxedo?"

He laughed. "Yes. What's this about?"

"Can you escort me to a party at the Spanish Consulate in Edinburgh? It starts at eight o'clock."

"I'll pick you up at seven, and we'll take the train down. What's your address?"

I recited it and gave him the phone number at the flat. A pause followed. "Should this stay between us?" he asked.

"It should, Evan. It most definitely should."

I thanked him and rang off. Dialing again, I RSVP'd for the consulate reception, making sure the receptionist knew I was attending in Kinnon's place.

I'd impulsively committed to representing Kinnon in an unknown capacity and to dragging along an unsuspecting accomplice. But it was the only way I'd learn if the event held a connection to whatever Kinnon was investigating.

At one o'clock, I opened the connecting door. Darach picked up a visitor's chair and set it beside his desk chair. He was doing a better job of not hounding me about the letter than I was of not worrying why he wasn't hounding me.

"Did you get through the bids?" he asked.

"I did." I sat and flipped open the top file. "I used what you taught me and studied Kinnon's spreadsheet of this year's jobs-to-date to analyze sequencing to get an idea of how long each phase takes. I haven't worked out all of the nuances, but I asked the sales department and Frank a few questions, so the bids should be pretty close."

While he checked my figures, I looked around his office then looked again. His walls and shelves held no personal photos. The artwork looked like something a decorator would pick out, tasteful and traditional.

"Remarkably well done," he finally said, tapping his pen on the files. "Here's where you can improve."

I made notes. Finally, I stood.

"You don't trust me," he said out of the blue, his words a statement, not a question.

"Right now, I don't know *who* to trust."

He nodded slowly.

"Is there something work-related I can do this afternoon?"

He stood. "Put on your trainers and we'll finish touring the manufacturing floor."

"Okay."

He followed me into my office, where I changed shoes. I looked up from tying my laces. "Are you trying to establish trust between us?"

His arms crossed. "MKI will function more efficiently if we can establish trust."

"And it might improve your odds of convincing me to sell at the end of thirty days?"

His first genuine smile was devastating. "Aye, there's that."

We walked downstairs and picked up hardhats in the locker room. I pushed through the double doors and turned toward the place we'd broken off my last tour of the floor.

"You remembered," he said.

"It would be hard to forget. I still feel bad about ruining that safety record."

"I looked it up. Your middle name is not Grace."

"Smart aleck." Without thinking, I playfully punched his bicep. Were we becoming friends?

Energized, I returned to my office. I'd completed the tour without a single scratch, and I'd had a genuinely pleasant time with Darach. He grew animated when he talked about pipes and fittings. I checked my watch. The Dallas branch of the James Wiseman Company was finally open. I dialed and asked the receptionist to transfer me to the European energy analyst.

"Robert Davis."

"Hi, Robert, it's Lyssa."

"Lyssa! Hey, Jackson told us about Megan and her husband. I'm sorry."

I squeezed my eyes shut then opened them. Jackson. Of course, he'd have heard. "Thank you. I'm still in Scotland. Events are complicated, and I have some questions I hoped you could answer." I picked up a pen.

"Shoot."

"Are you familiar with MacKendrick Industries?"

"Sure. Privately owned and successfully operated." I heard him tap computer keys. He gave a low whistle. "If they issue an IPO, I'm buying in. Do you have a line on them?"

"More than a line. I'm now half-owner."

Silence stretched. "Robert?"

"Did you say half-owner?"

"Yes. Megan's husband was a partner."

"Lyssa, you're rich."

"I'd trade it all to have Megan back."

"Sorry, I wasn't thinking. We'll miss you here."

I straightened. How was I going to explain this to my supervisor? "Can you transfer me to Janey when we finish talking?"

"Sure. Now, what's up?"

"Why might the Spanish energy minister court MacKendrick Industries?"

The James Wiseman financial analysts ranked as the best in the business, and Robert didn't disappoint me.

"Spain's developing additional offshore natural gas resources. Your company could bid on pipe and valve contracts."

My company. I leaned over my notepad. "What might make MKI special to Spain, and what can you tell me about our competitors?"

"Well, for starters—"

I wrote furiously as he talked. When he'd shared all he knew, he transferred me to Janey, and I again related the basics about my inheritance and Megan's and Kinnon's murders.

"You said you have a month to decide whether you'll keep it or not, although I'd want your head examined if you turned it down. I know it's not your field, but you're capable of taking this on and succeeding. MKI would be lucky to keep you," she said

Warmth filled me. Janey didn't offer compliments

lightly.

"On the other hand," she said, "your bereavement leave, sick leave, and vacation days won't hold you until the end of your month. Daniel and I are filling in for you, but I can't guarantee you the full thirty days. I hope you understand."

A pit opened in my stomach. I enjoyed my job. "I do. I'll try to make my decision before then."

"Sounds good. Keep in touch."

"I will."

I hung up. I *would* be giving up MKI. I just hoped it happened before I had to give my notice in Texas.

CHAPTER FIFTEEN

Wednesday came and went with hours spent memorizing sequencing, cruising through files, and visiting with department heads and staff. The more I learned, the more obvious it became that Darach was committed to the business and respected by his employees. Management at MKI was a full-time job. I couldn't imagine Greer coming to work every day, but in her defense, I still didn't know her very well.

No one mentioned their police interviews, though I had the impression Gavin, Sabrina, and Frank were going out of their way to avoid me. Darach was the exception. He took me down to the floor for another hour of orientation.

Afterward, back in my office, I pulled out the copy of Megan's letter I'd concealed inside an inter-office envelope and froze. The string on the closure was wound in figure-eights. I'd wound the string in oval loops.

Darach knew I'd made a copy.

I stood at my window and visually retraced the route we'd taken on the manufacturing floor. My office window wouldn't have been visible most of the time. Had he chosen that path on purpose?

Suspicion gave way to acceptance. I closed the planner. DI White had interviewed everyone Megan had listed by now.

All anyone might have learned was that Megan thought Kinnon had suspected them. Maybe that knowledge would make them vulnerable to exposure.

Thursday morning, I sat in on a sales meeting. The staff patiently answered my questions. Afterward, I returned to my office and reviewed more of Kinnon's computer files.

Evan, my solicitor, arrived at eleven-thirty. He sat across from me, and we kicked back with our feet on my desk. His bill lay between us. I tapped it with my finger.

"I can't tell you how much I appreciate all of your help. But unless Scots solicitors have extremely different rates, I doubt you charged me enough to justify the hours you spent on me, or with Gavin and Sabrina."

The corners of his eyes crinkled. "It's been a bit dodgy, but I've enjoyed it. And some of my hanging about was on my own time." He tapped my bare foot with his foot. "Sabrina is warming up to me."

"Really?" I'd met Evan in the lobby when he'd arrived. Sabrina had breezed by on her way to the canteen, and he'd greeted her cheerfully. She'd cold-shouldered past him without a word. I began to warn him about Darach's apparent relationship with Sabrina, but Evan continued.

"Unless you decide to write a new will between now and Saturday, I won't see you again until our date. And it is a date—I won't be billing you."

It would be my first date since—

The connecting door opened. Darach's stare took in our

lounging forms. Sabrina joined him in the doorway. "Are we interrupting?" she asked. Evan swung around and beamed at her. She scowled and leaned into Darach. He absorbed her weight but continued to stare at me.

Without hurrying, I lowered my feet and searched for my shoes. "Evan was dropping off his bill."

"Are you letting him go?" Sabrina sounded pleased.

"Lyssa knows I'll always be available for her should she need me," Evan said.

"Give the bill to Mrs. Gibson to turn in to accounting," Darach said.

Why was he scowling? "No. I hired Evan before I joined MKI. I'll pay him." Properly shod, I stood. "Did you need something?"

"We're off to lunch. Would you care to come?" Darach's stiffly delivered invitation matched his posture.

Eating at the same table with Sabrina obviously held appeal for Evan, but I'd rather face an SEC audit. While most of the staff members were warming up to me, Sabrina still seemed to have her claws out whenever I was around.

"Thanks, but I have errands to run. I'll grab something while I'm out. Evan may be free." I walked to the coat rack, but Evan didn't seize my setup.

"I'll join you, Lyssa," he said, helping me with my coat. "I can direct you to whatever shops you need. I'm a male anomaly—I enjoy shopping." He leaned in and whispered. "Spontaneity is an attractive quality."

Darach and Sabrina frowned. Because of Evan's whisper or his enjoyment of shopping?

"Thanks," I said. "I'd appreciate a guide."

Darach stepped forward. "The wind is brisk. Don't forget your scarf." He plucked the MacKendrick battle plaid from the rack and looped the cashmere around my neck, a little too tight for comfort.

Sabrina's eyes narrowed. "Darach, isn't that your—" She cleared her throat and walked to my desk to scribble on a notepad. "If you need clothing, Lyssa, try this shop. Evan can help you with the location."

For lunch, Evan chose Chinese. We squeezed in at a table for two as the noon crowd packed in, causing chairs to bump one another. The man at the table behind Evan sat so close I heard him order triple delight in a voice that grated like tires on the chipped-rock driveway that led to Darach's manor.

I sipped hot green tea and dug into General Tso's chicken. Unable to get my weekly Tex-Mex fix, I'd ordered the dish extra-spicy.

"I wasn't joking about needing to run errands," I warned Evan. "I need clothes, and I need to stop by the Inland Revenue Office and get a National Insurance number."

"I know someone there," Evan said. He dialed his phone. The conversation was brief. "She'll meet us when we arrive. That should save some time."

I signaled for the check and pulled Sabrina's note from my purse. Taking her shop recommendation made me nervous, but I didn't know where else to go. "Where is Fia's?"

Evan glanced at the address. "I like neat penmanship. The shop's here in city centre. I'll drop you there and do some shopping of my own across the way." He propped chopsticks on his plate and laid cash on the table before I could open my wallet. "My treat. Did you see Sabrina's face when I offered to accompany you?"

I nodded, reluctant to quash Evan's optimism. In my experience, Sabrina frequently frowned like that.

Evan's friend at the Inland Revenue Office whisked us in and out in fifteen minutes. We returned to city centre: a collection of shops and cafes that surrounded a large concert hall. Evan parked outside the pedestrian-only shopping area. He pointed out Fia's then headed off to run his errands. I studied Fia's window display—a trio of mannequins dressed tastefully for spring—and relaxed. Maybe Sabrina *didn't* have an ulterior motive.

A bell jangled as I entered. Racks of clothing, ranging from casual to workplace to evening wear, filled the space without crowding it. Megan would have loved browsing here. A tall blonde turned from arranging skirts. "Can I help you?"

"I hope so. I need jeans, a business suit, something casual, lingerie, and black evening gloves." I gave her my size and let her figure the European conversion.

The model-slender woman with enviably translucent skin set a hand on her hip and studied me. "I have what you want. Follow me." She lifted items from the racks as we made our way to the dressing room. "Try these." She hung the clothes inside.

I shut the door, undressed, and started with a skirt-and-jacket set. The woman's exactly-right choices reminded me of shopping with Megan whose color and fashion sense led her to what I needed before I grew frustrated and gave up.

"These are keepers." I passed them out the door and moved on to the lingerie. "Are you Fia?" She was too good at this to be an employee.

"Yes. You're American?" She draped three pairs of black gloves over the door.

"I am. From Texas." I picked my three favorite sets of lingerie and swung them over the door. "I'll take these." I tried on gloves, then a leggings-and-sweater set. My reflection agreed—she was good.

"Are you here on business?"

I shed the sweater and replaced my blouse. "Kind of." I hesitated and then added, "My sister and her husband died last week."

Instead of an obligatory condolence, Fia gasped. "What were their names?" Her voice wasn't smooth anymore.

I fastened my skirt. "Megan and Kinnon MacKendrick."

"How did you hear about me?" she demanded.

"Sabrina Cameron suggested your shop."

"That cow. She would."

The shock of her words was followed by the click of a cigarette lighter. Smoke drifted into the dressing room.

"You know Sabrina?" I opened the door. Fia leaned

against the wall, looking as if someone had slapped her. Her professional politeness had disappeared.

"I know them all. Well."

"How well?"

She took a drag from the cigarette. "Some better than others. Some better than they thought."

"Kinnon and Megan?"

"Megan, not so well." She remained silent while I made the connection.

"You and Kinnon were—"

"Lovers. For three years. He insisted he wasn't the committing type." Her lips twisted. "And then he met Megan."

Her bitterness almost knocked me back. But these days I had a certain sympathy for jilted lovers.

"Sabrina knew we'd discover our common ground," I said.

"That's Sabrina for you." Fia cupped a hand beneath the cigarette and walked briskly to the counter. "Have you met her father? Cruelty runs in that family."

I followed her and laid gloves, sweater, and leggings alongside my other selections. "I'll take these, too."

Fia smirked. "Patronizing my shop is one way to get back at Sabrina."

"Sabrina has nothing to do with it. I like your inventory." I handed her my credit card. "What did you mean about cruelty running in the family? I'm obviously not on good terms with Sabrina, but her father seems dedicated to the MacKendricks."

"To Darach, you mean." Her long fingers jabbed the register keys as she rang up my clothes. "The things I could tell you about those two families—"

I perked up. "For instance?"

Her eyes narrowed as she blew a veil of smoke upward. "Why are you interested?"

The dancing entry bell announced another customer. "I'll be right with you," Fia called, stubbing out her cigarette and grabbing an aerosol can from under the counter. A prolonged blast made the air smell like a ripe fruit bowl.

Fia ran my card, and I signed. "Kinnon's plane was sabotaged. The police are investigating," I said.

She closed the register drawer. "I read the paper."

"Have you thought about who might have killed them?" It was a long shot but worth a try.

She wrapped my purchases in fire-orange tissue paper and popped them into a large fuchsia bag. Her attention turned toward the woman browsing dress racks.

"Please, Fia?" I begged.

She stared at me and then leaned in. "Come back Monday at noon. But keep this to yourself. It's a private offer."

I was still mulling over Fia's former relationship with Kinnon when Evan pulled into the MKI parking lot.

"You're sure we ran all of your errands?" he said.

I'd been a terrible conversational partner on the drive back, so I smiled. "I found everything I needed, thanks. Did you?"

"And then some. I was only after batteries from the electronics shop, but when the owner asked what I did for a living, I answered and received a detailed account of the break-in at his shop several weeks ago. Turns out the thieves were friends of his son. If he presses charges against the thieves, he'll also have to press charges against his son. There's pretty strong evidence the boy let the others into the shop." Evan shook his head. "The things families get into could sour one on the institution."

I nodded. Either that or slam you into investigating your sister's murder.

CHAPTER SIXTEEN

Friday, I received and deposited my first paycheck. I'd deliberately left my copy of Megan's letter at the flat, and the day passed without incident.

Saturday morning, I removed most of Megan's photos from their frames and placed them in an envelope to mail to Texas. I'd take the others to my office. The activity proved a good distraction from over-thinking the evening's consulate reception, but it was time to get dressed.

Once I removed the basted tucks, Megan's black velvet dress fit me perfectly. I fought the urge to continually tug up the bodice. This was my first strapless gown—I didn't quite trust the engineering.

Evan picked me up on time, looking at ease in his tuxedo. He still reminded me of an eager Irish Setter, and an attractive one at that. We conversed easily on the train ride to Edinburgh and took a taxi to the Spanish Consulate.

The consulate, a Mediterranean-style masterpiece, featured intricate ironwork that followed the curve of the large foyer's staircase. I hoped to avoid meeting Darach and Sabrina until we were inside where they'd have to tolerate our presence.

We entered at a pace somewhere between Evan's inclination to stroll and enjoy the experience and mine to charge forward and start interrogating guests. I held our place in the receiving queue while he checked his overcoat and my cloak and evening bag.

Given my experience in dealing with Latin American businessmen, I knew I could handle a Spanish Energy Minister. That didn't stop me from whispering a quick prayer for an evening without a blunder on my part.

"All set," Evan said as he returned.

We inched toward Spain's energy minister, a tall, nice-looking, brown-haired man.

Evan murmured to the minister's assistant.

"Miss Lyssa Eastin of MacKendrick Industries and Mr. Evan Murray," the man said, checking a line on his list.

The minister's firm hand gripped mine. "A pleasure, Senorita Eastin," he said in an equally firm voice.

Mannerisms I used south of the American border, slipped into place. I looked up through my lashes into hazel eyes. *"El gusto es mío, señor."*

He smiled. *"Habla Español, senorita?"*

"If you allow for a bit of Texican," I said in Spanish.

"I look forward to speaking and dancing with you."

The minister released my hand. I moved on to shake hands and exchange pleasantries with local consulate dignitaries. Their expressions didn't change when I mentioned Kinnon and MacKendrick Industries.

Evan touched my elbow and nodded to the far wall.

"There's the bar. Would you care for a drink?"

"White wine, please."

An immense wrought-iron chandelier matched the ironwork in the foyer and lighted the ballroom. The polished marble floor and high ceiling amplified the soothing chords of the string quartet along with the murmur of conversations generated by the thirty or so people in the room. The women—a rainbow of silks, satins, and sequins—wound among the men.

Evan returned, bearing two champagne flutes. "Cava. White, sparkling, and Spanish. I thought you might enjoy the bubbles." He moved closer as I took a glass. "Over my left shoulder. Standing at the bar. The redheaded man is Fergus Douglas, owner of Douglas Manufacturing. He's your competition. The attractive female at his side is not his wife, so one must presume she is his 'Sabrina.' I hear Minister Alba has an eye for beautiful women." He smiled. "Ah, speak of the devil."

I turned, expecting to meet the minister's eyes, which had shone with interest. Instead, Sabrina's eyes held restrained temper.

"Lyssa and Evan. What a surprise." She employed a drawl worthy of a Texan. I looked past her to Darach. His tightening lips almost made me regret my decision to come. I straightened my shoulders.

"We have the presentation under control." Sabrina said, her voice sharp enough to cut through my faltering confidence.

An awkward silence fell.

"What may I bring you to drink, Sabrina, Darach?" Evan asked. Both requested Scotch. "I'll need an extra hand then. Sabrina, do you mind?"

"I'm not a waitress."

"Please assist Evan, Sabrina," Darach said. "I need to speak with Lyssa."

Sabrina's complexion approached the red of her daringly cut gown, but she turned and walked regally beside Evan.

I added my half-full glass to a passing waiter's tray. Darach took my arm and led me through tall, carved, double doors along the back wall. Outside on the patio, the brisk night air nipped the exposed skin above my elbow-length gloves. I hugged my bare shoulders.

Darach settled his jacket around me, sharing his warmth and spicy aftershave. "Your hair looks nice," he said, as if the compliment had emerged of its own volition.

"Thank you." I'd used every skill Megan had taught me regarding makeup and style. I raised a hand to check the tendrils escaping the loose knot. The last time a man had commented on my hairstyle, he'd suggested my preferred twist symbolized a repressed nature.

The muted light softened Darach's strong profile. I drew his jacket close, catching a finger in the chain holding the garnet pendant I wore.

I raised the pendant toward him. "I found this necklace in Megan's jewelry box, along with other pieces I didn't recognize. You should go through them so any MacKendrick heirlooms stay in your family."

His jaw hardened.

I cringed. Darach would view the family business as

infinitely more valuable to the family, and I'd kept that against their wishes.

"Why are you here?" His voice lost all warmth.

"To help you promote MKI. And to ask the Spanish minister and the other men in the receiving line if and how well they knew Kinnon."

His eyes narrowed. "Why?"

"Kinnon received an invitation. Someone here may have planned to talk to him tonight."

"About what?"

My temper heated. "You've read Megan's letter, so you know what."

"Megan's—the letter you gave to White? You were there. He wouldn't let me see it. Why would you think I had?"

"Didn't you have someone search my briefcase while we toured the floor on Thursday?"

"No. But I might have if I'd suspected you carried your copy there."

If not Darach, then who? I glanced toward the doors. Sabrina? Gavin? Frank?

Darach frowned. "Did Megan's letter mention this party?"

I looked back at him. "No."

His exhale sounded like a sigh. "Then why pester the minister with questions? He offered his condolences when I arrived. Perhaps you aren't aware that I'm here tonight to—"

"To pitch MKI for the contract for the 823 miles of pipe the Spanish need for their offshore gas pipeline." I silently thanked Robert at my former job for his briefing.

Darach crossed his arms. "Since you researched the project, you understand its significance. Why are you risking our chances?"

"There is no risk. I'll slip my questions into the conversation, and if anyone seems suspicious, I'll follow up."

He scowled.

"This is about finding Megan and Kinnon's murderer." I heard the pleading in my voice, but I wasn't letting him discourage me from finding answers.

"The police are working on that, and Kinnon's killer certainly isn't here. I'm socially acquainted with the ambassador and his assistants."

"Did any of them know Kinnon?"

"It's doubtful, but if it will keep you from harassing them, I'll ask tonight."

"Will you follow up if any of them admit to knowing Kinnon?"

"Yes."

My options were few. Darach's acquaintance with the men would make his questions seem natural, but my priorities ranked the murders first and MKI second, while his appeared to rank MKI first.

"Deal." I held out a hand. He shook his head then shook my hand.

"By the way," I said, shrugging off the warmth of his coat and handing it back. "I recommend a low-key approach toward the minister. He knows we're interested because we showed up. Latins enjoy courtships."

Darach put his jacket on and worked the buttons. "We've no time for a courtship. Tonight, is about business. Our competition is here to lobby for the project. Douglas will fire all guns, starting with the blonde on his arm. I don't want MKI lost in the resulting smoke screen, so we'll employ similar tactics. Sabrina is doubtless already charming Minister Alba."

I shook my head. "Douglas's approach won't achieve results tonight. I'm not saying the minister will ignore his pitch or his blonde, but Latins approach business almost as an afterthought. We can stand out by not talking shop. It sounds counterintuitive, but I'm sure he'll call us next week."

"How many contracts have you negotiated?" Darach asked, slowly walking toward me.

I backed up. "None, but I've—"

"Come inside, Lyssa. Watch and learn."

CHAPTER SEVENTEEN

As Darach predicted, Sabrina *was* flirting with the minister when we walked inside. She wasn't alone. Mr. Douglas, his blonde, and even Evan spoke to him when opportunity allowed. I straightened my gloves and kept pace with Darach.

The minister favored me with a smile, the sensuality of which failed to alarm me. Either appreciation for all women truly ran in Latin males' blood or they enjoyed perpetuating the myth.

"Senorita Eastin, here you are at last."

I replied as he had addressed me, in Spanish. "Minister Alba, you have a wonderful memory for names."

"I remember what is important."

A blue blaze raked my peripheral vision, but I ignored Darach. He could jump in at any time. And if the minister paid no attention to Sabrina, at least he wasn't paying attention to Mr. Douglas's blonde either.

I smiled and looked toward the musicians as an acoustic guitar riffed into a song I recognized from past business trips and dinners. The minister switched to English.

"Would you care to dance, Senorita Eastin? All day I have contemplated building natural gas pipelines. Perhaps you have some suggestions?"

"It would be my pleasure to dance, but could we

postpone the discussion? Señor de Falla deserves attention."

A smile highlighted his attractive laugh lines. "You know Manuel de Falla's compositions?"

"*La Vida Breve* is a favorite of mine. His music translates your culture more vividly than words."

The minister offered his arm.

Ignoring the women's glares, Darach and Douglas's dark looks, and Evan's broad grin, I surrendered to the music's expressive power, the room's Old-World beauty, and Alba's graceful steps. When we glided to a stop at the last decisive note, he signaled a slow dance and once again set us in motion.

"This is the first government affair in several years that I have truly enjoyed. You are new to MacKendrick Industries?"

I saw my opportunity. "Minister Alba—"

"Call me Alonso. May I call you Lyssa?"

"Of course, Alonso." I continued. "My sister married Kinnon MacKendrick recently."

"Ah, the plane crash last week, yes?"

"Yes." I followed another abrupt pivot and blinked back the pain that stabbed every time I thought about Megan's death.

"That explains the sadness in your golden eyes." His hold eased. "I must ask, since you mourn your sister, why do you attend tonight?"

"I inherited Kinnon's half of MacKendrick Industries." I waited another beat. "Did you know Kinnon or meet my sister?"

"No, I'm afraid not." The tilt of his head conveyed sympathy. "A loved one's death presents a complex burden.

I can assure you the burden lightens—but not soon. I lost my wife two years ago."

"I'm sorry," I said. "It's a very lonely time. Death sets you adrift from others."

Some of the earlier light left his hazel eyes. "If you will accept advice, don't let yourself drift too far. Seek a lifeline. And dance." He swirled me in a dramatic arc, and I smiled despite myself.

"Is dancing a grief-management technique?"

His shoulders performed a distinctive Latin shrug. "Yes. Very effective. Because one of the hardest parts of losing my Elsa was losing this." He drew me close then eased away.

I nodded. "Curling up in a blanket doesn't compare to a loved one's embrace. And the Scots aren't big on spontaneous hugging. This is the closest I've been to anyone since Megan died."

"Is there no one you can approach for comfort?"

A man's face came to mind, but I pushed it away. "I'm not inclined to seek contact for the sake of comfort. That's not how I want to handle Megan's death."

A smile curved his lips. "*Cuidado,* Lyssa. And I had better be careful myself."

The orchestra segued into another slow dance. The minister squeezed my hand but didn't step away. "Since I am creating a scandal by ignoring my other guests, we had best take advantage of this dance. What does MacKendrick Industries have to offer that Mr. Douglas's company does not?"

Back on comfortable ground, I condensed MKI's strong points. When the music ended, the minister led me off the floor and claimed Douglas's blonde for the next dance. Bemused, I watched them walk away.

"Well?"

Sabrina's urgency tensed my shoulders. I put on my partner face. "Where's Darach?"

She waved a hand. "Dancing with a client's wife. I sent Evan after champagne in case we had something to celebrate." She cocked her head. "I underestimated you. After three dances, you must have wrapped up the contract. Perhaps I should pick up my French lesson books again. A second language appears to be an asset."

I glanced at the dance floor and spotted Darach. "I'm not discussing my conversation with the minister here. We can talk tomorrow, or Monday at work."

Black eyes narrowed. "This is *business*, Lyssa. You're worse than a fool if we don't talk now—outside if necessary. Alba will probably ask me to dance next. I need a briefing on what you two discussed."

Evan interrupted with flutes of effervescing cava. "You were certainly a hit, Lyssa. I've never seen so many green-eyed females and males in one room."

"Hmpf." Sabrina claimed a brimming glass. "Lyssa captured the minister's attention with a second language and a flattering dress." She looked me over. "It's more stylish than your usual attire."

"It was Megan's."

Sabrina's eyebrows rose. I sipped. Delicate bubbles slid down my throat.

"Based on what I saw her wear," Sabrina said, "you should get a decent amount for her wardrobe. Will you also collect her royalties for the advertisements she's still in?" she asked.

"Sabrina, that's heartless. Lyssa didn't plan to profit from her sister's death," Evan defended me.

"No?" Sabrina continued to stare. "You claimed Kinnon's half of MKI quick enough. Whatever your intentions, you made out quite well inheriting Megan's *and* Kinnon's estates."

To keep from pulling a 'Greer' and drenching Sabrina, I handed my glass to Evan. "Excuse me."

I made for the ladies' room. Seeing the line, I instead exited the consulate's front door and fled down the stairs. Low voices and tobacco smoke drifted from my left. Head down, shaking with anger, I followed the sidewalk to the corner and turned right.

Not sharing my reasons for accepting the inheritance didn't make me an opportunist, but I had to admit it made me look like one. As the evening's chill pierced my anger, I rubbed my goose-bumped arms and wished Darach's jacket was handy.

I reached the end of the block and made another right turn. I heard traffic and saw the occasional set of headlights though no vehicles traveled my route. It wasn't very late, but the closed businesses and lack of other pedestrians caused me to jump at the smallest noise. Pale wisteria cascaded over a shop entry, scenting the air. The dark night sapped the petals' true color, imparting a forlorn quality.

My heels echoed down the empty street. I gathered my skirt and moved faster. Another right would deliver me back to the consulate.

A car door shut quietly.

I glanced back and stepped in a sidewalk crack. I teetered, and the three-inch heel broke loose. Lately, shoes with heels were my adversaries. I scooped up the heel, limped to the corner, and followed the consulate's front fence. Dense, dark-green holly bushes paralleled the iron bars.

To avoid an embarrassing hobble inside, I slipped off my shoes, winced as the chilly concrete sucked the remaining warmth from my feet, and pushed the ruined shoes into the holly bushes. My first distribution of Megan's belongings wasn't what I'd planned.

A rough hand clamped my neck. "Don't turn 'round," a harsh voice said. A hard shoulder forced me against the holly. Prickly leaves nicked my shoulders.

"I don't have a purse," I blurted, spreading my gloved fingers to protect my face.

"You'd best return to America, lass," he said as if we were chatting. "They remove obstacles. They took your sister and her husband. Don't cross them unless you're prepared to lose all."

My pulse pounded in my ears. "*They* who?" I turned my head and glimpsed a hand and sleeve before he shoved me deeper into the holly.

"Oi! You there! What are you doing to that lady?"

More shouts joined the alert. The man released me and ran.

Footsteps pounded closer and then past me and around the corner.

A set of hands freed me from the snagging shrubs clinging to Megan's beautiful dress. "Miss Eastin, are you hurt?"

"Ian?"

Darach's groundskeeper and handyman apparently moonlighted as Darach's chauffeur.

Free of the holly, I looked down the street. The man that knew who'd killed Megan and Kinnon was gone. I closed my eyes and tried to recall exactly what he'd said.

"Are you hurt, miss?" Ian's concern penetrated my concentration.

"I'm fine," I said, shaky but certain. A quick exam cataloged the scratches on my shoulders as superficial. "Did you see his face?"

"No." His hands continued to cup my elbows as two men in chauffer uniforms jogged toward us, breathing hard.

"He disappeared," one said. "Sorry, miss."

Disappointment engulfed me as my best lead to learning the killer's identity evaporated. No—*killers*. He'd said *they*. "It was brave of you to chase him," I said. As adrenaline ebbed, awareness of my bare feet increased.

I shivered. I didn't want to be here anymore. Minister Alba hadn't known Kinnon, and Darach would keep his word and ask the other two men. I needed to talk with DI White as soon as possible.

"I need a favor, Ian. Will you go in and ask Evan Murray to collect my things and meet me out here?"

"Of course." Ian handed keys to the man beside him.

"Put Miss Eastin in Mr. MacKendrick's car to warm up." He strode away.

"This way, miss."

Hugging my shoulders, I followed the man to Darach's BMW. Better a comfortable leather seat out of view than to continue standing on the numbing concrete.

The man settled me on the backseat, started the engine and heater, and withdrew to stand watch. The heater blasted away, and my trembling slowly subsided. I shook my hair loose to cover my shoulders and vigorously massaged my numbed feet.

My door jerked wide. Darach filled the opening.

CHAPTER EIGHTEEN

Darach leaned inside the car and glared at me. "What did you do?"

"Where's Evan?"

"He'll see Sabrina home. What possessed you to run off from the consulate?" His Rs rolled with an intensity I hadn't heard before. Cold air flowed past him. "Move over," he demanded.

I scooted to the other side of the car as he sat beside me and closed the door.

"I needed to clear my head, so I walked around the block." I wouldn't blame Sabrina—it was my decision to leave, and my being threatened had turned into a positive thing. I should probably thank her. "Listen—"

"Where is your brain, woman? Do people not get attacked on Dallas's back streets?"

I wasn't used to an assault on my intelligence. "Yes, but in Scotland, people are harassed in *front* of consulates."

He flipped on the dome light then gripped my chin, turning my face from side to side, studying me and making conversation difficult. "He didn't take your jewelry?"

I grabbed his hands. "No. He said I should go home because the people that killed Megan and Kinnon removed obstacles, and he implied I might be an obstacle too."

When I said it like that, it sounded ominous.

Darach's eyebrows drew together. "He knew you? The killers sent him?"

"Why approach me otherwise?"

"Did you see him inside the consulate?"

"I don't know—I never saw his face out here." I thought for a moment. "I don't think so. He wore a coat over a sweater, not formal evening wear."

Darach released my chin. "You have a leaf." I felt a gentle tug, and he pocketed whatever he'd removed. "When he told you to go home, do you think he meant home to Perth?"

"He specifically mentioned America. Can I borrow your phone? The man is long gone, but DI White needs to know he made contact."

Darach handed me his phone and exited the car. I dialed White and watched Darach open his wallet and pass money around, thanking the men for their assistance. White answered and agreed to meet me at the flat. Ian arrived and handed Darach my cloak and purse. Darach ducked back into the car. Anticipating the cloak's warmth, I lowered my feet to the floor.

His lips barely moved—as if he were practicing ventriloquism. "Where are your shoes?"

I told him.

"What is it with you and shoes?" he mumbled before stepping out to retrieve my footwear. I dug pen and paper from my purse and wrote down the gravel-voiced man's warning, as close to verbatim as I could remember.

Darach returned.

158

"I shouldn't take you away from the party and the minister. If you'll call a cab, I'll get back to Perth and meet with White."

He shook his head. "Sabrina will look after our interests, and Evan will look after her."

I sat back. Evan finally had a chance to try his luck.

Darach unearthed a silver flask from the seat-back pocket and uncapped the lid. "You're still shaking. Drink," he ordered.

I swallowed the smooth radiance. "Excellent Scotch," I said.

"You're difficult, but at least you're discriminating. That's a fifty-year-old private label." He held out his hand as Ian pulled away from the curb.

I returned the flask. "Why would someone think I'm an obstacle? All I've done since arriving in Scotland is bury Megan and try to deal with my inheritance." *The MKI shares.* The unwelcome thought wriggled into my consciousness. Greer had accused me outright of stealing Kinnon's estate. Darach was perhaps grudgingly tolerant because he wanted to buy Kinnon's shares, but he might feel the same. I glanced sideways. "The relevant question to ask is *who benefits from my leaving Scotland?*"

Darach deciphered the subtext and stared at me like I was a new species. "You're suggesting I hired someone to frighten you into returning to Texas?"

His anger seemed genuine.

"Given your desire to own every share of MKI stock, a better question is *why wouldn't you?*"

He passed the flask. "Fair enough. But my plan is to wait twenty more days and again ask you to sell. Until then, it's easier to run MKI with you here."

I believed him. Instead of feeling better, his explanation left me dispirited. "You're counting the days?" I asked.

"Absolutely."

The car's heater circulated a scent of leather, spicy aftershave, and blended Scotch. I sipped and returned the flask. He shook it and replaced the cap.

"I hoped to learn something tonight, but I didn't anticipate this." I drew the cloak up to my shoulders, and exposed my toes.

Darach muttered while unwinding the black wool scarf from his neck. He layered it across my feet. "All I need is you catching pneumonia and dying without a will."

I tried to lighten the mood. "Consider the bright side. If I die during the next twenty days, your mother will own Kinnon's shares."

"There's not much bright about that."

"But if your mother inherited the shares, you could buy them from her."

"Mother wouldn't sell to me. She knew Kinnon didn't want me to have his shares. She'd respect his wishes." He looked out the window. I couldn't read his expression.

"Why?"

"This isn't the time. Tonight's concern is your health and safety."

More than ever, I was eager to spend time with Greer.

Why would she support one son against the other?

"Don't worry about me. The flat's entry gate and Mrs. Donnel act as primary and secondary security systems."

He looked surprised. "Mrs. Donnel?"

I nodded. "I think she's installed a motion sensor that alerts her when people are in the common hall. This morning I tiptoed out of the flat with my garbage. On my fifth step down the hall, her door opened, and she wished me a good morning."

He emitted an indistinct sound, and we lapsed into silence as the Scotch served its purpose. I leaned into the seat. Light and dark patches alternated inside and out as Ian drove, leaving Edinburgh behind. I shut my eyes.

When I woke, my head rested on Darach's shoulder. I covered a yawn and moved away. "Sorry. But it's partly your fault for being built like you can support the weight of the world."

Had I just said that out loud?

A grim smile stretched his lips. "Is that how you see me? As Atlas?"

I shrugged. "If the world fits—but not always. Only when I'm not contemplating your control issues."

"I've no idea what you're referring to," he said, making me smile.

Ian parked in front of my apartment building. I slipped the shoes on, and Ian helped me from the car.
A few spaces away, DI White exited his car.

"Hello," I said.

The stone-faced inspector followed us to the gated entry. "Busy evening?" he asked.

"And they say Scots have no sense of humor," I said.

Darach entered the code and opened the gate. I unlocked the entry door and hobbled to my flat. Before I could unlock that door, Mrs. Donnel peeked out. "More police?"

"Yes, but everything's fine," I said, shooting Darach an I-told-you-so smirk.

Darach, Ian, DI White and I settled in the living room. Darach sat beside me on the couch.

Five minutes into our conversation, White asked, "You didn't see your assailant?"

I picked another holly leaf from the folds of my dress and deposited it on the coffee table, pretending he hadn't asked the question before. "Only his left hand. He wore a rough, dark coat over a heavy, light-colored sweater. Caucasian. Oh! He wore a ring."

"A wedding band?" Ian suggested.

"No. Bigger. A dark stone held by—" I touched the heels of my hands together. "Fingers? Maybe?"

"Was the stone black or red?" White asked.

I opened my eyes. "It could have been either—or dark green or blue."

"Gold or white gold band?"

I shook my head. "It happened so fast."

"None of us saw his face," Ian said from his seat on the couch beside Darach. "He wore a dark coat and a muffler about his neck. Light hair—blonde, maybe, or gray or white."

"Anything distinctive about his voice?"

"Yes! It was rough, like he'd swallowed gravel. I heard a similar voice when Evan and I ate lunch at a Chinese restaurant last week. The man sat behind Evan, facing away. I didn't see his face, but I heard him order." I frowned. "If it's the same man, he's following me."

"What did you and Evan discuss?" White asked.

"Shopping and other errands. Evan called a friend and set up an appointment for me. And he may have mentioned our date tonight."

Darach had been looking down at his hands, but his eyes shot up to my face at this announcement. White finished writing and closed his notepad. "That's all for now. Call if you think of anything else. And in future, don't walk alone on dark streets at night. We don't want you hurt."

I nodded. "I'll be careful."

I walked him to the door and returned upstairs. Darach and Ian stopped talking, and Ian pulled keys from his pocket and walked toward me. "Good night, miss."

They were leaving already?

"Thank you for sitting through all that." I hugged him. "And thank you for your help tonight."

He hugged back. "I'm glad I was there, lass."

"And thank you, Darach." I didn't try to hug him.

He nodded. Both men walked downstairs. I turned off the living room lights except for a table lamp. In the soft light, I collected coffee cups and carried them to the kitchen. When I finished washing up, I returned to the living room and nearly screamed.

Darach stood at the window, staring into the night, arms folded and posture rigid.

I lowered the hand I'd pressed to my chest. "I thought you left with Ian."

"I sent him home. He'll pick me up tomorrow morning. If the man is following you, he likely knows where you live."

I'd thought of that, too.

"I appreciate your company, but I'm over the scare. If he didn't hurt me while I was shivering and barefoot in an evening gown, he probably won't hurt me tonight."

I joined him at the window. Beyond the parking lot, reflected lights shimmered on the River Tay. Night hid the distant hills.

"Do you plan to leave Scotland?" he asked.

"No. I want a front-row seat when the killers are caught." The mantle clock struck midnight. "It's Sunday." I briefly closed my eyes. "Megan and I always called one another on Sundays."

Darach didn't respond.

Fatigue drained the remainder of my energy. "It's late." I stepped back. "You're welcome to the couch or the master bedroom."

Outside, a car, headlights off, parked. Darach pulled me behind the curtain and stretched to turn off the lamp. I leaned to peek. A slimly built man in dark clothes and a stocking cap exited the vehicle and walked to the security gate. He seemed to have difficulty punching in the code and then fumbled with the latch.

"Have you seen him before?" Darach asked.

"No. But I haven't met many neighbors."

"Stay here."

Darach crossed the living room and tested the heft of a fireplace poker. Carpet muffled his descent of the stairs. Barefoot, I made no sound as I followed, stopping halfway down. He unlocked the entry and opened the door a crack to watch the hallway.

When I heard Mrs. Donnel's door open, I gripped the railing. What if she—

"Late night again, Jamie Grant?" I heard her disapproval.

The man sighed. "Good morning, Mrs. Donnel."

She tsked and shut her door. Across the hall, a key scraped a lock. Darach closed my door.

"I told you she installed sensors," I said, walking down.

He started, and then turned. "And I told you to stay upstairs."

I folded my arms. "What if you'd needed help? I'm your partner."

"I can manage on my own." He started up the stairs and then hesitated. I opened my bedroom door and turned to see what delayed him. As he resumed his climb, his words carried down.

"Do you think Kinnon put in the red carpet to welcome himself home?"

"What a sad thought. I hope not," I said, but he'd climbed beyond my sight.

CHAPTER NINETEEN

Don't cross them unless you're prepared to lose all.

I lay in bed Sunday morning, replaying last night's encounter and warning until I remembered Darach had stayed the night.

I wasn't alone!

I scooted from beneath toasty covers, mentally reviewed my pantry contents, and decided I could manage breakfast.

Minutes later, dressed in jeans and a sweater, hair secured, I jogged upstairs. The sofa was vacant. My chest tightened. I should have asked Darach to wake me before he left.

I jumped as the master bedroom door opened. Darach emerged, hair damp and smoother than his creased dress pants and shirt. My morning suddenly brightened.

"How did you sleep?" I asked.

He glanced at the clock. "Surprisingly well. I haven't slept past six in years." He buttoned his cuffs. "I forgot to ask last night—what did you and Minister Alba discuss for three dances?"

Back to business. That suited me. "We started with life and loss." Darach's eyebrows rose. "The third dance, he asked what MKI can offer Spain. I think I covered everything."

Darach nodded. "I spoke to the minister before Ian came in and told me you were outside. You impressed him, and your instincts were correct, he didn't want to discuss business with me. Care to say *I told you so*?"

"No."

Darach had recognized my assessment; that was enough. I straightened a packed box in the living room, ready to address another issue. "Do you know an estate agent that works on Sunday? After last night, I'm ready to move."

"Do you want to visit flats today?"

His offer held appeal, but if he came along, I'd have to explain why I wasn't signing a long-term lease. "I doubt there will be time after the estate agent is through. I'll spend a couple of nights in a Dundee hotel while I research what's available."

"MKI has an account at a hotel near city centre. We use it when clients visit. I'll make the call if you'll make coffee."

"Deal."

I headed for the kitchen while Darach called. A few minutes of muted conversation later, he joined me. "You have a reservation guaranteed for late check-in." He named the hotel. "Do you know where it is?"

"Yes. I noticed it when Evan took me shopping."

His voice sharpened. "The estate agent will arrive at eleven to give you an estimate. If you agree, her crew can come at one this afternoon. Would you like me to be here?"

"Thanks, but no. I've taken enough of your weekend." I handed him a steaming mug. "What will you do today?"

"Ian and I are updating the electrical and plumbing in the upstairs west rooms of the manor."

"You're a handy pair." I sipped coffee. "How about breakfast? I have bacon and eggs. No baps, but I can manage toast."

"That's not necessary. Ian will be here soon. I called him when I woke. But go ahead and start your breakfast."

"I'll wait." My mood dimmed. As stiff as Darach's company and conversation were, I'd looked forward to both.

His phone rang. He checked the screen and answered. "I'll be right down." He swallowed his coffee and set the mug in the sink. I followed him downstairs.

"You'll be all right?" Darach faced me, his hand on the doorknob, a furrow between his eyes.

I forced a smile. "Absolutely. I have a busy day."

"Then lock the door and call if you need anything."

"I will."

I closed the door behind him and peeked through the peephole. Darach stood in the hall, staring at what I presumed was the knob. I turned the deadbolt with force, and he receded from view. My appetite had vanished, and I had two hours to fill.

I carried the box of personal care items to the trash chute at the end of the hall, pausing to wish Mrs. Donnel a good morning. She must have seen Darach leave, but she didn't seem put off.

Back in the flat, I tapped a toe against the remaining box on the living room floor. I'd filled it with photos for

Greer. Maybe this was a good morning to visit her.

No overtly suspicious figures lurked in the parking lot as I settled the box in my rental's trunk and set out. Brilliant sunshine fell through the oak leaves, dappling my car's hood. Peter's reluctant invitation to visit had ended with a warning: "This will be Greer unfiltered. Do you understand?"

I did.

I checked the rearview mirror constantly until one of my tires scraped the curb. After correcting my course, I paid more attention to the road ahead than the vehicles behind.

When I arrived, Peter met me. "Let me take that." Relieving me of the box, he tilted his head to the left. "Greer's in her study. Before we join her, I'd like to ask a favor."

"Go ahead," I said.

"Greer's appetite is poor, and she doesn't sleep well. I'm mourning my stepson; I don't want to mourn my wife, too. I'm trying to buffer her and her grief, but she's grown unhappier. Would you talk to her about Kinnon? Perhaps she'll open up to you."

The only thing Greer was likely to open was the nearest bottle of Scotch to pour on me.

"Peter, I never met Kinnon. I don't think I'm the one she should talk to. A female friend maybe? Or Darach?"

"I've tried the first, and Greer and Darach observe the social niceties but little else."

"I've noticed. Why is that?"

He ignored my question. "A sympathetic ear is all I ask."

I pinched the bridge of my nose and reminded myself that I had come here to learn more about Greer. "I'll try," I promised.

"Thank you." He opened a door. "Sweetheart, Lyssa is here with Kinnon's photos."

"Hello." I walked in and froze.

Kinnon, blonde and handsome, progressed from childhood to adulthood via dozens of framed photos that covered the walls, desk, and tables. This wasn't a study—it was a shrine. I scanned for images of a dark-haired Darach and saw none. Nor did I see photos of Kinnon with Megan.

"I have their wedding photos," I said.

"They gave me a set."

Greer's disdain reminded me of Darach when I'd offered to return any family jewelry. I set the box on the coffee table.

"Thank you for bringing these," she said.

Her appreciation sounded rehearsed. I felt like we were both playing nice at Peter's request. She didn't offer tea, so I supposed this would be a short visit.

Greer opened the box and unwrapped the picture of Kinnon and Peter and their cars. Walking to a long table against the wall, she moved two frames to make room for the third. Peter nudged me. Time to make good on my favor.

"Mrs. Rand, I know that losing Kinnon has been difficult."

Greer swung around so quickly I took a step back.

"You can't possibly know what I feel. A mother spends her life loving and protecting her children, Ms. Eastin."

At least one of them. I immediately regretted my

pettiness. I didn't know all the facts, so I kept my voice even. "Megan was four years younger than me. I was still a child when our parents died, but I became more than a big sister. I know what it's like to sing a child to sleep, to hold their hand the first week at the new school, and to dry tears. From what Megan told me, Kinnon didn't take you or Peter, or your love for him, for granted."

During my conciliatory speech, she'd stared at a photo of Kinnon. But it appeared I'd opened a can of worms and they insisted on wriggling out. She turned, shoulders tense, voice sharp.

"Since he was a child, I made sure that Kinnon knew I loved him. Which is why your coming into this house and telling me how I feel is arrogant."

As we stared at one another, I recalled how angry I'd been with pretty much everyone but Megan after our parents died. "I apologize for presuming. You should mourn in your own way and time."

"Darach mentioned you lost your parents while young," Peter said. "Is that what made you so strong?"

Greer looked at him in surprise. So did I. Darach had shared that?

"It certainly contributed," I said.

"I'm sorry, I didn't know," Greer said.

"That's okay. Given time, you and Megan would have discussed it." My turn to change the subject. "I get the impression you're angry because you think I took what Kinnon meant for you. Do you *want* to work at MKI?"

She looked at the photos on the wall. "I wanted to do what Kinnon wouldn't do. I wanted to sell the shares to Darach. I hate that company, but Darach is his father's child. My first husband hurt Darach terribly when he left Kinnon that cursed bequest, and now you're hurting Darach further."

She couldn't have surprised me more if she'd begun dancing a tango. "Darach's under the impression you'd have followed Kinnon's wishes and kept the shares," I said.

"Why would he tell you that?"

"Because I asked."

Greer sat on the edge of her seat like she wanted to escape. But I still had questions.

"Do you think running the business alone is good for Darach? I haven't worked at MKI long, but he seems willing to let me help with the paperwork end of things."

She faced me, all signs of vulnerability gone. "He could hire someone for that. He's fond of Sabrina, and she's played a valuable role in his social life for the last year. She's already part of MKI. He could train her. And perhaps she could make him happy outside work as well. Gavin is already like family. Sabrina would make a good addition."

Peter slid a quick glance at Greer. Because of her reference to Sabrina, or Gavin, or both?

"Thank you for bringing the photographs," she said. "I'm going upstairs to rest now." She walked out the door while I stood speechless.

I looked at Peter. "She certainly opened up. That probably didn't unfold as you'd hoped."

His eyes brightened. "It was better than I'd hoped. She seldom mentions Darach, and when I do, she changes the subject." He squeezed my shoulders. "Did you hear her, lass? She'd have sold the stock to Darach! There's hope for them yet!"

I looked at the surrounding pictures. "I hope you're right."

"We weren't pleased that Kinnon rushed into marriage," he said, "but I noticed Megan brought out the positive in him. He was a different man with her, the man I knew he could be."

"Thank you. I like hearing that." I picked up my purse. "Did you have any thoughts about the note I found in Kinnon's handwriting? The one with letters and numbers?"

"I'm afraid not. If I do think of anything, I'll call you."

"Thanks. I need to get back to meet the estate agent. They're clearing the flat today."

Peter motioned me to precede him down the hall. "Have you found a new flat then?"

I spun. "Good Lord, I forgot to tell you."

I summarized the events that occurred outside the consulate. Peter's face blanched.

"We think they know I'm staying at Kinnon's flat. Darach has arranged a room at a Dundee hotel for me. Safety in numbers."

Peter shook his head. "What next?"

He closed the door behind us and stood with me on the porch. "I have another favor to ask."

"Which is?" His favors proved thornier than most.

"When you see him next, will you tell Darach what

Greer said about giving him Kinnon's MKI stock?"

"It's not my place. He should hear it from Greer."

"I doubt he'd believe her. But if you tell him exactly how you provoked Greer, he'll believe you, I'm sure. It could be the foundation they need to rebuild their relationship."

I'd provoked Greer? I thought I'd offered condolences. Still, Peter had played the family reconciliation card. I was vulnerable to family issues. Despite their strained relationship, Greer appeared to love Darach, and she didn't want to work at MKI. Giving my shares to Darach would minimize paperwork and attorney fees and fulfill Greer's wishes.

I glanced at Peter. "Okay. I will."

Preoccupied with my thoughts, I forgot to watch for a tail on my drive back to the flat. Darach and I had forged a working relationship, and even a friendship of sorts, which made working together relatively trouble-free. Would our relationship hold up if he knew that if I hadn't accepted the inheritance, he'd already own MKI?

I arrived at the flat without arriving at an answer. I visited the manager and told her Kinnon's flat would be empty tonight. I bade Mrs. Donnel a good afternoon in the hallway, told her to expect the movers, and entered the flat a few minutes before the estate agent arrived.

She was petite, with blonde hair that shot out in all directions as if she plugged herself into an electric outlet at night to start the day with a full charge. She flitted through the flat, making notations on her clipboard. We agreed on terms. Her crew arrived at one.

Four hours later, I closed the door. The flat was empty except for my suitcase, and silent except for my growling stomach. I'd missed breakfast and lunch. I walked through the empty flat one last time, glad that Megan had been happy here.

I gripped my suitcase and grabbed my keys. As I opened the door, a piece of paper fluttered. A receipt from the estate agent? A fumigation notice?

Mid-reach, I jerked my hand back.

Computer-printed block letters slashed across the white sheet.

"LAST WARNING."

CHAPTER TWENTY

I slammed and locked the apartment door, wrestled DI White's card from my day-planner, and dashed upstairs for the phone. My shaking hands forced me to dial twice.

"Detective Inspector White," he answered.

"It's Lyssa Eastin. There's a note on the flat door that's similar to the one mailed to Kinnon."

"Stay inside. Don't touch the note. We're on our way."

I retreated to the guest room taking the phone with me and wishing I'd kept the fireplace tools for weapons. Had the man from last night left the note?

That didn't make sense. If he was watching, he'd have seen the movers and would think I was leaving.

If the note was my last warning, what happened next? The hotel no longer seemed like a safe option.

I dialed again. Darach's answered.

"Lyssa?"

I breathed easier just hearing his voice. "Would it be all right if I spent a night or two at the manor instead of the hotel?"

His voice sharpened. "What's happened?"

"Someone left a threatening note on the door. I wouldn't be alone at the hotel, but could I stay at the manor instead?"

"I'll be there in twenty minutes."

"Thanks," I said, but he'd already hung up.

I checked my watch and leaned against the wall. How had the deliverer entered the building and avoided Mrs. Donnel's notice? She heard everyone. What if she'd confronted the note-carrier in the hallway?

A mental image of her tied up in her apartment, unable to call for help, prodded me into action.

I tiptoed to the door and peered through the peephole. No threatening forms lurked in my fishbowl view. Surely, if the person had hung around, he'd have grabbed me when I'd stepped out the door. I turned the deadbolt, eased the door open, scanned the empty hallway, and dashed out to pound on her door.

"Mrs. Donnel!"

Her door opened almost immediately.

"Thank goodness!" I kissed her forehead.

"Miss Eastin! What a surprise! Would you care to join me for dinner? It's just shepherd's pie, but I have enough for two." My fear must have been obvious. Her magnified eyes blinked up at me. "Is something wrong, dear?"

"Did you see anyone in the hallway after the movers left?"

"No, I took a shower. They were gone when I finished." She pulled her wavy white hair aside and pointed. "I take my hearing aid out when I bathe, and I didn't put it back in until just before you knocked. But I was very good yesterday—wore it all day."

I darted another look up and down the hall.

"For the next few days, if you see a strange man or men in the hall or at my door, don't ask them their business. Just get a good look at them through your peephole and call the police."

"But why, dear?"

The buzzer in my flat bleated. "That's probably DI White, but just in case, lock your door."

Her door slammed in my face. When I heard the deadbolt click, I ran for my flat, locked myself in, and answered the buzzer.

"Can you let us in?" White asked.

Eye to the peephole, I watched until the detectives' familiar faces filled my view. They removed and bagged the note. Anticipating their knock, I opened the door.

"You're moving?" Detective Gilly asked, glancing into the guest room.

"Yes. An estate crew emptied the flat today."

"I'll visit with the neighbors," he said.

"Please start with Mrs. Donnel. When I checked on her, she said she didn't see anyone, but I think I scared her."

"Made her day, more likely," Gilly muttered, closing the door behind him.

I pointed at the stairs. "Best seat in the flat." DI White sat beside me on the steps. "I saw the moving crew out about thirty minutes before I found the note." I filled him in with the time line and the name and phone number of the estate agent.

"Simple enough to follow one of the movers in and wait for a chance to leave this." White lifted the bagged note.

"It looks like the same font used for Kinnon's note,

doesn't it?" I said. "The man last night wasn't exactly civil, but I thought *they* would give me time to get out of Dodge. Wouldn't seeing me empty the flat give that impression?"

"It does seem illogical and heavy-handed," White agreed.

My stomach rumbled for the umpteenth time. "Have you asked Gavin about the argument Megan mentioned witnessing in her letter?" I said.

"He attributes it to a misunderstanding," he said, watching me. "Are you planning to leave?"

"This flat, yes. Scotland, no."

"Where will you stay?"

"At Darach's manor. You said his alibi checked out, right?"

"His and the Rands'." White nodded. "I'm comfortable with your arrangement."

That was a relief since I'd already invited myself to stay at Darach's.

The outdoor buzzer sounded. "It's me," Darach said.

I buzzed him in. DI White waited at the open flat door with me. The sight of Darach, jaw set, striding closer, made me feel safer than any number of policemen could. Fortunately, he didn't seem to notice.

"We're done here," White said. "Call if you need us." He looked at Darach. "I suggest you feed Ms. Eastin."

As White walked out, Darach lifted my suitcase. "Ready?"

"Almost. I need to say one good-bye."

I picked up my purse and briefcase. He waited while I locked the deadbolt and took a few steps down the hall and knocked.

"Mrs. Donnel, it's Lyssa." After a full fifteen seconds, the door opened about three inches. "I've come to say good-bye," I said.

She opened the door wider and tipped her head toward Kinnon's door. "It's been an interesting flat, that one. I wonder who will move in next."

I leaned to hug her. "Take care."

"You, too, dear. With all this going on, it's nice you have a strong lad to look after you."

I smiled and gave her my key to leave with the manager. Darach and I walked down the hall.

"She's right, you know," I said as we walked outside. "First you're Atlas, now you're a guardian angel. I'm glad to know that you'll keep me safe—at least until I write a new will."

"And I suppose you'll name my mother your beneficiary, so I'll keep up the protection."

I smiled at his humor but mentioning Greer reminded me of the promise I'd made to Peter.

"I visited her and Peter this morning to drop off Kinnon's photos," I said. "She told me that if she'd inherited the MKI shares, she would have sold you Kinnon's stock."

Darach stopped, one hand gripped the iron security gate. "Why would she tell you that?"

"Because something I said upset her. Her outburst wasn't planned. But she knows that owning all of MKI would make you happy, and she wishes that Kinnon had sold you his shares."

He stalked to his car, beeped open the trunk, and stowed my bag. Turning, he crossed his forearms and settled them on my car's roof. I faced his confused hostility.

"Why are you telling me this?"

"Peter asked me to."

He looked surprised. "Why?"

"Because he thinks it's time to reconcile whatever differences you and your mother have."

He nearly succeeded in staring a hole through me. I'd overstepped our partnership boundaries.

"My relationship with my mother hasn't changed since she and Kinnon left," he finally said.

"It sounds like she desires your happiness. Maybe you should explore that."

"And perhaps you should explore minding your own business."

That served me right for stepping outside my glass house. I had to swallow before I could speak again.

"Would you prefer I check into the hotel?" I'd invited myself to his house. I owed him a chance to change his mind.

His laugh was filled with sharp edges. "And throw a lamb to the wolves? Although I suspect they'd be surprised by the lamb." He pushed away from my car—away from me. "There's more than enough room at the manor, and Anice will enjoy having another mouth to feed." He turned away. "Follow me."

I did, and frustration followed me down the road.

I'd upset his world again, but he'd needed to know what Greer had said.

On the narrow roads outside the city limits, my speedometer climbed to a dangerous pace. The rental car shuddered as I shot past a sign indicating an upcoming curve. *Enough.* Whatever demons pursued Darach—my revelation about Greer or his realization that he'd own MKI outright now if not for me—they weren't worth a wreck. I eased off the accelerator and coasted to a reasonable speed.

Darach raced ahead. One—two—three—

His brake lights flashed when I counted eight. I caught up to him as he turned onto the familiar gravel track that snaked between towering pines. The setting sun cast a red-gold tinge over MacKendrick Manor, warming the stone's strong lines. I parked beside his BMW in the detached garage and joined him as he lifted my suitcase from the trunk. Purse and briefcase in hand, I walked with him toward the house.

"Your home is magnificent. The history must be fascinating," I said.

"History costs a small fortune to maintain, and the recent manor history has been bleak."

I'd never heard Darach call the manor "home". It was *the house* or *the manor.* "At least it's not a shrine," I said without thinking.

His lips tightened. "You saw Mother's sitting room."

"Peter is worried about her," I said.

"Kinnon was a major part of her life, but people grieve

and move on. Look at you."

"Don't confuse my desire for justice with strength. I'm motivated by my mental picture of a judge sentencing Megan's and Kinnon's killer to the electric chair."

"We don't have the death penalty here."

"The rack?"

A corner of his mouth lifted. "Not for some time now."

The front door opened. Anice smiled at us. "Dinner's ready, and Ms. Eastin is in her usual room."

Darach handed my things to Ian. I walked inside and inhaled. "Dinner smells delicious."

I crossed to the buffet and filled my plate with salmon, green beans, and potatoes. I added a hot roll and a mound of salad. I was too busy eating to mind the lack of conversation. I'd given him plenty to think about. Two empty plates later, the chill between us faded.

He leaned back. "Do you have a mobile phone?"

"Yes, but I need to buy one here. My former employer owns my current phone, so I prefer not to use it for personal calls."

"Mrs. Gibson will set you up on our MKI plan." He pushed away from the table. "I need to finish some electrical issues."

"That's okay. I'll unpack and clean up. Unless you need help?"

He shot me a surprised look. "Not this time, thanks."

CHAPTER TWENTY-ONE

Monday morning, I sat down to breakfast and a chat with Anice. A few minutes later, Darach walked into the kitchen, dressed for work, keys in hand. He plucked a slice of toast from the stainless rack that reminded me of an upright file holder.

"Do you want to ride with me?" he asked before taking a bite.

The idea of carpooling appealed. It would give us time to talk. "Don't you have a meeting tonight?"

"Aye. MKI sponsors the Dundee Extraordinary Athletes chapter. We're meeting to discuss fundraising. You could come with Sabrina and me. We're having dinner afterwards."

He'd aimed the last sentence at Anice, who nodded acknowledgement.

Mentioning Sabrina made my decision for me. I chose my own four wheels over becoming a *third* wheel tonight. "Thanks, I'll pass this time, but I'd like to hear more about the chapter."

He finished his toast and snagged a second slice as he headed outside. "We'll talk at work." The door closed behind him.

Anice beamed. "That's the best breakfast I've seen him eat since Kinnon passed."

When I arrived at MKI, I called Evan. When he asked why

I'd left the consulate suddenly, I suggested he come over. He arrived mid-morning, sat, and extended his legs until his shoes joined my stocking feet on the desk's edge.

"I called your flat last night but couldn't get through."

"Sorry. The estate agent emptied the flat, and the phone service canceled this morning."

"Then let's start with your rushing off Saturday night. MacKendrick's man came in and said you were outside needing your things. Then he whispered to his boss, and MacKendrick grabbed your claim ticket from my hand and told me to escort Sabrina home." He grinned. "She was exceedingly annoyed at his desertion and equally annoyed that he'd left her with me. I can be entertaining, though. She got over it."

I grinned back. "That obviously appeals to you."

"Many things about Ms. Cameron appeal to me." His grin faded. "However, many things about Ms. Cameron also frighten me."

Picturing Darach and Sabrina as a couple opened an unexpected void in my stomach. The thought hadn't bothered me before.

I tapped a foot against his loafer. "What if Darach asked Sabrina to the party for personal reasons, not just business? They spend non-business time together, and his parents are encouraging the relationship. That may present a problem."

"A challenge, not a problem. It's possible Sabrina considers Darach husband material, but that challenge is easily met. All I have to do is show her what she's missing."

"Like your optimism, sense of humor, and readiness to escort deserted damsels?"

"Precisely. Now, why did you leave?"

His grin faded as I related Saturday night's events and Sunday's note on the door.

"You're taking precautions?"

"I am. I'm paying attention to my surroundings, and I'm staying at MacKendrick Manor until I find a new flat."

"That's considerate of MacKendrick—keeping you safe by keeping you close."

"Don't even go there. Anything that affects me affects MKI. Darach's just looking out for the business." I reached for a notepad. "By the way, I need a realtor to help me find a new flat."

Evan consulted his phone then wrote on my notepad.

"What happened at the consulate after I left?" I asked.

"The minister danced with Douglas's lady friend and with Sabrina. When Douglas finished a private chat, Sabrina managed one, during which the minister inquired after you. I explained that you weren't as ready for a festive atmosphere as you'd thought. He understood."

"Thanks for covering for me."

He pushed his glasses up the bridge of his nose. "In the interest of full disclosure to my favorite client, Sabrina offered to help me choose new glasses frames if I hounded you to write a will."

"Bribery, huh? Well, you asked, so she owes you her assistance. I'll let you know when I'm ready." I fiddled with the notepad. "Did you tell anyone you were escorting me to the Spanish consulate?"

His expression was a combination of disappointment and affront. "No. I wouldn't let my pursuit of Sabrina supersede any personal promise or professional obligation to you." His face lightened. "On the other hand, when I catch her, I may occasionally put her first. For example, when she needs rushing to hospital to deliver our children."

Sabrina as a mother was hard to imagine. She seemed too career oriented.

Evan swung his feet to the floor. "I have a meeting to get to."

I slipped into my shoes. "I'll walk you to the lift."

I left Evan at the elevator and backtracked to Mrs. Gibson's desk.

"Darach said I should talk to you about a company cell phone," I said.

"I'll order it now. The mobile company will deliver it tomorrow."

"Thank you. I'm off to lunch."

It was time to pump Fia for information.

City centre bustled with the lunch crowd. I watched for someone paying me too much attention but didn't spot anyone suspicious.

Fia was standing by the door when I arrived. She set the sign in her shop window to read, "Back at 12:15."

"I usually stay open and eat at the front counter," she said. "I can't afford to miss customers."

Inside, a pink and white uniformed teen held two paper bags. "That'll be six pounds two pence, miss," she told me.

"I ordered salads from next door," Fia said. "You don't mind paying since you inherited Kinnon's half of MKI?"

I gave the girl several bills. "Keep the change," I said.

Fia locked the door behind her.

"Before I leave, can you pick out an office dress? Most of my clothes are still in Texas." It wouldn't hurt my cause to purchase something, and her taste suited mine.

"I have just the thing." Fia selected a simple white shift, hung it by the cash register then led me to the back room. She poured hot water from an electric kettle over a tea bag and added artificial sweetener.

"I'll eat later," I said, joining her at the small table.

Fia pulled a salad from one bag. "Suit yourself. Anything new on the investigation?"

"Not that the police are sharing. But I was threatened twice this weekend." I gave her the short story. "Any idea why *they* might think Kinnon and Megan were obstacles?"

She picked up a fork, clearly unmoved. "Sounds to me like *they're* cross about you inheriting MKI."

"Any guesses on who *they* might be?"

"Plenty of people at MKI have ice water in their veins, but my guess is Gavin MacDonald."

"Gavin?" If Fia had intended her words to astonish, she'd succeeded.

She impaled a lettuce leaf. "After Kinnon inherited his MKI shares, Gavin bullied him to write a will and name a

beneficiary. Probably under duress, he named Darach."
But then Kinnon changed—he grew secretive."

I leaned forward. "And he revised his beneficiary to Greer?"

"At Christmas dinner last, Kinnon shocked everyone by
telling Gavin to write a new will that benefitted Greer
instead of Gavin's beloved Darach." She leaned forward,
her face animated. "How's that for rubbing salt in the
wound!"

Her smile dimmed. "He also announced he'd quit
gambling and was making other *life changes*. I turned out
to be one of those changes. He shouldn't have shut me out.
I was helping him."

I tried to guide the conversation back on track. "The families
must be close if they celebrate Christmas dinner together."

"Not as close as some of them would like." Fia stared at
her salad as if it had lost its flavor.

"That might explain why Kinnon went to a new attorney
for his last will instead of using Gavin, but I don't see a
motive for murder. Gavin is obviously—maybe even
obsessively—loyal to Darach, but I gather he's been a
MacKendrick friend for years."

Fia reached for her tea. "Gavin and Greer hope Sabrina
and Darach will marry. So Gavin prefers that Sabrina's
husband controls the business."

Darach and Sabrina again? I was suddenly cross.

Fia set down her cup. "After Kinnon changed his will,
Gavin began chatting up Kinnon on ponies, asking if he'd
heard of any sure things, and calling to compare notes.

I knew he wanted Kinnon to fall so far into debt that he'd have to sell some of his stock to get out. All Darach needed was one share to change the power balance. I warned Kinnon, but he laughed and said he could handle Gavin." She skewered a tomato with her fork. "I think that after Kinnon married, Gavin decided Darach should have *all* the shares."

I sipped my tea. For that to work, Gavin would have had to know that Greer would sell to Darach. Since Peter hadn't known, I doubted Gavin had either.

"I'm not convinced. None of Kinnon's family has mentioned Gavin pressuring Kinnon. It's your word against Gavin's."

"I have proof." Even her smug expression was elegant. "Emails from Gavin to Kinnon asking for specific horses and races to bet on. I told Kinnon he should show them to Greer and Peter and Darach. He refused."

I too wished Kinnon had told someone. Then I wouldn't be sitting here trying to extract information from an ex-girlfriend who certainly wasn't over his dumping her. And since I was the sister of the woman who'd won Kinnon—

"Why are you helping me?" I asked.

"Oh, I'm not doing it for you. You just—inspired me." She stirred her tea. "I thought about it over the weekend. Murder changes things. I won't be betraying Kinnon's trust now if I go to the police. They'll question Gavin, and he'll be exposed as a rotter. It might stain Sabrina, too."

I lost my appetite. "This isn't about finding Kinnon's killers for you. It's about payback."

She gave me a look of faux-shock. "Would you rather

the police not know?"

"Of course they need to know, but—"

"Serves them right afterthe way they treated me," Fia snapped. "When Kinnon announced the terms of his will at Christmas dinner, Sabrina and Gavin were dumbstruck. I thought Darach would break the stem of his wine glass. But Greer simply rang for dessert. And Peter, diplomat that he is, changed the subject."

I easily pictured the scene. "That sounds like Peter."

"Don't let him fool you. The man can play hardball." She attacked her salad again.

After all the help he'd given me, I wanted to defend Peter. "He's very protective of Greer."

"That's certain."

I contemplated her accusations and revelations. Once she went to the police, I might never see her *evidence*. The emails didn't sound murder-related, but—

"Will you forward the emails to me?

"Sure."

I wrote my e-mail address on a napkin and passed it across the table. "Do you really consider Gavin capable of murder?"

She tapped a red fingernail on her teacup. "I consider him capable of *hiring* a murderer."

I'd opened a can of retribution labeled "Fia," and it threatened to explode and injure MKI by setting Darach and the Rands against Gavin. But I had to let it play out. All leads needed to be followed, no matter who they involved.

Fia reached for a pack of cigarettes, hesitated, and

picked up lipstick and a mirror instead.

I nudged the cigarettes. "You smoke the same brand as Kinnon."

"He didn't smoke." She stood and tossed what remained of her lunch into the trash.

"I found a pack in his car." I picked up my lunch bag and followed her to the register.

She shrugged. "Maybe I left it somewhere and he put it aside. A week before Christmas, I reached under his car seat for my purse, and pulled out a carton. He said a deliveryman left it at the office. He gave it to me." She paused. "Come to think of it, the carton was open, and one pack was missing. Maybe that's the one you found." She paused.

"They were his final gift to me—I'll run out today." She turned the pack over in her hand as if seeing it for the first time then smiled a smile I wouldn't want her to direct at me.

"Will you call me?" I asked. Now that I'd set her in motion, I wanted to keep tabs on her.

"No. You can call me later this week."

What a control freak. No wonder Kinnon chose Megan. She rang up my purchases.

"Did you ever meet my sister?" I asked as she walked me to the door and released the lock.

She tensed. "Kinnon introduced us. He expected me, as a *friend*, to be happy for him—for *them*. He expected me to like her because he loved her." Her eyes revealed the depth of her pain.

"I'm sorry. That must have been difficult for you."

Her gaze hardened. "You're nice—like your sister. I managed to behave while we stood face-to-face. But the whole time I was wondering when Kinnon would realize I loved him best."

I drove toward MKI. Fia was clearly bitter and her evidence weak. The further away from her I got, the more I felt I'd made a mistake asking for her help. I'd started her down payback road, and it didn't seem fair to not warn Gavin— and gauge his reaction.

. As I parked, I spotted Gavin and Sabrina standing in the sheltered entry. I walked towards them.

"What do you mean you don't have the money?" I heard Sabrina ask.

Startled by the accusation in her voice, I froze.

"Something came up that had to be dealt with. It's taken me longer to recoup the principal than I'd anticipated."

"How are we supposed to loan Darach money to buy out Lyssa at the end of her thirty days? *If* she'll sell." Sabrina sounded annoyed.

"Given the murders and the note on the flat door that Darach mentioned, I'm sure the stock will be Darach's sooner rather than later," Gavin said.

The doors opened, and I gave them a head start. If they were planning to buy me out, Gavin must have spent or leveraged a substantial amount of money. Hearing that Darach was giving them updates wasn't surprising—so why did it hurt?

I caught up to them at the lift. "Gavin, do you have a moment?"

His eyes widened. "Of course."

Sabrina looked curious as I joined them in the lift.

"I have a legal question," I said.

"Why not ask Evan?" Sabrina said.

"It doesn't involve Evan. Shall we go to my office?" I said as the door opened on the second floor.

Sabrina walked out first. "I'll catch up with you later, Dad."

She walked ahead of us, not bothering to knock before opening Darach's door. Gavin followed me. I closed my door and watched him carefully. "I spoke with Fia Cullen today."

Gavin's fingers twitched. "How on earth did you meet her?"

"Sabrina recommended her store last week, and I shopped there again today. Fia described in detail how you encouraged Kinnon to gamble."

A muscle jumped in Gavin's jaw. "That's slander."

"Not if she really possesses the emails that support her claim." He hadn't denied the accusation, just renamed it slander.

"Gavin, you're the lawyer, but if I were you, I'd talk to Darach and the Rands soon. Fia plans to contact the police." I held his glare until he exited.

After work, Evan's realtor friend and I visited furnished flats for rent. Two hours later, I'd narrowed my options to two choices. Grateful for the realtor's time and efforts, I bought us dinner at a busy café.

Now, having left Dundee behind, I signaled a turn onto the single-lane road that eventually led to MacKendrick Manor. Bordered by fields of grazing livestock and gentle hills, the rural road felt safe, and the May sun wouldn't set for another half-hour. I'd begun to relax when a commercial van barreled up behind me and flashed its headlights.

"Hold on to your kilt," I muttered, aiming for one of the pull-offs to let him pass. I accelerated and almost overshot the wide spot that doubled as a scenic overlook. I stomped on the brakes.

The seat belt locked, holding me secure. The van roared past, clipping my rear fender and jolting the Ford forward.

"Jerk!" I shouted.

My foot still tried to mash the brake pedal through the floorboard. I gripped the wheel to control my shaking. The van kept going.

After another few breaths, I slid across the seat, shoved the passenger door open, and lurched outside to survey the damage. The Ford's right front tire sat perilously close to a steep drop-off of at least thirty feet to a field where nervous sheep bleated. Red fragments of shattered taillight littered the road. Worse, the crushed fender was jammed fast against the tire. Only a tow truck could move the car now, and my new phone wasn't arriving until tomorrow.

I wrapped Darach's scarf around my neck, drawing courage from his lingering scent. It would be a long hike to the manor.

I stuffed my purse into my briefcase and retrieved the

bag from Fia's. With luck, I'd arrive in time to call Darach before he could pass my car and panic.

An engine grumbled from the direction the van had traveled. The gravelly sound reminded me of the man who'd threatened me at the consulate. Feeling exposed and vulnerable, I grabbed my things. I scrambled across the road and up the hill to a cluster of boulders. I watched from behind a rock.

A van approached. The same van? It slowed and passed. Then stopped and backed toward my Ford at a reckless speed.

I slapped a hand over my mouth.

The van's bumper butted my car's trunk. My rental pitched off the overlook, diving hood-first down the embankment.

CHAPTER TWENTY-TWO

The van reversed then idled.

The driver jumped out and looked over the edge of the drop-off, a bottle in his hand. He stuffed a strip of cloth into the bottle's neck. I glimpsed his face in the flame of the lighter and gasped. He threw the bottle over the embankment and sprinted to the van.

I ducked.

A muted *KAFOOM* sounded, followed by an explosion. A scorching blast of air flew past the boulders. I locked my forearms over my head. When I looked again, the van was gone.

I stood on shaky legs. Metal popped as the remains of my rental car expanded and warped. I searched the empty road, replaying the last few minutes in my head. Molotov man's dark hair, slender build, and face matched the description of the plane saboteur. If I'd stayed in the car, I'd be dead. Had *they* canceled my deadline to leave town?

By twilight and firelight, I picked my way down the outcrop, and ran across the road. Flames fed on the Ford's interior, along with my coat and another pair of high heels. The grass, damp from recent rains, confined the blaze. The sheep had fled to safer pastures.

If I cut across the fields, I'd reach the manor sooner, but

I'd risk losing my way in the heather and taller clumps of gorse with who knew what kind of livestock. Bleating sheep I could handle, but not the shaggy red cattle with horns that looked capable of skewering me like a kebab.

After trudging for an hour, I banged the manor's heavy brass knocker. Ian had locked up for the evening, and I didn't have a key.

He opened the door, covering a discreet sniff by rubbing a finger under his nose. I probably smelled like a bonfire. "We left the curtains open, but I didn't see your lights at the garage. Do you want me to put away your car?" He looked past me and frowned.

I walked in. "There was an incident."

Anice joined us.

"Here, Miss Eastin, sit down." Ian pulled out a chair. Their kindness undid me.

"Please, call me Lyssa," I said, nearly sobbing. "I need to call Detective Inspector White. His number is in my briefcase." I fumbled with the clasp until Ian eased the strap off my shoulder.

"What happened?" Anice knelt beside me.

I'd practiced a matter-of-fact explanation during my walk, so I made it through the story. When I finished, Ian left to call the police and fire department.

Anice walked me upstairs and started the bathwater running. While I waited for the tub to fill, she brought me a warm mug. "A whisky toddy will put strength back in your legs. You have at least forty-five minutes before the police arrive, so enjoy a nice soak. I'll check on you in a bit." She left the bathroom door ajar and closed my bedroom door as she left.

I poured a generous amount of liquid from a green glass bottle into the water. Almond-scented bubbles blossomed beneath the cascading tap. I eased into the tub. The Scotch heated me inside while the bathwater warmed me outside.

The wall-heater hummed on a relaxing frequency.

Sabotage, murder, the letter in Kinnon's mail, the man who'd threatened me outside the Spanish consulate, the note on Kinnon's flat door, the physical similarities between the van driver and the man seen near Kinnon's plane—all raised goose bumps. I slipped under the water and came up searching for shampoo and answers.

Had the person who'd pilfered my briefcase and read Megan's letter and her list of suspects decided to act?

I'd angered Gavin with Fia's allegation, and he'd told Sabrina he was short on money. Was Fia right? Was Gavin so desperate for Darach to own all of MKI and for Sabrina to marry Darach, he'd encouraged Kinnon's gambling——or gone further than that?

Fia had loved Kinnon, but he'd married Megan. I'd unwittingly provided Fia a means to publicly humiliate the Rands, Gavin, and Sabrina. Fia had resented and perhaps hated Kinnon and Megan, but why would she want me dead?

I rinsed then squirted a dollop of conditioner onto my

palm and worked it through my hair. I ducked under the water and rinsed again. As I surfaced, I added one more suspect. The man outside the Spanish consulate.

I shut off the water and leaned back. Taking another sip of toddy, I closed my eyes. I was close to falling asleep when I heard the bedroom door open.

"How much time do I have, Anice?" I asked, opening my eyes.

Darach stood in my bedroom, his hair rumpled and his eyes narrowed.

I sank to my chin under the bubbles. "Now is *not* a good time. Leave."

He advanced, grabbed a towel off the counter and tossed it into the tub. I tucked it around me.

"Ian called. *You* should have called. Is that whisky?" He pointed at the glass on the tub's rim.

"Whisky toddy."

"It'll do."

He snared the glass, downed its contents in one toss, pulled off his jacket, slung it on the sink counter, and settled beside it to stare at me.

His arms crossed. "What happened?"

I told him, ending with my suspicion that the plane saboteur and the van driver were the same man. "Did you see my car when you drove by?"

He nodded abruptly. His gaze skimmed my shoulders. As bubbles popped, I fluttered my feet to regenerate froth.

"How can you live in Texas and have skin so fair?" he

asked quietly.

My heart jumped. He was looking at me—not as a nemesis or partner but as a woman. His intensity literally curled my toes.

"Ow!" Pain shot through my calf. I grabbed it and sloshed a small tidal wave onto the floor.

"What?" He looked confused.

"Charlie horse," I gasped.

"Charlie what?"

"Leg cramp!" I frantically rubbed my calf, both relieved and disappointed I'd interrupted whatever had just been happening.

His hands plunged into the water. One hand flexed my foot, the other kneaded convulsed calf muscles.

"*Ouch*!" I spoke through clenched teeth. "No, don't stop. You're helping."

"Does this happen to you often?" His voice, like his hands, soothed. Lord have mercy, what was it about MacKendrick men that appealed to Eastin women?

"Leg cramps or car demolitions?"

"Either."

"Rarely on the former, first time on the latter." I eased Darach's hands away. "Thanks, it's passed. Now I need to get dressed. DI White will be here soon."

He stood. Wet sleeves molded his forearms, exposing dark hairs beneath the fine white cotton. He picked up a dry towel and blotted his arms. The doorbell rang below.

"I'll show White to the study," he said, leaving without a

backward glance.

When the door snicked shut, I exhaled. A glow that shouldn't have existed warmed me inside. Darach MacKendrick had ditched Sabrina and their dinner to see how I fared. The concern he focused on MKI extended to me. I liked it.

I was as delusional as Evan.

I threw on jeans and a blouse and headed downstairs. Anice intercepted me outside the door, holding another whisky toddy.

"Mr. Darach said you'd be needing an extra nip."

"Thanks. I believe I do."

I entered the study, greeted White, avoided Darach's eyes, and sat near the fire. Darach excused himself. By the time I'd recited a third telling of the evening's events, my hair was nearly dry.

"Did you notice you were being followed?" White asked.

"No. I try to stay alert to what's going on around me, but sometimes I forget."

He nodded and pulled out a sheet of paper. "Is this the man you saw tonight?"

I looked at the sketch. My pulse kicked up. "Is this the saboteur suspect?"

"It is."

"The man who rammed my car and set it on fire certainly resembles this man. I don't know if I'm relieved or horrified."

"A mix is healthy." He set the sketch beside me. "If you

remember any more details, let us know."

"OK. Now *I* have questions."

"No promises but ask anyway."

"Did you find video of the phone booth and whoever called Kinnon and convinced him to fly home early?"

He shook his head. "No security cameras in that area of Muirhead have a view of that phone box."

"Where in Muirhead is the phone box located?" I could ask the neighbors if they remembered anything. DI White read my mind.

"We are questioning everyone that might have seen anything, Ms. Eastin. Let us do our job."

"Did the movers notice anyone else entering the building?"

"One saw a man follow him in. Indeterminate age. Stocky. Cap pulled low. No one saw his face." He stood. "You need to take precautions. I'll speak with Mr. MacKendrick about that. Call if you remember anything else."

A chill shook me. "Don't worry, I will."

I still sat by the fire when Darach joined me. He knelt in front of the fireplace and used more force than necessary to toss in another log. Sparks erupted, and he looked at me, close enough that I saw the anger darkening his navy eyes. "Do you regret accepting the inheritance?" he asked.

"No."

"Is it worth your life?"

"It won't come to that." I prayed.

He slid the poker onto its stand. "You haven't been here long enough to have formed an attachment to MKI."

"My attachment is to Megan. I want to know who killed her." Was it hard for him to understand family loyalty? I met his stare. "Did you tell anyone at the office your mother wanted to sell you Kinnon's shares if she inherited them?"

He shook his head.

"Well I've given someone a reason to want me out of the way. I just have to figure out what I said to who." I still needed to ask Gavin if he knew Greer would sell.

I'd had time to review MKI's financials, including partner salaries and MKI's value. I didn't know Darach's personal financial situation, but I did know the value of Kinnon's stock.

"I've told you I won't sell, but if something happened to me before the thirty days are up and Greer inherited, do you have enough cash and liquid assets to buy the stock from her?"

The corner of his mouth lifted. "You don't think she'd accept an IOU?"

Concern overrode my pleasure at his making a joke. "I'm serious."

He rubbed his temples. "We'd work something out. I'd probably sell the manor and its furnishings and finance the remainder or buy the stock in increments. Since Kinnon and then you turned me down and Mother never mentioned it, I hadn't put a pencil to the numbers. And it's moot. I'll not let anything happen to you." He took a deep breath like he'd made a difficult decision. "Forget about renting a flat. Stay here until the police catch the killer."

His admission of non-premeditation pleased me more than his offer to let me stay.

"I accept."

If I stayed thirty days, I could give Darach one share and Greer the rest or split the shares between them. If I decided on Darach only, Greer wouldn't have to act against Kinnon's wishes. If I decided on Greer, Darach would have to raise the cash to buy her out.

A yawn took me by surprise.

Darach offered a hand. "I'll walk you up."

I'd easily hugged Peter, Ian, and Evan, and I'd even considered hugging DI White this evening, but I hesitated to touch Darach. Touching Darach elicited something deeper. I held my breath as I fit my palm to his and let him tug me to my feet.

CHAPTER TWENTY-THREE

Tuesday, low clouds scudded in the gray sky and flung occasional raindrops onto the windshield and road. Industrial warehouses, converted into offices, lined the street onto which Ian turned. "It's there," he said, pointing to the right.

I gathered my briefcase and purse. "I appreciate your rearranging your morning after my late start."

I hadn't heard whoever came in and turned off my alarm.

"Mr. Darach didn't want you taking a taxi. And we all thought you'd want a lie-in after last night's ordeal."

I smiled at his euphemism. "The extra sleep was appreciated. Now I'm ready to accomplish things."

"Here you are then." He double-parked at the curb.

I'd called ahead for an appointment. Evan's umbrella sprung open as he hurried from the building's doorway.

"Shall I wait?" Ian said.

"No, thanks. Evan will drive me to MKI when we're done, and I'll ride back to the manor tonight with Darach." I wasn't ready to rent another car.

Evan walked me to the elevator.

"Good to see you're still an intelligent businesswoman and not a roasted grouse," he said, handing me the morning paper. A photo of my charred rental dominated the front page. I folded the paper, hiding the picture. "Been there, survived that. And I'm ready to write a new will."

"Smart girl."

We exited the elevator and entered his corner suite where he introduced me to his legal assistant, requested coffee, and ushered me into his office.

Sand-textured walls complimented the patina of his cherry desk and shelving. The room was businesslike but not overly formal. "You and your office reflect one another."

His grin returned. "Thanks for helping me afford it." He pointed. "Have a seat."

Coffee arrived, and we sorted out the details of my will. We chatted over a second cup of coffee until his legal assistant returned with the typed document. I signed.

The assistant made two copies and handed me three manila envelopes. I looked over each set of papers then put them back into the envelopes and wound the string on each in loops to close them. I slid the original to Evan. "Thanks for hanging on to this for me."

I tucked the copies into my briefcase and stood, satisfied I'd protected MKI, and nervous in case the man from last night eventually succeeded. "I appreciate your driving me to work."

"Not at all." Evan grinned. "You never know who you'll bump into."

His assistant came in with a note. Evan read it and smiled. "Let me call MacKendrick and tell him we're on our way."

"He knows I'm here? Ian must have told him."

It felt odd, all these people looking out for me.

Evan let me off at MKI's entrance before parking. I obliged my aching feet by walking to the elevator instead of the stairs. The doors opened.

"Hold the lift."

Darach strode toward me, frowning. His hand flattened on the small of my back, producing an unexpected jolt as he ushered me inside.

"You should have stayed at the manor and rested," he said.

I pushed the second-floor button. "Physically, I'm fine. I had to settle the insurance with the rental car company. And I visited Evan, but you already know all that."

"Are you complaining?" He looked genuinely curious.

"No. I'm grateful for your concern."

The elevator reached the second floor and Darach pushed and held the "Close Doors" button. "You need to be careful."

"I'm not deliberately putting myself in harm's way. Until I arrived in Scotland, I'd managed to avoid threats and Molotov cocktails. I'd never even had someone stop an elevator to talk to me." I smiled at him, trying to lighten the mood.

He shot me a reluctant smile and released the button. The doors slid open. I saw the office workers look away. The canteen would be gossiping today.

Evan emerged from the stairwell.

"Someone held the lift. I had to take the stairs." His glance moved between me, Darach, and the elevator.

"Well, it is your lift." He trailed us toward the executive offices.

"Miss Eastin?" Mrs. Gibson said, tentative.

"Yes?" I approached her desk a step ahead of the men. Something had shaken her.

"I'm so glad you're safe. You received flowers. I put them on your desk."

"Flowers?"

"Aye. And there's a Mr. Green waiting in your office," she said, rushing the words.

"*Jackson* Green?" The name echoed in my head like I'd spoken into a well.

She nodded.

Surprise slid into dread then rose to reluctant curiosity.

"Who?" Darach asked, glancing from me to Mrs. Gibson.

"He says he's Miss Eastin's fiancé."

I nearly snorted. Typical Jackson. But why was he here? It had been hard to get him to drive across town for a dinner date, and now he'd flown to Europe? I started toward my office.

Darach caught my arm, his earlier concern replaced by something darker. "You never mentioned a fiancé."

"Ex-fiancé. We broke up months ago. He probably said that to get inside."

"That's good," Evan said. "MacKendrick-Green Industries just doesn't have the same ring."

"I'll escort him out," Darach said.

Tempting, but if Jackson had come on business, I couldn't afford to burn that bridge. I'd need my job back when I returned to Texas. I sighed. "No. I'll see him."

Neither Darach nor Evan moved. I squeezed between them to walk down the hall. I paused in my open doorway. Jackson stood at my window-wall, engrossed in the factory view.

We'd worked together three years, dated during the past year, and been engaged for the first month of this year. I waited, expecting to feel—what? His presence didn't inspire anticipation or devastation. My heart neither raced nor ached. I was over him. I wished I could call Megan and tell her.

I hung my coat and closed the door. "Hello, Jackson."

"Lyssa!" He walked over and enveloped me in a familiar and comforting hug.

I inhaled his mown-grass scent and leaned away. "I can't believe you're here." Attractive sun lines bracketed his hazel eyes. A sun-streaked wing of light brown hair fell across his forehead. Four months ago, I'd have swept it back off his brow.

"I'm sorry about Megan. How are you holding up?"

"I'm coping. What brings you to Scotland?" I stepped out of his embrace and set my purse on my desk.

"I'm on my annual tour, checking out the European manufacturing sector. Robert told me you now own part of the most interesting private companies in Scotland." His gaze shifted to the factory floor. "MacKendrick Industries is quite an operation. Any plans to take it public?"

"No." I smiled, imagining Darach sharing management

decisions with a board of directors.

"I called your cell, but it wasn't working."

"My new phone arrives today. I didn't feel comfortable using my James Wiseman phone, so I blocked all calls except the office. In fact," I dug the phone from my purse. "Would you return this for me?"

He took the phone. "I wasn't sure how you'd feel about my stopping by."

"Pleased to see a familiar face. Though less pleased you said we were still engaged."

Jackson shrugged. "I had to convince her to let me wait for you; that thing was heavy." He pointed to the box on my couch. "I brought your personal items from work."

I panicked. "You cleaned out my desk?"

"It was the least I could do."

"You shouldn't have," I said, meaning it. I wanted to go back to my job. Now my department head would think I'd quit without notice. I looked at the wall clock. The Dallas office wouldn't open for another hour.

The connecting door opened.

"Lyssa, we need to review—sorry, you have a visitor."

I rolled my eyes. Darach could forget about an acting career. "Darach, Jackson Green. Jackson, Darach MacKendrick, my partner."

Darach offered Jackson his hand. I couldn't help comparing them as men. Jackson's lean, spear-tosser body contrasted with Darach's solid, caber-tosser physique. The unexpected image of Darach in a kilt, hefting a telephone pole, sent me spinning to examine the stunning roses occupying the center of my desk. I searched for a card among the velvety, fire-orange blooms blushed with pink and yellow.

"What brings you to Scotland?" Darach asked Jackson.

"Business, but I'm grateful for the opportunity to check on Lyssa."

"Are you staying long?" Darach asked.

"I'm flexible." Jackson turned to me. "Where are you living?"

"With me," Darach said.

My fingers jerked away from the card and caught a stabbing thorn. Wide-eyed, Jackson's glance moved between Darach and me.

I glared at Darach then faced Jackson. "Darach lives in the MacKendrick family manor, and recent circumstances make my staying there prudent. I'll eventually rent a flat." For reasons I couldn't begin to sort through, I didn't want Jackson to think I'd undertaken a rebound fling.

"You're safer at the manor than at a flat," Darach said.

"Safer?" Jackson folded his arms and looked Darach up and down. "Or easier to take advantage of while she grieves?"

"*Enough*," I said. They seemed to view one another as rivals, but neither man was available. I faced Darach. "What did you want to review?"

"Next month's production schedule. I gave you the file yesterday."

I pulled the file from my outbox and handed it to him.

His eyebrows climbed as he flipped through the pages.

"You finished it?"

"Yes."

"Lyssa's, intelligence and efficiency are sorely missed at James Wiseman," Jackson said.

"If you care, why are you her ex-fiancé?" Darach asked.

"Darach," I warned.

His shoulders remained tense, but his glower eased. "Who sent the flowers?"

I opened the card and translated the bold strokes of Spanish: *When tragedy crescendos, remember that the troubled cadence will, in time, change. Alonso Alba*

"They're from the Spanish minister. He's obviously read today's paper."

"A minister sent you flowers?" Jackson said. "I didn't know clergy did that."

"Alonso Alba is Spain's minister of science and technology," I said.

I lowered my face to a bloom and inhaled sympathy.

Jackson gave a low whistle. "You're hanging with some heavy hitters. What were you saying about being safe? Is someone threatening your factory?"

Darach shut the file. "MKI is safe. Someone sabotaged my brother's plane and is now threatening Lyssa."

Jackson's expression went from shocked to grim. "We need to talk, Lyssa. Can you get away for lunch?"

Darach cut me off. "She needs to be careful. Lunch out isn't a good idea."

Some amount of concern and protection was good, but

I wasn't letting Darach dictate my schedule. I faced Jackson. "Do you mind driving, and can you bring me back afterwards?"

"Of course. I've always walked you to your door."

I had to admit Jackson still had a charming smile. He picked up my coat as I picked up my purse.

"See me when you get back and we'll go over the schedule," Darach said. He closed the connecting door with unnecessary force

The afternoon threatened rain as Jackson drove to city centre. We walked to a pub and threaded through patrons to claim an empty table near the front window. I studied every face, but no one resembled the saboteur.

Jackson requested ale. I ordered mineral water. We both ordered sausage rolls. Outside, the heavy mist condensed into drizzle.

"I need to buy an umbrella," I said. Fia's shop wasn't far, but I wasn't pushing my luck or her tolerance by visiting two days in a row.

Jackson handed me a napkin. The waitress arrived with our drinks. As she walked away, I asked the question nagging at me. "You were pretty provocative in my office. Does Cassie know you're seeing me?"

Jackson smiled. "Sorry. Your partner set me off. And yes, Cassie knows. She said to tell you she's sorry about Megan."

I relaxed, finally comfortable with him. "Tell her I appreciate that."

He aligned the salt and pepper. "Megan called me a

week after you and I broke up."

"What?" I stared. "She never mentioned it. What did she say?"

"She delivered a justifiably indignant lecture on my not deserving you."

I smiled. "That sounds like Megan. I won't apologize for her."

"Should I apologize to you?"

I considered it. "You did already. And you could have been much worse. You were honest with me about Cassie. You didn't drag things out."

"That's forgiving of you."

"I'm viewing it through the perspective of time and death."

"I remember Megan saying, 'It's those closest to us that can hurt us the most.' I told her there was more to our breakup than a cliché. She said she wasn't being cliché."

My heart accelerated. Jackson and I had broken up a couple of weeks after Megan met Kinnon. Had she confided in my ex-fiancé, of all people?

"Did she mention names?"

"No." He continued. "Lyssa, it isn't my business, but MacKendrick strikes me as possessive. Are you sure you should stay at his house?"

I waved away his concern. "Darach doesn't favor change, and his life has been upended several times in the last few weeks. Your showing up probably has him worried that I'll get—distracted."

"That we'll pick up where we left off? I'm pretty sure

that if I asked, you'd decline." He smiled. "There's something different about you. You're stronger. Part of it is probably Megan's death, but the rest—management suits you."

"Thanks." I leaned back as the waitress delivered our lunch.

Jackson picked up his fork. "Was MacKendrick trying to keep you away from me when he said you were safe with him?"

"No." I filled him in between bites. When I came to the Molotov and the car, he lowered his fork.

"Good Lord, Lyssa."

"Yep," I said. I scanned the tables and the bar. My gaze slid past several men and then jerked back. "Jackson, there's a man at the bar—light blue sweater, light hair. Can you look at him without being obvious?"

Jackson glanced. "I see him."

"He's wearing a large ring on his left hand." I poured the rest of his ale into my mineral water. "I'm going to get a better look. If he's the man from outside the consulate, I'll nod and you call 9-9-9 for emergency services."

"That's a bad idea. Let me—"

"You don't know what to look for."

Barely registering his colorful curse, I carried the empty pint glass across the room. I leaned against the bar beside the man and lifted the glass in the bartender's direction. "Another McEwan's, please."

My quarry's fingers tightened around his beer. He appeared to concentrate on the soccer match playing on the corner television. The bottles lining the mirror-backed bar hid his reflection.

I glanced down. His heavy gold ring held a dark red stone nestled between spread wings that could pass for fingers if glimpsed at night. "Is this a popular brand of cigarettes?" I asked. My pulse pounded as I tapped the pack beside his hand.

"Chat up someone else."

His cement-mixer voice churned chills up my spine. I glanced at Jackson and nodded. He picked up his phone.

"One McEwans." The bartender set the glass in front of me. I thanked him. The boisterous group of office workers at the table behind me instilled courage. Surely he wouldn't create a scene with this many witnesses.

"I believe we've met," I said. "Outside the Spanish consulate? Your ring and your voice are memorable."

"Shove off," the man muttered.

He still hadn't looked at me. I hoped Jackson had a better view.

"My car made the front page today—"

"That was you?" He seemed genuinely surprised.

That threw me. If he hadn't known my car was torched—

"You said *they* removed obstacles. Why did they think Kinnon was one? Why do they think I am? And why did they kill Megan and Kinnon?" I heard my voice getting louder. I saw Jackson pocket his phone and stand. Gravel Voice ignored me. Like Megan was nothing. Like her death was nothing.

"Intimidation isn't your only night job, is it?" I said. "Did you help sabo—"

He shoved me. I regained my balance as he shouldered roughly through indignant diners, slapping away the hands that tried to hold him on his way to the door. I sprinted outside after him.

His pale blue sweater and shadow-gray pants blended with the now-pelting rain. I caught a lamppost, kicked off my heels, and took off again.

Jackson shouted. I sped up. If I kept the man in sight until the police arrived, the murders might be solved today.

He turned left. I heard the clang of metal. I sprinted into the alley and spun in a circle.

He'd disappeared!

I opened dumpsters and twisted locked doorknobs. I slapped the last unhelpful door with the palm of my hand and then shook away the pain. *I'd been so close.*

Sirens approached as Jackson pounded up behind me and grabbed my arm. "Do you know how stupid that was?" Breathing hard, he braced his free hand on his knee.

My frustrated tears mixed with rain. "I know, I know. But that man knows who killed Megan and Kinnon."

He straightened. "You've definitely changed."

Patting my shoulder, he waved down the patrol car.

CHAPTER TWENTY-FOUR

A constable escorted Jackson and me back to the pub, where we paid our bill and collected our things from the waitress. I traded my wet suit jacket for my dry overcoat but could do nothing about my soaked skirt or ruined shoes.

The constable began interviewing witnesses. DI White arrived. I introduced him to Jackson as I removed the combs from my wet hair and raked my fingers from my scalp to the ends. The waitress, bless her, delivered a round of hot coffee.

I went through the story for White and was explaining why I'd suspected the man of being Gravel Voice when the pub door opened and Darach stormed in. He took in my bare feet and damp clothes, and skewered Jackson with a lethal stare. "You were to watch out for her," he accused.

"He tried," I said. "It was my fault."

Jackson stood and squared off with Darach. "Lyssa saw the man who threatened her outside the Spanish consulate. I called the police, but he ran. We followed but lost him in an alley."

"It was my fault, Darach," I repeated.

White sat back and watched the show.

"You call that taking care of her?" Darach said.

I stood and glared at Darach. "I am responsible for my actions.

I should be apologizing to Jackson for involving him."

Darach turned to White. "Was the man following her?"

"Possibly. A waiter saw him enter after Ms. Eastin and Mr. Green. We're checking CCTV to determine if he followed her from MacKendrick Industries."

"Can she leave?"

The corners of White's mouth twitched in amusement at Darach's refusal to speak directly to me. I couldn't see the humor. "Aye. But before you go, Mr. Green used his mobile to photograph the man in profile. We'll work up a full-face likeness with the bartender and witnesses." White showed Darach the shot he'd shown me minutes before.

I held my breath, but Darach shook his head. "I don't recognize him."

I sighed and touched Jackson's arm. "I owe you a calmer, drier lunch."

He covered my hand with his. "Not a problem. Just slow down for me next time."

"I'll take her back to MKI," Darach said to White.

"If you prefer, I'll drive you," Jackson said.

I stepped into my wet shoes and grimaced. Riding with Darach would be as much fun as having a tooth filled. "Thanks, Jackson, but you need to change clothes."

Leaning in, Jackson surprised me with a quick hug and kiss on the cheek. I smiled as he walked away. A silent Darach escorted me outside, one hand firmly on my back during the march to his car. This time I didn't feel the jolt.

He seated me, started the engine, and pulled away from

the curb. He handed me a phone and paper. "Your mobile and the number," he said, passing them to me. Anger clipped his words. "My numbers and White's are programmed in, as well as 9-9-9 emergency services."

"Thanks." A sudden question made me face him. "How did you know to come to the pub?"

"White called me."

"Why would he do that?"

"We made an arrangement last night."

"What kind of arrangement?"

Darach braked for a light. "I'll keep him informed of your schedule if he calls me when you get into trouble."

My anger evaporated as subtext surfaced. "White will make deals for information?"

A horn honked behind us. Darach waved an apology and drove.

"Not with you," he said. "He thinks you're too disposed toward trouble as it is."

I threw my hands up. "I'm asking questions. I can't help how other people react. That man knows the murderer. I had to follow him."

"You weren't trying to catch him?"

"I wouldn't have known what to do with him if I had. My plan was to keep him in view until the police arrived to arrest him."

"You outran your fiancé."

"Ex-fiancé. And I had a head start."

"What if those alley doors hadn't been locked and you'd

found him?"

I returned his glare but had no answer.

"What did you say in the pub to provoke him?"

"What makes you think it was something I said?"

"You have a provocative mouth, Lyssa."

That shut me up. But only for a moment.

"The man seemed surprised when I mentioned the car demolition. He didn't run until I suggested his night job might involve assisting with airplane sabotage."

"Intelligent move," Darach said.

"Sarcasm isn't attractive."

He glanced at me then looked away. "I don't want to see you hurt."

His words sounded sincere; like he cared.

"And the employees don't need another shock," he added.

Pleasure deflated. Back to business. At least I could ease his mind in one respect.

"Evan wrote my new will this morning. Your copy is in my briefcase at the office."

He swerved to the curb and braked, twisting toward me. "Forget the bloody will, although you seem determined to place yourself in situations that make having one prudent."

"I didn't plan anything that happened." I settled my feet next to the floor vent, appreciating the blasting heat. Darach must be sweltering, but he didn't complain.

"Since you and White are buddies now, did he tell you what was in the letter I gave him, and who wrote it?" I asked.

"Yes."

That surprised me. White was supposed to let me know when I could share the letter with others. "Has he told anyone else?"

"Not to my knowledge."

"What do you think of Megan's suspect list?"

He pulled back onto the street. "I'd say Kinnon deliberately misled her, perhaps to keep her safe. I know everything that goes on at MKI. No one there would kill them."

I hadn't considered that Kinnon might intentionally mislead Megan. "But if that's true, the only viable leads we have are the ones I've motivated."

Darach said something that sounded like *provoked* under his breath.

I could wish in vain for quid pro quo with White, but Darach had it—meaning White trusted him. I looked out my window and didn't recognize the street.

"Where are we going?"

"To the first women's clothing store I see. You need dry clothes."

"This is the second pair of shoes I've ruined while running into that man with the gravelly voice."

"Shoes can be replaced."

Meaning I couldn't? Before I could ask, he took my hand. The jolt was back, running up my arm.

"You're not wearing Jackson's ring," he said.

"I returned it when we broke the engagement."

"Did he ask if you'd wear it again?"

"No. Neither of us is going backwards."

His eyes thawed, and he released my hand.

"Don't you want to know who my will's beneficiary is?" I asked.

"Yes."

"You."

The tensing of his jaw could have meant pleasure or an ulcer.

I straightened the skirt of my new dress as we pulled into MKI. Fia would never carry the green synthetic material I wore, but it was warm, and it fit.

Darach parked in his space and told me to wait while he walked around the car to open my door.

"Thanks," I said as he closed the door behind me. Arriving at MKI felt comforting—like coming home. Inside the entry, Darach said, "See you later," and walked to the manufacturing-floor entrance—no doubt happy to return to the machines, which probably gave him less trouble than I did.

I took the stairs to the second floor and slipped into my office. I hung my jacket and skirt to dry and toed off the clammy shoes. I dug my tennis shoes from my briefcase.

"Hey, Sis." I smiled at the photos of Megan on the wall. I had no future at MKI, but that hadn't stopped me from transforming Kinnon's office into my own space. I'd replaced his racehorse prints with photos from the flat. Minister Alba's flowers added a burst of color.

I flipped through a short stack of mail, all addressed to Kinnon except for an oil-and-gas publication with my name on the label. I was still smiling at it when the connecting door opened and Darach walked through, followed by Sabrina and Evan. They weren't smiling.

"What's up?" I set the magazine aside.

"Minister Alba visited Douglas's plant today," Darach said, sending my stomach into free fall.

Sabrina glanced past me. "Your flowers must be a consolation prize." Accusation and a hint of "I told you so" flavored her words.

My ears buzzed. Darach had warned me to stay out of the negotiations, but I'd been so sure I could handle them.

"Since the minister hasn't called for an appointment to visit MKI, it looks like we're out of the running," Sabrina said. I shrank to about two inches tall as she crossed her arms. "At least the day wasn't a total loss. Darach says you wrote a will."

He hadn't wasted any time sharing the news with Sabrina.

"I would have loved to sign as a witness," she said.

"That wasn't necessary," Evan said sharply.

I didn't know if he meant we hadn't needed her as a witness or if he referred to her dig. Either way, her smile disappeared. She walked back to Darach's office and Darach followed.

Evan shut the door behind them. "What happened? You've changed clothes."

I ran him through it. "So that was my lunch. How was yours?"

He shook his head. "I took Sabrina to the Chinese place.

She acted like I'd taken her slumming, but the food pleasantly surprised her. She's a bit spoiled."

"Does that daunt you?"

"No. I can work with spoiled." He walked to the door. "Don't let the news get you down. I have a friend on Douglas's legal staff. The minister hasn't signed a contract yet. Could be he's saving the best for last."

I appreciated his words but didn't feel any better. "Nice glasses," I said. The rimless style blended in, making his jaw and cheekbones the first thing I now noticed about him. "Sabrina made a good choice."

He smiled. "Aye, when she's nice, she's verra, verra nice."

After Evan left, I finished paperwork and again reviewed the files from Kinnon's flat. If they held clues, I still couldn't recognize them.

The connecting door opened. Darach was alone this time.

"Has Minister Alba called?" I asked, hopeful.

He shook his head. "You'd best let me deal with future potential clients. After you've a bit more experience, and when you haven't so many distractions, you can assist with negotiations."

Even knowing he was right, I bristled. "I'm capable of handling everything that's going on."

"Between the murder of your sister, the destruction of your rental car, the return of your fiancé, and a second encounter with the man who threatened you, you're having an eventful week."

"Ex-fiancé." I sighed. "And it's only Tuesday."

His smile pleased me. He nodded at the box on my couch. "What's that?"

I walked to the carton. "Jackson brought my personal items from the Texas office."

"Do you want to keep them here or take them to the manor?"

"I hadn't thought about it." I lifted the lid. Nestled on top was the framed wedding photo Megan had sent. It had arrived a week before she died.

We stared for a long moment before I picked it up and propped it on my desk.

"We'll leave for the manor at six," Darach said, walking out.

I used my new smart phone to call Evan's realtor friend and let him know I wouldn't need a flat for a while. Next, I called Jackson at his hotel. He assured me he was drying nicely.

I checked my email, found one from Fia, and opened the attachment containing the emails from Gavin that Kinnon had copied her on. All carried a December date.

Gavin wrote, "Who do you like in the third race? An acquaintance has mentioned…" I read and scrolled to the next and the next. By the fifth email, Kinnon and Gavin were practically pen pals, but I hadn't read a hint of coercion. Gavin seemed to have a genuine interest in learning the ins and outs of horse racing. Did that explain his sudden financial setback?

In the last email, Kinnon wrote: "Are you setting me up to sell stock to Darach?" Gavin denied the accusation.

Nothing struck me as incriminating. I saw nothing but an excuse for Fia to embarrass Gavin in front of the Rands, Darach, and in public by instigating a visit to or by the police.

I printed the emails to read again later.

At six thirty, I closed my bedroom door at Darach's manor. I'd have traded my Roth IRA for a scented soak in the tub, but he'd asked me to meet him in the study in half an hour. Fifteen minutes wouldn't do a bath justice, so I opted for a shower.

Twenty minutes later, warm in leggings and a sweater, I kicked off my flats and prowled the study. Flames danced in the fireplace. Tawny light filtered from amber-shaded wall lamps onto heavy masculine furniture and chairs upholstered in a navy-blue plaid striped with dark green and shocking red lines. The room reflected Darach: traditional with jolts of the unexpected.

One section of mahogany shelves held a sophisticated sound system. Darach's old-school collection of CDs ranged from classical to modern Celtic. I fed a disc into the player. A haunting harp wove a spell through the speakers. The horizontal blue bars on the stereo's equalizer rose and fell with the music like heartbeats—like the EKG that had monitored the end of Megan's life.

The door opened. I turned, eager to replace bleak memories with Darach's vital reality. He had changed into jeans and a black mock turtleneck. He opened a cabinet, poured two measures of Scotch, and handed me one. "*Slàinte mhath.*" He touched his glass to mine. "Shall we sit?"

I chose an armchair. He nudged its mate closer and settled.

"You need a minder," he said.

I ignored the insult and considered the substance of his remark.

"Can you recommend a bodyguard service?"

I only half-joked. Confirming the gravel-voiced man was following me, bothered me more than I wanted to admit.

"What about me?"

"Do you have a handgun or a black belt in some form of martial arts?"

"No. But I'm large and, they tell me, intimidating. We're partners. We're living in the same house. We can ride to and from work together. If you eat lunch or dinner out, I'll go with you. Merging our social schedules is easy enough."

"Especially since I don't have one."

I sipped. Warmth raced down my throat. Spending more time with him appealed on several levels. Protection for one. The other—attraction—was better left unexplored.

"Darach, I admire your dedication to the company, and I trust you to do what's best for MKI—"

"But you don't trust me to do what's best for you."

"It's not that." I walked to the fireplace.

"Then what?"

When I didn't answer, he set his glass on a table and approached. His hands gripped the mantel, trapping me between braced arms. My heart immediately sprinted. Up close, I could see the blue glints in his black hair. I wondered about the feel of its texture and stopped myself from raising a hand to explore.

"This isn't about who owns the stocks. It's about my preferring you safe, not dead," he said.

"And I appreciate that." I struggled to keep my voice level. Between the fire at my back and Darach at my front, I was overheating.

His head tilted. "But?"

But? I focused.

"But you're already helping me by letting me stay here, and by offering to carpool. I won't be reckless about it, but I'll continue asking questions. I don't mind Minister Alba or Jackson or you reacting to my damsel-in-distress situation by offering help or suggestions when I need a sounding board, but I'll determine my own solutions."

I expected him to challenge me. Instead he said, "Alba and Jackson are offering help?"

"In one form or another," I hedged, seeing a sudden alertness in his expression. I jumped as someone knocked on the door. Anice's voice followed, announcing dinner.

I ducked under Darach's arm. "Coming, Anice," I called, needing time to cool my thoughts and body.

Darach picked up my shoes and held them out.

"Thank you," I said.

The weight of his watching me—like he was trying to work out a complicated puzzle—followed me to the dining room and continued throughout the polite small talk during dinner and dessert. Afterwards, I declined a nightcap, climbed the stairs, and fell fast asleep.

Megan's cardiac monitor hiccupped a brief warning, resumed its rhythm, hiccupped again, and bleated an urgent alarm. A flat line replaced the weak peaks and valleys.

Gavin, Sabrina, Frank, Peter, Greer, and Fia—all dressed in nurse smocks and pants—converged on Megan.

"No!" I tried to hold them back.

On the opposite side of the bed, a man with short black hair closed on Megan with cardiac paddles. "Clear!" he warned.

Megan's broken body jerked. I screamed.

The gravel-voiced man from the pub grabbed my arms.

"Don't worry," he said. "He'll see to you when he's through with her."

CHAPTER TWENTY-FIVE

Wednesday morning found me distracted. It wasn't just last night's dream that had me rattled. There was Darach's behavior toward me yesterday.

He'd been solicitous because I'd had a tumultuous day by anyone's standards. He'd been angry because I'd chased a man who'd threatened me before. He'd been frustrated because I'd apparently spoiled MKI's consideration for the Spanish gas pipeline project. But I couldn't formulate an explanation for his recent possessiveness—from last night's scene by the fireplace, to his reaction to my mentioning that Alba and Jackson had also offered help—what was that about?

Did Darach still count the days until he could ask me to sell again, or was he getting used to me? Given the escalating threats, I couldn't blame him for wanting to keep an eye on me. I must be pushing every button he possessed.

He didn't know how quickly I wished I could disperse my shares, or how little he needed to worry about all of this while we had more important things to focus on, like accelerating the slow progress of finding Megan and Kinnon's murderers.

I opened my briefcase and pulled out a copy of my will. Maybe having the document in his possession would ease his mind.

I found him in the dining room. He offered a good morning but continued reading the newspaper. I dropped the envelope in front of him.

"What's this?" he asked.

"Your copy of my will."

Anice breezed in and placed full plates before us.

"I enjoy making breakfast," Anice said. "I prepare it so rarely."

I inhaled the aroma of fresh baked scones. "That's a shame. You excel at it."

"Thanks for noticing."

"I've noticed, too," Darach said. Setting the paper aside, he split a currant-studded scone. "Butter, cream, or jam?"

"Jam, thanks." I accepted the jar. "I've been thinking about your offer to help keep me safe. I agree to stay, and we can carpool to work. However, lunches, dinners, and meetings are as needed."

Predictably, he didn't look satisfied. "How am I supposed to protect you if I don't stay close?"

"We're business partners. That keeps us close."

"Closer." He leaned in and caught my chin. I inhaled his spicy aftershave. My pulse jumped, and I nearly dropped my knife. Darach up close was compelling.

I pulled away before I embarrassed myself. "We don't want anyone getting the wrong idea." I primly licked citrusy Dundee jam from my thumb.

His eyebrows climbed. "You've lost your sister to murder,

been targeted by an assassin with a Molotov cocktail, and twice confronted a man with ties to killers. I doubt your accepting the security the manor and I offer will surprise anyone." He leaned back. "Word is already getting 'round the employees that you're living here."

I sat up straight. "How did they find out?"

He shrugged as if gossip were inconsequential. "You changed your payroll address to mine yesterday."

"Word traveled that fast?"

He nodded and took a bite of scone. I set mine aside. "I'll probably blush when I walk into work today, and that will only encourage the rumors."

"As I said, most of the employees will understand."

"And the rest will suspect that half of MKI isn't enough for me."

I blurted out the thought uppermost in my mind. "Aren't you and Sabrina dating? You don't want to let office gossip mess that up."

He gave me one of his rare smiles. "It won't."

When he didn't elaborate, I wondered if his words boded well for Evan's pursuit of Sabrina. My appetite suddenly increased.

"Does your mother know I'm staying here?"

"I haven't mentioned it."

I recalled Greer's expression when she talked about Megan and how much the surprise of Kinnon's elopement had hurt her. Darach wasn't her favorite son, and our living arrangement certainly wasn't marriage, but—

"We should tell her before someone else does."

"Why?" He seemed surprised I'd suggest it.

"Trust me, she'll want to know, and it's better if she hears it from you."

Darach called Peter. Twenty minutes later we parked behind the silver Jaguar. Once again, we gathered in the sunroom amid the bright furniture and flourishing plants.

"Have the detectives discovered something about Kinnon?" Greer asked.

I could see dark circles under her eyes from across the room.

"No. We're here on another matter," Darach said. He briefly outlined what had happened over the past two days and didn't downplay the danger. "Lyssa will be staying at the manor until the killers are caught."

Greer shot to her feet and stalked out of the room. Both men stood.

"Let me talk to her, Peter," Darach said. Peter's jaw didn't relax, but he nodded.

I exhaled as Darach walked out. "That didn't go well."

"Did you really expect it to?" Peter said. "First Kinnon and Megan. Now Darach and you."

"We're not Kinnon and Megan," I said. "We're not getting married. We're not even together. With all that's happened we just want another set of eyes keeping watch. We're trying to help catch Kinnon's killer, not hurt Greer."

Peter looked down the hall. "I believe that wasn't your intent.

However, I doubt Darach fully realizes his intentions. He has *never* behaved impulsively like this."

I fought back the urge to defend Darach. "At any rate, I feel safer at the manor."

"You *are* safer at the manor." Peter patted my hand.

"While we wait, I have a few questions," I said.

Peter sat beside me. "It seems that questions are all that are left. Ask."

"Last week, Sabrina suggested I shop at Fia Cullen's store. Fia told me she and Kinnon were lovers."

He snorted. "She felt more for Kinnon than he felt for her. That became obvious the minute he met your sister. You'd think some of my diplomatic training would have rubbed off on him." He shook his head. "Why he thought Fia and Megan should meet and become friends is beyond me."

"Fia admitted she didn't react well to the news," I said.

"An understatement. She raked her keys down the side of his Porsche."

That explained the car repairs. "What did Kinnon do?"

"He wasn't inclined to press charges. I felt Fia shouldn't get away with vandalism. I told her that if she didn't pay for the damage, I'd insist Kinnon go to the police. She promised to pay—I wonder if she did."

I pictured Darach's handing cash to the surly mechanic. I told Peter about the Porsche.

"She didn't mention paying," I said. "But she did say you played hardball. I guess she meant your holding her accountable. Did you mention her vandalism to DI White?"

"No, but I will." Peter glanced down the hall. "If you'll excuse me, I want to check on Greer. Then I need a cigarette. It's a poor time to be trying to quit."

I rose as well. "Darach and I should go."

We stopped in the doorway of Greer's sitting room. Darach spotted us and stood. Greer's face went blank as she said good-bye.

Back at MKI, I'd completed the morning's paperwork when Darach opened our connecting door and invited me to lunch. We drove to a bistro downtown. I picked at a Greek salad.

"Are you feeling all right?" he asked.

"Nothing capturing a murderer wouldn't cure," I said.

"If I help keep you alive until the police arrest someone, will you be grateful enough to sell me your stock?"

The question was so unexpected, and asked in such an uncharacteristically lighthearted manner, I laughed. "Don't hold your breath."

"I wasn't planning on it." His face relaxed. "You've a nice laugh."

I didn't know what to say to that, so I was grateful when he changed the subject.

"There's an Extraordinary Athletes track-and-field event in Dundee this weekend. We could use another competition assistant if you're available. An athlete's father is bringing her and picking her up, but he can't stay for her events. Aileen needs a coach."

"I don't have many athletic talents," I said.

"You possess kindness and enthusiasm; those are enough."

I liked that he thought me kind and enthusiastic. "What makes the athletes extraordinary?"

"Different challenges. Aileen has Down syndrome. The young man I'm coaching is autistic."

"How old are the kids?"

"Aileen is seventeen, my athlete is eighteen. The events are age and gender specific and accommodate young children up to adults. It's about competition, socializing, exercising and confidence-building."

"What would I do?"

"You would make sure Aileen's on time for her events, follow along from the edge of the track while she competes, and shout encouragement. I can have the volunteer director call and talk you through what you need to know."

"Okay." I looked forward to spending an afternoon thinking of something other than murder.

He checked his phone's display and answered. "Yes, Mrs. Gibson."

He signaled for the check. "We'll be there in ten minutes."

I threw my napkin over the remainder of my salad. "Duty calls?"

His eyes shone. "Minister Alba will be at MKI in thirty minutes. He'd like a tour."

CHAPTER TWENTY-SIX

Darach and I met the minister in MKI's lobby. The men shook hands, then Alonzo held mine between his.

"Lyssa, I was very saddened by the news of the plane being sabotaged. How are you?"

"Determined to continue letting the music carry me until this song ends and another begins. Your flowers added a beautiful note. Thank you, Alonzo."

He gave my hands a squeeze. "I am sorry to rush, but I have an early-evening flight to Spain. Shall we start?"

"Of course," Darach said, eyeing me. I'd forgotten to mention the minister and I were on a first-name basis. "Lyssa, if you'll lead the way to the locker room, we'll pick up hats."

I'd already stashed my hat and tennis shoes under a locker-room bench, making a quick change easy. Darach started the tour as we entered the plant. His presentation included specifics pertinent to Spain's requirements. I liked listening to his voice: strong and animated, with the added appeal of his Scots burr. We ended the hour in his office.

"Most impressive," Alonzo said, sitting beside me on the couch. Darach leaned against his desk. "Both your factory and Mr. Douglas's are well-run and capable of handling our needs."

Darach nodded. Alonzo pulled folded papers from his pocket. "These are the specifications for the four facilities and pipelines. I would appreciate a bid as quickly as you can put one together. Send it to the consulate; they will forward it to my engineering team. A decision will be made soon." He stood to shake Darach's hand then faced me. "Lyssa, will you walk me out?"

"Of course."

Darach left his door open, which I took as an invitation to return and debrief after Alonzo's departure.

Alonzo switched to Spanish as we walked to the elevators. "I have enjoyed seeing you again."

"And I you," I said in Spanish. "We heard that you'd visited Mr. Douglas's plant. I'll confess, I thought you might have already made your decision."

He smiled. "My assistant sets my appointments."

The elevator doors opened, and we stepped inside. I pushed a button.

"He watches you with many emotions in his eyes."

I blinked. "Who?"

"Señor MacKendrick."

I smiled. "He was probably nervous I'd say or do something wrong. And not without reason; I'm still new to all this."

His warm, hazel eyes crinkled in the corners. "You are intelligent. It won't take you long."

"Thank you. I've known Darach only slightly longer than I've known you. Our partnership is strengthening."

The elevator opened. We stepped out, and Alonzo stopped me. "Have you not realized that his interest in you involves more than your partnership?"

I felt myself blushing. "Forgive me, but I don't think so."

With an indulgent smile, he took my elbow and walked me outside. Alonzo's driver pulled to the curb.

"It is too bad that I did not meet you first, Lyssa." His smile was that of a man putting down something he couldn't have. I extended my hand. Instead of shaking, he lifted it to his lips. "*Adios.* May your life's path soon return to happiness."

I smiled. I'd miss him. "Thank you—for everything."

As the car pulled out of the lot, I put aside his comments. Latins loved romance. He'd told me what I wanted to hear, but that didn't make it true.

I walked upstairs and entered the hall as Gavin walked into Darach's office and closed the door. He looked grim.

I detoured to my office and glanced at the connecting door. If Gavin was confessing he'd encouraged Kinnon to gamble, or complaining about my confrontation in the parking lot, tonight's drive to the manor could be frosty.

I picked up the ringing phone. "Hello?"

"It's your fiancé, Miss Eastin," Mrs. Gibson said politely.

"Thank you."

I had to correct the fiancé rumor. Employee gossip must be wild, having me engaged to Jackson and living with Darach. And Mrs. Gibson had stopped calling me "Miss Lyssa."

I switched lines. "Hi, Jackson. How go the business calls?"

"Faster than I anticipated. I'm packed, checked out of my hotel, and driving to the airport. I'm nearly to MacKendrick Industries. Can I stop to say good-bye?"

My stomach twisted unexpectedly. Jackson was a slice of home, and I'd barely seen him. "I'd be disappointed if you didn't."

"See you in a few." He disconnected.

I walked to Mrs. Gibson's desk, glancing at Darach's still-closed door. Her smile was respectful, but I sensed a hint of censure.

"Mr. Green is coming by, and I wanted you to know that we aren't engaged. We were planning to marry at one time, but that ended before I came to Scotland."

"Oh?" The lines by her mouth eased and then reformed. "The scoundrel lied to me?"

"He wanted you to let him wait for me the day he arrived. And I'm glad you did. It's been nice seeing someone from home."

Mrs. Gibson looked around at the cubicles. "I'm very discreet," she said. "But if you don't mind, I may mention about that Mr. Green isn't your fiancé."

"Thanks. That's easier than working it into the company newsletter."

She beamed. "Don't worry, Miss Lyssa. I'll still the wagging tongues."

I met Jackson at the elevator. "Do you have time to sit down?"

"Fifteen minutes." We walked to my office. "I didn't mean to cut it this close, but I was able to get a seat on an earlier flight."

We settled on the couch.

"Cassie's ready for your return?"

"Definitely. She said to tell you hello, and she halfheartedly suggested I stay a little longer if you were in danger. I'll admit the pub incident made me uneasy, but given what I saw from MacKendrick afterwards, you're in good hands."

I frowned. "Because he pretended I didn't exist?"

"In man-action, that means you scared him, so he must care about you. And I've seen the way you watch him."

Jackson's observation, following Alonzo's, almost made me a believer. Almost. "We're partners. I don't see us going beyond that."

"I know I'm a hard act to follow but give him a chance."

I tagged his shoulder with a gentle fist. "Megan just died. I don't know why I'm feeling attraction."

"It's because you're alive. And life will hunt you down to reaffirm itself."

"You know, Jackson, I really am glad you came to Scotland."

I looked at the wall clock and stood. "You'd better get started before traffic picks up."

He stood. "Could you use a hug?"

"More than anything."

He obliged with a warm and comforting embrace.

"Jackson?"

"Mm-hmm."

"The answer is yes."

"Yes? To what?"

"To the last question you asked me when you broke our engagement."

His head shook. "What did I ask?"

"If we could be friends. The answer is yes."

I felt his smile against my hair. "Good."

"I need to find a way to get hugged more often," I said as the connecting door swung in. Darach filled the opening. Jackson and I stepped apart.

"Come see me when you've a moment," he said stiffly before walking back into his office and closing the door.

Jackson let me go. "I know the way out. Take care of yourself, and let him help. Guys like defending and protecting."

"I'll try." I walked him to the door. "Thank Cassie for sharing."

"Will do."

I felt a little lost as he left, and the link to my old life—the life that had included Megan—weakened. I turned to the connecting door and went through without knocking. Darach stood at his window-wall.

"You wanted to see me?"

He turned to me, his face a carefully neutral mask. "You may not realize that Fia Cullen is not a family friend."

"So I've learned." I crossed my arms. "I saw Gavin come in. What did he say?"

"That Kinnon misinterpreted their conversations about horse racing as encouragement to gamble. Gavin's been placed in a difficult position. If you'd mentioned Fia's fantastical theory to me—"

"It wouldn't have changed anything. I won't dismiss a potential lead or suspect no matter who stands accused. Gavin's situation is currently embarrassing, but it's only difficult if the police decide her evidence supports her position more strongly than the emails illustrate."

"You've seen the emails?" He looked surprised.

"I asked her to send them to me. I can print them for you if you'd like."

He followed me to my office. I pulled up the emails and started printing.

"Are you and Gavin okay?" I asked.

"We are unless Fia's accusations prove true." He started reading as the pages emerged. I sat on my desk and waited for him to finish.

"I see nothing incriminating here," he said.

"Neither did I. My impression is that she holds a grudge, and she's determined to humiliate Gavin by making him talk to the police and defend himself to you and your parents."

Darach folded the papers in half. "You and Jackson seem to be getting closer."

I glanced at my watch. "Actually, we're getting further apart. He's flying home tonight."

Darach's shoulders relaxed. "Do you think you'll ever consider Scotland home?"

I planned to leave when the police caught the killers, and no matter what, I'd always be an American. But I could picture myself living here—under different circumstances.

"I'm pretty adaptable," I said.

He walked toward the door. "You never said why the engagement ended."

"It's not important now."

His words came softly, and I thought he said, "Good to hear."

CHAPTER TWENTY-SEVEN

The rest of the workweek's surprises were the good kind. Jackson called to check on me after he returned to Dallas. Thursday, when I exited Darach's car at MKI, I saw my name painted in shiny black letters in the space beside his. Friday, I found a personalized hardhat—proportional to my head—in my office.

Darach's behavior remained attentive but guarded—not surprising, since I'd unintentionally helped Fia direct police attention to his longtime friend and solicitor, Gavin. Off and on, I'd caught Darach staring at nothing, and I hoped that he, too, was analyzing everyone's motives.

Gavin was conspicuously absent Thursday and Friday. Judging by the glares Sabrina shot at me the few times she couldn't avoid me, he'd told her about my talk with Fia.

Friday afternoon, I followed up with DI White about Jackson's photo of Gravel Voice. It hadn't produced any hits in the criminal databases. Whoever my sometime shadow was, he didn't have a record. Yet.

When I asked about Fia's email evidence, White commented only on the thoroughness of Gavin's legal training and said he would explore all leads, etc., etc.

Tired of being outside the loop, I called Fia.

"Fia's," she answered.

"It's Lyssa. Can I stop by today?"

"Hang on." I heard the cash-register drawer open. Moments later, it closed. "I found something you'll like, but I'm busy with a weekend sale. Come by Monday after eleven."

She hung up, still a control freak.

Darach charged through the connecting door. "Minister Alba called my mobile. He was disappointed you weren't with me."

The gleam in his eyes propelled me to my feet. "Did he offer you the contract?"

"He offered *us* the contract and made it clear you sold him."

He grinned like a boy, and I couldn't stop myself—I hugged him. It was the first time I'd acted on my attraction for him, and it shocked me.

He tensed but hugged back. Unsure what to do next, I awkwardly patted his back and stepped away.

Darach recovered first. "We're allowed a bit of celebration."

My mood launched like a rocket. "I agree. That's fabulous news! When will the job start?"

"Late July."

"Oh!" A month and a half away. I expected the killer to be caught before then. I'd probably be back in Dallas and miss out on seeing the job I'd helped secure become pipe and valves.

Darach misread my faltering smile. "It's the earliest our production schedule allows."

I resuscitated my smile. Knowing that MKI employees were manufacturing for a deal I'd participated in would help make my missing it bearable. "I understand. I'm happy for all of us."

Darach clapped a hand on my shoulder. "Then let's find Sabrina and start the contract."

Saturday, I rode with Darach to Edinburgh, where crisp temperatures and clear skies favored the Extraordinary Athletes track-and-field meet. An impressive turnout swelled the stands and grounds of a soccer field divided into event venues.

I found Darach's presence across the track reassuring in the crowd of unfamiliar faces. More than once, I looked for him, his height and breadth were easily spotted in the throng. The smiles and laughter that regularly creased the corners of his eyes and mouth mesmerized me.

"Lyssa!"

Aileen, my teen-aged athlete, waved enthusiastically, sending the fingertips of my gloves flapping on her hands; she'd left hers in her father's car. She crouched at the starting line of her final event, the equivalent of a fifty-yard-dash. I waved back.

The starting gun fired. Aileen and six other girls ran, focused and determined. I jogged with the other coaches, calling encouragement. "Come on, Aileen! Great stride, way to move!"

She advanced from fourth place to third as the first two athletes crossed the finish line. The winner stopped and threw kisses to the crowd. As soon as everyone crossed,

I joined Aileen and gave her a hug. "Great job!"

She looked at me, her expression serious. "I didn't win."

"No, you won't always win, but with practice and trying your best, who knows what will happen the next time? You ran bravely and with focus."

"Thanks!" Her smile brightened.

I checked my watch. "Your father will be here soon. I'm sorry he couldn't see you compete, but I'm glad I got to be your partner."

"Me, too. Look, there's Mr. Darach!" She pointed to the end of the adjacent track where he waited with open arms for his runner. I'd noticed all the Dundee kids knew him, and he knew them all by name.

"Do you like Mr. Darach?" I asked as we walked toward him.

Aileen nodded. "Do you like Mr. Darach?"

I smiled at her. "I do."

"Are you going to marry him?"

My pulse jumped. "No. We're business partners."

"I'd marry him," Aileen said.

Darach exchanged a high-five with his athlete's parents then turned to us. "Hello, ladies." He nudged between Aileen and me and settled his arms on our shoulders. I liked this open and relaxed side of Darach. Spontaneous and playful looked good on him.

He looked at Aileen. "Thanks for keeping an eye on Lyssa. She's a terrible tendency to get into trouble."

Aileen poked him in the ribs. "No, she doesn't."
She looked past Darach. "Oh! There's my Da!"

She darted away. We caught up as the thin man she hugged straightened to face us. "Thank you for supporting her, miss. I couldn't turn down an extra work shift."

I shook his hand. "It was my pleasure. You have a wonderful daughter."

"Aye." His grip eased. "Your hands are freezing, miss."

"I'll take care of that." Darach gathered my cold hands in his. Even gloveless, his hands were warm. We watched Aileen and her father join the crowd in the awards area.

"Are those your gloves she's wearing?" Darach asked.

"She needed them more than I did. And I believe a young boy is wearing your cap."

"Tam, woman. Scots wear tams." His gaze followed the kids. "The committee chair told me you presented them with a generous check in memory of Kinnon and Megan."

I hadn't expected it to become common knowledge. "It was the proceeds from their estate sale less the bills that have come in. I thought Megan and Kinnon would approve."

He nodded and released my hands. I tucked them into my pockets, savoring his lingering warmth as we walked toward the presentation stage.

"Did you enjoy yourself?" he asked.

"I did. Megan would have loved this. She ran track in high school, and she loved kids. She wanted at least four."

Darach's mouth thinned. "I considered Kinnon capable of fathering children but not of being a father. Do you want children?" he asked.

"Definitely. How about you?"

251

"Yes and no," he said. His pace and voice slowed. "I'm very like my father. I might put work first and parenting second."

"The fact that you're concerned about it indicates you'll do all right."

He bumped me. "Optimist."

For the rest of the afternoon, he watched me with an undecipherable expression.

CHAPTER TWENTY-EIGHT

Sunday, I helped Anice spring-clean the large pantries and then offered to carry lunch to Darach and Ian while she took a breather.

I found the men rewiring a bedroom on the second floor. "I come bearing sustenance," I said, setting the tray on an ornate walnut dresser. "Sandwiches and ale."

Ian reached for a bottle and an opener. "If you haven't eaten, stay for a bite, lass. My wife made enough to feed a clan gathering."

"Thanks, I will." I opened another bottle and stepped over a coil of electrical wire and a toolbox to hand it to Darach. "How goes the renovation?"

He took a long pull on the bottle and swallowed. "Snaking the new wire through the existing routing is challenging but easier going in this room than the last."

Ian looked inside his sandwich. "Does anyone else want pickles?"

Darach and I answered no, and Ian headed for the kitchen.

I examined an uncovered electrical box that sprouted shiny copper wires. Darach picked up one sandwich as I helped myself to another. Anice's chicken salad was delicious.

"Did you learn to wire electrical boxes in engineering school?" I asked.

Darach chased his bite with ale. "I was wiring when I was twelve. Frank taught me."

"A handy talent."

"Aye." He took another bite, chewed, and swallowed. "Several other students and I once disassembled a professor's Mini Cooper and reassembled it in his third-story office."

"Why?"

He leaned against the wall. "We disagreed with the grades he gave us on an exam. The disputed problem involved a Mini Cooper. We proved our point."

"Did he catch you all?"

"He suspected. But we wore gloves. No fingerprints."

"How did he get it back outside?"

"He hired me to disassemble it and reassemble it outside."

"If he suspected you, why did he hire you?"

"Winter holidays started the next day. Everyone else was going home. I didn't have any plans, so I was available."

I laughed so hard I had to set my ale down to keep from spilling it. Darach joined in.

"I gave him a good price," he said, setting us off again.

I looked out my bedroom window, watching night slowly conceal the landscape. I could barely make out the crushed-rock drive, the neatly mown lawn, and the trimmed hedge that paralleled the walk from the garage to the manor. It was a beautiful house and grounds. And its owner was an impressive man.

I rubbed goose bumps from my arms but couldn't erase the epiphany racing to a tipping point. When had I started falling in love with Darach? When he came bearing baps? When he wrapped his scarf around my feet in the car outside the consulate? When he rushed over after I found the threatening note on the flat door? Or when he'd interacted so easily with the extraordinary athletes?

Megan's death didn't cut as deeply when I was with Darach—at work, at meals, or just talking. Megan would want me to be happy—want me to fall in love. Still, guilt bit. I was alive and she was dead. Exhaling hard enough to fog the glass, I moved to another pane and checked my reflection, patting my loosely upswept hair—the style Darach had complimented at the Spanish consulate.

I started downstairs.

When I'd moved in, Darach and I began meeting before dinner.

Tonight, I was worried about giving away my feelings.

I paused inside the open study door. Darach stood at the fireplace, handsome in pressed jeans and a navy-blue sweater. One elbow rested on the mantel, a peaceful expression softened his face. He looked as if he'd put something troubling behind him.

"Am I intruding?" I said.

"Not at all." He studied my face. "What are you thinking?"

That living here with you holds more appeal every day.

I plucked a forest-green throw from the couch and swung it around my shoulders. "That either Megan's killer lacks a sense of urgency or your protection is working. I haven't suffered so much as a stubbed toe in the last few days."

"You don't sound happy with that."

"I don't *want* to run into any of them again but, at least while Gravel Voice was delivering threats, I felt like the investigation was moving forward. Now, I'm wondering if the killers are going to get away with murder."

"Patience isn't your strong suit."

"No. But I'm getting plenty of practice."

As I paced by, Darach caught an end of the throw and tugged me toward the fire. "You'll warm up faster here." He released the throw and crossed his arms. "Whoever killed them has made it plain that they still want something," he said.

I held my hands toward the fire. "I wish I knew what that something was, and how I'm an obstacle to them."

Darach shook his head. "Peter is sure that Kinnon settled all of his gambling debts. The only valuable assets he owned were his Porsche, his plane, and his stock. And he managed to hold on to all three." I heard his grudging respect. He picked up the poker and nudged a log in the fire.

"I agree that the gambling angle is a dead-end."

Darach's eyes, made bluer by his sweater, met mine. "I'm finding it hard to believe Kinnon's murder involves his stock," he said. "The first right of refusal protects us from an outside takeover. And I'd hate to think that if Father hadn't split the company, Kinnon might still be alive."

"From what I've heard, your father was an astute businessman." I tucked both hands into the throw. "Since you read her letter, you know Megan thought he'd thrown you and Kinnon together to give you a chance to be brothers."

"A kind assumption, but Father didn't think that way. Business came first, family second."

"Then it doesn't make sense that he'd change his plan to leave you all of MKI."

"We'll never know."

"Maybe he recognized an opportunity." I snapped my fingers. "Kinnon's marketing background? Would he throw Kinnon into a briar patch and presume he'd eventually apply himself? Megan's datebook entry implied he was making tangible changes. And several people at MKI have mentioned that Kinnon had become more involved at work."

The grandfather clock tolled seven. Darach turned toward the door, ending our conversation. "It's time for dinner."

I tossed the throw onto the couch and followed him.

We ate in silence, though I caught his occasional glance. I regretted stirring the pot regarding his family, but the murders left me no choice except to ask questions and to occasionally behave *provocatively*, as he'd accused me of.

When we finished, I stood, ready to excuse myself and retire early to give him some alone time, but he invited me back to the study. When we entered, I was pleased to see that Ian had rebuilt the fire.

I slipped my shoes off as we sat on opposite ends of the couch. Darach's outstretched arm rested along the back.

"When did you decide to become a financial analyst?" he asked, surprising me with his choice of a personal topic.

"At age sixteen. When I learned to drive, I drove Aunt Sally everywhere, including meetings with her financial planner. The charts, reports, and statements fascinated me. I started researching stocks and sectors and making portfolio recommendations. I enjoyed the analysis."

"That's why you can complete in hours the paperwork that takes me all day." He studied me. "What an odd child you must have been."

"You're one to talk, being similarly driven in your own field."

"I'm driven by many things," he said. "What else drives you, Lyssa?" His eyes and voice held a deeper question as his hand left the couch back and reached toward me, palm up. I hesitated then twined my fingers with his. When he tugged, I slid over until I leaned against him. Contact felt reasonable by firelight.

"I heard you tell Jackson you needed hugging up." Warm lips pressed my temple, firing every nerve in my body.

"I like hugging."

"So, you hugged me Friday because I was handy?"

"No. That was right-place, right-time spontaneity at hearing good news."

"Without the good news, it would have been business as usual?"

I looked at him. "Until now, you never seemed to need or want a hug. And I was pretty sure you resented me."

His breath warmed my forehead.

"I resented your questions about Kinnon that required answers I didn't want to revisit. I resented you asking

Mother if she'd sell because I'd never asked. But I no longer resent your presence in my business or my home."

"What changed?"

His shrug held a touch of stiffness. "You accepted what was legally yours to accept." One side of his mouth lifted. "And you stand up to me. And you don't gloat when you prove right. And you admit when you're wrong. If I must have a partner, you'll do."

Maybe Jackson *had* done me a favor by cleaning out my Dallas desk. That I shouldn't have inherited MKI in the first place wouldn't matter if Darach fell in love with me.

He leaned closer. Pleasure consumed my body, but a question consumed my brain. "So, you're about to kiss me because?"

"Because I want to. Stop me if you wish."

Our lips met. Eyes open, we gauged one another's reaction, willingness, the next step. Kissing Darach was like savoring dark chocolate. Complex. Smooth. A bittersweetness held on the tongue and allowed to melt, allowing me to appreciate its addictive pleasure.

I missed hearing the door open behind us.

"Darach, we've come to invite you to dinner—"

Peter's abrupt silence, followed by Greer's angry gasp, sprang my eyes open. I hadn't realized I'd closed them.

"I'm sorry, we should have knocked," Peter began.

Darach stood, holding me in place with a hand on my shoulder.

She whirled to face Peter. "He's resorted to this."

"Mother," Darach warned.

Her head whipped toward him. "I'm ashamed of you."

Darach jerked as if she'd struck him. I was too shocked to speak.

"Greer," Peter said, trying to intervene, but she never looked away from Darach.

"You asked her to sell?" she said.

"Yes." Darach's shoulders tensed.

"She turned you down."

"Yes."

"Gavin told us her former fiancé visited her from America. You knew if she married anyone else, MKI would face a divided future."

Darach's hand tightened on my shoulder as Greer continued.

"You're making love to her because you want to keep control of MKI."

My breath stalled. I stared up at the muscle jumping in Darach's jaw and waited for his denial.

"I did consider the possible division of MKI," he said.

My hands clenched. "Since you couldn't keep me out, you invited me in?"

Darach looked at me, his eyes shadowed. "That wasn't my only reason."

"Which means it was part of your reason."

Anger vied with embarrassment. I shoved his hand away and stood.

Greer reached a hand toward her son. "She only wants more money."

Darach's face hardened. "Speaking of wanting money, I understand you would have sold to me if you'd inherited Kinnon's shares."

"Yes. I would have." She seemed to be appealing to him.

"Either way, I'd be paying."

She flinched. I glared.

"That's enough." A head shorter and fifty pounds lighter than his stepson, Peter bristled. "She's your mother. If you can't be kind, you will be respectful."

As usual, Darach's expression gave nothing away. He moved to the sideboard and poured a neat Scotch.

I stepped into my shoes.

Silence followed me out the door.

CHAPTER TWENTY-NINE

At breakfast Monday, Darach sat at one end of the kitchen island with Ian, discussing plans for the next room remodel. I sat at the other end, beside Anice, trying to focus on her chatter. If she noticed my distraction, she didn't comment. Who knew how far last night's confrontation had carried with the study door open?

Today, I'd keep things all business. After all, I lied to myself, nothing of real importance had changed. Murderers still needed to be identified and captured. If that meant hanging on to Kinnon's stock for another year, that's what I would do.

When it came time to leave for work, I walked beside Darach to his BMW. Whatever he'd plotted the night before, he didn't seem interested in kissing me today.

As he drove, I studied papers pulled at random from my briefcase. Not a word that I read registered. I kept trying to come up with another reason for his reaction to Jackson and Alonzo and their comments to me about Darach. Part of my courage for reacting to Darach last night was their assurances of his interest in me.

"Tell me when you're ready for me to explain," he said as we turned onto the road to Dundee.

His annoyingly calm offer made holding my tongue

impossible in the face of my righteous indignation. I'd leave as soon as the murderers were found. I saw no point in filtering my feelings from now on.

"Your mother laid it out succinctly. You want to keep the family business in the family. It's unromantic, but it makes business sense."

"Were you expecting romantic?" He glanced at me.

"I'm female with a healthy self-esteem. Of course I expected romantic."

"You have feelings for me?"

I refrained from socking the satisfied smile that formed on his mouth.

"Had—perhaps. Whatever I felt is gone, so it can't have been serious."

I stared out at the last of the morning mist hovering over the heather. A sudden realization narrowed my eyes. "Wait, I've been thinking short term. A married partner's children would divide and complicate MKI's future—unless the children belonged to both partners. Good lord, you *would* do anything to protect MKI."

A flush climbed his jaw.

"Aye," he said. "There's that."

The revelation silenced us for the remainder of the drive.

When we reached MKI, I glanced at my personalized parking space, seeing it as Darach's attempt to lure me into compliance. Inside, we retreated to our offices. I checked emails. Three departmental messages required no immediate action, so my brain drifted back to last night.

Greer's rant proved the pointlessness of my giving her all or part of the shares if she planned to sell them to Darach—unless she needed the money. Kinnon wouldn't want his mother left high and dry. I'd have to ask, and wouldn't that be fun?

The intercom buzzed.

"Yes, Mrs. Gibson," I said.

"Mr. Rand is on line two."

"Thanks." Last night's embarrassment resurfaced, but I picked up the call. "Hello, Peter."

"Lyssa, I'm glad you answered. You're either very polite or very curious."

"You took my calls when you didn't want to. I'm returning the favor."

"Then let me thank you for your forbearance last night. That conversation was the most therapeutic those two have ever shared." Excitement saturated his words.

Greer's therapy at my expense still hurt, but I managed to say, "You're welcome."

"The other reason I'm calling is to issue an invitation that Greer and I hope you will accept. She's speaking with Darach now."

"What—" The connecting door opened. Darach stopped in the doorway. "He just walked in. If you'll give us a moment, I'll give you an answer." I put Peter on hold. "What's the invitation?"

"Dinner Wednesday at their home. If you're agreeable."

I'd rather eat grain with mules. I reconnected the phone line. "What time would Greer like us to arrive?"

"Seven o'clock. And thank you, Lyssa."

"By the way," I said. "Did you talk to the police about Fia?"

"No, but now that you've reminded me, I'll call them immediately."

I turned my back to Darach and lowered my voice. "Can you wait until lunch? I'm seeing Fia this morning, and she'll be in a better mood if she doesn't know the police will be visiting."

"I can do that. Be careful. And take someone with you."

"I will. See you tomorrow." I hung up.

"Are you sure you're okay with this?" Darach stepped into my office.

I stopped him with words. "Yes. Despite our differences, she's making an *honest* effort." And I'd have a chance to ask about their finances because right now, I was motivated to find a reason to give her Kinnon's shares.

The connecting door closed behind Darach. A tap on my office door made me turn.

Gavin peered in. "Lyssa, do you have a moment?"

He seemed cordial enough. Curiosity got the better of me. "Of course."

He stepped inside and closed the door. "I want you to put a leash on Murray."

"What's Evan done?"

"He's harassing Sabrina. She went through a difficult

divorce a few years ago. She doesn't need him following her about like a puppy."

"I won't interfere in my solicitor's personal life." It wasn't smart, but I had to ask. "Are you sure you're not projecting your romantic desires *for* her *onto* her?"

"What desires?"

"It would be advantageous for you both if Sabrina married Darach. Even more so if he were the sole owner of MKI."

Gavin chuckled, but his voice held no humor. "Absolutely not. And since you won't sell, and your will names Darach as your beneficiary, the only way he can become sole owner now is, as they say, over your dead body." He smiled, showing his teeth. "That was a statement of fact, not a threat."

"Duly noted." Still, I wouldn't present my back to him any time soon. "If I die before I've held the shares thirty days, Greer gets them. Did you know that she would sell to Darach?"

"Darach mentioned it. Sabrina's saved enough to help him buy the stock should you decide to sell."

"You've all thought this through."

"Aye, for the sake of MacKendrick Industries' stability."

I pulled an envelope from my briefcase and walked to my printer. "Darach has a copy of my will. You should too."

His eyes lighted. "That's an excellent idea."

I ran the pages through, picking up the copies as the machine spit them out, and put them into an inter-office envelope, which I left open.

"Here you go." I handed the envelope to Gavin.

"Thank you, Lyssa." He turned to leave.

"Gavin."

He turned back, his fingers playing with the loose string on the envelope.

"Evan's a nice man," I said. "He won't hurt Sabrina. And she's capable of avoiding him if she wants to." She'd certainly shunned me since the mess with Fia.

The connecting door opened. "What's this?" Darach said, walking in.

"Lyssa gave me a copy of her will," Gavin said.

Darach looked at me. "I'm attending that charity luncheon today and need to leave shortly. Are you coming?"

"No, thanks. I'm seeing Fia. I need a dress to wear to your parents'." And Fia became almost forthcoming when I spent money with her.

Gavin exchanged a glance with Darach, while winding the string on the envelope with nervous fingers.

"Wait until three, and I'll go with you," Darach said, folding his arms.

As if I'd want to go shopping with him. Besides, if he came, speaking privately with Fia would require telepathic abilities I was pretty sure neither of us possessed.

"I'll ask Evan. He's seen the police sketches of the man from outside the consulate and the plane saboteur, so he knows who to watch for."

"Darach, Fia's is not a good place for Lyssa to visit anymore," Gavin protested, quieting when Darach nodded at me. My partner was backing me up?

"Ah, here you are, Darach. Father."

Sabrina lounged against the connecting doorjamb, her dark gaze darting between the three of us. "Time to go, Darach. The luncheon begins in an hour, and the director asked that we arrive early to review donations for Thursday night's fundraiser."

When everyone left, I sat on my couch. Gavin had wound the closure on the envelope I'd given him into a figure eight.

CHAPTER THIRTY

I walked to Mrs. Gibson's desk. When I saw Frank speaking to her, I returned to my office and stuffed some bids I'd been working on into another inter-office envelope. I hurried to join them.

Frank looked my way and offered a brief nod. "Ms. Eastin."

"Call me Lyssa. How is your wife?"

"Fine. Why do you ask?" His eyes narrowed. I'd picked the wrong topic for small talk.

"I heard you postponed retirement to pay for her care. That's very admirable."

He shrugged. "Aye, well, I'll be working a few years more." His glare returned, daring me to say otherwise.

"I'm sure that's as much of a relief to Darach as it is to me. He speaks highly of you and your part in training him." His face relaxed. I'd finally said something he liked.

"Darach's a good lad. He could run MKI solo."

I caught his meaningful look. "I'm sure he could. But sometimes it helps to spread the workload. Did you help Kinnon learn the business, too?"

"His work interests were different. As are yours."

"True." I dropped the bids into Mrs. Gibson's inbox. "I'm mechanically challenged, but I'd still like to increase my knowledge when you have time to show me around."

I could also increase my knowledge of Frank.

I couldn't tell if frustration or consternation drew his brows together. "Aye? Well maybe later this week."

Mrs. Gibson smiled at us playing nice.

"Oh," I said, stopping his retreat. "Do you mind glancing at these bids I'm working up?" I pulled the copies a few inches out of the envelope and handed it to Frank.

He tapped the papers back inside. "No need, lass, Darach says you're doing fine." He secured the envelope string with loops and handed it back. "I hear you've rewritten your will in the lad's favor. It's a good thing you've done," he said before walking away.

Persuading Evan to let me visit Fia alone proved impossible—less, I suspected, because he thought I was in danger there than because he feared what Darach would do if he found out I'd gone in alone. "I have a question for her about Kinnon," I said as we passed through city centre.

"Are you sure you want to see her?" Evan asked me. "Sabrina mentioned that she threatened Gavin."

"I'm sure. If she knows anything at all, I want to hear it."

He put a hand on the entry. "Then I'll stay by the door." He raised a finger. "Inside, not out."

Fia's perfunctory smile became a frown when she saw Evan follow me inside. "Can I help you, Miss Eastin?"

"I need a cocktail dress," I said.

Evan stationed himself by the entry. I followed Fia to the clothing racks.

"This one will suit you." She lowered her voice. "I'm not

discussing anything in front of your—who *is* he?"

"My attorney." I held up the topaz dress. "I had to bring either Evan or Darach. I've received threats and couldn't come alone. What have you found out?" For Evan's sake, I added more loudly, "I like the cut, but won't the color wash me out?"

"You'll be surprised," Fia said meaningfully. "Try it on."

We wound between racks to a dressing room, and I changed quickly. My reflection made me pause. *Wow.* Even with my hair in its business knot, I looked sophisticated. Pretty, even.

I stepped out and Fia circled. "Play up your lipstick and wear your hair in the same style, only looser." Her head tilted. "Gold jewelry—necklace, bracelet, earrings. Where are you going?"

"Dinner at the Rands'."

"You're joining a uniquely connected family." Fia tugged the zipper a little too forcefully.

She stepped back, looked me up and down, and smiled smugly. "Having you in the office adjacent to Darach's must upset Sabrina."

"I'm Darach's partner, not his romantic interest."

"Yours is a subtle beauty. And you've depth. A man would wonder about you."

"I'm in deep, all right. But the main thing everyone seems to wonder about me is if I'll sell Darach my stock and go home to Texas." I turned my head and checked out the back of the dress. It was still a wow.

Fia's eyes glittered. "The police seemed very interested in my emails. Do you think Darach will fire Gavin?"

Predictably, DI White hadn't shared with Fia his opinion about the potential of her emails.

The entry bell saved me from answering. Evan threw an alarmed glance at me then stared hard at the older woman who entered. I smiled. He made a terrible bodyguard.

Fia looked over her shoulder. "It's my lucky day. I can take a nice holiday on what she spends. And after what I remembered, I'll need one." She stepped behind me and lowered the zipper.

"What did you remember?"

"Sorry," she said, not sounding it. "Come back around one and leave the guard dog outside. He's glaring at my best client." She nudged me toward the changing room and leaned in. "You can tell a lot about a man by the company he keeps."

"What does that mean?"

She shoved the door shut, missing my nose by an inch.

"Hand the dress out. I'll bag it, select the proper lingerie, and ring you up."

A short walk later, I sat across from Evan at an upscale bistro around the corner from Fia's shop. I pushed my half-eaten chicken and vegetables away and sighed. Why hadn't Fia just told me what she'd remembered? Was she making it up as she went along?

Evan asked the same question when I told him I needed

to go back to her shop after lunch.

"I don't suppose you'd stay outside this time? She might be more forthcoming," I said, hopeful.

Forehead furrowed, he leaned his fork against his plate. "MacKendrick said I'm not to let you out of my sight upon penalty of castration." His hands dropped to his lap. "The boys and I are rather attached."

"I'm sure you are." I fought a smile. "You can look inside before you stand outside, but I need to talk to Fia in private. I promise nothing will happen that might separate you and your boys." I intercepted the lunch check. "It's my turn to pay."

Evan's hands remained in his lap. "Why do I feel I'll regret agreeing?"

A crowd of pedestrians slowed our walk to Fia's. "Sorry!" I rebounded from another unavoidable shoulder bump.

"Must be a festival or outdoor sale," Evan said. He glanced at the leaden sky. "Brave souls." He clasped my elbow as we wound through the crowd. Snippets of conversation filtered through.

"Imagine, in broad daylight!"

"Stand back. The ambulance wants through!"

"What's happened?" Evan asked a deli-uniformed teen. I recognized her as the girl who'd delivered lunch to Fia's last week.

Horror dilated the girl's pupils. "Fia Cullen was murdered in her shop!"

"Are you sure it was Fia Cullen?"

Evan's question barely penetrated my sudden shock and the wail of the approaching ambulance siren.

"Positive. She ordered a salad. Mary carried it next door when the rush slowed. That's when the screaming started. She found Fia on the floor in the back room with one of those expensive silk scarves she sells wrapped about her neck."

"No." Slipping Evan's hold, I pushed through the crowd to the yellow police tape.

He caught up and recaptured my arm. "Don't run off again."

I'd made him angry, but I had to know. I scanned the police for a familiar face.

"Detective Gilly!"

If my presence surprised him, he hid it well. Fat raindrops anointed us and slid off the occupied body bag carried out by EMTs. My stomach lurched. "Is it really Fia?" I asked, unable to look away.

Gilly frowned. "Did you speak to Ms. Cullen recently, Ms. Eastin?"

"I was in her store before lunch."

Gilly looked surprised. "Why?"

"I bought a dress, and she said she'd remembered something related to the murders, but another customer came in, and she told me to come back after lunch."

I absorbed Gilly's reproving stare. "Something more than what she told us when we interviewed her this week about Gavin MacDonald?" he asked.

"Yes."

Gilly raised the crime-scene tape. "We need to visit."

I slipped under. Evan followed.

Gilly frowned. "Who are you?"

"Ms. Eastin's solicitor. I was also in the shop earlier. I got a good look at the woman who came in as we left."

My throat tightened. "Can we talk somewhere else?"

"You're familiar with the station," Gilly said.

When Gilly finished asking questions, clearly disappointed I had no idea what Fia had remembered, Evan drove me back to MKI. He offered to walk me in but seemed relieved when I declined.

When I entered my office, Darach stormed though the connecting door.

"What have you stumbled into now?" he demanded.

"How did you—" *Evan.* I walked past Darach and dropped into my chair. "I can't believe she's dead."

"What happened?"

I retold the afternoon's events. "That's all I know," I finished.

"Was she robbed?"

"According to Detective Gilly, the till was intact, but the memory card for her shop's security camera was missing."

His jaw tightened. "Whoever looks at that video will know you were there and think that she passed you information."

I nodded. "Gilly mentioned it. He came to interview her and arrived at a murder scene."

He frowned. "Interview her about what? Her emails were

inconclusive at best."

"He was following up on her keying Kinnon's Porsche."

"*Fia* damaged Kinnon's Porsche?"

"Yes, after Kinnon introduced her to Megan. Didn't Peter or your mother tell you?"

"No." His expression darkened. "Kinnon didn't confide in me. You don't confide in me. So why would you think Peter and Mother would share information with me?"

"Let's not get into trust."

He stared without effect. I was immune, I told myself.

He crossed his arms. "You didn't say anything last night when I admitted wanting to keep MKI in the family."

"I was embarrassed. But I've had time to think about it, and I'm glad you told the truth. There's no point in complicating our partnership."

After a long pause, he asked, "When Mother arrived, before she spoke. Were you sorry we were interrupted?"

I wasn't poking that hornets' nest.

"Darach, I kissed you because I wanted to. And you should know by now that I won't deliberately hurt MKI—no matter what our relationship."

"Thank you." He turned and walked back to his office.

CHAPTER THIRTY-ONE

Unless they've had military or medical training, most humans aren't wired to immediately move ahead after exposure to a violent death whether witnessed or described.

Tuesday, I didn't think anything could divert my thoughts from Fia's death and its probable ties to Megan's and Kinnon's murders. But I hadn't considered Darach. He kept a steady flow of personnel from the sales and marketing departments visiting my office.

Though I appreciated his diversions, I didn't forget he was attracted to me because of what I possessed, not who I was.

He left me to my meetings the rest of the workday. And later he insisted on eating dinner with Anice and Ian, which kept the conversation neutral and impersonal. I didn't join him in his study. Instead, I wandered the garden in the diminishing light, breathing the blossom-scented air and contemplating tomorrow night's dinner with the Rands. I felt as comfortable around Peter as I felt uncomfortable around Greer. I had no doubt whose side Peter would take in a confrontation, but I admired his loyalty. Greer was fortunate in her husband.

I turned back and followed the path to the manicured lawn. What was left of the sunset reflected off the manor windows, and I thought I saw a curtain fall into place in Darach's study.

We left MKI early on Wednesday to give me time to dress for dinner. When I stepped into the foyer, Darach stared so long and hard my face heated. "Nice dress," he finally said, reaching for the doorknob.

"Thank you." I offered silent gratitude to Fia as we walked outside.

"How are you holding up? I should have asked Mother to reschedule after Fia's murder," he said.

"I'm fine," I lied.

Since we would be drinking, Ian drove us to the Rands'. As usual, Peter answered the door.

"Welcome!" he said.

I waved good-bye to Ian before Peter ushered us inside.

Darach held out his hands, a bottle of cabernet in one, sauvignon blanc in the other. Peter smiled. "Take them to your mother. She's in the kitchen overseeing the caterer. Bring her to the sitting room. I'll prepare cocktails."

Darach nodded and turned away. One hand on my elbow, Peter walked me down the hall.

"I guess you've heard about Fia," I said.

"Yes, Darach mentioned that you visited her shortly before she died. I'm glad you weren't there when her killer arrived."

"Me, too." An image of Fia's body bag on the gurney flashed in my mind.

Peter sighed. "Fia was far from a favorite of mine, and Greer spent more than a few anxious moments worrying that she would convince Kinnon to propose. It's callous, but I'm glad she's gone. She caused this family, and others, pain. Gavin said she slandered him to the police."

"She told me she considered Gavin capable of arranging Kinnon's murder." I shivered. "She wanted to tell me something else, only she never got the chance."

"Likely another diversion." Peter stopped at the bar. "What can I get for you?"

"Chardonnay, please."

Peter filled a glass halfway. "How are you fitting in at MKI?"

"Pretty well, except for the tension with Gavin and Sabrina."

"You're a catalyst." He poured another chardonnay and a Scotch and finally mixed a vodka tonic with a squeeze of lime.

"I intend to be," I said.

He picked up the vodka tonic. "It's not necessarily a bad thing. Diplomats sometimes introduce subjects or people to steer a negotiation or topic in a premeditated direction. And you aren't the only catalyst. I don't know what their father expected when he made Kinnon Darach's partner, but he set in motion a catastrophe waiting to happen." He exhaled deeply. "The sooner the murderers are caught, the sooner Greer will accept happiness. I'll assist you however I can."

I touched my glass to his then sipped. "Thanks. I'll call if there's a problem you can help with."

Footsteps approached, and Peter set his drink down. He handed wine to Greer and Scotch to Darach. "Cheers,"

Peter said. We all clinked glasses.

Peter proved his diplomat skills during cocktails and the meal, introducing and redirecting conversation, keeping us all civil. Halfway through the meal, he leaned toward me, voice low. "They're talking," he said.

Between bites of asparagus, I glanced at Greer and Darach. Mother and son were indeed chatting, but they didn't seem comfortable doing it. Both sat arrow straight, their expressions controlled.

When the unobtrusive catering crew appeared again, it was to pour a tawny port and whisk away the remnants of a perfectly roasted prime rib to quickly replace it with small plates of sliced pears and Stilton cheese.

Candles and gleaming silver cast and caught reflections. The Rands had spared no expense. And I hadn't yet found an opportunity to ask about their finances.

The port removed a layer of restraint. I missed the words that preceded Greer's response, but I was pretty sure Darach had spoken them.

"Kinnon was happy pursuing his own interests," she said. "Your father never should have included Kinnon in MKI."

"I agree, but it's too late to change that." Darach tilted his head. "Do you know why Father gave Kinnon the shares?"

"No." Greer's shoulders sagged.

"Megan had a theory—" I blurted.

"What did she think?" Peter asked.

I looked between the three faces. Peter and Greer watched me, and Darach watched his mother.

"That he was trying to reconcile his sons."

"I wonder what might have happened," Darach said, "if I'd asked Father to let me leave with you when you left him."

Greer turned toward him. "But then he'd have been alone. We each needed someone, and you were better suited to live with your father. Your interest in MacKendrick Industries pleased him."

Everyone was quiet for a long moment.

"I appreciate your telling me, Mother," Darach said, laying his napkin beside his plate. "I would also appreciate you and Peter making time to know Lyssa better. She is part of the business that is so important to me."

His request surprised—and pleased—me.

Greer didn't answer, but Peter put an arm around her shoulders and faced Darach. "Your mother did what she thought best for you and Kinnon. Her intentions were good, even if they didn't work out as she'd hoped."

Greer's chin quivered, and Darach's face settled into severe lines. Things were about to fall apart. I raised my glass. "To Kinnon and Megan."

Everyone looked surprised but glasses rose.

"Kinnon and Megan," they echoed.

Peter put a hand on Darach's shoulder. "Darach, would you have a cigar in the library?" Darach nodded and followed, leaving me alone with Greer.

"Thank you for the lovely dinner," I said.

"Not at all," she said, not looking at me.

The port made me brave. "I know I'm being personal,

281

but I wondered if your desire for Kinnon's inheritance was due to financial need?"

Her gaze widened then hardened. "No. I don't need the money. I receive an annual allowance from MKI's profits, and Peter provides more than adequately for us."

"I'm sorry, but when you said you'd sell Kinnon's shares to Darach, I wondered if you needed the money."

She shot me an indignant look. "Would you have me just give the boy the shares? He worked ten years to earn the first half of MKI from his father. I'd not spoil Darach like I did Kinnon. Paying for the rest would ensure he appreciates them."

I was sure he'd appreciate them regardless, but I couldn't fault her logic.

"I might have needed the money," she said, making an obvious effort at conversation. "But Peter advised me against an investment that was exposed as a fraud. You wouldn't have seen the story. It happened months ago." She rushed on. "Do you know what Gavin's done to irritate Peter? He called the other day, and Peter refused to take his call."

I guess the port was affecting her, too. I shook my head. Perhaps Peter was upset with Gavin because, thanks to Fia's accusations, he now thought Gavin had encouraged Kinnon to gamble. If Peter hadn't shared that knowledge with Greer, it wasn't my place. While I searched for another topic to keep things rolling, Greer stood.

"If you'll excuse me, I need to see to the caterers."

As she walked out, I wondered how long it would take

Darach and Peter to finish their cigars.

Thursday morning, to assist Peter's plan of reconciling Darach and Greer, I told Darach I wanted to take flowers to his mother as a thank-you for dinner. He looked at me funny but agreed. I called Peter before we started over and he enthusiastically approved.

When we arrived, Peter and Greer stood in the driveway, next to the open driver's window of an unfamiliar car. I handed her the flowers. "Thank you again for dinner," I said.

"They're lovely. And you're welcome." Her gaze moved to Darach. "Darach, you remember Anne Gleeson?"

Darach leaned in to speak to the woman in the car.

Greer handed the flowers to Peter and walked around to the passenger side. Darach followed to help her inside. He shut the door then leaned in to answer a question from Anne.

I figured I was dismissed so I joined Peter.

"Did she accept Anne's invitation before or after you told her I was coming?" I asked.

Peter patted my arm. His mood seemed lighter than at any time since I'd met him. "Let's just say she had offers to choose between, and Anne won. Shall we go inside?"

He took my arm and steered me to the front door. "You've done it again, Lyssa. It's Greer's first venture out since the crash. I feel like celebrating. Do you fancy a coffee?"

I tried to see my catalyst role in Greer's life in the positive way Peter did. Finding the killer was my priority, but helping this family was a good project too. "No, thanks, but you go ahead."

He filled a cup in the kitchen and escorted me to his library. The comfortable room looked lived in. Correspondence lay atop the desk. A newspaper occupied an end table. The French doors to the patio stood open to the fine spring morning.

I paused beside a bookshelf and studied the contents. Classics and modern thrillers mixed with thick books with plain bindings and titles containing the names of countries that ended in *ia*—Estonia, Croatia, Bulgaria, Macedonia.

"Are these from your diplomatic service days?"

He set the cup on his desk and joined me. "Yes. I doubt I'll ever pick them up again, but they make an impressive shelf in a library." He put a hand on my shoulder. "Your diplomatic appearance today was very thoughtful."

"It was my pleasure," I assured him. "I, also, want Darach and Greer to improve their relationship."

He was silent for a moment then squeezed my shoulder. When he spoke, his voice sounded thick.

"It's nice to have an ally."

CHAPTER THIRTY-TWO

After we left the Rand's, Darach drove us to work. I visited the marketing department and sat in on online meetings with buyers. I was getting the hang of this business.

That was of little consolation later in the afternoon when I called my supervisor at James Wiseman and resigned. My combined work leave didn't run out until tomorrow, but given the time difference, why delay the inevitable?

At four o'clock, I closed the file I'd reviewed. Manufacturing required a different kind of analysis. I reveled in the challenge of my work. But for how much longer?

The connecting door opened and Darach came in.

"Are you sure you won't come tonight?" he asked.

I stared, afraid my jaw would drop and never recover from the fall. Darach looked so—Scots. He wore his kilt with confident ease. His—what was the name of the animal-skin pouch that Scots men wore around their waists over their kilts? Knee socks flattered his strong calves. My eyes widened. Was that a knife in his sock?

Sabrina glided in behind him in a royal blue evening gown that clung like a second skin. "Ready, Laird Auctioneer?"

"Lyssa?" he said.

I swallowed. Dinner wouldn't digest well if I had to sit next to Sabrina.

"Thanks, but the week has caught up with me. I'll make it an early night. I hope you raise millions."

"I'll settle for thousands. Our local fundraisers rarely produce beyond that." His blue eyes quizzed me. "Ian will pick you up at six. I'll be home by ten thirty. Wait up, and we'll share a nightcap."

Sabrina and I both stared at him. Then Sabrina circled him, possessively tugged at the back of his short black jacket, and said what I'd thought. "I've never heard you call the manor 'home.'"

Darach looked startled then adjusted the front of his coat, not commenting. He stepped toward my desk and swept a hand above the paperwork. "What's all this?"

"The files from Kinnon's flat."

"Find anything illuminating?" Sabrina asked.

"Just more questions. For instance, when did we start accepting after-hours raw-material deliveries?"

"About a year ago," Darach said. "You've noticed how close we are to the railway?"

"Yes."

"We accept the containers on the railroad's schedule. Their drivers and lorries deliver upon arrival, so we minimize holding charges. The savings are substantial."

"Does Frank always meet the deliveries?" He had signed for each of the deliveries in Kinnon's files.

Darach nodded. "He prefers to supervise all aspects of a job."

"A trait with which you relate," I said.

"Absolutely."

"Do you have your keys in your sporran?" Sabrina asked.

Ah, that was the name of the pouch.

"Aye." Darach tapped the animal skin, setting off a faint jingle.

"Then give me your phone, or you're sure to vibrate during the auction." She slipped his phone into her evening bag. "Let's go." She linked an arm through his.

Though she hustled him out the door, the image of Darach in a kilt remained. I needed a distraction until Ian arrived.

I pulled up the week's raw-material delivery schedule and scanned for delivery details for the Spanish pipeline. They weren't posted yet. The report did show an after-hours delivery of raw material scheduled for this evening, though. Frank would be pulling some overtime.

To be thorough, I opened my JOBS spreadsheet and added a row for after-hour delivery dates. The first was 1/13, then 2/22, 3/12, 4/5 and 5/2—

I grabbed my day-planner and found my copy of Kinnon's sticky note.

AHD1132223124552. After-hours deliveries!

The numbers in the column matched Kinnon's note. The zero was missing from the end of the note, but the paper *had* been torn.

May twentieth. Tonight.

I picked up the phone, stabbed three numbers, and stopped.

I had no proof Kinnon's note pertained to after-hours

deliveries or that anything would happen tonight.

If I called Darach, he'd turn his auctioneer duties over to Sabrina and return to watch with me. Being alone with him in a dark room for hours would be difficult, but worse, he'd probably insist I return to the manor while *he* checked out my theory. If my theory was a bust, I'd have wasted his evening and jeopardized the fundraiser.

I tapped the receiver on the desk then hung up.

Frank would be here, along with the guard at the gate. And I could watch the materials delivery from my office.

I picked up the phone and dialed. "Hi, Ian, it's Lyssa."

"Are you ready for me to fetch you?"

"That's why I'm calling. I'm working late. I'll catch a ride home with Darach after the fundraiser."

"I'll drive in and keep you company."

"Thanks, but the guard is at the gate, and Frank will be here overseeing a delivery. I'm covered."

After silent consideration, Ian said. "Then I'll see you in the morning."

I'd need a ride home, so I'd call Darach after the shipment arrived. He'd be annoyed, but I'd know by then whether the delivery dates held significance.

I called the guard at the gate, told him I was staying, and that Darach would be picking me up. Next, I visited the canteen vending machines and bought a bottle of water, a coffee to reheat when needed, and a bag of chips.

Hands full, I returned upstairs. If the letters and numbers on Kinnon's note indicated something important,

I might learn what had caused him to buck his 'status quo'.

I settled into my office. I had a good view of the receiving dock doors. I sipped water and watched the employees leave the plant floor for home. The delivery was scheduled for nine.

I turned out my lights and sat far enough from the windows that I could see but not be seen. Like Darach, I always kept my curtains open; no one below would think it unusual.

To fill the time, I named the equipment and recited the detailed pipe-manufacturing process from start to finish. The low-wattage, after-hours lighting shaped the hulking machinery on the plant floor into futuristic mechanical monsters.

I kicked off my flats and touched my toes. Straightening, I glanced at the wall clock. Eight forty-five. I yawned and gave up counting support beams; it was too much like counting sheep. I checked my watch. Nine o'clock.

At nine-ten, afraid I'd miss my ride if I waited any longer, I dialed Darach's cell, got his voice mail, and left a message to swing by on his way home.

My hypothesis was a bust.

One of the large bay doors clanged open. A light came on downstairs. I saw Frank toss his cap onto a filing cabinet. He spoke with the man who followed him in, signed some papers, and waved him out.

My shoulders fell. I don't know what I'd expected, but it wasn't the abrupt, mundane conclusion I'd witnessed. Frank fussed with a few more items then reached for his cap. A different man entered through the open door.

Frank gestured with his hands, seeming upset. The other man's hands moved in an apparent attempt to calm him. Frank crossed his arms and shook his head as a second man walked through the door.

I stepped into my flats. Was there a problem with the delivery? If the issue wasn't something the delivery drivers could solve with my foreman, perhaps an owner could help.

I took my cell phone, in case Darach called, and trotted downstairs, through the dimly lighted locker room, and entered the factory. The familiar scents of oil and grease surrounded me as I navigated a shadowy path between machines toward the arguing men.

"I'll not do it." I heard Frank say.

"I'm sure we can work something out." The gravelly voice froze me in place. Still shielded by a machine, I pulled out the phone and dialed as I backpedaled.

"DI White," he answered.

I cupped a hand to muffle my words. "It's Lyssa Eastin. I'm at work. The man who threatened me outside the Spanish consulate—the man I chased into the alley—is here."

Leather soles whispered across the concrete floor behind me. Hands clamped my arms. My phone crashed to the floor. A boot heel crushed the case.

"Frank, help!" I shouted.

A thud and a grunt sounded nearby.

"Frank can't help you, lass." The grating voice was conversational. He shoved me against the cinder-block wall. "I need tape and a blanket," he yelled.

He leaned into me until my lungs burned. Tape secured my wrists. He slapped more across my mouth and around my ankles then covered my head with a thick gray blanket that smelled of exhaust fumes. Fear overwhelmed me.

He spun me around. His shoulder connected with my stomach and I jackknifed against his back as he lifted me. "Subdued Frank, did you?" he said.

"Aye," a brusque voice answered.

"Pick up his tam and lock the door."

They had Frank, too! I squirmed and attempted a tape-garbled protest while feeling the cool night air on my calves.

"Pop the boot."

My brief free fall ended on thin carpet that smelled of oil, dirt, and tobacco. The car trunk slammed with a hollow thud that sent my heart to my throat.

"Get in," Gravel Voice said.

"Let her go," Frank answered, shaky.

"I won't ask again."

A car door shut, the engine started, and we moved. I kicked both feet toward where taillights should be, but something crackly padded the trunk's interior. I'd lost my shoes when Gravel Voice carried me to the car, and I couldn't make enough noise to alert the guard at the gate as we rolled over the speed bump.

I counted to estimate time and distance. In roughly ten minutes, the car stopped. Only one door opened. Several thunks and a metallic screech later the trunk opened. A rush of cold air chilled me. Someone hoisted me, blanket and all, and swung me onto a hard surface. Again, metal screeched.

I lay on my side, listening. The car engine's growl faded.

I shook free of the blanket's smothering weight and encountered complete darkness. Cold penetrated my skin. I wiggled until I worked my bound hands under and in front of me and painfully peeled the tape from my mouth. I lowered my hands for balance. A wood floor. Elevated, because I hadn't fallen far when they'd swung me. Where *was* I?

The tape around my ankles resisted my efforts, but eventually I freed them, lurched onto my legs, and stood. Despite my teeth's best efforts, the tape binding my wrists wasn't coming off.

I reached out and touched a metal wall. They'd tossed me in here through a door. I shuffled in a rectangle until I stumbled into a short stack of rough, slatted wood. Pallets? I inched around them and shuffled on. My fingers finally bumped over a wall seam that ran to the floor and up farther than I could reach. Interior locking rods but no handle. A barefoot stomp produced a hollow echo that ricocheted inside my stomach. They'd locked me in a semitrailer!

I pressed an ear to the metal and listened to silence. Panic lessened. The trailer wasn't moving.

Where was I? *Where was Frank?*

"Hello? Frank!"

I walked the perimeter again, extending a tentative foot

every other step, searching the trailer's center for Frank and finding nothing. It was just the pallets and me. If they'd thrown Frank into another container, he might hear me shout.

I pounded the walls with my fists. "Help! Frank! Can anybody hear me?"

No one answered. I needed a survival plan.

Though chilly, the temperatures weren't life-threatening. My stomach growled, but I was far from starving. The only immediate danger was the possibility they'd come back.

I worked my way around the trailer again, collecting and dragging the blanket and two pallets to a corner away from the doors. One pallet became a seat, the other a backrest that kept me from leaning against cold metal. I wished in vain for my MacKendrick battle-plaid scarf.

Wincing at splinters, I wrestled a loose pallet board free and rhythmically pounded the trailer floor.

DI White must be at MKI. Encouraged by the thought, I readjusted the blanket across my shoulders and resumed pounding the floor, rocking my body in time with the beat.

Thud, thud, thud. Had Darach checked his messages? *Thud, thud, thud.* Or was he still enjoying a three-course dinner with Sabrina in the comfort of a warm room? *THUD, THUD, THUD!*

CHAPTER THIRTY-THREE

I woke from a jumbled dream. Amazed I'd fallen asleep, I rubbed the crick in my neck.

A car door slammed. The muffled sound startled me out of the smelly blanket.

I stood and lost my balance. On my knees, I groped for my pallet slat and gripped it as best I could with my bound hands.

"Hey!" I croaked. I cleared my throat and tried again. "*Hey*!"

I pounded wood against metal, producing as much racket as possible before stopping mid-thump. If the men who'd kidnapped me had returned to finish me off, I'd just let them know I was awake.

The trailer's outside latch groaned.

I struck a batter's stance and backed away as the doors swung wide. Morning light blinded me.

"Lass, how'd you get in there?"

I squinted at the silhouette of a tall man wearing a pea coat and a stocking cap. His eyes locked on my taped wrists and club.

"Where am I?" I asked.

"The Dundee docks," he said. "Are you American?"

"Yes." My legs steadied. I wouldn't die in this container. Overhead, gulls called. Salt-sea air filled my lungs.

I lowered the club. "Is there a phone nearby?"

"Aye, miss. In the office."

The tall man raised his arms to help me down.

Darach answered on the first ring.

"It's Lyssa," I said.

I heard something crash to the floor.

"Are you all right? Where are you?" I could barely understand him through the thick burr. He was worried. Without warning, I teared up.

"I'm okay. I'm at the docks."

"Which docks?"

"I'll put someone on to give you directions."

"Lyssa!"

Ignoring his roar, I handed the phone to my tall rescuer.

"Hello—We found her locked in a container—She hasn't said. Shall I call the police?"—"Aye? I'll put on more coffee."

Twelve minutes later, the door banged open and Darach burst in, followed by DI White and DS Gilly. Darach still wore his dress kilt. His usually smooth hair held deep furrows.

"Are you hurt?" he said, his voice as rough as the blue-black stubble darkening his jaw.

"No."

Just when I thought he'd reach for me, he planted his feet and thrust his face inches from mine. "Don't ever pass the phone again until I'm finished speaking to you."

"Getting cut off is frustrating, isn't it?" I snapped, realizing I'd expected him to gather me close. I'd been ready to make a fool of myself and hug him back. Kiss him even.

Weary blue eyes studied me. "Aye, you're all right." He touched a finger to the sticky residue on my cheek. "What's this?"

"They taped me up, and then put me in a freight container. Have you seen Frank?" My voice rasped, hoarse from last night's shouting.

His frown answered first. "No. He didn't come into work this morning. I've been calling, but I haven't reached him."

I faced DI White, who watched our reunion with open interest. "MKI had an after-hours delivery last night. Frank signed the manifests then got into an argument with the men at the receiving dock. I went downstairs to see what the problem was."

"You planned to defend Frank against quarreling men?" Darach asked.

"No. But for all I konw Frank regularly shouts at truck drivers. I thought it was a delivery problem. The second I recognized Gravel Voice, I called DI White."

"You should have called me too." Darach leaned in, the better for me to catch the irritation in his words.

"I left a message on your voice mail earlier asking you to pick me up after the fundraiser," I said.

"Sabrina had my mobile. She was checking my messages. You should have said I needed to pick you up immediately."

"Even if you'd left when I called, you couldn't have

arrived in time." I looked at White. "Frank may be stuck here, too. I heard them hit him, and it sounded like they put him in the car."

"I'll start a search," Gilly said, walking outside.

"Our forensics team will secure the container you were held in," White said. "We need to talk, Ms. Eastin. Are you ready to leave for the station?"

I was getting tired of that interrogation room. "Can we talk at MKI instead?"

"That's acceptable," White said.

"We both need a change of clothes. I'll have Anice send some with Ian. Until then..." Darach shrugged out of his short black jacket and wrapped it—still holding his body heat and scent—around me.

"Thank you," I said.

"Your shoes?" he asked.

"I hope they're near the loading dock."

I gripped the jacket's lapels as he picked me up. I felt my face heat.

"I can walk."

"Stop wiggling."

"I'm not exactly petite."

"No, you're a definite handful."

He carried me to the waiting car.

I refused to let Darach carry me farther than MKI's front doors—I walked barefoot from the elevator to my office, followed by Darach, the detectives, the plant nurse, and the employees' stares.

I sank into my chair and held out my hands for the nurse to remove splinters. While she applied antiseptic, Darach studied the manufacturing floor. Shortly, the nurse put away her supplies, leaving me with a handful of wet wipes.

White cleared his throat. "I need to talk with Ms. Eastin alone."

I expected an argument, but Darach merely nodded and exited through our connecting door.

"Where would you like me to start?" I asked.

"With why you stayed late."

I booted up my computer and noticed the intercom line to Darach's office was open. He must have toggled it while the nurse treated me. Good. I'd rather not tell the story twice.

"Several weeks ago, I created a spreadsheet using the files I found in Kinnon's flat. Last night, I added a column for raw-material delivery dates. Those dates matched the numbers on the note I found under this desk. The last number had been torn off, but since an after-hours delivery was scheduled for last night, I stayed to see if anything would happen."

"It appears you were right."

I opened the folder and angled the screen toward White.

"Maybe. Or maybe Gravel Voice snuck into the plant with the delivery truck when he noticed I didn't leave. Maybe Frank was arguing that I wasn't here. Then I showed up and proved him wrong. All I accomplished was getting us both kidnapped."

"Can you print that for me?" White said.

"Sure." I pushed keys and the printer spit out a sheet of paper. "Maybe I was supposed to die in the container. The dockworkers said it wouldn't have been reloaded until next week. Or maybe the kidnapping was another warning and I was *supposed* to be rescued."

"Start again, at the beginning."

I told him, in as much detail as I could, everything that had happened.

"Did anyone you saw look like the van driver who destroyed your rental?"

I shook my head. "One man's build was right, but they all wore hats. I couldn't see their faces from up here. What about the security cameras?"

"As you said, they wore hats; and they took Frank's car. It wasn't helpful."

White asked questions until we'd covered every angle of the story at least four times. He left with a vague promise to keep me informed.

"You can come in now, Darach," I said, switching off the intercom. I closed my eyes, pillowed my forehead on my arms on the desk, and tried to quiet the pounding in my head.

The door opened. "Do you want to see a doctor?" Darach asked.

"No. It's nothing a hot bath and aspirin can't fix."

I opened my eyes and immediately felt grungier. Darach wore a clean shirt and pants, and his jaw was shaved. He hung a skirt and blouse on the coat rack and set a paper bag on the desk.

He glowered at me. "I would have skipped the bloody auction if you'd told me what you suspected."

"I know. But it was a wild hunch." I opened a wet wipe and scrubbed my face and neck, grimaced at the dirt, and threw it away. "Is any MKI property missing?"

"Nothing except Frank and the security footage."

I groped for the lower desk drawer. "When we cleaned out Kinnon's car, I threw his aspirin in here." I piled Kinnon's collection of personal items on my desk until I spotted the white tablets. "Thank goodness." I opened the bottle, tossed two aspirin into my mouth, and chased them with lukewarm coffee and a shudder. My empty stomach protested the mix. "Ugh. I haven't eaten since lunch yesterday."

"I'll take you to eat after you change." Leaning in, he lifted the cigarette pack from my pile. "Where did you get this?"

"From Kinnon's glove box. They were Fia's. She said he gave her a carton at Christmas."

He stared at them and turned them over in his palm—like Fia had.

"Is something wrong?"

"They're unmarked."

"What are they supposed to be marked with?"

"All UK tobacco products carry a duty-paid mark to show they've been taxed. That package has never been taxed. Kinnon probably bought it at a boot sale."

"A shoe store?" I rocked my head from side to side. The neck crick I'd woken up with had returned.

"Boot as in *car boot*. *Trunk*? Contraband that smugglers dispense from their boots."

"Kinnon told Fia a deliveryman left them at the office." An elusive memory waved from a dark corner in my mind.

Darach's eyes suddenly resembled blue ice. "If a deliveryman is selling contraband cigarettes here, I need to know who he is."

"*We* need to know," I said. "What brand does Peter smoke?"

"Hennies. And every pack I've seen him with was legal."

The aspirin were taking their sweet time kicking in. I dropped the cigarettes and massaged my temples. "Would you shut the drapes? I want to change."

He walked past as I worked the buttons on his jacket. Behind me, the drapes ratcheted shut, darkening the room.

"Thanks." I held out his jacket.

He took it. "Call when you're dressed."

After the door closed, I undressed, opened the other wipes, and lined them up on my desk. I used every single one and finally felt sufficiently clean. I shook the paper sack's contents onto the desk. Bless Anice—she'd added my makeup bag.

Moving slowly, I eased my arms into the blouse sleeves. My night of board banging and splinters had left my fingers stiff and raw. I coordinated the top three tiny buttons with their buttonholes before pain shot through my fingers. I stepped into my skirt, raised it to my hips, and barely managed the zipper.

I dialed Mrs. Gibson.

An unfamiliar male voice said she'd left for lunch. I tried the nurse and struck out again. Gripping the blouse's edges, I opened the connecting door and stuck my head inside Darach's office.

"I need help." I said.

CHAPTER THIRTY-FOUR

He stood motionless for so long that I felt my face heat. I'd embarrassed us both.

"I tried Mrs. Gibson and the nurse, but they've gone to lunch. My fingers are too tender to work the buttons. Can you call Sabrina or another female to help me?"

He shook his head and walked into my office. "No need. Stand still."

He worked the small buttons with enviable ease as I silently recited every blue-chip stock ticker I could recall. "Why would someone smuggle cigarettes?" I asked when I ran out of tickers.

"Profit margins are enormous if you're not caught. And if you are caught, the penalties are a wrist slap compared to a drug-smuggling penalty."

His touch elevated my body temperature as if he were removing my clothes instead of dressing me. He tried to work my blouse under my skirt's waistband, but the silky material defied him. He blew out a frustrated breath. "Every time I get it tucked, it pulls out with my hand."

"Don't worry about it," I said, my voice a pitch higher. "Women typically pull shirttails down from under a skirt. The same way you must do with a kilt."

"A kilt gives a man room for everything a man needs

room for," he muttered. "Not like this sausage casing." He stepped away.

My sigh of relief turned into a gasp as he pulled pantyhose from the paper bag.

"Another sausage-casing device. Sit down."

"I'll skip them and wear my sneakers. I've never gone through shoes so fast."

As I remembered running barefoot in the rain, a memory clicked.

"Oh! When I confronted Gravel Voice in the pub, he had a pack of the same brand of cigarettes! But I didn't notice if his had a tax stamp. If contraband cigarettes were being routed through MKI, that could explain Kinnon having job files. Maybe he'd figured out the delivery system. Maybe Gravel Voice was dropping off cigarettes last night. Does the guard know how many containers are supposed to arrive when deliveries are made?"

"Yes. Two trucks arrived last night and neither driver matched the police sketches. Constables searched the new and existing flatbeds in our holding yard while we searched for you. They would have mentioned finding contraband cigarettes."

"They were looking for me, not cigarettes disguised as a steel shipment. How did Gravel Voice and his accomplice get in?"

"Probably slipped in on foot while the guard checked in the deliveries."

He knelt and eased my feet into my sneakers. I braced

one hand on his shoulder as he continued. "If the steel ingots are hollow and the cigarettes are stuffed inside, the trailer won't ride as low."

"We're going to look now, right?"

"Of course," he said.

He stood and held my jacket. I angled my arms into the sleeves then followed him out the door. We took the stairs down to a door that led outside.

"Wait here," he said.

He returned with a cordless drill and opened the door.

"The lot holds three rows of ten flatbeds. Each flatbed holds tons of steel. After last night's deliveries, the lot is nearly full. The security guard said Frank arrived at nine-o-eight; the two trucks came five minutes later. After ten minutes, two cabs—minus their trailers—left. Frank's car left shortly after."

We walked between flatbeds, scanning levels. None rode high.

"Maybe they compensated by adding weight. Which steel came in last night?" I asked.

He pointed. "The two loads on the end." Shrugging out of his jacket, he handed it to me. With the grace of a large cat, he vaulted onto a flatbed and randomly drilled holes in steel rods.

"They are what they appear to be," he said after checking the second load. His stare slowly traveled the yard and suddenly backtracked.

"Two scrap containers," he muttered.

"Is that unusual?"

"Aye."

I followed him to a pair of open containers—the kind that would haul gravel or sand in Texas. He climbed the ladder welded to the outside of the first and looked over the top. "This one is three-quarters full." He jumped down and climbed the second. "This one is full. It should have been removed when the empty one arrived. He strained, trying to pick up a piece of scrap.

He tried another piece and then climbed to stand in the container. "Someone's welded scrap into a massive cap."

Careful of my hands, I slung his jacket across one shoulder and climbed. When my head cleared the top, he was walking the cap's perimeter.

"How would they get the cap off?" I asked.

"I imagine they use a crane." He looked down at me. "Of course, you climbed the ladder—sore hands, tight skirt, and all." He pulled me up to stand beside him. "There's a gap, but I can't reach in past my forearm."

"Let me try." I handed him his jacket and took off my own.

"You're not poking about down there. If the cap shifts, you'll lose your arm."

"Would you rather ask the police to search?" I asked, knowing potential negative publicity for MKI would give him pause.

"Give me your hand."

I took his hand. He gripped hard enough to make me wince and then jumped up and down, trying to shift the cap. When it didn't move, he let me go. "You have ten seconds. Mind yourself."

I folded my suit jacket, knelt on the makeshift pad, and reached into the gap. "I'm touching rectangular boxes the right dimensions for cigarette cartons." I stretched farther. "Got one."

"Up with you." Darach caught my skirt's waistband and tugged.

I withdrew my arm and a carton. "It's the same brand. Without a tax stamp!"

"If the container is even half-full, we're talking contraband cigarettes worth millions of pounds." He shook his head. "Kinnon must have used the schedules in those job files to piggyback the smugglers' cargo with our legitimate deliveries."

"Megan wouldn't condone smuggling," I defended.

"He could have lied to her. The only reason for Kinnon to conceal the deliveries from me and the police is if he worked with the smugglers."

"But why would they kill their inside man?"

Darach rubbed his hands over his face. "You seem determined to unearth a decent trait in my brother."

I spread my arms. "Of course I am. I want to believe that Megan loved a man who deserved her."

Darach held up his fingers and counted off arguments. "The note you found that threatened Kinnon, ordered him to maintain the status quo. You found unmarked cigarettes in his Porsche, and he gave an unmarked carton to Fia. He had the pertinent job files. If Kinnon wasn't participating, he was likely trying to blackmail the smugglers and got himself and Megan killed for his greed. And maybe Frank as well."

"Does Frank's wife know he's missing? Mrs. Gibson mentioned she requires continuous care."

"The home nurse called last night. She'd promised to stay until ten and wasn't happy when Frank didn't arrive to drive her home. I hired a taxi to carry her and Kathleen— Frank's wife—to a private care facility. The taxi took the nurse home after she saw Kathleen settled. She'll be well-looked-after until we find Frank."

"A private facility must be expensive. I'll split the costs with you."

He stared then gestured to the ladder and followed me down. "Frank will appreciate that," he said when our feet touched the ground.

I matched his quick stride back to the building.

Mrs. Gibson called on the intercom as we entered his office. "Mr. Darach?"

"Aye," Darach answered.

"There's a man on the phone who insists on speaking to you and Miss Lyssa. He won't give his name, but he mentioned meeting her outside the Spanish consulate."

My mouth fell open.

"Thank you." Darach activated the speakerphone. "Darach MacKendrick."

"Where's the American lass?"

I flinched at the familiar gravelly voice. "I'm here."

"Miss Eastin, you Americans are a resilient lot. I'm ringing because I want to trade someone you want for something I want."

Darach's frame tightened. "You have Frank."

"That's right."

"How much do you want?" I asked.

"Don't be thick. You've been outside looking at what I want."

"You saw us?"

"Just keeping an eye on my property."

"The cigarettes are yours?" Darach asked.

"I'm the middleman. The owner's not a patient or good man, so don't call the police. Just give me what's his."

"What's your offer?" Darach said.

"Tonight, I pick up the container with no daft or courageous acts on your part. I call by five in the morning and let you know where to find Frank."

"Unacceptable," Darach said. "Bring Frank with you and leave him here."

"Nonnegotiable. I need the cargo tonight, and I need to know you won't have the police waiting for me. You can have Frank when I'm well away. Take it or leave it."

"We'll take it," Darach said. I opened my mouth to protest, but he silenced me with a raised finger. "I'll see you're let into the yard unmolested."

"Then Frank will be back in time for Friday-morning sausages. If we're followed, you'll never see him again."

Darach quieted the disconnect tone with a finger stab.

"We have to call DI White," I said.

He shook his head. "I'll not jeopardize Frank or land MKI in the news connected to the smuggling of illegal tobacco."

"But if the saboteur works for Gravel Voice—"

"Not likely." He pointed at the phone. "That man is tame compared to whoever pays him to smuggle. That's who probably hired the killer."

"He can identify his boss. If we let him get away, we might never see him again." I folded my arms. "I won't risk losing a solid link to Megan and Kinnon's killer."

"We need the cigarettes relocated. If the authorities find out Kinnon allowed contraband to be stored here, we could be made to forfeit half, if not all, of MKI to Customs and Excise. We'd have to close the factory and put our employees out of work."

He gave me time to consider. It didn't take long to put the needs of the living before the dead.

"What's your plan?" I asked.

"I'll let the guard know the scrap container will be picked up tonight, and I'll follow whoever picks it up. When I know where Frank is, I'll call DI White. The police will catch the men, and, if one of them is the plane saboteur, we'll have the killer. Can you agree to that?"

"With two conditions. We call Evan, tell him what's happened, explain the plan, and tell him he'll receive an hourly check-in call. If a call is missed, he's to call DI White."

Darach shook his head. "Evan is a solicitor. If he agrees to be informed about illegal activity before it happens, he's ethically compromised. The same goes for Gavin and Sabrina. I'll call you hourly after the container is picked up. What's your second condition?"

"We stop by a shop after lunch. I need black jeans. I'm going with you tonight."

He folded his arms. "Absolutely not."

CHAPTER THIRTY-FIVE

"Is anything happening?" I yawned. Once again, I'd fallen asleep on Darach's shoulder.

"Not yet."

"What's the time?"

"Nearly eleven."

"Think he's changed his mind?"

"He can't afford to."

Pole-mounted lights illuminated MKI's holding yard. From our vantage point behind another sedan in the narrow street, we could see a corner of the container that held several million pounds' sterling worth of contraband cigarettes.

"After last night's kidnapping and a full day at the office, I'm surprised you didn't nod off sooner. A less stubborn woman would have let Ian drive her home and spent her evening soaking in a tub." I felt his fingers clench and extend behind my head.

I sat up and stretched, difficult in my new jeans. During our afternoon shopping trip we'd bought dark shirts, work jackets, and dark tennis shoes.

Darach lowered his arm and stole the warmth from behind my neck. "I never thought my life would include an evening spent watching for smugglers," he said.

I patted his hand. "It's a temporary aberration. Your life will smooth out after they're caught and Frank is found and the killer is behind bars."

"I like your optimism, but you're wrong about my life smoothing out. You'll still be here."

I heard the tease in his voice, but his underlying acceptance interested me more. We teetered on the brink of exposing the smugglers' and the killer's identities, which put me on the threshold of giving away my part of MKI and leaving Scotland.

"I only half-heard your conversation with Peter," I said, reworking my loosened ponytail.

We'd compromised on using Peter as our safety valve, calling him on the hour.

"He protested that I wasn't telling him enough, and when that proved futile, he cautioned care. He'll plead insomnia and sleep on the library couch with his mobile."

"That's good."

I looked outside. During my nap, a light mist had fallen. Beads of moisture dotted the BMW's windshield and waxed hood.

Darach crossed his arms. "Do you have any regrets about unfinished business with Megan?" he asked. His voice was low and strained as if he'd introduced the subject against his will.

"Yes. I wish I'd flown to visit her every time she'd called and invited me to whatever exotic location she was working for her modeling job. I wish she hadn't toned down her excitement and happiness about Kinnon just because my engagement hadn't worked. She deserved every blissful moment between meeting and marrying Kinnon."

I looked over. "How about you?"

His left hand clenched the steering wheel as if his grip could crush his confession. "I regret that I never tried to help Kinnon become a responsible partner or a responsible man. If I'd been a better brother, Kinnon and Megan might be alive, and I might not be hiding in an alley waiting for smugglers to pick up illegal cigarettes. And I wouldn't be cursing Kinnon and the part he played in us being in this situation."

"After my parents died," I said, "I was angry at just about everyone and everything except Megan. Aunt Sally took as much of my anger as she could stomach then said it was time to move on. 'You choose what to hang on to and what to let go of. If you don't accept the Lord's trials, you'll never appreciate His treasures,' she said. Overcoming anger was the hardest thing I've ever done. And the most rewarding."

"Divine plans aside, I don't know if I can forgive myself or Kinnon," he said.

The night darkened his eyes to black.

"Maybe it's still too soon. But you might set a future goal to forgive whatever Kinnon did that led to tonight. You'll feel better for it."

The corner of his mouth lifted. "Aye, I would at that."

I didn't get to appreciate his smile for long. Down the street, a diesel engine rumbled.

"Get down." Darach slouched as headlights glanced past the street and over the car. When he raised his head,

I peeked, too. A truck cab had braked at the MKI gate. The guard was unlocking the yard.

In less than ten minutes, the truck pulled out towing the scrap container holding contraband cigarettes. Darach reached for the ignition then froze.

A second truck, pulling a similar container, flashed its bright lights as it rolled up behind the first truck. Our quarry had backup.

When they drove on, Darach started the car.

I fastened my seatbelt as he backed down the street and onto the street behind us. Moving forward, we now paralleled the big rigs. We drove four blocks and braked behind a car stopped for a red light.

A truck passed on the street ahead of us.

"It's the one from MKI."

"Do you see the other lorry?" Darach asked.

"No."

"Bird in hand," he said, turning right when traffic moved. The car in front of us had also turned. It signaled to park.

Darach braked hard and swore as his unrestrained body rocked forward.

"You need to buckle up," I said.

"Watch for the second lorry."

I twisted to look out the back window. "Nothing yet."

We started moving again. The truck in front had a healthy lead with three vehicles between it and us.

"Here." Darach pulled the seat belt across his body as

the road ahead curved and the truck disappeared. I clipped his buckle into place. He swerved to the left and back as a horn blared. We reached the curve and merged into a roundabout. Circling, we rubbernecked at each of the four exits. The truck wasn't in sight.

Darach slapped the steering wheel. "We know he didn't double back, and I doubt he's headed to Perth. That leaves Arbroath or Forfar. Both roads lead to Aberdeen, a good place to hide the containers in plain sight, given the harbor and the size of the city. The best road for a lorry to travel is the A90."

He accelerated and shot left, cutting off a smaller car.

Finally, we caught sight of the truck and slowed. I glanced back. "If the second truck fell back to watch for a tail, he's taking his time."

Darach's phone rang. He glanced at the screen and dropped it into my lap. "Peter."

I checked the dash clock. "Shame on you, Darach. You missed your check-in call. Hi, Peter," I said.

"Lyssa? You're with Darach? I thought he was doing something dangerous. Is he daft?"

"No, I'm persuasive."

"What are you doing?"

"We're driving north on the A90 following a—" Darach touched my hand, stopping me. "We're following a lead that may help us find Frank. When we know more, or in an hour, one of us will call back."

"Don't behave irresponsibly. I don't think Greer could

316

recover from losing Darach, too, and I've grown rather fond of you."

"Thank you. We'll be careful, I promise. Bye."

I used the phone's map function to trace our route. The truck pulled off the A90 well before Aberdeen and bypassed the town of Forfar. We found ourselves on a sparsely traveled road, so when the truck turned left, Darach followed the vehicle ahead instead.

We turned around half a mile down the road, sped back, and followed the constricted lane into a gentle valley. Faint moonlight pierced the overcast. Darach cut the headlights, coasted down into the valley, and started up the rise on the other side.

Thorny gorse, its yellow blossoms faded to cream by the night, defended both sides of the rural lane. Ahead, light glowed inside a chain-link fenced compound at the top of the rise. Taillights flashed as the truck braked then turned into the compound.

Darach pulled to the side of the road." Keep watch here. I'll check out the location."

I reached for binoculars. "What if the other truck shows up? If the driver sees your car, he'll tell the others."

Darach backed the BMW through stabbing branches that screeched against the door panels until our view of the road disappeared. Draping the binoculars around my neck, I retrieved a few items from my purse and stuffed them into my pocket.

We exited the car. My adrenaline surged as we trotted

up the road. As the gorse on our right thinned, I touched Darach's arm and pointed.

He followed me through the break; thorns tugged at my jeans. I raised the binoculars. "It's a lumberyard," I said.

A single pole-mounted security light failed to penetrate the darkness between the metal-roofed sheds. A diesel engine idled. Light glinted off the truck cab and trailer facing the back fence.

I passed the binoculars to Darach. "The driver parked toward the back. Unless there's a rear gate, he'll have to reverse out the same way he went in."

Darach returned the binoculars. "I need to get closer."

"Okay." I turned, but he gripped my shoulders.

"Not you."

"We agreed to stick together. It's time to call DI White."

"Not until I know Frank is alive. If the police roar in, he's in danger." He pressed his phone into my palm. "I'm safe as long as you're here watching out for me. If I'm not back in thirty minutes call for help. And then drive back to town."

I opened my mouth, my next argument already formed, but his hard kiss startled me into silence. When I opened my eyes, he was jogging uphill.

"You did that on purpose," I accused.

Heart in my throat, I watched him run uphill without stopping or slowing. He easily climbed the fence and disappeared into the darkness.

I used the binoculars to scan the lumberyard. It was difficult to judge size. The yard might go on forever or end on the other side of the idling truck. Five minutes passed with no sign of Darach. I checked his phone. No signal. My stomach lurched. Did a tower exist out here? If I sneaked closer, I'd gain elevation and perhaps a signal—and be nearer if Darach needed help.

My uphill approach lacked Darach's speed and aerobic ease. Bracing my hands on my knees, I paused to catch my breath. The ratcheting roar of a down-shifting standard transmission drowned made me jerk around. On the other side of the hedge, the second rig rumbled into the lumberyard.

CHAPTER THIRTY-SIX

Regardless of what Darach had said, the bad guys now outnumbered him. I dialed his phone, but the call didn't go through. The phone displayed a single, intermittent signal bar. I needed higher ground.

I jogged to the deepest shadows and climbed the chain-link fence. I hung the binoculars on a metal post so I'd know where to escape if the need arose. I checked the phone. One bar.

Time to find Darach.

I ran into the yard and hid beside a four-post shed. I counted three rows of four sheds between me and the far fence. Darach must be nearby. The pungent scent of pinesap, with an underlying note of fermentation, reminded me of a Tennessee distillery I'd visited with Megan.

The two trucks, lights off, idled one behind the other two rows away. I circled a forklift and climbed a few feet up a wood stack to gain a clear view of the truck cabs. Both appeared empty. Easing down, I crept forward and pulled a pen from my pocket. I wrote the license plates on my arm.

Easing along the right side of the trucks, I slipped out my lipstick and scribbled on both containers. My eyes adjusted to the faint light. I spotted Darach crouched beneath the partially open window of what appeared to be the lumberyard office.

Suddenly, he sprinted toward the fence. I followed. He slid to a stop, staring at the hanging binoculars.

"Darach!" I called in a loud whisper. He turned, and I ran to him.

"Lyssa? Why didn't you stay put?"

I ignored his questions. "Did you find Frank?"

"He's here, and he's not bound. He's working with them."

The pained expression on his face was obvious, even in the shadows. My brain tried to work Frank into the scenario.

"When will the police arrive?" Darach asked.

"The phone signal is weak," I said. "If I climb to a shed roof, I think I can call out."

He shook his head. "It's too risky. There are four of them, including Frank. We'll drive back toward town until we get a signal."

"No." I backed away. "If these men escape we've lost another chance to identify the killers. The only place we can watch them *and* call is from here."

I ran to a shed where the stacked wood protruded beyond the roof overhang. I started climbing.

Darach stalked out of the darkness. "That's a good seven meters up."

He was right; it was at least twenty feet. "The signal should be better there."

His hands gripped my waist. "Get over the fence and wait for me at the car. I'll climb and make the call."

I didn't let go. "I'm not leaving you alone, and I'm safer hiding on the roof than on the open slope."

"Then move," he said, lifting me two feet up the stack. He followed close behind. I'd gained four feet when the wood underfoot rocked. I grabbed a shed brace. Darach jumped to the ground.

"It's not properly balanced," he said. "Keep climbing. When you reach the top, stand toward the back and hang on to a post in case the stack tumbles."

Compromising speed for stability, I reached the top, hugged a post, and acted as a counter-balance while Darach climbed to my side.

"You still have my mobile?" Darach asked.

"Yes." I patted my jacket pocket.

"Let's get you on top."

I rubbed damp palms on my jeans. "I wasn't very good in gymnastics."

"You pull, I'll push."

I grabbed the edge of the metal roof. Darach boosted me to his shoulder, and I hooked an arm on the rooftop. He pressed me over his head until I could belly-crawl up the easy slope of the roof.

Boards clattered to the ground.

"Darach!"

"Do you have a signal?" he asked.

I checked. "Two bars."

"Make the call," he said calmly. "They're coming."

"Oi!" A flashlight beam raked the alley. "See that pile!

Told you I heard something."

Three additional flashlight beams swept between the sheds. I found DI White in Darach's contact list and connected. The first ring dragged into a second.

Frank's voice carried. "Coates, let's take the lorries and leave. It could be Customs and Excise."

"The yard would be swarming with agents if they were here," Coates said—my gravel-voiced adversary now had a name. "Surround the shed."

DI White answered. I spoke as loudly as I thought safe.

"It's Lyssa. Darach and I are in a lumberyard."

As I gave directions, a thud sounded on the adjacent roof. I spun, and a flashlight beam blinded me.

"Well, look who's here," Coates said. "I suppose MacKendrick's around somewhere."

I scrambled to my feet. "Detective Inspector," I said loudly. "I'm facing the man who threatened me outside the Spanish consulate and kidnapped me yesterday. His name is Coates. Frank, two other men, and two trucks carrying contraband cigarettes are here." I recited the license plates scribbled on my arm. "Fifteen minutes would be great." Having fudged twenty off the detective's ETA, I pocketed the phone.

"Anyone spot MacKendrick?" Coates called to the men below, easing closer to the edge of his roof.

"Leave them. Let's get out before the police come." Frank sounded worried and more than a little anguished. Whatever his relationship with the smugglers, he loved

Darach—which made him an ally of sorts.

"She's bluffing," Coates shouted. "You can't get a mobile signal from here, I've tried."

"Have you stood on a roof and tried?" I smiled. Doubt furrowed his forehead.

He took out his phone, checked the display and cursed as he put it away. "Time to come down, lass."

I took a step back. "I believe I'll wait up here."

"Then *I'll* join *you*."

"There he is!" a man called. Someone scrambled onto the stacked wood below. Seconds later, a board arced up from under the edge of the roof and landed beside me.

"Thank you, Darach!"

I grabbed the wood and held it like a bat.

Coates easily jumped the four feet separating our roofs and pointed to my awkward weapon. "What do you plan to accomplish with that?" He switched off his flashlight and tucked it into his pocket.

"I'm hoping for serious damage."

I swung. He dodged. I swung. He feinted, toying with me. Between fear and exertion, I was already breathing hard.

Beneath us, lumber groaned and shifted. Planks crashed. A wooden avalanche tumbled, blocking the gap between the shed and the fence. A surprised yell merged with a pain-filled bellow. Coates looked down.

I swung and connected with his arm. He staggered. I stumbled and lost my grip. The board clattered to the roof's edge. Coates grabbed me, twisted my arm, and forced me toward the roof's edge. "After tonight's delivery, I was leaving on an extended vacation," he said. "I was ready to forgive and forget."

I tried to jerk away. One of the truck engines revved and a transmission ratcheted. Someone was getting out of Dodge.

"You bloody fool!" Coates screamed.

The vehicle reversed. The panicked driver headed toward the corner of our shed.

I threw my head back and connected with his face as the truck struck the shed. Coates howled and let me go. I spun to see him cupping his nose, blood dripping from between his fingers.

I scrambled to the roof peak. The truck changed gears and inched forward. The structure gave an ominous creak.

Coates lost his balance and gravity took over. His hands left dark smears on the metal roof as he slid to an awkward landing atop the container. He crept toward the cab as the truck lurched over fallen timber, drowning his shouts.

I prayed that Darach's voice wasn't one of the cries I'd heard when the stacked wood collapsed. My watch showed sixteen minutes until the police arrived.

I glanced back at the creeping truck. Coates was no longer in sight. Beneath me, roof supports creaked as the building leaned. I stood and balanced, gauging the distance I'd have to jump to reach the adjacent roof. I heard another engine.

A forklift trundled into view. I watched as it dropped a

pallet of lumber behind the trucks, blocking them, and then raced toward me. I couldn't make out a face, but the shoulders looked broad enough to be Darach's.

Friend or foe, I needed off this roof.

I scooted down the slope toward the elevating forks and stepped onto the metal rails. As the forks came down, I saw Darach's face. The machine's motor quieted when I was close enough to the ground to step off. He jumped from the seat and tossed the keys over the fence.

"Are you hurt?" he asked.

"No." I brushed wood shavings from his jacket, needing to touch him. He was alive and unhurt, and I was grateful. "Good to see you're still in one piece," I managed.

His arms circled my shoulders and pulled me close. I pressed my face to his chest.

"You had time to worry about me?" he asked.

"I didn't know if you were caught in the lumber slide."

"Coates, Frank, and the other truck driver are skulking about. I tied the fourth man to the fence."

"Is he—"

"No. He's not the saboteur. He's too heavy and—"

A weak groan rose from the debris followed by, "Darach? Lad?"

"Frank?" Darach ran to the wood heap. I dodged the lumber he flung aside and helped him tear into the rubble.

Frank, scratched and bleeding, lay beneath more wood. Darach gripped him under the arms and pulled. Frank screamed.

"What's wrong?" Darach asked.

"It's my leg, lad."

I shifted more wood and caught my breath. A splintered stake pierced Frank's upper thigh; bright red blood spurted from the wound.

"Lay him down and cover him with your jacket," I said.

"Can we pull the stake out?" Darach's voice carried emotional strain.

"No." I struggled to recall the emergency first-aid class I'd taken last year. "I need your belt and shirt."

Darach draped his jacket over Frank's torso then unbuckled his belt. He dragged his shirt over his shoulders and handed both to me. I wrapped and tightened the belt around Frank's leg, above the puncture. His bleeding slowed but didn't stop. I rolled the shirt and used it to pad the wound around the stake.

"Ah-h-h-h!" Frank's back arched.

Darach flattened a hand to his mentor's chest. "Easy, Frank."

I'd never seen so much blood. Frank's labored breathing worried me, but the clammy look and feel of his face worried me more.

"—chose a poor way to make money and poorer friends," Frank said.

"You did this for money? Why didn't you come to me?" Agony filled Darach's words.

"You're not the sort one asks for help," Frank wheezed. "Coates paid to overnight containers. He said only a few shipments, but he kept coming back. I'd made a bad investment, so I let him."

"When did Kinnon get involved?" Darach asked.

"December. He slept off a pub crawl at work—the watchman said he was fair keeled over with drink when he came in. Thought I was safe—but Kinnon saw us in the plant. He asked questions—I saw him nosing around the scrap containers."

I pressed with the heel of one hand between Frank's groin and the tourniquet. "Darach," I said quietly. "This is arterial bleeding. Put your hand where mine is and apply pressure." We traded places. Darach stared at Frank's colorless face, his own a tortured mask.

"Told Coates Kinnon suspected—I demanded an end to—arrangement. Coates said discourage Kinnon—or they'd do it—Mailed notes that Kinnon ignored—Afraid he'd tell you."

"He should have." Darach ducked his head to his knee and wiped sweat from his face.

"I'm cold, lad," Frank said. "Kathleen?"

I shrugged out of my jacket and laid it over Darach's. Frank was losing too much blood.

"We're taking care of her. Hang on. We'll get you to hospital," Darach said.

"Saw the files on your desk, lass—Kinnon all over again."

"You told Coates about Lyssa?" Darach asked.

"To my shame." Frank's head lolled toward me. "You had no business taking half of MKI—sent you a warning, too." He fought to refocus on Darach. "I'm paying the piper."

"Aren't we all," Darach murmured.

I wiped the blood on my hands onto my jeans and leaned over Frank to slip Darach's phone from my jacket pocket.

"He needs medical help. If there's not a phone in the office, I'll try to climb to another roof."

Darach caught my wrist. "I'll go. Coates—"

"Is busy," I said. We could hear the wood Darach had dropped being tossed.

Frank groaned and Darach leaned over him. I twisted away and backed out of Darach's lunging range.

"I'll be back as soon as I can," I said.

"Misjudged you, lass." Frank's thready voice barely carried over the diesel trucks' idling engines.

I sprinted into the darkness.

CHAPTER THIRTY-SEVEN

I darted between the sheds and the fence, pausing at each corner to scout for danger. I glimpsed Coates and another man wrestling with the wood barricade created by Darach. Without the forklift, their task would take a while.

I wanted to see the other man's face—to see if he was the killer.

Instead, I slipped past and ran to the unlocked office. I spotted phone jacks but no phones. The forklift was now useless, and Darach couldn't leave Frank alone to help me climb another shed.

I ran outside, climbed the fence, and dialed. A choppy ring stuttered, followed by static.

I whispered a prayer as I ran to the open cab door of the truck furthest from the men. I clambered to the top of the cab. Finally, a signal! I dialed 9-9-9 and left terse directions for an ambulance.

I secured the phone in my pocket and ducked as someone closed the door of the other truck. Seconds later, that truck slowly backed toward the entrance.

I scrambled inside the other cab and groped the smooth steering column. My heart sank—a manual transmission.

"Brake, clutch." I used both hands to shift into first gear. I gripped the oversize steering wheel. "Gas."

The truck jumped forward, hit the fence, and jolted to a stop. My feet flew off the pedals. The engine coughed and went silent.

I yanked the keys from the ignition and reached for the door handle. The door flew open and a rough hand clamped my arm.

"Come to say good-bye?" Coates snarled.

He ripped the keys from my hand, shoved me across the bench seat, and took my place behind the wheel. Restarting the engine, he shifted into reverse. Metal squealed as the chain-link protested the cab's release.

I levered my head and shoulders out the passenger window. Coates dragged me back by my belt.

"You don't want to do this." I slapped at his hand.

"Two days ago I didn't want to do this," he said. "Now I'm wanted for kidnapping."

A fist jabbed through the window and Coates' head snapped to the side. Darach jerked the door open and dragged Coates out of the truck. Coates crumpled. I'd never seen anything so fierce.

"About time you met someone your own size," Darach said to Coates' still form.

I scooted to the door. Darach helped me out and over Coates' prostrate form. Then it dawned on me.

"Frank?" I looked at Darach as he searched beneath the truck's seat. He came up with a frayed bungee cord.

"Gone. Frank's gone."

His words held more self-control than I could have rallied.

"I'm sorry," I said. "I'm sure he appreciated your being at his side."

Darach knelt and tied Coates' hands behind his back. My partner looked tense enough to shatter. He remained kneeling, staring at Coates.

"How could Frank—I trusted a man who didn't deserve trust, and I suspected my brother of crimes he didn't commit. It seems I've misjudged almost everyone."

Darach nodded at Coates. "Let's move him while he's unconscious and manageable."

"It would be my great pleasure to drag Coates anywhere you choose. In fact, I'd enjoy the job more if we dragged him by his heels."

His shadow of a smile lifted my spirits.

"Lass, sometimes you scare me."

We hooked our arms through Coates' and were halfway to the lumber office when the second truck rolled out of the yard and accelerated up the road.

"Both trucks are getting away!" I protested.

"The fellow I tied to the fence must have escaped." Darach stared after the truck. "They're probably bound for Aberdeen," he said, his breathing aggravatingly even as we lugged Coates.

At the office door, we released our holds. Coates dropped to the ground with a satisfactory thud. "He must weigh as much as you," I gasped.

"I'd agree, although I'm in better shape."

"Maybe. I'd have to chase you down an alley to be sure."

He treated me to a severe stare. "I'm still in a fair rage about your daft chase."

"Yes. Well," I managed between breaths.

The distant wail of sirens heralded the approaching police. The first squad car screeched to a halt at the front gate. While Darach guarded Coates, I ran toward the flashing lights to report the escaping smugglers.

Following our interviews with DI White, Gilly approached.

"We caught the lorries," he said.

"You're sure you got the right trucks?" I asked.

"They were the only lorries with 'I'M A SMUGGLER' written in red lipstick on the side of their containers. Both held contraband cigarettes, but neither driver is the saboteur."

What little energy I possessed drained in a sudden rush.

"Are we done then?" Darach asked.

White nodded. Gilly closed his notebook.

Darach put a hand on my shoulder. "Let's go home," he said.

We retrieved his BMW from the gorse and drove southwest. As soon as the cellular signal permitted, he called Peter.

"We're safe. We found Frank. I'll fill you in tomorrow."

Empty roads and Darach's heavy foot on the gas pedal made quick work of the miles. My spirits lifted at the sight of light spilling through the long, narrow windows that bordered the manor's front door. He parked and followed me inside to the foot of the stairs.

"Should we call the solicitors before the press reads tonight's police reports?" I asked. The yawn that followed didn't catch me by surprise, but Darach's warm palms cupping my face did. Strong thumbs stroked my cheeks before his hands dropped to his sides.

"Go to bed," he said. "We're meeting Gilly at MKI at eight. I'll call Gavin and Sabrina first thing tomorrow and have them meet us there at eight-thirty."

"I'll invite Evan, too. His contact list is impressive, and we'll need all the public-relations goodwill we can get."

Darach nodded. "Aye. We will."

I woke Saturday morning thinking about MKI's future and mine. In five days, when my thirty-days were up, Darach would again ask me if I'd sell. When I told him the shares were his when the killers were caught, would he feel a twinge of "what if she'd stayed?" Or just relief that he was finally the sole owner of MKI?

When we arrived at MKI, DS Gilly looked like he hadn't slept. He searched Frank's locker and left. Darach and I stayed to empty it. I folded the foreman's red overalls and placed them in the plastic bag at our feet. Darach lifted Frank's hardhat, turned it over, and pulled a piece of stiff paper from inside.

"What's that?" I asked, stepping closer.

He turned a faded photo toward me. A much younger Frank draped a beefy arm across Darach's teenage shoulders.

"When was it taken?" I asked.

"Twenty years ago, when I began working the floor. Before the shutter released, Frank whispered, 'Don't you worry, lad. I'll teach you what you need to know.'"

Darach's hand crumpled the photograph. "Frank should have come to me. *Kinnon* should have come to me."

He dropped the hat and photo into the plastic bag and knotted the top closed.

"Frank said I'm not the sort one asks for help." His words sounded like a challenge, and his stare demanded the truth.

I answered carefully. "You can come across as intimidating, but you're not unapproachable. You're a good man, Darach. Frank and Kinnon *should* have come to you. I won't guess at Frank's choices, but maybe Kinnon didn't confide in you because he'd already confided in Megan. If his plan for redemption involved proving himself to you and everyone at MKI by exposing the smugglers, then handing you the problem would have lessened his achievement."

Darach didn't seem comforted or convinced. He picked up Frank's bagged belongings and opened the stairwell door for me.

"After we meet with the solicitors, I'm visiting Frank's wife and making his funeral arrangements. I won't be back until after two."

"I can go with you."

The lines across his forehead eased a bit. "Thank you, but Kathleen is easily agitated by strangers, and she might not recognize me today. I'd best do this alone."

We started up the stairs.

"Is there anything I *can* do for you?" I asked.

"With all that needs attending to, I've let Mother's and Peter's messages go to voice mail. Would you go to Perth and explain last night to them? And tell Mother I'll stop by Tuesday."

I forced my smile to remain in place. "Of course."

"If Evan is free, take him with you. I don't want you to travel alone."

"Okay."

We found our solicitors gathered in the conference room. Darach summarized our discovery of the contraband in the MKI lot and our night at the lumberyard.

"Since there's a chance one container of contraband can be traced back to MKI we should prepare a statement that emphasizes Darach didn't know the containers were being held here," Gavin said.

"We told the police last night that Kinnon planned to expose the smugglers," I said.

"That's supposition," Sabrina said. "We need the press on our side in case government law enforcement pays a call. Smuggling always interests them."

"I'll arrange interviews with *The Scotsman* and the BBC," Evan offered. "And I've another friend who might help."

Evan retreated to a corner with his phone. Gavin and Sabrina continued to brainstorm damage control. Media spin fell outside my area of expertise, so I followed Darach's lead and listened.

A few minutes later, Evan sat beside me, his phone pressed

to his chest. "Lyssa, if MI5 offers Coates immunity in exchange for revealing who he provided transportation services for, would you agree to drop assault and kidnapping charges?"

The others stopped talking.

"Is that up to me?" I asked.

"Your day in court is guaranteed—unless you forfeit it."

"For MI5 to propose involvement, they must think Coates is connected with a terrorist organization or crime family," Sabrina said.

"That's a fair assumption," Evan agreed.

"What would I get in return?" I asked.

"The gratitude of queen and country. And, I suggest an expedited official investigation to quickly clear MKI from legal action by Customs and Excise."

"Agree," Sabrina urged. Gavin nodded. Darach met my gaze but offered no opinion. Giving up a personal day in court didn't bother me, but there was something else.

"I also want them to look into Fia's murder."

Gavin's alarmed expression registered in my peripheral vision. It appeared he still didn't approve of anything to do with Fia. "Kinnon gave her some of the smuggled cigarettes," I continued. "Given her behavior the last time we met, I think she'd figured out a link. I owe her this."

Evan relayed my request and nodded. "Agreed."

I pressed my palms to the table. "Okay."

"That will work," Evan said to his contact. "Thanks." He hung up.

"You all realize that I'm sparking an inter-agency rivalry

between MI5 and Detective White," I said.

"You're also saving MKI's business reputation." Sabrina looked genuinely impressed. "I'd call that a solid bargain."

Darach stood. "Evan, can you drive Lyssa to visit my mother and Peter? She'll fill them in on the last forty-eight hours."

"Of course—"

"Do you need a lift to Perth, Lyssa?" Gavin interrupted. "I'd like to speak to Peter. I can drive you to the manor afterwards."

"Or I could—" Evan began, but Sabrina put a hand on his arm.

"Father, you and Lyssa riding together is a lovely plan." She turned to Evan. "Who do you know at MI5?"

He grinned. "If I tell you about her, she might feel obligated to kill me."

Sabrina's eyes narrowed. "She?"

CHAPTER THIRTY-EIGHT

Gavin and I sped past bright yellow fields of flowering rapeseed. Their joyous color clashed with my mood. We'd caught the smugglers, but unless one of them talked, we were no closer to finding the murderer.

I leaned back, appreciating Gavin's silence. His thoughts, whatever they were, occupied him as fully as mine occupied me.

At the Rands', Gavin parked beside Peter's Jaguar.

"We shouldn't be long," I said, preceding him up the red-brick walk.

Peter opened the door.

"Come in, come in." He took my hands and cocked his head. "You're pale. Time to quit testing fate and start trusting the police."

"I do trust the police. And you don't look any more rested than Darach or I. Sorry we kept you up—thanks for acting as our security blanket."

"Not at all."

"Did you tell Greer about last night?" I asked.

He nodded. "What little Darach mentioned. Three captured and Frank's involvement and death. I can't quite believe it. Frank was dedicated to Darach—to MKI." He stepped back. "You know your way to the sitting room.

I'll find Greer and join you."

In the sitting room, Gavin and I ignored the couch that faced the fireplace and the wingback chairs that anchored two corners of an Oriental rug. Finally, Peter led Greer into the room, holding her hand.

"Would either of you care for a drink?" Peter asked.

Gavin and I declined.

"I'm glad you and Darach are unharmed," Greer said stiffly.

She and Peter took the couch; Gavin and I sat in the chairs. While Greer stared out the window, I focused on Peter and started with the kidnapping and ended with the lumberyard. "I spoke to DI White this morning. None of the smugglers are identifying who hired them. That may change with MI5's involvement."

"MI5?" Greer looked at me.

"They think the smugglers may work for terrorists or a crime family," Gavin said.

"The type of people who might hire someone to kill Kinnon." Greer covered her mouth with her hand.

Peter jumped up. "Let me get you a glass of water, dear. I'll just be a minute." His gaze swung to mine, his plea for help unmistakable. I nodded.

Gavin stood. "I'll walk with you, Peter," he said. "I need a moment of your time."

The men left. The silence grew awkward.

"Is there anything I can do for you?" I asked.

Sharp blue eyes focused on me. "You're bringing news Darach should have brought."

"He'll stop by Tuesday. I'm here today because he wanted you to know what happened last night. He's at the nursing home, breaking the news of Frank's death to his wife. Afterwards, he'll arrange Frank's funeral."

Greer's face lost its angry pink tinge. "I didn't realize—" She deflated in front of me.

I took the opportunity to plant a seed. "You and Darach have endured a terrible month. When he's here Tuesday, maybe you can share your worries with him and encourage him to share his."

"When I look in his eyes, I see accusations. Darach is like his father. Even as a boy, my oldest son wasn't easy to know or get close to."

"What I've learned about Darach in less than a month is that he's principled, hard-working, and dependable. He considers what's best for the situation, not what's best or easiest for himself. He's considerate, attentive, and passionate in his beliefs. You may be confused about where you stand with him, but you always know he'll have your back."

"He's constant," Greer said.

"Exactly."

She looked directly at me, all signs of weakness gone. "Do you love Darach?"

"I—" Truth was truth, but to admit it to Greer of all people? "Yes. But as you guessed, it's unreciprocated."

"Thank you for being honest. I wished only for my sons not to endure in their marriages what I endured in my first marriage."

All I could do was blink. Obviously, neither of the Eastin girls was good enough for Greer's sons.

Peter's voice carried from the hall. "Gavin, I said I'd think about it. That's the best I can do today." Peter's voice lost its angry edge as he came through the door and handed a glass to Greer. "Here's your water, darling."

I picked up my purse. "It's time we left. Peter, Darach is coming by on Tuesday if you have more questions. No need to see us out."

I evaded Peter's surprised look and breathed a relieved sigh when Gavin followed me outside.

We took the A90 out of Perth, the drive back as silent as the drive over. As we neared the turnoff for the lane that would deliver us to the manor, Gavin spoke.

"Do you mind a side trip? I'd like to talk with you about Fia."

I held suspicions about Gavin, but the smugglers were now the prime suspects. "I have questions, too. We can trade answers, but I still need to be careful. Where did you have in mind?"

He pointed at two distinctive mounds rising from the landscape. "The first is Balgay Hill. The Mills Observatory there is surrounded with paths and, it being a Saturday and nearly lunchtime, is probably full of picnickers."

A public place with plenty of people around. "Sounds safe," I said.

We entered Dundee, exited a roundabout, and passed through residential neighborhoods. The homes on our right gave way to a cemetery studded with upright stones.

I looked away from the reminder of Megan's and Kinnon's deaths. Gavin noticed.

"Sorry, I should have taken the long way 'round. I cut through here because the car needs petrol."

He entered a commercial area and pulled into a self-serve gas station. "I'll just be a moment."

I watched in the side mirror as Gavin inserted a credit card. When he didn't start pumping gas, I looked around. He stared at the pump display.

His eyes shut tightly and then opened. He examined the contents of his wallet then knocked on my window.

"It seems I have an issue with my credit card. Could I borrow forty pounds until Monday?"

Looking away from his flushed cheeks, I pulled out my wallet.

"No problem. I insist on paying since you are kind enough to act as my taxi and escort."

"Thank you."

Again underway, and a few turns later, a retaining wall rose, holding back thick woods on our right while suburbia blurred by on our left. A right turn took us through the woods along the base of the hill. Another turn and we climbed a narrow road and followed other cars into the Mills Observatory parking lot. A small motorcycle scored a parking spot near the entrance while we weaved farther into the lot.

Gavin chose a slot in the far corner. "We're closer to the path here," he said.

The observatory, a light-colored sandstone building with

an off-white dome and railed-roof terrace, occupied the hill's summit. A stream of people walked toward the entrance.

I stepped out of the car. Gavin indicated a sign for the Planet Trail.

"This path has benches where we can find a seat and a quiet place to talk," he said.

We followed the sloping asphalt trail past stands of redwoods, cypress, and cedars. The path wound past a series of standing stones, each representing a planet in the solar system.

Maybe it was the cemetery's lingering influence, but the stones reminded me of grave-markers, and I thought about Darach picking out a stone for Frank.

"This is the place I had in mind." Gavin nodded at a succession of benches. The woodlands limited the downhill view to an occasional glimpse of Dundee and the River Tay.

I walked to the middle bench. Sunshine warmed my shoulders as I sat. Gavin sat beside me.

"You said you had questions," Gavin offered.

So had he, but I was glad to start this discussion.

"Did you go through my briefcase and read Megan's letter?"

"What makes you ask?" Red tinted the tips of his ears and cheeks.

"Because Frank and Darach wind office envelope closures in ovals while you use figure-eights."

"I'm hardly the only one at MKI to do that."

"Yes, but only a few people knew I'd received the letter. Darach, Sabrina, and you."

"When was this?"

I sensed he was bluffing for time to recover, but I tugged my notepad from my purse and thumbed through the pages.

"Wait! What was that?" Gavin asked.

He snatched the pad from my hands and flipped back two pages. My purse fell to the grass. He'd glimpsed notes from my conversation with Fia. I'd written: *Could Gavin have hired someone to kill Kinnon?"*

His compressed lips barely moved. "What you have here is slander."

A couple strolled by and claimed the downhill bench. I wrenched the notepad from Gavin's fist. "What I have are personal notes from a conversation with a woman who was murdered. And now it's time you take me home."

I leaned and picked up my purse. As I stood, so did Gavin.

"Lyssa, I—"

I heard a faint *pop* and all six feet of Gavin crumpled into my arms. I staggered under his weight. Beyond his shoulder, someone moved in a stand of cedars about a hundred yards back in the direction we'd walked. I glimpsed black hair and black clothing and heard the popping sound again. Something disrupted the air beside my cheek.

I quit trying to prop Gavin up and let his weight carry us down the hill until untrimmed brush halted our momentum and offered some cover. He lay face down and still. Blood darkened his suit's back right shoulder.

"Are you all right?"

The couple from the next bench peered down the hill at us.

For the second time in less than twenty-four hours, I tried to recall my emergency first-aid training. "I need you both down here, now!"

They scrambled downhill and slid to a stop beside Gavin. "Is it a heart attack?" the woman asked.

"No. Get down. He's been shot."

Eyes and mouths wide, the couple dropped to their stomachs.

"What are your names?" I asked, digging through my purse.

"Tom and Mary," the man said.

"Tom, I need you to call an ambulance and the police."

He fumbled a phone from his pocket and punched 9-9-9. Within seconds, he was talking to emergency services.

"Good Lord," Mary said faintly. "Is he dead?"

"No. Just unconscious."

My heart pounded. I tore the wrapper off travel tissues and pressed the entire pack against the entry wound in his shoulder.

"Hold these firmly in place please, Mary."

Her expression held shock, but she covered my makeshift compress with her palm.

I wiped my hand, warm with Gavin's blood, on the grass and then worked it between Gavin and the ground to probe the front of his chest and shoulder. The bullet hadn't gone through.

Mary looked around wildly. "Who? Why?"

Tom looked at me, his phone still pressed to his ear.

"Because the shooter missed *me*," I said.

I hadn't thought either of them could get any paler. I was wrong.

How had the shooter known I would be here? Gavin chose this place, this path. Had he made the arrangements before we left MKI or while we were at the Rands? Had the shooter shot his employer by mistake? I could no longer see the trees to our left. If the shooter was working his way toward us, I'd put Tom and Mary in danger.

"Keep pressure on the wound and stay down," I said. "If the shooter is still out there, you're safer without me here."

I slung my purse to my back and raced uphill.

CHAPTER THIRTY-NINE

I reached the path and sprinted toward the observatory. Sunlight had reflected off the shooter's dark clothing. Leather maybe? Like the motorcycle rider who'd ridden into the lot?

I paused at the intersection where the planet trail crossed the road. I saw the observatory through the trees.

I heard a motorcycle engine start. I left the trail and ran up the road. If the shooter was already on his bike, my chances of reading the license plate were slim.

I picked up a fallen tree limb. If he'd put his rifle away, I had a chance.

The motorcycle revved for a gear change. The black-clad rider rounded the curve. I stepped from behind a tree and heaved the limb onto the road in front of him.

The motorcycle jerked sideways in a spectacular slide. The bike and rider parted company. Rolling and spinning into the woods, both connected with trees. The engine sputtered death throes.

Two patrol cars screamed into view. I waved my arms. Tires squealed, and four officers ran toward me. I pointed. "The shooter's there."

Three constables cautiously approached the shooter's prone form. The fourth pulled me away from the action.

"Where's the ambulance?" I asked.

"On its way." The officer eyed the blood on my hands.

"I can show you where the wounded man is," I said.

"We have it under control. I need you to sit here until we're ready to talk to you."

I sat in the cruiser's backseat and rubbed my palms together to ease their tingling. I called DI White and then, since Darach might still be meeting with the funeral director, I called Evan. He said he'd find Darach, contact Sabrina, and take her to the hospital to meet Gavin's ambulance.

"I'll join you all there after I give my statement," I said.

A third siren approached. The ambulance appeared to know where I'd left Gavin. Mixed reactions skittered through me. I didn't want Darach to lose another close friend. Accidently or not, Gavin *had* saved my life, but what if he'd inadvertently blocked a shot he'd arranged and paid for?

The conversation I'd overheard between Gavin and Sabrina at MKI earlier, took on terrible significance. Had the money missing from Gavin's account paid for an assassin? Had his confidence that my stock would soon belong to Darach been based on more than optimism?

The afternoon sun threw short shadows beside the other cruiser. A second ambulance arrived.

Two policemen angled toward the ambulance with the shooter clutched between them. A third followed, carrying a short rifle. I leaned so close to the window that my breath fogged the glass. The shooter's head lolled. The police secured his wrists with handcuffs before the emergency techs took over.

DI White and DS Gilly arrived. White approached the shooter. Gilly made his way toward me.

The first ambulance trundled past. I murmured a quick prayer for Gavin's recovery as the siren fired up and the vehicle drove away.

Gilly opened the door. "Last night wasn't enough excitement for you?" He softened the question with a quick smile.

"Last night I knew our decision was risky." I nodded toward the shooter. "That fellow came without notice."

Gilly stopped in the act of pulling out his notebook. "You didn't recognize him?"

I looked again. The shooter's head still hung forward. "I haven't seen his face. Is it—"

"Give the EMTs a moment, then I'll let you tell me. In the meantime," Gilly tapped my shoulder. "Turn around and let's get started. Why were you and Mr. McDonald here?"

"Gavin wanted to discuss Fia Cullen."

"What about her?"

"We never talked. The shots came minutes after we reached the bench. My theories range from innocent conversation to a setup. The shooter either followed us or he knew to come here."

As he scribbled his shorthand, I continued glancing at the shooter. A few minutes later, the constables escorted him toward the other cruiser.

"Is that him?" Gilly asked.

Our eyes locked as he passed. The shooter's hard stare made me glad I sat inside a cruiser with Gilly beside me.

"Yes, it's him," I said.

I jumped when White opened my door and looked in. "Are you two through?"

"Aye. Miss Eastin made a positive identification," Gilly said.

"Then the constables will drive you wherever you need to go, Ms. Eastin," White said.

"What about Gavin's car?" I asked.

"Do you have his keys?"

"They're in his pants pocket. Maybe Sabrina has a spare set."

Gilly snapped his notebook shut and sent me another smile. "You've managed to clear up our next week's schedule."

I smiled back. "Always happy to assist law enforcement."

He slipped out and closed the door.

"We're off to interrogation," White said, exiting.

"Will you call me later and tell me what he says?"

"Pop by the station tomorrow at ten. With luck, it will be a late night. If he'll talk, we've quite a few questions." He closed the cruiser door as the constables took their seats in the front. "Where to, miss?" the driver asked.

I met his eyes in the rearview mirror. "The hospital, please." I entered the waiting room and spotted Sabrina on a couch, bookended by Darach and Evan.

"They just took him into surgery," Evan said.

He stood and enveloped me in a hug. Darach stayed beside Sabrina with her grip tight on his hand.

"Tell me what happened," Sabrina demanded.

I shared the shooter's identification as the plane

saboteur, details of the shooting, answered questions, and mentioned tomorrow's appointment with DI White.

"I'll take you," Darach said.

"What did Gavin say about Fia?" Evan asked.

"The shooter hit Gavin before that conversation started," I said.

Sabrina's frown deepened my suspicion. If she knew why Gavin wanted to talk to me, did she also know where he'd taken me and why? Until now, I hadn't suspected her of more than speaking her mind in a rude way and being possessive of Darach.

We sat mostly silent for the next few hours. Finally, the surgeon came out and told Sabrina that he'd removed the bullet and stabilized Gavin. Much relieved, we waited again, this time until he woke up in the recovery room. The staff allowed only Sabrina in for a brief visit.

When she returned, the tightness of her face had eased. We all stood.

"He's sleeping off the anesthesia and resting comfortably," she said.

Evan initiated a hug that she broke off. "I'm staying tonight. When he's moved into his room, I'll have a cot there."

"Can I fetch us something to eat from the canteen?" Evan said.

Sabrina turned to Darach. "Would you wait with me?"

Evan was visibly shocked, and I wasn't far behind. Darach met the uncharacteristic plea in her eyes and nodded.

"Of course. I'll stay as long as necessary."

"I'll stay, too," Evan offered.

"That won't be necessary. And Lyssa needs a ride." Sabrina dismissed us with her usual brusqueness.

I walked beside Evan through the visitors' parking lot. The sun, still above the horizon, surprised me with its presence. I glanced at my watch. Four forty-two.

"Are you hungry?" Evan asked.

"No." Though I'd missed lunch, my appetite had fled. And judging by the halfhearted way he'd offered, his appetite wasn't any greater than mine. I'd been looking forward to talking everything over with Darach—and maybe hearing him say he was glad I was alive.

Evan drove me to the manor, each of us silent, lost in contemplation of the implication of Sabrina choosing Darach to stay with her. Had Gavin's shooting made Darach and Sabrina realize that they depended on one another for more than work and friendship?

I hadn't wanted to fall in love with Darach, but I accepted that I had. I wasn't sorry I'd rejected a personal relationship with him after that confrontational night in his study, but that hadn't stopped me from hoping for a second chance.

CHAPTER FORTY

I slept as long as I could before rising Sunday morning to ride with Darach to the police station for our meeting with DI White.

I hadn't heard Darach come in last night, so I presumed he'd stayed with Sabrina at the hospital. He appeared deep in thought.

"How is Gavin doing?" I asked.

"His pain is managed, and he's coherent. He wants to talk to you so we'll see him after you finish with the police."

He'd answered succinctly, but I could tell his mind was elsewhere. If he and Sabrina had realized any personal insights last night, he wasn't sharing.

DI White didn't keep us waiting. Two minutes after entering his compact, beige-walled office and asking my first question, I jumped from my chair, incensed by his report.

"Confronted with the rifle under his jacket and the bullet casings in his pocket that he didn't have time to dispose of, he *still* won't tell you who hired him?"

White massaged his neck, the first sign of frustration I'd seen him exhibit. "We can prove he shot Gavin. He denies sabotaging the plane, ramming and burning your hire car, and strangling Fia Cullen. However, some of that may change if his DNA matches what we found under Ms. Cullen's fingernails." He straightened his tie. "He stopped talking altogether once his high-powered solicitor arrived."

"What does he do that he can afford a high-powered defense attorney?" I asked.

"He claims he's a laborer at the Aberdeen docks."

"Is he local?" Darach asked.

"East of here."

Darach leaned forward in his chair. "Are we talking Tayport or further east?"

White shook his head. "Lyssa and Gavin were fortunate with the distance of the shot and the brush between them and the shooter. Closer, and with an unobstructed view, he could have killed them both."

"Really? I saw the rifle. It looked like a toy," I said.

White snorted. "The police should be so well-provisioned with *toys*. The man's a professional. Based on his choice of weapon, he's well-funded."

I recognized a dead end when I butted my head against one. "How about Coates? Did he say anything useful?"

"No. And if he does now, he'll say it to MI5." White shot me a censuring look.

"I'm sorry about that, but they made me an offer I couldn't refuse."

He shrugged. "They have resources we don't. We'll cooperate fully."

"Thank you," I said.

"I understand that Mr. McDonald's surgery went well,"

White said. "Detective Sergeant Gilly will pay him a visit later this morning."

"How about Fia's murder?" I said. "I've seen CCTV all over the Dundee city centre. I presume you've checked them?"

"Despite public opinion, the closed-circuit cameras don't capture every centimeter of the town on video. Fia's shop doesn't receive direct coverage. We've looked at a great many things, Miss Eastin, and will look at many more. Be patient with us."

"Are you saying that real police work isn't like television, where murders are solved in an hour or two?" I said with mock shock.

He surprised me with a laugh. "We have a superb force and the Dundee Forensic Lab's support, but we still need evidence and clues. Assumptions simply won't do."

We all stood. "You'll let us know if the shooter's memory improves?" Darach asked.

"We'll be in touch," White said.

I was beginning to hate those words.

Darach drove to the hospital and guided me to Gavin's private room. Gavin lay in bed, pale but alert. His head and shoulders were elevated. Sabrina and Evan stood beside him.

Darach hugged Sabrina and spoke into her ear.

"Gavin, I hope you'll be up and around soon," I said. "How are you feeling?"

"Like I've been shot." He didn't smile or look confused, so I interpreted his words as confrontational.

"Dad, a detective is coming to speak with you shortly," Sabrina said. Concern and aggravation mixed in her voice.

A little more color faded from Gavin's face. He looked at me, chin lifted. "I had nothing to do with what happened yesterday."

Sabrina glared at me. "He took the bullet meant for you. Do you seriously think—"

"It crossed my mind," I said. My honesty quieted the room.

"It's time for that talk I promised you on Balgay Hill," Gavin said to me. "Darach, I'd like you to stay." Gavin looked at Evan. "This is a private conversation."

Evan's expression went carefully neutral. "I'll wait outside."

Sabrina's focus darted between her father and Darach. Gavin must have told her what he planned to say. His confession would ease his soul and, I feared, further burden Darach's.

Sabrina watched the door until it closed behind Evan. She positioned Darach at the foot of the bed. "Lyssa, if you'll stand next to Darach, Dad won't have to turn his head."

I moved to Darach's right and looked at Gavin. He gave a small nod.

"First, I want you to know that I did what I did for Darach and MKI," he said, almost pleading.

"What exactly did you do?" I asked.

Gavin seemed to shrink into the bed, and Sabrina shot me a dirty look as she sat in the chair beside the bed. Gavin looked at Darach and spoke.

"Since they've both passed, I'm comfortable sharing with you that I advised your father against giving his MKI shares to Kinnon. I also counseled Kinnon against accepting the shares. You often spend twelve hours a day at MKI. One could see that Kinnon wasn't prepared to make the same commitment. My intent was to protect MKI and your and your mother's incomes."

While also protecting his and Sabrina's incomes and jobs? I glanced sideways at Darach, catching his barely perceptible nod. Gavin continued.

"Last fall, I realized that Kinnon's gambling was getting out of hand. I suggested he consider selling some of his shares to you—just enough to cover his losses. Kinnon wasn't happy with what he termed my 'interference,' and I'm sure he shared my suggestion with Fia."

He paused and reached for the cup on the table beside him. Sabrina got there first and angled the straw so he could drink. When he lay back, I could tell the effort had winded him.

"As Fia said, I contacted Kinnon in January for tips on horse racing but not to encourage his gambling or to force him to sell MKI shares to Darach. I used his tips to try to recover my own financial losses.

"Where did your money go?" I asked.

Sabrina's foot swung in angry, swift arcs. "Not to pay that horrid man who probably killed Kinnon and Megan and who almost killed Dad," she snapped.

Gavin licked his lips and started again.

"I assembled a group to invest in commercial real estate. In December, my group closed on a property. A month later, the surrounding properties were zoned for council houses and our property immediately lost two-thirds of its appraised value."

"What are council houses?" I asked.

"Public housing projects," Sabrina said.

Gavin looked at Darach. "Peter wisely kept your mother out of it, but the group included Frank."

I started. Frank had said he'd made a bad investment with a colleague he'd trusted.

"How much did you both loose?" Darach asked calmly.

"Our entire pensions," Gavin said.

"I see." Darach didn't sound upset, but the tic in his jaw suggested otherwise.

I gripped the rail at the foot of the bed. "If you invested your entire retirement in real estate last December, you couldn't afford to hire the shooter."

Sabrina raised her hands. "Finally."

Gavin looked at me. "I'm guessing that the argument Megan heard between Kinnon and me was Kinnon lecturing *me* to quit gambling and to talk to Peter about proper investments. I wasn't kind in my response."

"So, the reason you wanted to drive me to the Rands was to talk to Peter about investments?" I said. "Why did you want to talk at Balgay Hill afterwards?"

"I asked Peter for help with solid, safe investments that might help me recover financially. He was angry about those emails Fia produced—the ones she thought proved I'd encouraged Kinnon to gamble. I thought that if I could explain to you my argument with Kinnon and our email conversations, Peter might be more inclined to advise me. He likes you."

"Were you planning to explain it to me?" Darach asked.

"That's enough," Sabrina said. Gavin closed his eyes.

Darach walked to the window, though I doubted he took in the view.

Little wonder that he walled off his emotions. No one had confided in him. Greer chose Kinnon over him, though for well-thought-out reasons. His father reneged on leaving Darach all the MKI stock, perhaps also for a good reason. Kinnon hadn't shared the presence of smugglers at MKI. Frank had chosen betrayal instead of asking for help, and I had swooped in, taking half his company. It was a wonder Darach trusted anyone anymore.

When Gavin's eyes opened again, I said, "Thank you for explaining. I'm glad my suspicions were unfounded."

"You shouldn't have had them to begin with," Sabrina snapped.

"I had my reasons. And I understand your father wanting to keep his circumstances private, but I wish I'd known earlier."

"As you said, I had my reasons." Gavin looked toward Darach who stared out the window.

Turning away, I picked up someone's copy of the morning paper. The latest exploits of an Eastern European crime family filled the front page. Below the fold, the paper also covered Gavin's shooting.

I opened the door and let Evan in. He looked at Sabrina then joined me.

"I guess Gavin's shooting proves the smugglers' boss *is* responsible for the kill orders," I said quietly. "It's a relief because the people I've suspected—"

"Didn't include me, right?" he said, his grin lopsided.

"No, but pretty much everyone else I've met here." I tossed the paper onto a chair. "Any news from your friend at MI5?"

"No. But it's early. I do know an agent was assigned to look over the forensic evidence of Fia Cullen's death."

"DI White said the video cameras covering city centre didn't cover her shop."

Evan perked up. "Maybe something else did."

"Like what?"

"Maybe that wasn't the only camera. I'm going to run down to city centre and see what I can find."

I shrugged. "Okay. I'll grasp at straws."

Unable to help ourselves, Evan and I looked across the room. Darach and Sabrina stood close together, talking softly.

"I'm off," Evan said, his face unusually sober. "Can I drop you at the manor?"

"Yes, please."

CHAPTER FORTY-ONE

Monday morning, on the ride to MKI, I listened as Darach spoke on the phone to Mrs. Gibson and arranged to tell the employees what had happened over the weekend. Neither of us had much to say after he finished his call. Our relationship was slipping backward to the remote politeness of strangers, and I didn't know how to stop it.

At MKI, we rode the lift upstairs and walked to Mrs. Gibson's desk. Up close, I could see that she'd been crying.

"The staff has assembled in the canteen," she said.

I tossed my briefcase and purse into my office as we walked past on our way to the stairs. When we entered the canteen, the room went silent.

Darach explained what had happened to Gavin and assured the workers that the solicitor would make a full recovery. His announcement that the shooter was also suspected of sabotaging Kinnon's plane, and was in police custody, evoked approving murmurs.

When Darach revealed Frank's death, I felt a wave of shock wash through the room and saw more than a few tears. As Darach explained what the papers would soon report about the smuggling operation, heads lowered.

"Details of Frank's wake on Wednesday will be posted," Darach finished. "We'll celebrate his many years of service to MKI and the good he did—and try to forgive the rest." I preceded him to the stairwell.

We started up the stairs, and he came alongside me. I tugged him to a stop. He faced me, his expression set but his eyes tortured. I wrapped my arms around him. Four breaths later, I let go. He hadn't hugged back.

"You looked like you needed that," I said.

"I did. Thank you."

We continued upstairs and separated at our offices.

Hours later, Darach and I walked out to the MKI parking lot. The evening-angled sunlight lent crisp definition to the contours and colors of the parked cars and brick walls. I raised my face to the radiance. Darach opened the BMW's passenger door for me. Moments later, we sped away from Dundee's brisk traffic.

The sun flirted with the hills when we arrived at MacKendrick Manor. "Ian and Anice have the evening off," Darach said. "I can make omelets."

"I'll take you up on that, but can we walk in the garden first?"

"Of course."

We circled the house. Soon, our footsteps crunched on the rock path. April's buds were now May's blossoms. I brushed a hand through a cluster of rhododendron petals and released a sweet fragrance that couldn't fill the void inside me.

I stopped beside the bench where we'd held our first real conversation.

"I'm flying to New York to resolve Megan's apartment and belongings," I said.

Darach shoved his hands in his pockets. "When do you leave?"

"Wednesday, after Frank's wake is in full swing."

He scooped a leaf from the granite birdbath. "When will you return?"

"I'll let you know," I said. "Before I leave, I'll make sure all pending bids are in, and the financial paperwork is caught up."

Darach stood quiet. His lack of a protest left me feeling empty.

My stomach growled.

"Come inside," Darach said. "It's time to feed you."

We turned toward the house.

"Lyssa?" he said.

"Yes?"

"Don't ever get shot at again."

Darach prepared a delicious omelet, and his company—if not relaxed—was at least pleasant as we ate at the kitchen island. And then he got personal.

"I'd like to apologize for my behavior in the study the night I kissed you," he said. "I shouldn't have. I'm not sure why I did."

My heart sank. "You've experienced a lot of shocks this past month. I understand your desire to keep MKI intact, but it was a move that could have left us both unhappy," I said.

"Perhaps I'm the type of man a woman wouldn't enjoy

being married to."

"I didn't say that." I fiddled with my napkin until I'd sorted my thoughts.

"They say there's someone for everyone, but workaholics generally have to work even harder at finding and keeping a spouse," I said.

He rested his fork on his plate. "You're saying that marriage to me would be difficult?"

The too-casual note in his voice tugged at me. Was he worried Sabrina might think so? Though loath to encourage him in her direction, I shook my head.

"I was referring to my own engagement debacle. I paid more attention to U.S. consumer durables than I did to Jackson, which might be what rekindled his attraction to his former girlfriend."

I carried my plate to the sink. That was probably more sharing of flaws than he'd needed. I shifted the conversation back to him.

"If anything, Darach, I suspect you'll be overly cautious in your decision-making process. But in the end, you'll make a good choice."

He didn't say anything as we washed up, leaving Anice's kitchen as clean as we'd found it.

"Join me in the study?" he said, one hand on the light switch.

"I'm tempted," I said, and I was. "But the last few days and nights have worn me down. I want to shower before I fall asleep on my feet."

"You've had more than your share of frights this week."

"This lifetime."

"Tomorrow night, we need to have a serious talk," he said.

"About what?"

"The future."

Was he ready to ask me to sell again? Was he ready to see me leave?

He switched off the light and fell into step beside me. We parted at the foyer as he turned toward his study. His words carried behind him. "Sleep well, Lyssa."

"After that?" I muttered, climbing the stairs.

All hope of Darach loving me evaporated during my mirror-steaming shower. By the time I cut off the water, I'd made my decision.

I'd accomplished what I'd come for. Megan's killer sat in jail. It was time to give Kinnon's shares to Darach.

CHAPTER FORTY-TWO

"What are your plans?" Darach asked during our Tuesday morning drive into Dundee.

"I'm reviewing upcoming jobs with the sales department. Afterwards, I'll call DI White for a progress report on the shooter then ask Evan who I can call for information at MI5."

He changed lanes. "You should have all that finished by lunchtime."

"Yes, and your mother is expecting you today. Lunch may be a good time for your visit."

His jaw tightened. "I'll call her and ask."

Just before lunch, Darach opened the connecting door and stepped into my office.

"I'm off to Mother's. You can come if you'd like," he said.

I found his hopeful expression appealing but shook my head. "Greer and I talked on Sunday. She wants to see you. Please tell her and Peter hello for me."

For lunch, I bought a sandwich in the canteen and ate in my office. A few hours later, I closed a file of pending bids and carried it to Mrs. Gibson.

"We're getting twice as many bids out now that you're figuring them," she said.

I returned her smile. "I like estimating and calculating

the raw-material requirements. Please buzz me when these are ready to sign. I'd like to get them in tonight's mail."

Having failed to reach DI White this morning, I dialed again and got through. "Is the shooter talking?" I asked.

"MI5 whisked him away. No doubt they're interviewing him now." White's tone verged on testy. "On the bright side, the Newcastle Airport employee identified him as the man he saw around Kinnon's airplane."

"Do you think that means MI5 found a link between the shooter and Coates?"

"If you thought I was unforthcoming, wait until you try to extract information from MI5." White chuckled. "But don't give up. They wouldn't have transferred him without good reason."

We hung up. I reviewed the summer job schedule until my phone rang. "Yes, Mrs. Gibson."

"Mrs. Rand is calling. And your bids are printed. Shall I bring them to your office?"

Greer? Calling me?

"No, thanks. I'll be out to sign them in a few minutes." I pushed the blinking button on the phone. "Mrs. Rand, this is Lyssa. How are you?"

"I'm not sure."

Her distracted tone surprised me. As her pause stretched on, worry set in. What had happened during her lunch with Darach?

"Mrs. Rand?" I coaxed.

"Darach's just left. Could you come by the house? I'd

like to talk with you."

She sounded surer of herself now. I drummed my fingertips on the desk, uncomfortable with her request. Unable to justify a refusal, I looked at my watch. "I can be there by three-thirty."

"Thank you."

I hung up. My transportation options were limited. Evan was at the hospital with Sabrina and Gavin. Ian had mentioned running errands, and Darach was driving back from Perth. I wouldn't ask him to turn around and drive right back, especially since I wasn't sure how his lunch with Greer had ended.

Had Darach declared his intentions regarding Sabrina?

Certainty was better than imagining scenarios, so I called a cab then carried my briefcase and purse to Mrs. Gibson's desk to sign the bids. When I finished, she handed me a new phone to replace the one destroyed when Coates kidnapped me.

"I've programmed the office numbers and Mr. Darach's numbers into your address book. Mr. Darach also asked me to include the detectives' numbers."

"Thanks." I placed the phone in my purse. "I'm going to visit Mrs. Rand. She said Darach is on his way here. Please tell him that I'll return via cab after my visit."

"All right."

I walked downstairs and outside, slipped into the waiting cab, and gave the driver the Rands' address. To distract myself from worrying about what Greer wanted, I dialed Evan.

"I have a new phone," I said when he answered. "The number's the same as the old. I'm on my way to visit Greer. How's Gavin?"

"He almost looks healthy today. And he's more relaxed. Something's perked him up. Even Sabrina is chatty again."

I heard the hope in his voice and feared we were both in for a letdown soon.

At the Rand's house, I paid the cab driver and dismissed him. I had no idea how long I'd be here. I rang the doorbell and admired the fragrant red roses that bordered the entry. Greer answered the door, surprising me. I was used to greeting Peter.

"Come in," she said briskly. "We'll talk in the sitting room. Would you care for coffee or tea?"

"No, thank you." I set my briefcase beside an antique console table in the foyer and followed her. We settled in adjacent chairs.

"Darach and I had that talk you suggested," she said. "We clarified some false perceptions. He even agreed to let me help arrange Frank's funeral. I asked you over because I wanted to thank you."

It took a moment to find my voice. "You're welcome. I'm very happy for you both."

"Thank you." Her face lost some of its tension.

She fussed with a flower arrangement then pulled her hands back to her lap. Her blue eyes finally met mine.

"Peter admonished me for what I said to you the last

time you were here. So, I want to tell you what I told him, and what I told Darach today.

"I blamed Megan for Kinnon's death. God help me, I resented her surviving when Kinnon died. And I resented your opportunity to see her alive one last time when I'd never have that opportunity with Kinnon. I'll never have the chance to tell Kinnon how sorry I am for being cross about his marriage."

I relaxed for the first time in her company. "That's survivor guilt," I said. "I was angry, too. I still am sometimes, even though I know anger won't change anything that's happened."

"Darach mentioned that he's making some personal changes soon. The recent deaths—Kinnon and Megan, and Frank—have changed him and his priorities. He spoke of discussing his decisions with you. I hope you will hear him out and carefully think about your part in that future."

Meaning he'd marry Sabrina? My heart plummeted, but I sat tall.

"I will—"

"I've wasted so many years with him," she broke in. "I'm hoping you—"

Ah, now I understood. "Don't worry. I won't get in the way of you two reconciling."

"Thank you."

"Mrs. Rand—"

"Please, call me Greer."

"If you'll call me Lyssa."

The sitting-room door opened. Like children caught whispering in class, we quieted as Peter entered.

"Lyssa, what a pleasure." He pecked my cheek then kissed Greer. "Is everything all right, dear? I thought you were lunching with Darach."

"I did. Afterwards, I asked Lyssa to come by. We've been having a nice chat."

I nodded confirmation, and Peter's eyes widened. He covered his surprise with a smile.

"In that case, would either of you ladies care for a drink? I've been to see Gavin, and hospitals depress me."

When we declined, Peter crossed to the bar and mixed a vodka tonic.

"How is Gavin?" Greer asked.

"Alert and improved. The doctor is releasing him. Gavin is to walk and move around as much as he's able. Sabrina and your solicitor friend, Evan, is it?"

I nodded.

"They're taking Gavin to her flat." Peter sipped his drink.

Greer turned to me. "Darach told me about the shooting. He said the man intended to shoot *you*." She looked sincerely concerned for me.

"He's the same man who pushed my car off the road. And DI White said that the Newcastle airport employee identified him in a lineup."

"Thank God they've caught him," Greer murmured.

"We still need the arrest of whoever gave him his orders." I glanced at my watch and stood. "I need to get back to work.

May I use your phone to call a taxi?"

"I'll drive you," Peter said.

He caught my glance at his unfinished cocktail. "It's more tonic than vodka. And I've only had a sip," he said, extending a hand to Greer and pulling her to her feet.

"I'd rather Peter drove you than a stranger," Greer said.

"I've never driven a Jaguar," I hinted.

Peter burst out laughing. "You want to drive us to MKI? By which time I will have metabolized the wee bit of alcohol in my system? One would think you were the one with diplomatic training after that tactful designated-driver offer. I accept." He handed me his keys.

"Does the Jaguar have a manual transmission?"

Peter nodded.

I handed his keys back and picked up my purse. The Rands followed me to the foyer where I retrieved my briefcase. Peter opened the door.

"I enjoyed our talk," I said to Greer.

"Let's do it again soon." She beamed, and I saw where Darach had gotten his smile.

The door closed. Peter and I walked down the steps. My phone rang and displayed Evan's number. "Excuse me, I need to take this."

"I'll be at the car." Peter walked ahead.

"Hi," I answered. "What's up?"

"Remember the electronics store across the way from Fia's? The one I visited when you first went to her shop?" He sounded excited.

"Yes."

"Well, I stopped by just now because the last time I was in, the owner mentioned that after his shop was broken into, he'd installed a series of hidden cameras. The one inside is aimed at his shop's front door—you can see Fia's shop entrance across the street. The camera is backed up to its own hard drive, and the video is time-marked. Since Fia's murder is still Detective Inspector White's case, I'm delivering the hard drive to him. We should know who entered her shop within the hour."

I smiled, imagining Evan's grin. "Congratulations, counselor! You may have solved Fia's murder. Call me when you hear anything more?"

"Of course. And from now on you may refer to me as 'super-sleuth solicitor.'" He rang off.

"Good news?" Peter asked, reading my face as I sat next to him in the Jaguar.

I swung my briefcase and purse into the back seat. "The best!" I buckled my seatbelt as he started the car. "Fia's murder might be solved soon. Evan visited the electronics store across the street from her shop. The store has security video footage from the day of her murder. He's taking it to DI White as we speak."

Peter pulled onto the street. His eyes locked on the rearview mirror. I turned and saw his house. He stared as if committing every detail to memory.

"Do you want to go back and share this news with Greer?"

"I expect I'll receive a call soon," he said.

"They'd better call us both when they have a name to match the face."

Peter's shoulders straightened. "I'll be on that video."

"You saw Fia that day?"

"She rang me that morning to tell me Kinnon had given her a carton of contraband cigarettes he'd gotten from someone at MKI. The first day you visited her store and asked questions was the day she noticed they lacked a tax stamp. She suggested we meet."

"*You* were her lunch meeting? Why didn't you say something earlier?"

"Because when we did meet, I couldn't talk her out of telling the police that Kinnon had found contraband cigarettes on MKI property. MKI sustains Greer's income and Darach's livelihood. Fia knew that."

I pressed a hand to my chest. "Fia tried to blackmail you?"

His laugh held no humor. "Yes. But she'd also remembered that when she and Kinnon came for dinner at Christmas—while the rest of us were busy preparing dinner—she'd answered the phone at my request and taken a message. The caller was cross at my failure to locate a storage facility and strongly recommended that I find one quickly. She'd put two and two together."

He shook his head. "Our meeting ended badly."

CHAPTER FORTY-THREE

"Peter, did you kill Fia?" I asked.

He took a moment to refocus.

"I'm sorry, Lyssa. What did you say?"

Panic shook my words. "Did you kill Fia?"

"God help me—I did."

I glanced around, hoping to see another vehicle. No such luck. And I didn't recognize the road we traveled.

"Video and DNA will be hard to dispute," he said, almost to himself.

I pressed my palms against my thighs as I recalled Peter's diplomatic service in Eastern Europe and DI White saying the shooter's nationality was "east of here."

"Where does the crime family you work for call home?" I glanced at the speedometer. If I tried to jump, I could be killed.

"I don't work for them. I was returning a favor for a friend. A favor that got out of hand."

"I don't understand."

"In the diplomatic service, you meet people in diverse areas of politics and commerce. Mid-December, a politician who'd used unorthodox methods to help me with a diplomatic issue approached me for a return of his favor. His 'associate' required a secure, temporary storage facility in southeast Scotland.

"One doesn't delve too deeply into the backstory of a

376

favor. I made inquiries and came up with options. The politician passed them on, and each was vetoed by his 'associate.' As Fia unfortunately discovered, their patience was running out. I didn't dare disappoint the politician. So, at dinner one night, when Kinnon, with Fia as his date, mentioned Frank's wife's illness and their financial situation, I thought I saw a solution. I suggested that my acquaintance contact Frank."

He turned onto another deserted road.

"My acquaintance promised his client would locate another storage facility after no more than two shipments. I didn't know the shipments had continued until you exposed Frank. I never suspected that Kinnon had found out and was trying to catch them."

He slowed to negotiate a rough patch of road. "I'd arranged enough degrees of separation between the operation and myself that my involvement shouldn't have been traceable—except for Fia."

I felt my face flush. "You should never have suggested using MKI."

He nodded. "You're right. But I never imagined Frank would lose his money in that real estate deal of Gavin's and continue the relationship. Or that Kinnon would notice anything amiss. I never imagined he and Megan would die because I'd settled my debt with the politician." His voice broke. "I never imagined this last month."

My phone rang inside my purse on the backseat.
Peter continued talking in a flat tone.

"Even after we knew that the plane crash was murder, I didn't suspect the Albanians until you and Darach exposed the smugglers." He slapped the steering wheel. "I'm cornered, Lyssa. All because of that blasted video. When the police start looking for me the Albanians will start tying up loose ends. They don't care if you helped them in the past—only if you can hurt them in the present or future."

I tugged at the door handle. Nothing happened. I glanced over my shoulder. The lock hid flush with the door panel. I tried the window button, but the glass didn't lower.

Running out of options, I aimed for Peter's soft spot.

"What about Greer?"

He fumbled a cigarette pack from the console. "My leaving could keep her safe. I'll not go back—never see her again. When she finds out what I did, she won't want to see me anyway. I love her. I didn't want it to come to this. But if you die, she'll inherit your MKI stock and sell it to Darach, which will bring them closer and ensure her financial security. It's the last gift I can give her."

He tapped the pack on the steering wheel and caught a cigarette with his lips. Pushing the lighter, he turned north.

"Where are we going?" I asked.

"To the airfield where Kinnon took flying lessons. I'll hire a plane and pilot there."

Peter lit the cigarette and replaced the lighter. He turned onto a narrow lane. The car slowed as we climbed.

I wouldn't die on Peter's schedule. A chance to escape from a car wreck was better than the certainty of whatever he had planned.

When Peter again raised the cigarette to his mouth, I reached across the console and wrenched the steering wheel right. The car careened toward a stony bank.

He wrenched back.

I pressed the car's cigarette lighter and again grabbed the steering wheel. His overcorrection jerked my hands loose, and he plowed an elbow into my chest. Gasping, I huddled against the passenger door.

He glanced from the road to me and back to the road. "Don't force me to hit you again, and I promise you'll suffer as little as possible."

The heated lighter popped out. I grabbed it and branded Peter's inner thigh. He roared and struck at my hands. The smell of burned meat and singed cloth filled the car.

A curve sign whipped past. As Peter slowed, I threw the lighter onto his lap.

He swatted and screamed.

I turned the ignition key, shutting off the car. Peter grabbed the steering wheel, but the steering column had locked. He pumped the brakes, but each pump reduced the braking power.

I covered my head with my hands as we flew off the road.

A string quartet screeched a jarring melody in my head. Fighting sluggishness that smothered like a too-heavy blanket, I opened my eyes. Powdery dust motes drifted through the car's interior. I pushed the deflating airbag away and looked to my right.

"Peter?" I whispered.

Held by his seat belt, Peter slumped amid his deflating air bags. I reached to test the pulse in his neck.

He groaned.

I released my seatbelt and grabbed the keys from the ignition. I pressed the unlock symbol twice then shoved my door open against a hedge of blooming gorse. I stumbled outside and wrenched open the back door. I slid onto the seat and upended my briefcase.

I flipped the MacKendrick battle-plaid scarf around Peter's chest and knotted the ends behind his seat. I kicked off my heels and shoved my feet into my tennis shoes.

"Lyssa?" Peter mumbled.

I stuffed everything into my briefcase and scrambled outside, slamming and locking the door. Peter's head lolled toward me, eyes open. His mouth formed words I had no wish to hear.

I dropped his keys into my pocket and ran to the road, clutching my briefcase like a life preserver.

I ran until I couldn't see the car then pulled out my phone. As I accessed my contact list, Megan's laugh and voice unexpectedly resonated in my head. *One heck of an afternoon, sis.*

My laugh sounded ragged to my ears. "Could be worse, Megan. Could be raining."

A thumping vibration rolled closer. I searched the sky as the sound became a steady *wop-wop-wop*. "Yes!" I screamed, reading POLICE on the belly of the approaching helicopter.

My briefcase hit the ground as I waved my arms overhead.

The helicopter touched down in the open field. Dirt and heather pelted me. Shielding my eyes, I watched as a door opened and a familiar figure jumped out, bent at the waist, and raced toward me.

"Darach!"

The idling helicopter drowned out his answering shout. I ran to meet him, knocking him back a step as I flung my arms around him.

"Are you all right?" He swept tangled hair back from my face, his own face creased with concern.

"Yes." Releasing him, I stepped back and faced the advancing detectives.

I handed the Jaguar keys to Gilly and pointed. "Unless he's recovered enough to free himself, Peter's still in his car."

DI White looked at me. "How did you manage—tell me later."

The detectives ran to find the Jaguar.

I faced Darach. "How did you find me? What are you doing in the police helicopter?"

"White recognized Peter on a video of Fia's shop that Evan gave him. When White called the house, Mother told him Peter was driving you to MKI. When he couldn't reach you or Peter, he called me. I traded him access to the GPS app on your phone for a seat in the helicopter."

"I have a GPS app? Thank you!" I wanted to kiss him, but I turned away instead. "Shall we go check on Peter?"

When the ambulance arrived, DS Gilly rode with Peter,

who had regained consciousness and profusely apologized to us all. Except for tenderness where Peter's elbow had connected, I was unscathed. We boarded the helicopter. Seated between Darach and White, I secured my harness. White handed me a headset. The pilot took off, and the questions started.

I was grateful when we landed at the police station and more grateful when Darach asked to sit in on the interview. DI White agreed. Inside his office, between sips of hot tea, I retold the drama.

When I finished, White leaned back. "Gilly and I were about to leave for the Rand's when your solicitor called and said he was bringing video of Fia's shop entry."

"Why were you going to see Mother and Peter?" Darach asked.

"Because Gavin McDonald remembered hearing a motorcycle as he left their cul-de-sac and again noticed one when he stopped for petrol. We were trying to determine if one of the Rand's neighbors has a motorcycle or if the shooter had been seen loitering around the area. It appears he was following Lyssa and waiting for an opportunity."

Darach stood. "Excuse me; I need to make a call." He stepped into the hall.

A few minutes later I said goodbye to DI White and joined Darach. "Is your mother alone?" I asked when he hung up.

"No, I asked Sabrina to sit with her before I boarded the helicopter. Evan is coming to pick us up."

"Your BMW isn't here?"

"No. The helicopter picked me up at the office."

I imagined the stir caused by a police helicopter landing in front of MKI.

We walked outside and waited. Evan pulled up and jumped out of the car. He wrapped me in a hug. "I can't believe this."

"Me neither."

"Where do you two need to go?" Evan asked, releasing me.

"Can you take me to the manor then take Darach to MKI to pick up his car?" I said.

Darach looked startled. "You aren't coming to Mother's?"

I shuddered at the thought of standing in that house again today. "She has enough to deal with without me there as a reminder. Tell her I'll visit when she's ready to see me."

He nodded. "You're right, it's probably best."

When we arrived at the manor, Darach walked me to the door.

"I'll call you tonight." He looked as if he might say more but instead returned to the car.

When I turned down dinner, Anice insisted on making tea and toast. I sat with her and Ian in the kitchen, comforted by their concern. When exhaustion and aftermath kicked in, I excused myself and went to my room. I couldn't imagine what Greer was going through. I hoped that the reconciliation she and Darach had reached earlier would help her cope with Peter's involvement and arrest.

The ringing phone woke me at 10:15 p.m. I saw Darach's name on the screen and answered.

"Hi. How's your mother?"

"Trying to sleep." He hesitated. "She's not sure she wants to visit Peter in the hospital."

I propped a pillow behind me. "I don't envy her the decisions she has to make."

"She'd like to see you tomorrow."

"Tell her I'll call before I come."

"Thank you. Now go back to sleep."

"Thanks for letting me know what's going on."

"Not at all." I heard fatigue in his voice as he reverted to formalities.

"We never managed that talk you mentioned," I rushed to add, holding him on the phone a moment longer.

He was silent for a heartbeat. "No. We didn't. Are you still flying to New York tomorrow?"

"Yes. Megan's landlord needs her apartment cleared by the end of the month."

"Then it will wait until you return. Pleasant dreams, Lyssa."

He hung up.

I lay awake, knowing I wouldn't be coming back.

CHAPTER FORTY-FOUR

I dreamed of Darach's familiar spicy scent, and felt the mattress dip as he gathered me close. A knock on the door woke me—alone in my bed. I rose to my elbows.

"Yes?"

The door opened and Darach looked in. Thankfully, the pre-dawn dimness concealed the blush heating my face.

"How was your night?" I asked.

"Long. I seem to be having a lot of those recently."

"Has something happened?" I asked.

He stepped inside and leaned against the door. "No. I came for a shower and change of clothes. Sabrina and I are meeting the press at Evan's office in forty-five minutes. That should delay the media from swarming you, Mother, and MKI."

I didn't insist on accompanying him. The press conference was a task I was happy to leave to the others.

"How are you holding up?" I said.

He looked surprised by my question.

"I've been so busy that I haven't thought about it. When I do, I suspect a glass of Scotch will be involved."

I nodded. "I'll tie up some loose ends before I come to work."

"No one will fault you if you don't come in today."

"And if it were any other day, I might not. But I have things to finish before I leave tonight."

"Ah." His hands sought his pockets. "I'd forgotten you were leaving tonight."

In between life-threatening events, leaving was pretty much all I'd thought about.

"See you later then?"

"Aye."

The door closed, and I replayed the decisions and circumstances that had swept an ever-widening group of Darach's family, friends, and employees into a deadly spiral.

If Peter hadn't suggested MKI as a storage facility to repay his debt to the politician—if Frank hadn't needed the smugglers' money—if Kinnon hadn't spent that night at MKI and seen the container delivered—if he'd told Darach— if Darach had answered Kinnon's call the night of the crash—if I'd come to Scotland immediately after Megan married—if Fia hadn't threatened Peter. Actions and consequences. None of which could be altered now.

Sighing, I rose and wrestled my suitcase from the armoire, swung it onto the bed, and began filling the case.

So much more was involved here than the way I felt about Darach. I was here because Megan hadn't known her in-laws well enough to decide who might deserve Kinnon's MKI shares.

No, not deserve. That was how *I'd* been looking at it, but Megan wouldn't have based her decision on an analysis of the business. She'd have based her decision on the people involved. I sank onto the bed beside the suitcase and stared at the empty armoire.

Forty minutes later, my packed suitcase stood at the foot of the bed. Over the last month, I'd ruined enough clothes and shoes to make room for their replacements.

"Ready, miss?" Ian asked from the doorway.

"Ready."

I stayed a moment longer. Then I practiced walking away from the manor—from MKI—from Darach.

I said good-bye to Anice in the foyer. Kitchen towel to her eyes, she hurried away. I followed Ian outside.

"Sure you don't want me to fly to New York and help you pack up your sister's things?" he said, loading my suitcase into the trunk.

"I'd love that," I said, meaning it. "But Darach will need you more than I will over the next few days."

He nodded. "Aye, that's true."

He drove me to Evan's office. "I'll be right here when you finish, miss."

"Thanks, Ian."

I walked inside and took the elevator up. The press had moved on, and Evan was expecting me. When I told him what I wanted, he collapsed onto his chair.

"This has to be the biggest giveaway *ever*. Is there anything else you want to give away? Sabrina said Kinnon owned a Porsche."

"Too late. It's sold. I donated the money to the

Extraordinary Athletes." I leaned forward, seeking Evan's understanding. "I initially accepted Kinnon's and Megan's MKI shares so I could settle her affairs and make the choices she didn't have time for. When we learned they were murdered, I stayed to see their killer caught. I've accomplished everything and my thirty days of MKI ownership are up tomorrow. It's time to return the shares."

Evan crossed his forearms on his desk, his Irish Setter eyes concerned. "That's noble if a bit daft. You've taken to the place like a salmon to the Tay. You're not doing Darach a favor by leaving."

"It's not about my doing a favor for Darach. It's about me doing what Megan would have wanted." My usually neat signature sprawled across the document giving away MKI. I pushed the papers back across the desk.

"Have you told Darach?" Evan asked, his grin missing.

"Not yet."

"You're making a mistake."

I picked up my briefcase and stood. "I'll see you tonight at Frank's wake?"

He nodded slowly.

I recognized the tall, solid woman who guarded the front door. Greer's friend, Anne—instigator of Greer's first day out of the house without Peter. Had it been only a week ago? She let me inside the foyer.

"Hello, Anne. How is Greer?"

The corners of her eyes crinkled with worry. "About as

you'd expect. She's in the solarium. I thought the sunshine would do her good." She glanced down the hall. "Can I bring you tea? It would be marvelous if you could get her to drink some. Lots of honey if you can manage it."

"I'll do my best," I promised.

Greer stood in front of the couch. She stepped forward tentatively. I spread my arms and we shared a hug.

"I'm sorry. I had no idea Peter would—that he could—" Her voice lifted and dipped like a carousel horse.

"I can hardly believe it myself. But it's over for me. Let's concentrate on you."

She gripped my hands as we sat, and rushed her words.

"After the way I've behaved—I don't know how to make any of it up to you."

The sharp tap of footfalls announced Anne's approach.

"You can start by drinking tea and eating biscuits. I didn't make time for breakfast, and I won't feel comfortable eating alone."

"Here you are, ladies." Anne smiled as she set the tray on the coffee table. "I'm off to make a phone call," she said, leaving us alone.

Greer squeezed my hands then released them. "Will you pour? I'm a bit unsteady."

"Of course."

I filled the cups, added honey to Greer's, and placed two cookies on each plate. She made an admirable effort, and though my stomach growled a protest, I only matched her bite for bite. I could pick up coffee and a bagel when I drove to MKI.

"I'm trying hard to believe that something good will come out of everything that's happened," she said.

"I'm right there with you."

"It's difficult."

"But not impossible."

As we ate, I launched into an explanation of the papers I'd signed relinquishing MKI. When I finished, Greer's mouth worked soundlessly. I waited for her to find her voice, expecting anything but what finally emerged.

"You're what?" Blue eyes flashed as her chin lifted. "You don't want to be my son's partner? He depends on you. *You said you loved him.*"

The imperious Greer had returned. I wished Darach could witness her indignation on his behalf. I smiled at her.

"I meant what I said. But I made Megan's decision, not mine. My leaving will give you and Darach a chance to work out your relationship and decide what you want for your futures."

"When will you tell him?"

"Tonight, at Frank's wake."

I made one last stop.

The cemetery's stone entry arched overhead, casting a shadow on the rock path. My conscience scolded me for not visiting since the funeral. I found the double headstone and laid a bouquet of yellow daffodils and scarlet tulips in the center. I knelt and pressed my palms above Megan's name and Kinnon's. The marble radiated the sun's warmth.

"Hi, Megan, Kinnon. I know you've moved on, but this feels like the best place to let you know that the man who killed you is in jail. He won't hurt anyone else. Peter regrets his decisions. Greer and Darach are rediscovering one another; they'll be okay. Your families miss you." I closed my eyes. "We'll always miss you."

When we arrived at MKI, Ian transferred my suitcase to Darach's trunk. "Have a safe flight, miss," he said.

"Thank you." I gave him a hug.

I spent the afternoon clearing every task off my desk and taking a last walk around the manufacturing floor, exchanging greetings with the employees. At five, Darach opened our connecting door. A tired smile creased his face. He reached for my case. "Ready?"

I wasn't sure what to expect at a Scots wake. The pub was minutes from MKI, and Darach had hired the whole place for Frank's send-off.

Voices quieted when Darach and I entered and faded to silence when a bagpipe started playing behind us. Evan handed Darach and I each a shot of Scotch then lined up beside me. Sabrina stood opposite, next to Darach.

A lone piper entered, and bodies pressed close to form an aisle down which the piper slow-walked, playing a Celtic lament. I didn't know the words but others sang along, glasses lifted. A moment of silence allowed the echoes to fade. As Darach's glass met his lips, everyone drank.

Without warning, the band launched into a raucous tune. With solemnity cast aside, the party cranked up. The proficient bartenders briskly filled and handed off glass after glass of ale.

I mingled and visited. An hour into the festivities, I pulled Evan aside. "It's time."

He set his drink on a table and pulled me into a hug. "I'm not ready for you to leave," he said.

"I feel like Dorothy saying good-bye to the Scarecrow *and* the Tin Man." My hug tightened. "I know your brain's intact. Take care of your heart."

Evan managed a weak grin.

"Gavin's spirits are markedly improved," he said. "It's obvious that Sabrina and Darach spending time with him and each other is something he's long hoped for."

I glanced at Gavin seated at a table out of the way of jostling bodies.

"You'll keep in touch?" Evan said.

"Yes." I meant it, but we both knew my decision to leave was already distancing our friendship. "Now, I need your services one more time, Counselor. I need to find Darach, and I need a cab."

He nodded and disappeared. Minutes later, Darach appeared at my side.

"Evan has called my cab. I need to get my luggage out of your trunk," I said.

"Of course." Holding my elbow, he eased our passage to the entry. Outside, the remaining rays of sunlight glinted off his BMW. He swung my suitcase from the trunk onto the parking lot.

This was it.

A substantial piece of my heart chipped away.

"You'll call when you're ready to return?" he asked.

"That won't be necessary." I extended the rolling bag's handle.

He frowned. "What is that supposed to mean?"

"My thirty days are up tomorrow. All restrictions on my ownership of my MKI stock end then."

"Aye," he said, eying me cautiously.

I took a deep breath. "When she wrote her will, Megan wanted MKI to stay with the MacKendricks, but she couldn't decide if you or Greer should be her beneficiary. That's why she left me everything. I accepted Kinnon's shares because I needed time to make Megan's decision for her. And then I kept them until the killer was found. But I always planned to give them back."

I'd managed to stun him. His mouth opened and then closed. As he stared, his eyes narrowed in confusion. "Why didn't you tell me?"

"I couldn't risk you or Greer challenging me for the shares. And I needed a fair, unbiased look at how your family worked."

"Is that all this past month was about?"

"No. That's just the way it started." I looked him in the eyes. "I left paperwork with your mother that gives her my company shares."

A flurry of emotions flickered over Darach's face and settled into disbelief. I watched him swallow.

"Darach, if it were my decision to make for myself, I'd give you the shares. Up until Peter tried to kill me, that was my intent. But afterward, I realized I'd gone about my decision backwards."

He stepped back.

"Please understand," I pleaded, "this wasn't about me making *my* decision as a financial analyst. It was about me making *Megan's* decision—and she was all heart. We learned early the importance, preciousness, and fragility of family ties. I believe she'd have seen the shares as an opportunity for you and your mother to grow close, to learn to communicate and work together. Giving them to Greer is what Megan would have done."

He looked past me and lifted a hand.

A cab pulled to the curb. I indicated my luggage, and the driver loaded it into the trunk. I searched for something compelling to say to Darach, but an MKI mechanic stepped outside.

"Mr. MacKendrick, they're callin' for you, sir. The speeches are startin'."

Darach turned and walked away.

I tried to stay busy on the drive to Edinburgh. Evan had given my Texas numbers to his friend at MI5 to call me with a weekly update. I called DI White and gave him my numbers.

"Will you let me know when Peter's trial is scheduled?"

"There won't be a trial. Peter Rand is pleading guilty to

all counts," White said.

I processed this and smiled. "He's saving Greer and Darach from stress and publicity?"

"That's his stated intent. And this particular Albanian crime family will be history when MI5 convinces Coates or the shooter to talk. When they took custody of both men, they made sure each saw the other, so there's a bit of a race on now. They only need one of them to turn and take the deal off the table for the other. Personally, I'm betting that Coates folds first."

The cab arrived at Edinburgh Airport three hours before my scheduled departure time. An eternity later, I took one last look back before boarding the plane.

Darach hadn't come to stop me.

CHAPTER FORTY-FIVE

Tired after the overnight flight, I let myself into Megan's apartment and showered. Wrapped in her robe, I fell asleep in her bed, too exhausted to dream, let alone look around. I woke in the wee hours and walked through her rooms wondering how I'd accomplish yet another round of saying good-bye.

As hard as clearing her apartment was, it would have been harder a month ago. The shock of grief had passed, and the task kept me from relentlessly recalling the look on Darach's face when I'd told him I'd made Greer his partner. I wondered how or if they would work things out.

I missed the MKI manufacturing-floor melody, the mechanical hums and motorized percussion that performed Darach's private symphony. Maybe I could find similar work in Texas. If I mentioned MKI on an application, would Darach give me a favorable reference?

I spent three days sorting. On the fourth, having packed and shipped everything I wanted to keep, I called a local charity. They brought bags and boxes and returned the next day with a truck and volunteers who carried everything outside. I locked the door, turned in the key, and caught a cab to the airport.

A week later, I still hadn't acclimated to the Texas summer heat. The short walk to my apartment's communal mailboxes had me thinking of taking another shower when I returned to my air-conditioned apartment. I unlocked my box, reached inside, and had to tug to get the letters out.

The culprit was a heavy-stock, odd-sized envelope. As I closed the door, I scanned the return address and read Sabrina's name on what was obviously an invitation. Was this her final jab at me?

I thrust the invitation underneath the rest of my mail and walked to my apartment. I set the invitation aside while I scanned the other letters, but my eyes kept returning to the invitation. I spent three full minutes bracing myself to read confirmation of Darach and Sabrina's wedding.

Opening the envelope felt like ripping a Band-Aid off raw flesh. I read and reread the wedding invitation, confirming Evan's name beneath Sabrina's. He hadn't mentioned it during our last phone call. If his plan was to surprise me, he'd succeeded. The wedding was in August. Either the Scots didn't believe in long engagements or Evan wasn't giving Sabrina a chance to change her mind.

I tapped the RSVP card. Darach would attend the wedding, of course.

I parked in front of the Fed-Ex store and vented my windows a few inches. I fanned my face with the reply. I hadn't heard from Darach since I'd left, and Evan had avoided mentioning Darach during our phone calls.

A trickle of sweat rolled down my spine. I got out of the car and laid the reply on the hood. Digging in my purse, I found a pen and wrote my name in the space provided, paused, and checked *will attend*. Lightheaded with my leap of faith, I sealed the envelope and walked inside.

A blue-uniformed employee greeted me. "Can I help you?"

"I want to send this to Scotland." I handed him the envelope. For better or for worse, I'd soon face Darach. I smiled for the first time in two weeks.

In the ten minutes it took to drive back to my apartment, doubt invaded my thoughts. I got out of the car and locked the door. No longer distracted by traffic, I visualized my return to Scotland and my appearance at the wedding. What if Darach greeted me with stoic distance? What if I approached him and he turned away? I froze. What if he came to the wedding with a date?

"Hello, Lyssa."

I jerked toward the greeting, toward the man exiting a gray sedan.

Darach's pale blue shirt looked slept in, and his navy eyes held shadows. He advanced, a carryon dangling from his hand. He stopped a foot away, his expression unreadable.

"If Anice could see you, she'd cluck her tongue," he said. "Don't Texans eat?"

I steadied myself against the car and quickly stepped away from the hot metal. Darach must be sweltering. I pointed to my door. "Would you care to come in?"

"I would."

He followed me up the sidewalk. I fumbled my key into the lock. "Watch out for the boxes," I said. Megan's personal belongings still cluttered my entrance hall. "Can I get you anything?" I slipped into the kitchen and turned on the light.

Darach entered behind me. The galley-style layout instantly shrank.

"Do you have coffee?"

"Yes. It will just take a minute." The familiar actions of filling the coffeemaker failed to settle the butterflies in my stomach as I stared at the tediously dripping Kona.

"Where are your cups?" he asked.

I pointed to a cabinet. He reached for two mugs. I inhaled his spicy aftershave as he thumped the mugs down beside the coffeemaker.

My brain struggled to place him in Texas. "Why are you here?" I finally asked.

His mouth tightened. "You tossed your farewell speech at me bloody fast."

"I thought it would be easier that way. You had Frank's wake and funeral, Peter to deal with, and your mother to look after." I nudged the mugs closer to the coffeemaker. "How is Greer?"

"Struggling. She loved Peter. Part of her still does. I don't approve of anything he did, but I do appreciate his protecting her and MKI from the publicity of a trial."

The coffee maker pinged, and I poured. My hands trembled so badly I had to set the carafe down.

Darach took over and poured with a steady hand. "Gavin has healed. He and Sabrina are keeping in touch with Mother while I'm here. You'll be happy to know that MI5 is making arrests in that particular Albanian crime family."

I nodded. "Evan mentioned that during our last phone call. What he didn't mention was his engagement." Clutching my mug, I led the way to my living room and sat in an armchair. "I received their wedding invitation today. It surprised me. When I left, I thought you and Sabrina were getting serious."

He settled on my couch.

"Sabrina and I have always been serious about helping one another," Darach said. "When her marriage ended, she asked for my help discouraging male interest while she caught her breath."

"Escorting her also kept you off the market. Was that intentional?"

His cheeks reddened—a reaction I hadn't thought possible. "Actually, I hoped it would help me meet someone. But owning and operating a manufacturing business caused me to break or cut short more dates than I've seen to their doors. Are you coming to the wedding?"

"I just mailed my reply."

"And?"

"Miss Lyssa Eastin will attend."

"Then you can attend with me."

He said what I wanted to hear, but I lassoed my soaring heart.

"Why were you so distant those last few days?"

He ran a hand through his hair, making it stand higher.

After Peter tried to kill you, you seemed to withdraw. I thought you were rethinking your ties to the family that helped get Megan killed."

"That doesn't explain why you're here."

He made a frustrated sound in his throat then stood and left the room. I jumped up, ready to chase him if I heard the front door open, but he returned with his carryon, opened it, and withdrew—

"My scarf!"

His face serious, he unwound the scarf from around a picture frame, set the frame face down, and flipped the scarf around my neck. I caressed the MacKendrick battle-plaid colors. "Thank you. I regretted leaving it in Peter's car."

He picked up the frame and turned the picture toward me. Megan and me, looking at each other, happy.

"This was on your shelf. Since you didn't pack up your office, I went in to exorcise your lingering presence and instead found this." He tapped the photo. "Your love for Megan is obvious in your smile. I'm here because you've smiled at me that way."

He propped the frame on the coffee table then looked at me. "I'm here to prove to you that I love you. It took me a bit of time to figure out how after that fiasco when Mother and Peter walked in on us kissing."

He looked so tortured that I decided to help him out.

"It happened slowly, but about a week after that 'fiasco,' I was as much in love with you as before."

"Good to hear." His shoulders relaxed. "She gave them to me," he said.

"Sorry?" I set my mug on the coffee table.

He reached into the carryon again and brought out a legal-size envelope that he laid on the table between us. An envelope I'd last seen at Greer's.

"That's—"

"Mother told me that Kinnon and Megan gave me a gift she couldn't match. That gift was you. Then she gave me the envelope and said it was mine to do with as I saw fit."

He handed me the envelope that held ownership of my MKI shares. "You haven't filed, or whatever it is you do, to accept ownership?" I asked, turning the envelope over. "You haven't even opened it!" I looked at him. "I thought you wanted to be sole owner."

The corners of his mouth lifted in an appealing smile. "Apparently, being completely independent makes me unapproachable. Mother, Kinnon, Frank, Gavin, Peter, you—none of you came to me when you could have." He leaned forward, holding my gaze. "I don't want just any partner. I want you."

"Why?" The word popped out and dangled in the air.

"Because about halfway through your stay, I realized I once again anticipated my workdays with pleasure, not just duty. More than once, I reached for our connecting door without purpose. I enjoyed seeing you and talking to you.

I replaced our connecting door with one made of glass."

I smiled that smile.

Darach walked toward me.

Still holding the envelope, I held up both hands. He kept coming. His chest butted my hands, jolting an electric shock between us. He'd crossed an ocean and half a continent for me. But unfinished business literally lay between us.

"I want you to open the envelope," I said. "I want you to claim what's important to you."

He took the envelope from me and ripped it down the middle. The halves fell to the floor.

"There, it's open. And as for claiming what's important to me, I believe I could use a hug."

I stepped into his arms.

"And I have to warn you. I'm going to kiss you again."

"I'd be disappointed if you didn't."

Darach didn't disappoint me.

Sign up to join Dawn Smith's mailing list at
www.DawnSmithMysteries.com
and receive advance notice of her upcoming books.

Note from the author: Reviews are valuable to authors!
If you enjoyed this book, would you consider rating
and reviewing it on Amazon.com?

Read on for a preview of

INHERITING TROUBLE

Coming in December 2019

INHERITING TROUBLE

DAWN SMITH

What if you inherited a ranch house and land in the Texas Hill Country—and a drug dealer is hiding heroin on your property?

Darcy Cooper's dream of opening a bed-and-breakfast becomes a nightmare when she becomes as an unresolved problem for criminals that solve problems permanently.

Sheriff Eli Whitepath's looming reelection hinges upon catching the drug dealers and their suppliers in his county. As attacks against Darcy escalate, Eli fights to save his job—and Darcy's life.

INHERITING TROUBLE

Coming in December 2019

Made in the USA
Coppell, TX
08 February 2022